AUTHORS LOVE HIM

"Amazing."
—Michael Connelly

"Thrilling."
—Louise Penny

"Brilliant."
—Jeffery Deaver

"Watch for those twists—
they'll get you every time."
—Ian Rankin

"Edge-of-your-seat,
heart-in-your-throat suspense."
—Tess Gerritsen

"The novels of Peter Robinson are chilling,
evocative, deeply nuanced works of art."
—Dennis Lehane

CRITICS LOVE HIM

YOU'LL LOVE HIM

One of the world's most popular and acclaimed writers, **PETER ROBINSON** grew up in the United Kingdom, and now divides his time between Toronto and England. The bestselling, award-winning author of the Inspector Banks series, he has also written two short-story collections and three standalone novels, which combined have sold more than ten million copies around the world. Among his many honors and prizes are the Edgar Award, the CWA (UK) Dagger in the Library Award, and Sweden's Martin Beck Award.

PETER ROBINSON

AFTERMATH

AN INSPECTOR BANKS NOVEL

wm

WILLIAM MORROW
An Imprint of HarperCollins*Publishers*

AFTERMATH. Copyright © 2001 by Peter Robinson. All rights reserved. Printed in the United States of America. No part of this book may be used or reproduced in any manner whatsoever without written permission except in the case of brief quotations embodied in critical articles and reviews. For information address HarperCollins Publishers, 195 Broadway, New York, NY 10007.

HarperCollins books may be purchased for educational, business, or sales promotional use. For information please e-mail the Special Markets Department at SPsales@harpercollins.com.

A hardcover edition of this book was published in 2001 by William Morrow, an imprint of HarperCollins Publishers.

FIRST WILLIAM MORROW PAPERBACK EDITION PUBLISHED 2015.
FIRST AVON MASS MARKET PAPERBACK EDITION PUBLISHED 2002.

Library of Congress Cataloging-in-Publication Data has been applied for.

ISBN 978-0-06-240024-6

15 16 17 18 19   OV/RRD   10 9 8 7 6 5 4 3 2 1

To Richard and Barbara,
good friends and gracious hosts

The evil that men do lives after them.

—WILLIAM SHAKESPEARE, *Julius Caesar*

AFTERMATH

Prologue

*T*hey locked her in the cage when she started to bleed. Tom was already there. He'd been there for three days and had stopped crying now. He was still shivering, though. It was February, there was no heat in the cellar, and both of them were naked. There would be no food, either, she knew, not for a long time, not until she got so hungry that she felt as if she were being eaten from the inside.

It wasn't the first time she had been locked in the cage, but this time was different from the others. Before, it had always been because she'd done something wrong or hadn't done what they wanted her to do. This time it was different; it was because of what she had become, and she was really scared.

As soon as they had shut the door at the top of the stairs, the darkness wrapped itself around her like fur. She could feel it rubbing against her skin the way a cat rubs against your legs. She began to shiver. More than anything she hated the cage, more than the blows, more than the humiliations. But she wouldn't cry. She never cried. She didn't know how.

The smell was terrible; they didn't have a toilet to go to, only the bucket in the corner, which they would only be allowed to empty when they were let out. And who knew when that would be?

But worse even than the smell were the little scratching sounds that started when she had been locked up only a few minutes. Soon, she knew, it would come, the tickle of sharp little feet across her legs or her stomach if she dared to lie down. The first time, she had tried to keep moving and making noise all the time to keep them away, but in the end she had become exhausted and fallen asleep, not caring how many there were or what they did. She could tell in the dark, by the way they moved and their weight, whether they were rats or mice. The rats were the worst. One had even bitten her once.

She held Tom and tried to comfort him, making them both a little warmer. If truth be told, she could have done with a little comforting herself, but there was nobody to comfort her.

Mice scuttled across her feet. Occasionally, she flicked her legs out and heard one squeak as it hit the wall. She could hear music from upstairs, loud, with the bass making the bars of the cage rattle.

She closed her eyes and tried to find a beautiful retreat deep inside her mind, a place where everything was warm and golden and the sea that washed up on the sands was deep blue, the water warm and lovely as sunlight when she jumped in. But she couldn't find it, couldn't find that sandy beach and blue sea, that garden full of bright flowers or that cool green forest in summer. When she closed her eyes, all she could find was darkness shot with red, distant mutterings, cries, and an appalling sense of dread.

She drifted in and out of sleep, becoming oblivious to the mice and rats. She didn't know how long she'd been there before she heard noises upstairs. Different noises. The music had ended a long time ago and everything was silent apart from the scratching and Tom's breathing. She thought she heard a car pull up outside. Voices. Another car. Then she heard someone walking across the floor upstairs. A curse.

Suddenly, all hell broke loose upstairs. It sounded as if someone was battering at the door with a tree trunk, then there was a crunching sound followed by a loud bang as the front door caved in. Tom was awake now, whimpering in her arms.

She heard shouting and what sounded like dozens of pairs of grown-ups' feet running around upstairs. After what seemed like an eternity, she heard someone prise open the lock to the cellar door. A little light spilled in, but not much, and there wasn't a bulb down there. More voices. Then came the lances of bright torchlight, coming closer, so close they hurt her eyes and she had to shield them with her hand. Then the beam held her and a strange voice cried, "Oh, God! Oh, my God!"

Chapter 1

*M*aggie Forrest wasn't sleeping well, so it didn't surprise her when the voices woke her shortly before four o'clock one morning in early May, even though she had made sure before she went to bed that all the windows in the house were shut fast.

If it hadn't been the voices, it would have been something else: a car door slamming as someone set off for an early shift; the first train rattling across the bridge; the neighbor's dog; old wood creaking somewhere in the house; the fridge clicking on and off; a pan or a glass shifting on the draining board. Or perhaps one of the noises of the night, the kind that made her wake in a cold sweat with a thudding heart and gasp for breath as if she were drowning, not sleeping: the man she called Mr. Bones clicking up and down The Hill with his cane; the scratching at the front door; the tortured child screaming in the distance.

Or a nightmare.

She was just too jumpy these days, she told herself, trying to laugh it off. But there they were again. Definitely voices. One loud and masculine.

Maggie got out of bed and padded over to the window. The street called The Hill ran up the northern slope of the broad valley, and where Maggie lived, about halfway up, just above the railway bridge, the houses on the eastern side of the street stood atop a twenty-foot rise that sloped down to the pavement in a profusion of shrubs and small trees. Sometimes the undergrowth and foliage seemed so thick she could hardly find her way along the path to the pavement.

Maggie's bedroom window looked over the houses on the western side of The Hill and beyond, a patchwork landscape of housing estates, arterial roads, warehouses, factory chimneys and fields stretching through Bradford and Halifax all the way to the Pennines. Some days, Maggie would sit for hours and look at the view, thinking about the odd chain of events that had brought her here. Now, though, in the predawn light, the distant necklaces and clusters of amber streetlights took on a ghostly aspect, as if the city weren't quite real yet.

Maggie stood at her window and looked across the street. She could swear there was a hall light on directly opposite, in Lucy's house, and when she heard the voice again, she suddenly felt all her premonitions had been true.

It was Terry's voice, and he was shouting at Lucy. She couldn't hear what he was saying. Then she heard a scream, the sound of glass breaking and a thud.

Lucy.

Maggie dragged herself out of her paralysis, and with trembling hands she picked up the bedside telephone and dialed 999.

Probationary Police Constable Janet Taylor stood by her patrol car and watched the silver BMW burn, shielding her eyes from its glare, standing upwind of the foul-smelling smoke. Her partner, PC Dennis Morrisey, stood beside her. One or two spectators were peeping out of their bedroom windows, but nobody else seemed very interested. Burning cars weren't exactly a novelty on this estate. Even at four o'clock in the morning.

Orange and red flames, with deep inner hues of blue and green and occasional tentacles of violet, twisted into the darkness, sending up palls of thick black smoke. Even upwind, Janet could smell the burning rubber and plastic. It was giving her a headache, and she knew her uniform and her hair would reek of it for days.

The leading firefighter, Gary Cullen, walked over to join them. It was Dennis he spoke to, of course; he always did. They were mates.

"What do you think?"

"Joyriders." Dennis nodded toward the car. "We checked the number plate. Stolen from a nice middle-class residential street in Heaton Moor, Manchester, earlier this evening."

"Why here, then?"

"Dunno. Could be a connection, a grudge or something. Someone giving a little demonstration of his feelings. Drugs, even. But that's for the lads upstairs to work out. They're the ones paid to have brains. We're done for now. Everything safe?"

"Under control. What if there's a body in the boot?"

Dennis laughed. "It'll be well-done by now, won't it? Hang on a minute, that's our radio, isn't it?"

Janet walked over to the car. "I'll get it," she said over her shoulder.

"Control to three-five-four. Come in, please, three-five-four. Over."

Janet picked up the radio. "Three-five-four to Control. Over."

"Domestic dispute reported taking place at number thirty-five, The Hill. Repeat. Three-five. The Hill. Can you respond? Over."

Christ, thought Janet, a bloody domestic. No copper in her right mind liked domestics, especially at this time in the morning. "Will do," she sighed, looking at her watch. "ETA three minutes."

She called over to Dennis, who held up his hand and spoke a few more words to Gary Cullen before responding. They were both laughing when Dennis returned to the car.

"Tell him that joke, did you?" Janet asked, settling behind the wheel.

"Which one's that?" Dennis asked, all innocence.

Janet started the car and sped to the main road. "You know, the one about the blonde giving her first blow job."

"I don't know what you're talking about."

"Only I heard you telling it to that new PC back at the station, the lad who hasn't started shaving yet. You ought to give the poor lad a chance to make his own mind up about women, Den, instead of poisoning his mind right off the bat."

The centrifugal force almost threw them off the road as Janet took the roundabout at the top of The Hill too fast. Dennis grasped the dashboard and hung on for dear life. "Jesus Christ. Women drivers. It's only a joke. Have you got no sense of humor?"

Janet smiled to herself as she slowed and curb-crawled down The Hill looking for number 35.

"Anyway, I'm getting sick of this," Dennis said.

"Sick of what? My driving?"

"That, too. Mostly, though, it's your constant bitching. It's got so a bloke can't say what's on his mind these days."

"Not if he's got a mind like a sewer. That's pollution. Anyway, it's changing times, Den. And we have to change with them or we'll end up like the dinosaurs. By the way, about that mole."

"What mole?"

"You know, the one on your cheek. Next to your nose. The one with all the hairs growing out of it."

Dennis put his hand up to his cheek. "What about it?"

"I'd get it seen to quick, if I were you. It looks cancerous to me. Ah, number thirty-five. Here we are."

She pulled over to the right side of the road and came to a

halt a few yards past the house. It was a small detached residence built of redbrick and sandstone, between a plot of allotments and a row of shops. It wasn't much bigger than a cottage, with a slate roof, low-walled garden and a modern garage attached at the right. At the moment, all was quiet.

"There's a light on in the hall," Janet said. "Shall we have a dekko?"

Still fingering his mole, Dennis sighed and muttered something she took to be assent. Janet got out of the car first and walked up the path, aware of him dragging his feet behind her. The garden was overgrown and she had to push twigs and shrubbery aside as she walked. A little adrenaline had leaked into her system, put her on super alert, as it always did with domestics. The reason most cops hated them was that you never knew what was going to happen. As likely as not you'd pull the husband off the wife and then the wife would take his side and start bashing you with a rolling pin.

Janet paused by the door. Still all quiet, apart from Dennis's stertorous breathing behind her. It was too early yet for people to be going to work, and most of the late night revelers had passed out by now. Somewhere in the distance the first birds began to chatter. Sparrows, most likely, Janet thought. Mice with wings.

Seeing no doorbell, Janet knocked on the door.

No response came from inside.

She knocked harder. The hammering seemed to echo up and down the street. Still no response.

Next, Janet went down on her knees and looked through the letter box. She could just make out a figure sprawled on the floor at the bottom of the stairs. A woman's figure. That was probable cause enough for forced entry.

"Let's go in," she said.

Dennis tried the handle. Locked. Then, gesturing for Janet to stand out of the way, he charged it with his shoulder.

Poor technique, she thought. She'd have reared back and

used her foot. But Dennis was a second-row Rugby forward, she reminded herself, and his shoulders had been pushed up against so many arse-holes in their time that they had to be strong.

The door crashed open on first contact and Dennis cannonballed into the hallway, grabbing hold of the bottom of the banister to stop himself from tripping over the still figure that lay there.

Janet was right behind him, but she had the advantage of walking in at a more dignified pace. She shut the door as best she could, knelt beside the woman on the floor, and felt for a pulse. Weak, but steady. One side of her face was bathed in blood.

"My God," Janet muttered. "Den? You okay?"

"Fine. You take care of her. I'll have a look around." Dennis headed upstairs.

For once, Janet didn't mind being told what to do. Nor did she mind that Dennis automatically assumed it was a woman's work to tend the injured while the man went in search of heroic glory. Well, she *minded,* but she felt a real concern for the victim here, so she didn't want to make an issue of it.

Bastard, she thought. Whoever did this. "It's okay, love," she said, even though she suspected the woman couldn't hear her. "We'll get you an ambulance. Just hold on."

Most of the blood seemed to be coming from one deep cut just above her left ear, Janet noticed, though there was also a little smeared around the nose and lips. Punches, by the looks of it. There were also broken glass and daffodils scattered all around her, along with a damp patch on the carpet. Janet took her personal radio from her belt hook and called for an ambulance. She was lucky it worked on The Hill; personal UHF radios had much less range than the VHF models fitted in cars, and were notoriously subject to black spots of patchy reception.

Dennis came downstairs shaking his head. "Bastard's not hiding up there," he said. He handed Janet a blanket, pillow and towel, nodding to the woman. "For her."

Janet eased the pillow under the woman's head, covered her gently with the blanket and applied the towel to the seeping wound on her temple. Well, I never, she thought, full of surprises, our Den. "Think he's done a runner?" she asked.

"Dunno. I'll have a look in the back. You stay with her till the ambulance arrives."

Before Janet could say anything, Dennis headed off toward the back of the house. He hadn't been gone more than a minute or so when she heard him call out, "Janet, come here and have a look at this. Hurry up. It could be important."

Curious, Janet looked at the injured woman. The bleeding had stopped and there was nothing else she could do. Even so, she was reluctant to leave the poor woman alone.

"Come on," Dennis called again. "Hurry up."

Janet took one last look at the prone figure and walked toward the back of the house. The kitchen was in darkness.

"Down here."

She couldn't see Dennis, but she knew that his voice came from downstairs. Through an open door to her right, three steps led down to a landing lit by a bare bulb. There was another door, most likely to the garage, she thought, and around the corner were the steps down to the cellar.

Dennis was standing there, near the bottom, in front of a third door. On it was pinned a poster of a naked woman. She lay back on a brass bed with her legs wide open, fingers tugging at the edges of her vagina, smiling down over her large breasts at the viewer, inviting, beckoning him inside. Dennis stood before it, grinning.

"Bastard," Janet hissed.

"Where's your sense of humor?"

"It's *not* funny."

"What do you think it means?"

"I don't know." Janet could see light under the door, faint and flickering, as if from a faulty bulb. She also noticed a peculiar odor. "What's that smell?" she asked.

"How should I know? Rising damp? Drains?"

But it smelled like decay to Janet. Decay and sandalwood incense. She gave a little shudder.

"Shall we go in?" She was whispering without knowing why.

"I think we'd better."

Janet walked ahead of him, almost on tiptoe, down the final few steps. The adrenaline was really pumping in her veins now. Slowly, she reached out and tried the door. Locked. She moved aside, and Dennis used his foot this time. The lock splintered, and the door swung open. Dennis stood aside, bowed from the waist in a parody of gentlemanly courtesy, and said, "Ladies first."

With Dennis only inches behind her, Janet stepped into the cellar.

She barely had time to register her first impressions of the small room—mirrors; dozens of lit candles surrounding a mattress on the floor; a girl on the mattress, naked and bound, something yellow around her neck; the terrible smell stronger, despite the incense, like blocked drains and rotten meat; crude charcoal drawings on the whitewashed walls—before it happened.

He came from somewhere behind them, from one of the cellar's dark corners. Dennis turned to meet him, reaching for his baton, but he was too slow. The machete slashed first across his cheek, slicing it open from the eye to the lips. Before Dennis had time to put his hand up to stanch the blood or register the pain, the man slashed again, this time across the side of his throat. Dennis made a gurgling sound and went to his knees, eyes wide open. Warm blood gushed across Janet's face and sprayed on to the whitewashed walls in swirling abstract patterns. The hot stink of it made her gag.

She had no time to think. You never did when it really happened. All she knew was that she couldn't do anything for Dennis. Not yet. There was still the man with the knife to deal with. Hang on, Dennis, she pleaded silently. *Hang on.*

The man still seemed intent on hacking at Dennis, not finished yet, and that gave Janet enough time to slip out her side-handled baton. She had just managed to grip the handle so that the baton ran protectively along the outside of her arm, when he made his first lunge at her. He seemed shocked and surprised when his blade didn't sink into flesh and bone but was instead deflected by the hard baton.

That gave Janet the opening she needed. Bugger technique and training. She swung out and caught him on the temple. His eyes rolled back and he slumped against the wall, but he didn't go down. She moved in closer and cracked down on the wrist of his knife hand. She heard something break. He cried out and the machete fell to the floor. Janet kicked it away into a far corner, then she took the fully extended baton with both hands, swung and caught him on the side of the head again. He tried to go after his machete, but she hit him again as hard as she could on the back of his head and then again on his cheek and once more at the base of his skull. He reared up, still on his knees, spouting obscenities at her, and she lashed out one more time, cracking his temple. He fell against the wall, where the back of his head left a long dark smear on the whitewash as he slid down and rested there, legs extended. Pink foam bubbled at the side of his mouth, then stopped. Janet hit him once more, a two-handed blow on the top of his skull, then she took out her handcuffs and secured him to one of the pipes running along the bottom of the wall. He groaned and stirred, so she hit him once more, two-handed, on the top of the skull. When he fell silent, she went over to Dennis.

He was still twitching, but the spurts of blood from his

wound were getting weaker. Janet struggled to remember her first aid training. She made a compress from her handkerchief and pressed it tight against the severed artery, trying to nip the ends together. Next she tried to make the 10-9 call on her personal radio: Officer in urgent need of assistance. But it was no good. All she got was static. *A black spot.* Nothing to do now but sit and wait for the ambulance to arrive. She could hardly move, go outside, not with Dennis like this. She couldn't leave him.

So Janet sat cross-legged and rested Dennis's head on her lap, cradling him and muttering nonsense in his ear. The ambulance would come soon, she told him. He would be fine, just wait and see. But it seemed that no matter how tightly she held the compress, blood leaked through to her uniform. She could feel its warmth on her fingers, her belly and thighs. Please, Dennis, she prayed, *please* hang on.

Above Lucy's house, Maggie could see the crescent sliver of a new moon and the faint silver thread it drew around the old moon's darkness. *The old moon in the new moon's arms.* An ill omen. Sailors believed that the sight of it, especially through glass, presaged a storm and much loss of life. Maggie shivered. She wasn't superstitious, but there was something chilling about the sight, something that reached out and touched her from way back in time, when people paid more attention to cosmic events such as the cycles of the moon.

She looked back down at the house and saw the police car arrive, heard the woman officer knock and call out, then saw her male partner charge the door.

After that, Maggie heard nothing for a while—perhaps five or ten minutes—until she fancied she heard a heart-rending, keening wail from deep inside the bowels of the house. But it could have been her imagination. The sky was a lighter blue now and the dawn chorus had struck up. Maybe it was a bird? But she knew that no bird sounded so desolate or godforsaken as that cry, not even the loon on a lake or the curlew up on the moors.

Maggie rubbed the back of her neck and kept watching. Seconds later, an ambulance pulled up. Then another police car. Then paramedics. The ambulance attendants left the front door open, and Maggie could see them kneeling by someone in the hall. Someone covered with a fawn blanket. They lifted the figure on to a wheeled stretcher and pushed her down the path to the ambulance, back doors open and waiting. It all happened so quickly that Maggie couldn't see clearly who it was, but she thought she could glimpse Lucy's jet-black hair spread out against a white pillow.

So it was as she had thought. She gnawed at her thumbnail. Should she have done something sooner? She had certainly had her suspicions, but could she somehow have prevented this? What could she have done?

Next to arrive looked like a plainclothes police officer. He was soon followed by five or six men who put on disposable white overalls before they went inside the house. Someone also put up white and blue tape across the front gate and blocked off a long stretch of the pavement, including the nearest bus stop, and the entire side of the road number 35 stood on, reducing The Hill to one lane of traffic in order to make room for police vehicles and ambulances.

Maggie wondered what was going on. Surely they wouldn't go to all this trouble unless it was something really serious? Was Lucy dead? Had Terry finally killed her? Perhaps that was it; that would make them pay attention.

As the daylight grew, the scene became even stranger. More police cars arrived, and another ambulance. As the attendants wheeled a second stretcher out, the first morning bus went down The Hill and obscured Maggie's view. She could see the passengers turn their heads, the ones on her side of the road standing up to get a look at what was happening, but she couldn't see who lay on the stretcher. Only that two policemen got in after it.

Next, a hunched figure shrouded in a blanket stumbled down the path, supported on each side by uniformed policemen. At first Maggie had no idea who it was. A woman, she thought, from her general outline and the cut of her dark hair. Then she thought she glimpsed the dark blue uniform. *The policewoman.* Breath caught in her throat. What could have happened to change her so much so fast?

By now there was far more activity than Maggie had ever thought the scene of a domestic argument could engender. At least half a dozen police cars had arrived, some of them unmarked. A wiry man with closely cropped dark hair got out of a blue Renault and walked into the house as if he owned the place. Another man who went in looked like a doctor. At least he carried a black bag and had that self-important air about him. People up and down The Hill were going to work now, driving their cars out of their garages or waiting for the bus at the temporary bus stop someone from the depot had put up. Little knots of them gathered by the house, watching, but the police came over and moved them on.

Maggie looked at her watch. Half-past six. She had been kneeling at the window for two and a half hours, yet she felt as if she had been watching a quick succession of events, as if it had been done by time-lapse photography. When she got to her feet she heard her knees crack, and the broadloom carpet had made deep red crisscross marks on her skin.

There was far less activity outside the house now, just the police guards and the detectives coming and going, standing on the pavement to smoke, shake their heads and talk in low voices. The knot of haphazardly parked cars outside Lucy's house caused traffic backups.

Weary and confused, Maggie threw on jeans and a T-shirt and went downstairs to make a cup of tea and some toast. As she filled the kettle, she noticed that her hand was shaking. They would want to talk to her, no doubt about that. And when they did, what would she tell them?

Chapter 2

*A*cting Detective Superintendent Alan Banks—"acting" because his immediate boss, Detective Superintendent Gristhorpe, had shattered his ankle while working on his dry-stone wall and would be off work for at least a couple of months—signed the first officer's log at the gate, took a deep breath and walked into 35 The Hill shortly after six o'clock that morning. Householders: Lucy Payne, age twenty-two, loan officer at the local NatWest branch up near the shopping precinct, and her husband, Terence Payne, age twenty-eight, schoolteacher at Silverhill Comprehensive. No kids. No criminal record. To all intents and purposes an idyllic, suc-cessful young couple. Married just one year.

All the lights were on in the house, and the scene-of-the-crime were already at work, dressed—as Banks was—in the obligatory white sterile overalls, overshoes, gloves and hoods. They looked like some sort of phantom house-cleaning crew, Banks thought—dusting, vacuuming, scrap-ing up samples, packaging, labeling.

Banks paused a moment in the hall to get the feel of the place. It seemed an ordinary enough middle-class home. The ribbed coral-pink wallpaper looked new. Carpeted stairs to the right led up to the bedrooms. If anything, the place smelled a bit *too much* of lemon air freshener. The only thing that seemed out of place was the rust-colored stain on the cream hall carpet. *Lucy Payne,* currently under observation by both doctors and police in Leeds General Infirmary, just down the corridor from where her husband, Terence Payne, was fighting for his life. Banks hadn't a lot of sympathy to spare for him; PC Dennis Morrisey had lost his struggle for life far more quickly.

And there was a dead girl in the cellar, too.

Most of this information Banks had got from Detective Chief Inspector Ken Blackstone over his mobile on the way to Leeds, the rest from talking to the paramedics and the ambulance crew outside. The first phone call to his Gratly cottage, the one that woke him from the shallow, troubled and restless sleep that seemed to be his lot these days, had come shortly after half-past four, and he had showered, thrown on some clothes and jumped in his car. A CD of Zelenka Trios had helped him keep calm on the way and discouraged him from taking outrageous risks with his driving on the A1. All in all, the eighty-mile drive had taken him about an hour and a half, and if he hadn't had too many other things on his mind, during the first part of his journey he might have admired the coming of a beautiful May dawn over the Yorkshire Dales, rare enough so far that spring. As it was, he saw little but the road ahead and barely even heard the music. By the time he got to the Leeds Ring Road, the Monday-morning rush hour was already under way.

Circumventing the bloodstains and daffodils on the hall carpet, Banks walked to the back of the house. He noticed someone had been sick in the kitchen sink.

"One of the ambulance crew," said the SOCO busy going through the drawers and cupboards. "First time out, poor sod. We're lucky he made it back up here and didn't puke all over the scene."

"Christ, what did he have for breakfast?"

"Looks like Thai red curry and chips to me."

Banks took the stairs down to the cellar. On his way, he

noted the door to the garage. Very handy if you wanted to bring someone into the house without being seen, someone you had abducted, perhaps drugged or knocked unconscious. Banks opened the door and had a quick glance at the car. It was a dark four-door Vectra, with an "S" registration. The last three letters were NGV. Not local. He made a note to have someone run it through the DVLA at Swansea.

He could hear voices down in the cellar, see cameras flashing. That would be Luke Selkirk, their hotshot crime scene photographer, fresh from his army-sponsored training course up at Catterick Camp, where he had been learning how to photograph scenes of terrorist bombings. Not that his special skill would be needed today, but it was good to know you were working with a highly trained professional, one of the best.

The stone steps were worn in places; the walls were white-washed brick. Someone had put more white and blue tape across the open door at the bottom. An inner crime scene. Nobody would get beyond that until Banks, Luke, the doctor and the SOCOs had done their jobs.

Banks paused at the threshold and sniffed. The smell was bad: decomposition, mold, incense, and the sweet, metallic whiff of fresh blood. He ducked under the tape and walked inside and the horror of the scene hit him with such force that he staggered back a couple of inches.

It wasn't that he hadn't seen worse; he had. Much worse: the disemboweled Soho prostitute, Dawn Whadden; a decap-itated petty thief called William Grant; the partly eaten body parts of a young barmaid called Colleen Dickens; bodies shredded by shotgun blasts and slit open by knives. He re-membered all their names. But that wasn't the point, he had come to learn over the years. It wasn't a matter of blood and guts, of intestines poking out of the stomach, of missing limbs or of deep gashes flapping open in an obscene parody of mouths. That wasn't what really got you when it came right down to it. That was just the outward aspect. You could, if you tried hard, convince yourself that a crime scene like this one was a movie set or a theater during rehearsals, and that the bodies were merely props, the blood fake.

No, what got to him most of all was the *pity* of it all, the deep empathy he had come to feel with the victims of crimes he investigated. And he hadn't become more callous, more inured to it all over the years, as many did, and as he had once thought he would. Each new one was like a raw wound reopening. Especially something like this. He could keep it all in check, keep the bile down in his rumbling gut and do his job, but it ate away at him from the inside like acid and kept him awake at night. Pain and fear and despair permeated these walls like the factory grime had crusted the old city buildings. Only this kind of horror couldn't be sandblasted away.

Seven people in the cramped cellar, five of them alive and two dead; this was going to be a logistical and forensic nightmare.

Someone had turned an overhead light on, just a bare bulb, but candles still flickered all over the place. From the doorway Banks could see the doctor bent over the pale body on the mattress. A girl. The only outward signs of violence were a few cuts and bruises, a bloody nose, and a length of yellow plastic clothesline around her neck. She lay spread-eagled on the soiled mattress, her hands tied with the same yellow plastic line to metal pegs someone had set into the concrete floor. Blood from PC Morrisey's severed artery had sprayed across her ankles and shins. Some flies had managed to get in the cellar, and three of them were buzzing around the blood clotted under her nose. There seemed to be some sort of rash or blistering around her mouth. Her face was pale and bluish in death, the rest of her body white under the bulb's glare.

What made it all so much worse were the large mirrors on

the ceiling and two of the walls that multiplied the scene like a fun-fair trick.

"Who turned the overhead light on?" Banks asked.

"Ambulance men," said Luke Selkirk. "They were first on the scene after PCs Taylor and Morrisey."

"Okay, we'll leave it on for the time being, get a better idea of what we're dealing with. But I want the original scene photographed, too, later. Just the candlelight."

Luke nodded. "By the way, this is Faye McTavish, my new assistant." Faye was a slight, pale, waif-like woman, early twenties perhaps, with a stud through her nostril and almost no hips at all. The old heavy Pentax she had slung around her neck looked too big for her to hold steady, but she managed it well enough.

"Pleased to meet you, Faye," said Banks, shaking hands. "Only wish it could be in better circumstances."

"Me too."

Banks turned to the body on the mattress.

He knew who she was: Kimberley Myers, age fifteen, missing since Friday night, when she had failed to return from a youth-club dance only a quarter of a mile from her home. She had been a pretty girl, with the characteristic long blond hair and slim, athletic figure of all the victims. Now her dead eyes stared up at the mirror on the ceiling as if looking for answers to her suffering.

Dried semen glistened on her pubic hair. And blood. Semen and blood, the old, old story. Why was it always the pretty young girls these monsters took? Banks asked himself for the hundredth time. Oh, he knew all the pat answers; he knew that women and children made easier victims because they were physically weaker, more easily cowed and subdued by male strength, just as he knew that prostitutes and runaways made easy victims, too, because they were less likely to be missed than someone from a nice home, like

Kimberley. But it was much more than that. There was always a deep, dark sexual aspect to these sorts of things, and to be the right kind of object for whoever had done this, the victim needed not only to be weaker, but needed breasts and a vagina, too, available for her tormentor's pleasure and ultimate desecration. And perhaps some aura of youth and innocence. It was despoilation of innocence. Men killed other men for many reasons, by the thousands in wartime, but in crimes like this, the victim always had to be a woman.

The first officer on the scene had had the foresight to mark out a narrow pathway on the floor with tape so that people wouldn't walk all over the place and destroy evidence, but after what had happened with PCs Morrisey and Taylor, it was probably too late for that anyway.

PC Dennis Morrisey lay curled on his side in a pool of blood on the concrete floor. His blood had also sprayed over part of the wall and one of the mirrors, rivaling in its pattern anything Jackson Pollock had ever painted. The rest of the whitewashed walls were covered with either pornographic images ripped from magazines, or childish, obscene stick figures of men with enormous phalluses, like the Cerne Giant, drawn in colored chalk. Mixed in with these were a number of crudely drawn occult symbols and grinning skulls. There was another pool of blood by the wall next to the door, and a long dark smear on the whitewash. *Terence Payne.*

Luke Selkirk's camera flashed and snapped Banks out of his trance-like state. Faye was wielding her camcorder now. The other man in the room turned and spoke for the first time: Detective Chief Inspector Ken Blackstone of the West Yorkshire Police, looking immaculate as ever, even in his protective clothing. Gray hair curled over his ears, and his wire-rimmed glasses magnified his sharp eyes.

"Alan," he said, in a voice like a sigh. "Like a fucking abattoir, isn't it?"

"A fine start to the week. When did you get here?"

"Four forty-four."

Blackstone lived out Lawnswood way, and it wouldn't have taken him more than half an hour to get to The Hill, if that. Banks, heading the North Yorkshire team, was glad that Blackstone was running West Yorkshire's part of their joint operation, dubbed the "Chameleon" squad because the killer, thus far, had managed to adapt, blend into the night and go unnoticed. Often, working together involved ego problems and incompatible personalities, but Banks and Blackstone had known each other for eight or nine years and had always worked well together. They got on socially, too, with a mutual fondness for pubs, Indian food and female jazz singers.

"Have you talked to the paramedics?" Banks asked.

"Yes," said Blackstone. "They said they checked the girl for signs of life and found none, so they left her undisturbed. PC Morrisey was dead, too. Terence Payne was handcuffed to the pipe over there. His head was badly beaten, but he was still breathing, so they carted him off to hospital sharpish. There's been some contamination of the scene—mostly to the position of Morrisey's body—but it's minimal, given the unusual circumstances."

"Trouble is, Ken, we've got two crime scenes overlapping here—maybe three, if you count what happened to Payne." He paused. "Four, if you count Lucy Payne upstairs. That'll cause problems. Where's Stefan?" Detective Sergeant Stefan Nowak was their Crime Scene Co-coordinator, new to the Western Division HQ in Eastvale, and brought into the team by Banks, who had been quickly impressed by his abilities. Banks didn't envy Stefan his job right now.

"Around somewhere," said Blackstone. "Last time I saw him, he was heading upstairs."

"Anything more you can tell me, Ken?"

"Not much, really. That'll have to wait until we can talk to PC Taylor in more detail."

"When might that be?"

"Later today. The paramedics took her off. She's being treated for shock."

"I'm not bloody surprised. Have they—"

"Yes. They've bagged her clothes and the police surgeon's been to the hospital to do the necessary."

Which meant taking fingernail scrapings and swabs from her hands, among other things. One thing it was easy to forget—and a thing everyone might *want* to forget—was that, for the moment, probationary PC Janet Taylor wasn't a hero; she was a suspect in a case of excessive use of force. Very nasty indeed.

"How does it look to you, Ken?" Banks asked. "Gut feeling."

"As if they surprised Payne down here, cornered him. He came at them fast and somehow struck PC Morrisey with that." He pointed to a bloodstained machete on the floor by the wall. "You can see Morrisey's been slashed two or three times. PC Taylor must have had time enough to get her baton out and use it on Payne. She did the right thing, Alan. He must have been coming at her like a bloody maniac. She had to defend herself. Self-defense."

"Not for us to decide," said Banks. "What's the damage to Payne?"

"Fractured skull. Multiple fractures."

"Shame. Still, if he dies, it might save the courts a bit of money and a lot of grief in the long run. What about his wife?"

"Way it looks is he hit her with a vase on the stairs and she fell down. Mild concussion, a bit of bruising. Other than that, there's no serious damage. She's lucky it wasn't heavy crystal or she might have been in the same boat as her husband. Anyway, she's still out and they're keeping an eye on her, but she'll be fine. DC Hodgkins is at the hospital now."

Banks looked around the room again, with its flickering

candles, mirrors, and obscene cartoons. He noticed shards of glass on the mattress near the body and realized when he saw his own image in one of them that they were from a broken mirror. *Seven years bad luck.* Hendrix's "Roomful of Mirrors" would never sound quite the same again.

The doctor looked up from his examination for the first time since Banks had entered the cellar, got up off his knees, and walked over to them. "Dr. Ian Mackenzie, Home Office pathologist," he said, holding his hand out to Banks, who shook it.

Dr. Mackenzie was a heavily built man with a full head of brown hair, parted and combed, a fleshy nose, and a gap between his upper front teeth. Always a sign of luck, that, Banks remembered his mother once telling him. Maybe it would counteract the broken mirror. "What can you tell us?" Banks asked.

"The presence of petechial hemorrhages, bruising of the throat, and cyanosis all indicate death by strangulation, most likely ligature strangulation by that yellow clothesline around her throat, but I won't be able to tell you for certain until after the postmortem."

"Any evidence of sexual activity?"

"Some vaginal and anal tearing, what looks like semen stains. But you can see that for yourself. Again, I'll be able to tell you more later."

"Time of death?"

"Recent. Very recent. There's hardly any hypostasis yet, rigor hasn't started, and she's still warm."

"How long?"

"Two or three hours, at an estimate."

Banks looked at his watch. Sometime after three, then, not long before the domestic dispute that drove the woman over the road to dial 999. Banks cursed. If the call had come in just a short while earlier, maybe only minutes or an hour, then they might have saved Kimberley. On the other hand, the timing was interesting for the questions it raised about the reasons for the dispute. "What about that rash around her mouth? Chloroform?"

"At a guess. Probably used in abducting her, maybe even for keeping her sedated, though there are much more pleasant ways."

Banks glanced at Kimberley's body. "I don't think our man was overly concerned about being pleasant, do you, Doctor? Is chloroform easily available?"

"Pretty much. It's used as a solvent."

"But it's not the cause of death?"

"I wouldn't say so, no. Can't be absolutely certain until after the postmortem, of course, but if it is the cause, we'd expect to find more severe blistering in the esophagus, and there would also be noticeable liver damage."

"When can you get to her?"

"Barring a motorway pileup, I should be able to schedule the postmortems to start this afternoon," Dr. Mackenzie said. "We're pretty busy as it is, but . . . well, there are priorities." He looked at Kimberley, then at PC Morrisey. "He died of blood loss, by the looks of it. Severed both his carotid artery and jugular vein. Very nasty, but quick. Apparently his partner did what she could, but it was too late. Tell her she shouldn't blame herself. Hadn't a chance."

"Thanks, Doctor," said Banks. "Appreciate it. If you could do the PM on Kimberley first . . ."

"Of course."

Dr. Mackenzie left to make arrangements, and Luke Selkirk and Faye McTavish continued to take photographs and video. Banks and Blackstone stood in silence taking in the scene. There wasn't much more to see, but what there was wouldn't vanish quickly from their memories.

"Where does that door over there lead to?" Banks pointed to a door in the wall beside the mattress.

"Don't know," said Blackstone. "Haven't had a chance to look yet."

"Let's have a butcher's, then."

Banks walked over and tried the handle. It wasn't locked. Slowly, he opened the heavy wooden door to another, smaller room, this one with a dirt floor. The smell was much worse in there. He felt for an overhead light switch but couldn't locate one. He sent Blackstone to get a torch and tried to make out what he could in the overspill of light from the main cellar.

As his eyes adjusted to the darkness in the room, Banks thought he could see little clumps of mushrooms growing here and there from the earth.

Then he realized . . .

"Oh, Christ," he said, slumping back against the wall. The nearest clump wasn't mushrooms at all, it was a cluster of human toes poking through the dirt.

After a quick breakfast and an interview with two police detectives about her 999 call, Maggie felt the urge to go for a walk. There wasn't much chance of getting any work done for a while anyway, what with all the excitement over the road, though she knew she would try later. Right now, she was restless and needed to blow the cobwebs out. The detectives had stuck mostly to factual questions, and she hadn't told them anything about Lucy, but she sensed that one of them, at least, didn't seem satisfied with her answers. They would be back.

She still didn't know what the hell was going on. The policemen who talked to her had given away nothing, of course, had not even told her how Lucy was, and the local news on the radio was hardly illuminating, either. All they could say at this stage was that a member of the public and a police officer had been injured earlier that morning. And that took second place to the ongoing story about the local girl, Kimberley Myers, who had vanished on her way home from a youth-club dance on Friday evening.

As she walked down the front steps past the fuchsias, which would soon be flowering and drooping their heavy purple-pink bells over the path, Maggie saw the activity at number 35 was increasing, and neighbors had gathered in little knots on the pavement, which had now been roped off from the road.

Several men wearing white overalls and carrying shovels, sieves, and buckets got out of a van and hurried down the garden path.

"Oh, look," called out one of the neighbors. "He's got his bucket and spade. Must be off to Blackpool."

But nobody laughed. Like Maggie, everyone was coming to realize that something very nasty indeed had happened at 35 The Hill. About ten yards away, across from the narrow, walled lane that separated it from number 35, was a row of shops: pizza take-away, hairdresser, mini-mart, newsagent, fish and chips; and several uniformed officers stood arguing with the shopkeepers. They probably wanted to open up, Maggie guessed.

Plainclothes police officers sat on the front wall, talking and smoking. Radios crackled. The area had fast begun to resemble the site of a natural disaster, as if a train had crashed or an earthquake had struck. Maggie remembered seeing the aftermath of the 1994 earthquake in Los Angeles, when she went there once with Bill before they were married: a flattened apartment building, three stories reduced in seconds to two; fissures in the roads; part of the freeway collapsed. Though there was no visible damage here, it *felt* the same, had the same shell-shocked aura. Even though they didn't know what had happened yet, the people were stunned, were counting the cost; there was a pall of apprehension over the community and a deep sense of terror at what destructive power the hand of God might have unleashed. They knew that something momentous had occurred on their doorsteps. Already, Maggie sensed, life in the neighborhood would never be the same.

Maggie turned left and walked down The Hill, under the railway bridge. At the bottom was a small artificial pond in the midst of the housing estates and business parks. It wasn't much, but it was better than nothing. At least she could sit on a bench by the water and feed the ducks, watch the people walking their dogs.

It was safe, too—an important consideration in this part of the city, where old, large houses, such as the one Maggie was staying in, rubbed shoulders with the newer, rougher council estates. Burglary was rife, and murder not unknown, but down by the pond, the double deckers ran by on the main road just a few yards away, and enough ordinary people came to walk their dogs that Maggie never felt isolated or threatened. Attacks occurred in broad daylight, she knew, but she still felt close enough to safety down there.

It was a warm, pleasant morning. The sun was out, but the brisk breeze made it necessary to wear a light jacket. Occasionally, a high cloud drifted over the sun, blocking the light for a second or two and casting shadows on the water's surface.

There was something very soothing about feeding ducks, Maggie thought. Almost trance-like. Not for the ducks, of course, who seemed to have no concept of what sharing meant. You tossed the bread, they scooted toward it, quacked and fought. As Maggie crumbled the stale bread between her fingers and tossed it into the water, she recalled her first meeting with Lucy Payne just a couple of months ago.

She had been in town shopping for art supplies that day— a remarkably warm day for March—then she'd been to Borders on Briggate to buy some books, and afterward she found herself wandering through the Victoria Quarter down toward

Kirkgate Market, when she bumped into Lucy coming the other way. They had seen each other before in the street and at the local shops, and they had always said hello. Partly through inclination and partly through her shyness—getting out and meeting people never having been one of her strong points—Maggie had no friends in her new world, apart from Claire Toth, her neighbor's schoolgirl daughter, who seemed to have adopted her. Lucy Payne, she soon found out, was a kindred spirit.

Perhaps because they were both out of their natural habitat, like compatriots meeting in a foreign land, they stopped and spoke to each other. Lucy said it was her day off work and she was doing a bit of shopping. Maggie suggested a cup of tea or coffee at the Harvey Nichols outdoor café, and Lucy said she'd love to. So they sat and rested their feet, their parcels on the ground. Lucy noticed the names on the bags Maggie was carrying—including Harvey Nichols— and said something about not having the nerve to go inside such a posh place. Her own packages, it soon became clear, were from British Home Stores and C & A. Maggie had come across this reluctance in northern people before, had heard all the stories about how you'd never get the typical Leeds anorak-and-flat-cap crowd into an upmarket store like Harvey Nichols, but it still surprised her to hear Lucy admit to this.

This was because Maggie thought Lucy was such a strikingly attractive and elegant woman, with her glossy black raven's-wing hair tumbling down to the small of her back, and the kind of figure men buy magazines to look at pictures of. Lucy was tall and full-breasted, with a waist that curved in and hips that curved out in the right proportion, and the simple yellow dress she was wearing under a light jacket that day emphasized her figure without broadcasting it out loud, and it also drew attention to her shapely legs. She didn't wear much makeup; she didn't need to. Her pale complexion was smooth as a reflection in a mirror, her black eyebrows arched, cheekbones high in her oval face. Her eyes were black, with flint-like chips scattered around inside them that caught the light like quartz crystals as she looked around.

The waiter came over and Maggie asked Lucy if she would like a cappuccino. Lucy said she'd never had one before and wasn't quite sure what it was, but she would give it a try. Maggie asked for two cappuccinos. When Lucy took her first sip, she got froth on her lips, which she dabbed at with a serviette.

"You can't take me anywhere," she laughed.

"Don't be silly," said Maggie.

"No, I mean it. That's what Terry always says." She was very soft-spoken, the way Maggie had been for a while after she left Bill.

Maggie was just about to say that Terry was a fool, but she held her tongue. Insulting Lucy's husband on their first meeting wouldn't be very polite at all. "What do you think of the cappuccino?" she asked.

"It's very nice." Lucy took another sip. "Where are you from?" she asked. "I'm not being too nosy, am I? It's just that your accent . . ."

"Not at all, no. I'm from Toronto. Canada."

"No wonder you're so sophisticated. I've never been any further than the Lake District."

Maggie laughed. Toronto, *sophisticated?*

"See," said Lucy, pouting a little. "You're laughing at me already."

"No, no, I'm not," Maggie said. "Honestly, I'm not. It's just that . . . well, I suppose it's all a matter of perspective, isn't it?"

"What do you mean?"

"If I were to tell a New Yorker that Toronto is sophisticated, she'd laugh in my face. The best thing they can say about the place is that it's clean and safe."

"Well, that's something to be proud of, isn't it? Leeds is neither."

"It doesn't seem so bad to me."

"Why did you leave? I mean, why did you come here?"

Maggie frowned and fumbled for a cigarette. She still cursed herself for a fool for starting to smoke at thirty when she had managed to avoid the evil weed her whole life. Of course, she could blame it on the stress, though in the end it had only contributed more to that stress. She remembered the first time Bill had smelled smoke on her breath, that quick-as-a-flash change from concerned husband to *Monster Face,* as she had called it. But smoking wasn't that bad. Even her shrink said it wasn't such a terrible idea to have the occasional cigarette as a crutch for the time being. She could always stop later, when she felt better able to cope again.

"So why did you come here?" Lucy persisted. "I don't mean to be nosy, but I'm interested. Was it a new job?"

"Not exactly. What I do I can do anywhere."

"What is it?"

"I'm a graphic artist. I illustrate books. Mostly children's books. At the moment I'm working on a new edition of *Grimm's Fairy Tales.*"

"Oh, that sounds fascinating," said Lucy. "I was terrible at art in school. I can't even draw a matchstick figure." She laughed and put her hand over her mouth. "So why *are* you here?"

Maggie struggled with herself for a moment, stalling. Then a strange thing happened to her, a sense of inner chains and straps loosening, giving her space and a feeling of floating. Sitting there in the Victoria Quarter smoking and drinking cappuccino with Lucy, she felt an immediate and unheralded surge of affection for this young woman she hardly knew. She wanted the two of them to be friends, could see them talking about their problems just like this, giving each other sympathy and advice, just as she had with Alicia back in Toronto. Lucy, with her gaucheness, her naïve charm inspired a sort of emotional confidence in Maggie: this was someone, she felt, with whom she would be safe. More than that; though Maggie may have been the more "sophisticated" of the two, she sensed that they shared more than it appeared. The truth was difficult for her to admit to, but she felt the overwhelming need to tell someone other than her psychologist. And why not Lucy?

"What is it?" Lucy said. "You look so sad."

"Do I? Oh . . . Nothing. Look, my husband and I," Maggie said, stumbling over the words as if her tongue were the size of a steak, "I . . . er . . . we split up." She felt her mouth drying up. Despite the loosened bonds, this was still far more difficult than she had thought it would be. She sipped some more coffee.

Lucy frowned. "I'm sorry. But why move so far away? Lots of people split up and they don't move *countries*. Unless he's . . . oh, my God." She gave her cheek a little slap. "Lucy, I think you've just put your foot in it again."

Maggie couldn't help allowing herself a thin smile, even though Lucy had touched upon the painful truth. "It's all right," she said. "Yes, he was abusive. Yes, he hit me. You can say I'm running away. It's true. Certainly for a while I don't even want to be in the same country as him." The vehemence of her words when they came out surprised even Maggie herself.

A strange look came into Lucy's eyes, then she glanced around again, as if looking for someone. Only anonymous shoppers drifted up and down the arcade under the stained-glass roof, packages in hands. Lucy touched Maggie's arm with her fingertips and Maggie felt a little shiver run through her, almost like a reflex action to pull away. A moment ago, she had thought it would do her good to admit to someone, to share what happened with another woman, but now she wasn't so sure. She felt too naked, too raw.

"I'm sorry if it embarrasses you," Maggie said, with a hard edge to her voice. "But you *did* ask."

"Oh, no," said Lucy, grasping Maggie's wrist. Her grip was surprisingly strong, her hands cool. "Please don't think that. I asked for it. I always do. It's my fault. But it doesn't embarrass me. It's just . . . I don't know what to say. I mean . . . *you?* You seem so bright, so in control."

"Yes, that's exactly what I thought: *How could something like that happen to someone like me?* Doesn't it only happen to other women, poor, less fortunate, uneducated, stupid women?"

"How long?" Lucy asked. "I mean . . . ?"

"How long did I let it go on before I left?"

"Yes."

"Two years. And don't ask me how I could let it go on for so long, either. I don't know. I'm still working on that one with the shrink."

"I see." Lucy paused, taking it all in. "What made you leave him in the end?"

Maggie paused a moment, then went on. "One day he just went too far," she said. "He broke my jaw and two ribs, did some damage to my insides. It put me in hospital. While I was there I filed assault charges. And do you know what? As soon as I'd done it I wanted to drop them, but the police wouldn't let me."

"What do you mean?"

"I don't know what it's like over here, but in Canada it's out of your hands if you bring assault charges. You can't just change your mind and drop them. Anyway, there was a restraining order against him. Nothing happened for a couple of weeks; then he came around to the house with flowers, wanting to talk."

"What did you do?"

"I kept the chain on. I wouldn't let him in. He was in one of his contrite moods, pleading and wheedling, promising on his mother's grave. He'd done it before."

"And broken his promise?"

"Every time. Anyway, then he became threatening and abusive. He started hammering at the door and calling me names. I called the police. They arrested him. He came back again, stalking me. Then a friend suggested I move away for a while, the further the better. I knew about the house on The Hill. Ruth and Charles Everett own the place. Do you know them?"

Lucy shook her head. "I've seen them around. Not for a while, though."

"No, you wouldn't have. Charles was offered a year's appointment at Columbia University in New York, starting in January. Ruth went with him."

"How did you know them?"

"Ruth and I are in the same line of work. It's a fairly small world."

"But why Leeds?"

Maggie smiled. "Why not? First, there was the house, just waiting for me, and my parents came from Yorkshire. I was born here. Rawdon. But we left when I was a little girl. Anyway, it seemed the ideal solution."

"So you're living across the road in that big house all alone?"

"All alone."

"I thought I hadn't seen anyone else coming and going."

"To be honest, Lucy, you're pretty much the first person I've spoken to since I got here—apart from my shrink and my agent, that is. It's not that people aren't friendly. I've just been . . . well . . . stand-offish, I suppose. A bit distant." Lucy's hand still rested on Maggie's forearm, though she wasn't gripping at all now.

"That makes sense. After what you've been through. Did he follow you over here?"

"I don't think so. I don't think he knows where I am. I've had a few late-night hang-up calls, but I honestly don't know if they're from him. I don't think they are. All my friends back there swore they wouldn't tell him where I was, and he doesn't know Ruth and Charles. He had little interest in my career. I doubt that he knows I'm in England, though I wouldn't put it past him to find out." Maggie needed to change the subject. She could hear the ringing in her ears, feel the arcade spinning and her jaw aching, the colored-glass roof above her shifting like a kaleidoscope, her neck muscles stiffening, the way they always did when she thought about Bill for too long. *Psychosomatic,* the shrink said. As if that did her any good. She asked Lucy about herself.

"I don't really have any friends, either," Lucy said. She stirred her spoon around the dregs of her cappuccino froth. "I suppose I was always rather shy, even at school. I never know what to say to people." Then she laughed. "I don't have much of a life, either. Just work at the bank. Home. Taking care of Terry. We haven't been married a year yet. He doesn't like me to go out by myself. Even today, my day off. If he knew . . . That reminds me." She looked at her watch and seemed to become agitated. "Thank you very much for the coffee, Maggie. I really have to go. I have to get the bus back before school comes out. Terry's a teacher, you see."

Now it was Maggie's turn to grasp Lucy's arm and stop her from leaving so abruptly. "What is it, Lucy?" she asked.

Lucy just looked away.

"Lucy?"

"It's nothing. It's just what you were saying earlier." She

lowered her voice and looked around the arcade before going on. "I know what you mean, but I can't talk about it now."

"Terry hits you?"

"No. Not like . . . I mean . . . he's very strict. It's for my own good." She looked Maggie in the eye. "You don't know me. I'm a wayward child. Terry has to discipline me."

Wayward, Maggie thought. *Discipline.* What strange and alarming words to use. "He has to keep you in check? Control you?"

"Yes." She stood up again. "Look, I *must* go. It's been wonderful talking to you. I hope we can be friends."

"I do, too," said Maggie. "We really *have* to talk again. There's help, you know."

Lucy flashed her a wan smile and hurried off toward Vicar Lane.

After Lucy had gone, Maggie sat stunned, her hand shaking as she drained her cup. The milky foam was dry and cold against her lips.

Lucy a fellow victim? Maggie couldn't believe it. This strong, healthy, beautiful woman a victim, just like slight, weak, elfin Maggie? Surely it couldn't be possible. But hadn't she sensed something about Lucy? Some kinship, something they had in common. That must be it. That was what she hadn't wanted to talk to the police about that morning. She knew that she might have to, depending on how serious things were, but she wanted to put off the moment for as long as she could.

Thinking of Lucy, Maggie remembered the one thing she had learned about domestic abuse so far: it doesn't matter *who* you are. It can still happen to you. Alicia and all her other close friends back home had expressed their wonder at how such a bright, intelligent, successful, caring, *educated* woman like Maggie could fall victim to a wife beater like Bill. She had seen the expressions on their faces, noticed their conversations hush and shift when she walked in the room. There must be something wrong with her, they were all saying. And that was what she had thought, too, still thought, to some extent. Because to all intents and purposes Bill, too, was bright, intelligent, caring, educated and successful. Until he got his Monster Face on, that is, but only Maggie saw him like that. And it was odd, she thought, that nobody had thought to ask why an intelligent, wealthy, successful lawyer like Bill should feel the need to hit a woman almost a foot shorter and at least eighty pounds lighter than he was.

Even when the police came that time he was hammering at her door, she could tell they were making excuses for him— he was driven out of his mind by his wife's unreasonable action in taking out a restraining order against him; he was just upset because his marriage had broken up and his wife wouldn't give him a chance to make it up. Excuses, excuses. Maggie was the *only one* who knew what he could be like. Every day she thanked God they had no kids.

Which was what she was thinking about as she drifted back to the present, to feeding the ducks on the pond. Lucy was a fellow sufferer, and now Terry had put her in hospital. Maggie felt responsible, as if she should have done something. Lord knows, she had tried. After Lucy's subsequent tale of physical and psychological abuse at the hands of her husband had unfolded during their many furtive meetings over coffee and biscuits, with Maggie sworn to absolute secrecy, she *should have done something*. But unlike most people, Maggie knew exactly what it was like. She knew Lucy's position, knew that the best she could do was try to persuade her to seek professional help, to leave Terry. Which she did try to do.

But Lucy wouldn't leave him. She said she had nowhere to go and no one to go to. A common enough excuse. And it made perfect sense. Where *do* you go when you walk out on your life?

Maggie had been lucky she had the friends to rally around her and come up with at least a temporary solution. Most women in her position were not so fortunate. Lucy also said that her marriage was so new that she felt she had to give it a chance, give it some time; she couldn't just walk out on it; she wanted to work harder at it. Another common response from women in her position, Maggie knew, but all she could do was point out that it wasn't going to get any better, no matter what she did, that Terry wasn't going to change, and that it would come to her leaving sooner or later, so why not leave sooner and spare herself the beatings?

But no. Lucy wanted to stick it out awhile longer. At least a little while. Terry was so nice afterward, so good to her; he bought her presents, flowers, swore he would never do it again, that he would change. It made Maggie sick to hear all this—literally, as she once vomited the minute Lucy left the house—the same damn reasons and excuses she had given herself and those few close friends who knew about her situation all along.

But she listened. What else could she do? Lucy needed a friend, and for better or for worse, Maggie was it.

Now this.

Maggie tossed the last crumbs of bread into the pond. She aimed for the scruffiest, littlest, ugliest duckling of them all, the one way at the back that hadn't been able to get at the feast so far. It made no difference. The bread landed only inches from his beak, but before he could get to it, the others had paddled over in a ferocious pack and snapped it right from under his mouth.

* * *

Banks wanted to get a look at the whole interior of 35 The Hill before the SOCOs started ripping it apart. He didn't know what it would tell him, but he needed to get the feel of it.

Downstairs, in addition to the kitchen with its small dining area, there was only a living room containing a three-piece suite, stereo system, television, video, and a small bookcase. Though the room was decorated with the same feminine touch as the hallway—frilly lace curtains, coral-pink wallpaper, thick-pile carpet, cream ceiling with ornate cornices—the videos in the cabinet under the TV set reflected masculine tastes: action films, tape after tape of *The Simpsons,* a collection of horror and science fiction films, including the whole *Alien* and *Scream* series, along with some true classics such as *The Wicker Man,* the original *Cat People, Curse of the Demon* and a boxed set of David Cronenberg films. Banks poked around but could find no porn, nothing homemade. Maybe the SOCOs would have better luck when they took the house apart. The CDs were an odd mix. There was some classical, mostly classic FM compilations and a best-of-Mozart set, but there were also some rap, heavy metal, and country-and-western CDs. Eclectic tastes.

The books were also mixed: beauty manuals, *Reader's Digest* condensed specials, needlecraft techniques, romances, occult and true crime of the more graphic variety, tabloid-style biographies of famous serial killers and mass murderers. The room showed one or two signs of untidiness—yesterday's evening paper spread over the coffee table, a couple of videos left out of their boxes—but on the whole it was clean and neat. There were also a number of knickknacks around the place, the sort of things that Banks's mother wouldn't have in the house because they made dusting more difficult: porcelain figures of fairy-tale characters and animals. In the dining room, there was a large glass-fronted cabinet filled with Royal Doulton chinaware. Probably a wedding present, Banks guessed.

Upstairs were two bedrooms, the smaller one used as a home office, along with a toilet and bathroom. No shower, just sink and tub. Both toilet and bathroom were spotless, the porcelain shining bright, the air heavy with the scent of lavender. Banks glanced around the plug holes but saw only polished chrome, not a trace of blood or hair.

Their computer expert, David Preece, sat in the office clacking away at the computer keys. A large filing cabinet stood in the corner; it would have to be emptied, its contents transferred to the exhibits room at Millgarth.

"Anything yet, Dave?" Banks asked.

Preece pushed his glasses back up his nose and turned. "Nothing much. Just a few pornographic Web sites bookmarked, chat rooms, that sort of thing. Nothing illegal yet, by the looks of it."

"Keep at it."

Banks walked into the master bedroom. The color scheme seemed to continue the ocean theme, but instead of coral it was sea blue. Azure? Cobalt? Cerulean? Annie Cabbot would know the exact shade, her father being an artist, but to Banks it was just blue, like the walls of his living room, though a shade or two darker. The queen-size bed was covered by a fluffed-up black duvet. The bedroom suite was assemble-it-yourself blond Scandinavian pine. Another television set stood on a stand at the bottom of the bed. The cabinet held a collection of soft-core porn, if the labels were to be believed, but still nothing illegal or homemade, no kiddie stuff or animals. So the Paynes were into porn videos. So what? So were more than half the households in the country, Banks was willing to bet. But more than half the households in the country didn't go around abducting and killing young girls. Some lucky young DC was going to have to sit down and watch the lot from start to finish to verify that the contents matched the titles.

Banks poked around in the wardrobe: suits, shirts, dresses,

shoes—mostly women's—nothing he wouldn't have expected. They would all have to be bagged by the SOCOs and examined in minute detail.

There were plenty of knickknacks in the bedroom, too: Limoges cases, musical jewelry boxes, lacquered, hand-painted boxes. The room took its musky rose and aniseed scent, Banks noticed, from a bowl of potpourri on the laundry hamper under the window.

The bedroom faced The Hill, and when Banks parted the lace curtains and looked out of the window, he could see the houses atop the rise over the street, half hidden by shrubs and trees. He could also see the activity below, on the street. He turned and looked around the room again, finding it somehow depressing in its absolute sterility. It could have been ordered from a color supplement and assembled yesterday. The whole house—except for the cellar, of course—had that feel to it: pretty, contemporary, the sort of place where the up-and-coming young middle-class couple about town *should* be living. So ordinary, but empty.

With a sigh, he went back downstairs.

Chapter 3

*K*elly Diane Matthews went missing during the New Year's Eve party in Roundhay Park, Leeds. She was seventeen years old, five feet three inches tall and weighed just seven stones. She lived in Alwoodley and attended Allerton High School. Kelly had two younger sisters: Ashley, age nine, and Nicola, age thirteen.

The call to the local police station came in at 9:11 A.M. on the first of January, 2000. Mr. and Mrs. Matthews were worried that their daughter hadn't come home that night. They had been to a party themselves, and hadn't arrived back until almost 3 A.M. They noticed that Kelly wasn't home yet but weren't too worried because she was with friends, and they knew that these New Year's parties were likely to go on until the wee hours. They also knew she had plenty of money for a taxi.

They were both tired and a little tipsy after their own party, they told the police, so they went straight to bed. When they awoke the following morning and found that Kelly's bed had still not been slept in, they became worried. She had never done anything like this before. First they telephoned the parents of the two girlfriends she had gone with, reliable in their estimation. Both Kelly's friends, Alex Kirk and Jessica Bradley, had arrived home shortly after two in the morning. Then Adrian Matthews rang the police. PC Rearden, who took the call, picked up on the genuine concern in Mr. Matthews's voice and sent an officer around immediately.

Kelly's parents said they last saw her around seven o'clock on the thirty-first of December, when she went to meet her friends. She was wearing blue jeans, white trainers, a thick cable-knit jumper and a three-quarter-length suede jacket.

When questioned later, Kelly's friends said that the group had become separated during the fireworks display, but nobody was too concerned. After all, there were thousands of people about, buses were running late and the taxis were touting for business.

Adrian and Gillian Matthews weren't rich, but they were comfortably off. Adrian oversaw the computer systems of a large retail operation and Gillian was assistant manager of a city center building society branch. They owned a Georgian-style semi-detached house not far from Eccup Reservoir, in an area of the city closer to parks, golf courses and the countryside than to factories, warehouses and grim terraces of back-to-backs.

According to her friends and teachers, Kelly was a bright, personable, responsible girl who got consistently high marks and was certain to land in the university of her choice, at the moment Cambridge, where she intended to read law. Kelly was also her school's champion sprinter. She had beautiful gold-blond hair, which she wore long, and she liked clothes, dancing, pop music and sports. She was also fond of classical music and quite an accomplished pianist.

It soon became clear to the investigating officer that Kelly Matthews was a most unlikely teenage runaway, and he instituted a search of the park. When, three days later, the search parties had found nothing, they called it off. In the meantime, police had also interviewed hundreds of revelers, some of whom said they thought they'd seen her with a man and others with a woman. Taxi drivers and bus drivers were also questioned, to no avail.

A week after Kelly disappeared, her shoulder bag was found in some bushes near the park; in it were her keys, a diary, cosmetics, a hairbrush and a purse containing over thirty-five pounds and some loose change.

Her diary yielded no clues. The last entry, on the thirty-first of December, 1999, was a brief list of new year's resolutions:

1. Help Mum more around the house.
2. Practice piano every day.
3. Be nicer to my little sisters.

Banks stripped off his protective clothing, leaned against his car out in the street and lit a cigarette. It was going to be a hot, sunny day, he could tell, only the occasional high cloud scudding across the blue sky on a light breeze, and he would be spending most of it indoors, either at the scene or at Millgarth. He ignored the people on the other side of the road, who stopped to stare, and shut his ears to the honking horns from the snarl of cars up The Hill, which had now been blocked off completely by the local traffic police. The press had arrived; Banks could see them straining at the barriers.

Banks had known it would come to this eventually, or to something very much like this, from the first moment he had agreed to head the North Yorkshire half of the two-county task force into the series of disappearances: Five young women in all, three from West Yorkshire and two from North Yorkshire. The West Yorkshire Assistant Chief Constable (Crime) was in overall charge, but he was at county headquarters in Wakefield, so Banks and Blackstone rarely saw him. They reported directly to the head of CID, Area Commander Philip Hartnell, at Millgarth in Leeds, who was the official senior investigating officer, but who left them to get on with the job. The main incident room was also at Millgarth.

Under Banks and Blackstone came several detective inspectors; a whole host of detective constables and sergeants, culled from both West and North County forces; skilled civilian employees; Crime Scene Coordinator DS Stefan Nowak; and, acting as consultant psychologist, Dr. Jenny Fuller, who had studied offender profiling in America with the National Center for the Analysis of Violent Crime at the FBI academy in Quantico, Virginia, and didn't look a bit like Jodie Foster. Jenny had also studied with Paul Britton in Leicester and was recognized as one of the rising stars in the relatively new field of psychology combined with police work.

Banks had worked with Jenny Fuller on his very first case in Eastvale, and they had become close friends. Almost more, but something always seemed to get in their way.

It was probably for the best, Banks told himself, though he often couldn't convince himself of that when he looked at her. Jenny had such lips as you rarely saw on anyone but a pouting French sex symbol, her figure tapered and bulged in all the right places and her clothes, usually expensive clothes, silky mostly in green and russet, just seemed to flow over her. It was that "liquefaction of her clothes" that the poet Herrick wrote about, the dirty old devil. Banks had come across Herrick in a poetry anthology he was working his way through, having felt a disturbing ignorance in such matters for years.

Lines like Herrick's stuck with him, as did the one about "sweet disorder in the dress," which made him think of DS Annie Cabbot, for some reason. Annie wasn't so obviously beautiful in the way Jenny was, not as voluptuous, not the kind to draw wolf whistles on the street, but she had a deep, quiet sort of beauty that appealed very much to Banks. Unfortunately, because of his new and onerous responsibilities, he hadn't seen much of Annie lately and had found himself, because of the case, spending more and more time with Jenny, realizing that the old feelings, that odd and immediate spark between them, had never gone away. Nothing had *happened* as such, but it had been touch and go on occasion.

Annie was also consumed with her work. She had found a detective inspector's position open in Western Division's Complaints and Discipline Department, and had taken it because it was the first opportunity that came up. It wasn't ideal, and it certainly didn't win her any popularity contests, but it was a necessary step in the ladder she had set out to climb, and Banks had encouraged her to go for it.

DC Karen Hodgkins edged her little gray Nissan through the opening the police made in the barrier for her and broke off Banks's chain of thought. She got out and walked over. Karen had proved an energetic and ambitious worker throughout the whole investigation, and Banks fancied she would go far if she developed a flair for police politics. She reminded him a bit of Susan Gay, his old DC, now a DS in Cirencester, but she had fewer sharp edges and seemed more sure of herself.

"What's the situation?" Banks asked her.

"Not much change, sir. Lucy Payne's under sedation. The doctor says we won't be able to talk to her until tomorrow."

"Have Lucy and her husband been fingerprinted?"

"Yes, sir."

"What about her clothes?" Banks had suggested that they take the clothes Lucy Payne had been wearing for forensic examination. After all, she wouldn't be needing them in hospital.

"They should be at the lab by now, sir."

"Good. What was she wearing?"

"Nightie and a dressing gown."

"What about Terence Payne? How's he doing?"

"Hanging on. But they say that even if he does recover he might be . . . you know . . . a vegetable . . . there might be serious brain damage. They've found skull fragments stuck in his brain. It seems . . . well . . ."

"Go on."

"The doctor's saying that it seems the PC who subdued him used a bit more than reasonable force. He was very angry."

"Was he, indeed?" *Christ.* Banks could see a court case looming if Payne survived with brain damage. Best let AC Hartnell worry about it; that was what ACs were put on this earth for, after all. "How's PC Taylor coping?"

"She's at home, sir. A friend's with her. Female PC from Killingbeck."

"Okay, Karen, I want you to act as hospital liaison for the time being. Any change in the status of the patients—either of them—and I want to know immediately. That's your responsibility, okay?"

"Yes, sir."

"And we're going to need a family liaison officer." He gestured toward the house. "Kimberley's parents need to be told, before they hear it on the news. We also need to arrange for them to identify the body."

"I'll do it, sir."

"Good of you to offer, Karen, but you've got your hands full already. And it's a thankless task."

Karen Hodgkins headed back to her car. If truth be told, Banks didn't think Karen had the right bedside manner for a family liaison officer. He could picture the scene—the parents' disbelief, their outpouring of grief, Karen's embarrassment and brusqueness. No. He would send roly-poly Jonesy. DC Jones might be a slob, but he had sympathy and concern leaking out of every pore. He should have been a vicar. One of the problems with drawing a team from such a wide radius, Banks thought, was that you could never get to know the individual officers well enough. Which didn't help when it came to handing out assignments. You needed the right person for the right job in police work, and one wrong decision could screw up an investigation.

Banks just wasn't used to running such a huge team, and

the problems of coordination had given him more than one headache. In fact, the whole matter of responsibility was weighing very heavily on his mind. He didn't feel competent to deal with it all, to keep so many balls up in the air at once. He had already made more than one minor mistake and mishandled a few situations with personnel. So much so that he was beginning to think his people skills were especially low. It was easier working with a small team—Annie, Winsome Jackman, Sergeant Hatchley—where he could keep track of every little detail in his mind. This was more like the kind of work he had done on the Met down in London, only there he had been a mere constable or sergeant, given the orders rather than giving them. Even as an inspector down there, toward the end, he had never had to deal with *this* level of responsibility.

Banks had just lit his second cigarette when another car came through the barrier and Dr. Jenny Fuller jumped out, struggling with a briefcase and an overstuffed leather shoulder bag, hurrying as usual, as if she were late for an important meeting. Her tousled red mane cascaded over her shoulders and her eyes were the green of grass after a summer shower. The freckles, crow's-feet and slightly crooked nose that she always complained ruined her looks only made her appear more attractive and more human.

"Morning, Jenny," Banks greeted her. "Stefan's waiting inside. You ready?"

"What's that? Yorkshire foreplay?"

"No. That's 'Are you awake?' "

Jenny forced a smile. "Glad to see you're on form, even at this ungodly hour."

Banks looked at his watch. "Jenny, I've been up since half-past four. It's nearly eight now."

"My point exactly," she said. "Ungodly." She looked toward the house. Apprehension flitted across her features. "It's bad, isn't it?"

"Very."

"Coming in with me?"

"No. I've seen enough. Besides, I'd better go and put AC Hartnell in the picture or he'll have my guts for garters."

Jenny took a deep breath and seemed to gird herself. "Right," she said. "Lay on, Macduff. I'm ready."

And she walked in.

Area Commander Philip Hartnell's office was, as befitted his rank, large. It was also quite bare. AC Hartnell didn't believe in making himself at home there. This, the place seemed to shout, is an *office* and an office only. There was a carpet, of course—an area commander merited a carpet—one filing cabinet, a bookcase full of technical and procedural manuals and, on his desk, beside the virgin blotter, a sleek black laptop computer and a single buff file folder. That was it. No family photographs, nothing but a map of the city on the wall and a view of the open-air market and the bus station from his window, the tower of Leeds Parish Church poking up beyond the railway embankment.

"Alan, sit down," he greeted Banks. "Tea? Coffee?"

Banks ran his hand over his scalp. "Wouldn't mind a black coffee, if it's no trouble."

"Not at all."

Hartnell phoned for coffee and leaned back in his chair. It squeaked when he moved. "Must get this bloody thing oiled," he said.

Hartnell was about ten years younger than Banks, which put him in his late thirties. He had benefited from the accelerated promotion scheme, which was meant to give bright young lads like him a chance at command before they became doddering old farts. Banks hadn't been on such a track; he had worked his way up the old way, the hard way, and like many others who had done so, he tended to be suspicious of the fast trackers, who had learned everything but the nitty-gritty down-and-dirty of policing.

The odd thing was that Banks liked Phil Hartnell. He had an easygoing manner, was an intelligent and caring copper and let the men under his command get on with their jobs. Banks had had regular meetings with him over the course of the Chameleon investigation and, while Hartnell had made a few suggestions, some of them useful, he had never once tried to interfere and question Banks's judgment. In appearance good-looking, tall and with the tapered upper body of a casual weight lifter, Hartnell was also reputed to be a bit of a ladies' man, still unmarried and tipped to remain that way for a while yet, thank you very much.

"Tell me what we're in for," he said to Banks.

"A shit storm, if you ask me." Banks told him about what they had found so far in the cellar at number 35 The Hill, and the condition of the three survivors. Hartnell listened, the tip of his finger touched to his lips.

"There's not much doubt he's our man, then? The Chameleon?"

"Not much."

"That's good, then. At least that's something we can congratulate ourselves on. We've got a serial killer off the streets."

"It wasn't down to us. Just pure luck the Paynes happened to have a domestic disagreement and a neighbor heard and called the police."

Hartnell stretched his arms out behind his head. A twinkle came to his gray-blue eyes. "You know, Alan, the amount of shit we get poured on us when luck goes against us, or when we seem to be making no progress at all no matter how many man-hours we put in, I'd say we're entitled to claim a victory this time and maybe even crow a little about it. It's all in the spin."

"If you say so."

"I do, Alan. I do."

Their coffee arrived and both took a moment to sip. It tasted wonderful to Banks, who hadn't got his usual three or four cups down his gullet that morning.

"But we do have a potentially serious problem, don't we?" Hartnell went on.

Banks nodded. "PC Taylor."

"Indeed." He tapped the file folder. "Probationary PC Janet Taylor." He looked away a moment, toward the window. "I knew Dennis Morrisey, by the way. Not well, but I knew him. Solid sort of bloke. Seems he's been around for years. We'll miss him."

"What about PC Taylor?"

"Can't say I know her. Have the proper procedures been followed?"

"Yes."

"No statement yet?"

"No."

"Okay." Hartnell got up and stared out of the window for a few moments, his back to Banks. When he spoke again he didn't turn round. "You know as well as I do, Alan, that protocol demands the Police Complaints Authority brings in an investigator from a neighboring force to deal with a problem like this. There mustn't even be the slightest hint of a cover-up, of special treatment. Naturally, I'd like nothing better than to deal with it myself. Dennis was one of ours, after all. As is PC Taylor. But it's not on the cards." He turned and walked back over to his chair. "Can you imagine what a field day the press will have, especially if Payne dies? Heroic PC brings down serial killer and ends up being charged with using excessive force. Even if it's excusable homicide, it's still the dog's breakfast as far as we're concerned. And what with the Hadleigh case before the court right now . . ."

"True enough." Banks, like every other policeman, had

had to deal more than once with the outrage of men and women who had seriously hurt or killed criminals in defense of their families and property and then found themselves under arrest for assault, or worse, murder. At the moment, the country was awaiting the jury's verdict on a farmer called John Hadleigh, who had used his shotgun on an unarmed sixteen-year-old burglar, killing the lad. Hadleigh lived on a remote farm in Devon, and his house had been broken into once before, just over a year ago, at which time he had been beaten as well as robbed. The young burglar had a record as long as your arm, but that didn't matter. What mattered most was that the pattern of shotgun pellets covered part of the side and the back, indicating that the boy had been turning to run away as the gun was fired. An unopened flick-knife was found in his pocket. The case had been generating sensational headlines for a couple of weeks and would be with the jury in a matter of days.

An investigation didn't mean that PC Janet Taylor would lose her job or go to jail. Fortunately there were higher authorities, such as judges and chief constables, who had to make decisions on such matters as those, but there was no denying that it could have a negative effect on her police career.

"Well, it's *my* problem," said Hartnell, rubbing his forehead. "But it's a decision that has to be made very quickly. Naturally, as I said, I'd like to keep it with us, but I can't do that." He paused and looked at Banks. "On the other hand, PC Taylor is West Yorkshire and it seems to me that *North* Yorkshire might reasonably be considered a neighboring force."

"True," said Banks, beginning to get that sinking feeling.

"That would help keep it as close as we can, don't you think?"

"I suppose so," said Banks.

"As a matter of fact, ACC McLaughlin's an old friend of mine. It might be worthwhile my having a word. How's your

Complaints and Discipline Department? Know anyone up there?"

Banks swallowed. It didn't matter what he said. If the matter went to Western Division's Complaints and Discipline, the burden would almost certainly land in Annie Cabbot's lap. It was a small department—Annie was the only detective inspector—and Banks happened to know that her boss, Detective Superintendent Chambers, was a lazy sod with a particular dislike of female detectives making their way up the ranks. Annie was the new kid on the block, and she was also a woman. Not a hope of her getting out of this one. Banks could almost see the bastard rubbing his hands for glee when the order came down.

"Don't you think it might seem just a bit *too* close to home?" he said. "Maybe Greater Manchester or Lincolnshire would be better."

"Not at all," said Hartnell. "This way we get to be seen to do the right thing while still keeping it pretty close to us. Surely you must know someone in the department, someone who'll realize it's in his best interests to keep you informed?"

"Detective Superintendent Chambers is in charge," said Banks. "I'm sure he'll find someone suitable to assign."

Hartnell smiled. "Well, I'll have a word with Ron this morning and we'll see where it gets us, shall we?"

"Fine," said Banks, thinking, *She'll kill me, she'll kill me,* even though it wasn't his fault.

Jenny Fuller noted with distaste the obscene poster as she went through the cellar door, with DS Stefan Nowak right behind her, then she put her feelings aside and viewed it dispassionately, as a piece of evidence. Which it was. It marked the keeper of the portal to the dark underworld where Terence Payne could immerse himself in what he loved most in

life: domination, sexual power, murder. Once he had got beyond this obscene guardian, the rules that normally governed
human behavior no longer applied.

Jenny and Stefan were alone in the cellar now. Alone with
the dead. She felt like a voyeur. Which she was. She also felt
like a fraud, as if nothing she could say or do would be of any
use. She almost felt like holding Stefan's hand. Almost.

Behind her, Stefan switched off the overhead light and
made Jenny jump. "Sorry. It wasn't on at first," he explained.
"One of the ambulance crew turned it on so they could see
what they were dealing with, and it just got left on."

Jenny's heartbeat returned to normal. She could smell incense, along with other odors she had no desire to dwell on.
So this was his working environment: *hallowed, church-like*.
Several of the candles had burned down by now, and some of
them were guttering out, but a dozen or more still flickered,
multiplied into hundreds by the arrangement of mirrors.
Without the overhead light, Jenny could hardly make out the
dead policeman's body on the floor, which was probably a
blessing, and the candlelight softened the impact of the girl's
body, gave her skin such a reddish-gold hue that Jenny could
have almost believed Kimberley alive were it not for the pre-
ternatural stillness of her body and the way her eyes stared up
into the overhead mirror.

Nobody home.

Mirrors. No matter where Jenny looked, she could see
several reflections of herself, Stefan and the girl on the mattress, muted in the flickering candlelight. *He likes to watch
himself at work,* she thought. Could that be the only way he
feels *real?* Watching himself doing it?

"Where's the camcorder?" she asked.

"Luke Selkirk's—"

"No, I don't mean the police camera, I mean his, Payne's."

"We haven't found a camcorder. Why?"

"Look at the setup, Stefan. This is a man who likes to look at himself in action. It'd surprise me a great deal if he didn't keep some record of his actions, wouldn't it you?"

"Now you come to mention it, yes," said Stefan.

"That sort of thing's par for the course in sex killings. Some sort of memento. A trophy. And usually also some sort of visual aid to help him relive the experience before the next one."

"We'll know more when the team's finished with the house."

Jenny followed the phosphorescent tape that marked the path to the anteroom, where the bodies lay, still untouched, awaiting the SOCOs. In the light of Stefan's torch, her glance took in the toes sticking through the earth, and what looked like a finger, perhaps, a nose, a kneecap. His menagerie of death. Planted trophies. *His garden.*

Stefan shifted beside her, and she realized she had been holding his arm, digging in hard with her nails. They went back into the candlelit cellar. As Jenny stood over Kimberley noting the wounds, small cuts and scratch marks, she couldn't help herself but found she was weeping, silent tears damp against her cheek. She wiped her eyes with the back of one hand, hoping Stefan didn't notice. If he did, he was gentleman enough not to say anything.

Suddenly, she wanted to leave. It wasn't just the sight of Kimberley Myers on the mattress, or the smell of incense and blood, the images flickering in mirrors and candlelight, but the combination of all these elements made her feel claustrophobic and nauseated standing there observing this horror with Stefan. She didn't want to be here with him, or with any man, feeling the things she did. It felt obscene. And it was an obscenity performed by man upon woman.

Trying to conceal her trembling, she touched Stefan's arm. "I've seen enough down here for now," she said. "Let's go. I'd like to have a look around the rest of the house."

Stefan nodded and turned back to the stairs. Jenny had the

damnedest sensation that he knew exactly what she was feeling. Bloody hell, she thought, the sixth sense she could do without right now. Life was complicated enough with the usual five at work.

She followed Stefan past the poster up the worn stone stairs.

"Annie. Got much on right now?"

"As a matter of fact, I'm wearing a mid-length navy-blue skirt, red shoes and a white silk blouse. Do you want to know about my underwear?"

"Don't tempt me. I take it you're alone in the office?"

"All on my little lonesome."

"Listen, Annie, I've got something to tell you. Warn you about, actually." Banks was sitting in his car outside the Payne house talking on his mobile. The mortuary wagon had taken the bodies away, and Kimberley's stunned parents had identified her body. The SOCOs had located two more bodies so far in the anteroom, both of them in so advanced a state of decomposition that it was impossible to make visual identification. Dental records would have to be checked, DNA sampled and checked against the parents. It would all take time. Another team was still combing through the house, boxing up papers, accounts, bills, receipts, snapshots, letters, anything and everything.

Banks listened to the silence after he had finished explaining the assignment he thought Annie would be getting in the near future. He had decided that the best way to deal with it was to try to put it in a positive light, convince Annie that she would be good for the job and that it was the right job for her. He didn't imagine he would have much success, but it was worth a try. He counted the beats. *One. Two. Three. Four.* Then the explosion came.

"He's doing *what?* Is this some kind of sick joke, Alan?"

"No joke."

"Because if it is you can knock it off right now. It's not funny."

"It's no joke, Annie. I'm serious. And if you think about it for a minute you'll see what a great idea it is."

"If I thought about it for the rest of my life it still wouldn't seem like a great idea. How dare he . . . You know there's no way I can come out of this looking good. If I prove a case against her, then every cop and every member of the public hates my guts. If I don't prove a case, the press screams cover-up."

"No, they won't. Have you any idea of what sort of monster Terence Payne is? They'll be whooping for joy that populist justice is served at last."

"Some of them, perhaps. But not the ones I read. Or you, for that matter."

"Annie, it's not going to bury you. It'll be in the hands of the CPS well before that stage. You're not judge, jury and executioner, you know. You're just a humble investigator trying to get the facts right. How can that harm you?"

"Was it you who suggested me in the first place? Did you give Hartnell my name, tell him I'd be the best one for the job? I can't believe you'd do this to me, Alan. I thought you liked me."

"I do. And I haven't done anything. AC Hartnell came up with it all by himself. And you and I both know what'll happen as soon as it gets into Detective Superintendent Chambers's hands."

"Well, at least we're agreed on that. You know, the fat bastard's been chomping at the bit all week because he hasn't been able to find anything *really* messy for me to do. For crying out loud, Alan, couldn't you *do* something?"

"Like what?"

"Suggest he hand it over to Lancashire or Derbyshire. *Anything.*"

"I tried, but his mind was made up. He knows ACC McLaughlin. Besides, this way he thinks I can hold on to some degree of control over the investigation."

"Well, he can bloody well think again about that."

"Annie, you can do some good here. For yourself, for the public interest."

"Don't try appealing to my better nature. I haven't got one."

"Why are you resisting so strongly?"

"Because it's a crap job and you know it. At least give me the courtesy of not trying to soft-soap me."

Banks sighed. "I'm only the advance warning. Don't kill the messenger."

"That's what messengers are for. You're saying I've no choice?"

"There's always a choice."

"Yeah, the right one and the wrong one. Don't worry, I won't make a fuss. But you'd better be right about the consequences."

"Trust me. I'm right."

"And you'll respect me in the morning. Sure."

"Look, about the morning. I'm going back to Gratly tonight. I'll be late, but maybe you could come over, or I could drop by your place on my way?"

"What for? A quickie?"

"Doesn't have to be that quick. Way I'm sleeping these days it could take all night."

"No way. I need my beauty sleep. Remember, I've got to be up bright and early in the morning to drive to Leeds. Bye."

Banks held the silent mobile to his ear for a few moments, then put it back in his pocket. Christ, he thought, you handled that one really well, Alan, didn't you? *People skills.*

Chapter 4

Samantha Jane Foster, eighteen years old, five feet five and seven stone three pounds, was a first-year English student at the University of Bradford. Her parents lived in Leighton Buzzard, where Julian Foster was a chartered accountant and Teresa Foster a local GP. Samantha had one older brother, Alistair, unemployed, and a younger sister, Chloe, still at school.

On the evening of the twenty-sixth of February, Samantha attended a poetry reading in a pub near the university campus and left alone for her bed-sit at about eleven-fifteen. She lived just off Great Horton Road, about a quarter of a mile away. When she didn't turn up for her weekend job in the city center Waterstone's bookshop, one of her coworkers, Penelope Hall, became worried and called at the bed-sit during her lunch break. Samantha was reliable, she later told the police, and if she wasn't going to come in to work because of illness, she would always ring. This time she hadn't. Worried that Samantha might be seriously ill, Penelope managed to persuade the landlord to open the bed-sit door. Nobody home.

There was a very good chance that the Bradford Police might not have taken Samantha Foster's disappearance seriously—at least not so quickly—had it not been for the shoulder bag that a conscientious student had found in the street and handed in after midnight the previous evening. It contained a poetry anthology called *New Blood;* a slim volume of poetry signed "To Samantha, between whose silky thighs I would love to rest my head and give silver tongue" and dated by the poet, Michael Stringer, who had read in the pub the previous evening; a spiral notebook full of poetic jottings, observations, reflections on life and literature, including what looked to the desk officer like descriptions of hallucinogenic states and out-of-body experiences; a half-smoked packet of Benson & Hedges; a red packet of Rizzla cigarette papers and a small plastic bag of marijuana, less than a quarter of an ounce; a green disposable cigarette lighter; three loose tampons; a set of keys; a personal CD player with a Tracy Chapman CD inside it; a little bag of cosmetics; and a purse containing fifteen pounds in cash, a credit card, student union card, shop receipts for books and CDs and various other sundry items.

Given the two occurrences—an abandoned shoulder bag and a missing girl—especially as the young DC who was given the assignment remembered something similar had happened in Roundhay Park, Leeds, on New Year's Eve—the inquiry began that very morning with calls to Samantha's parents and close friends, none of whom had seen her or heard of any change in her plans or normal routine.

For a brief time, Michael Stringer, the poet who had been reading his work at the pub, became a suspect, given the inscription he had written in his book of poems for her, but a number of witnesses said he carried on drinking in the city center and had to be helped back to his hotel around three-thirty in the morning. The hotel staff assured the police that he hadn't seen the light of day again until teatime the following day.

Inquiries around the university turned up one possible witness, who thought she saw Samantha talking to someone through a car window. At least the girl had long blond hair and was wearing the same clothes Samantha was when she left the pub—jeans, black calf-high boots and a long, flapping overcoat. The car was dark in color, and the witness remembered the three last letters on the number plate because they formed her own initials: Kathryn Wendy Thurlow. She said she had no reason to believe that there was any problem at the time, so she crossed over to her street and carried on to her own flat.

The last two letters of a car number plate indicate the origin of its registration, and WT signifies Leeds. The DVLA at Swansea were able to supply a list of over a thousand possibles—as Kathryn hadn't been able to narrow the search down to make or even color—and the owners were interviewed by Bradford CID. Nothing came of it.

All the searches and interviews that followed turned up nothing more about Samantha Foster's disappearance, and rumblings were starting on the police tom-toms. Two disappearances, almost two months and about fifteen miles apart, were enough to set off a few alarm bells but not a full-blown panic.

Samantha didn't have many friends, but those she did have were loyal and devoted to her, in particular Angela Firth, Ryan Conner and Abha Gupta, who were all devastated by her disappearance. According to them, Samantha was a very serious sort of girl, given to long reflective silences and gnomic utterances, with no time for small talk, sports and television. She had a level head on her shoulders, though, they insisted, and everyone said she wasn't the type to go off with a stranger on a whim, no matter how much she talked about the importance of experiencing life to the full.

When the police suggested that Samantha might have wandered off under the influence of drugs, her friends said it was unlikely. Yes, they admitted, she liked to smoke a joint occasionally—she said it helped her with her writing—but she didn't do any harder drugs; she also didn't drink much and couldn't have had more than two or three glasses of wine the entire evening.

She didn't have a boyfriend at the moment and didn't seem interested in acquiring one. No, she wasn't gay, but she had spoken of exploring sexual experiences with other women. Samantha might appear unconventional in some ways, Angela explained, but she had a lot more common sense than people sometimes imagined on first impressions; she was just not frivolous, and she was interested in a lot of things other people laughed at or dismissed.

According to her professors, Samantha was an eccentric student with a tendency to spend too much of her time reading outside the syllabus, but one of her tutors, who had published some verse himself, said that he had hopes she might make a fine poet one day if she could cultivate a little more self-discipline in her technique.

Samantha's interests, so Abha Gupta said, included art, poetry, nature, Eastern religions, psychic experiences and death.

Banks and Ken Blackstone drove out to The Greyhound, a low-beamed rustic pub with Toby jugs all around the plate racks in the village of Tong, about fifteen minutes from the crime scene. It was going on for two o'clock, and neither of them had eaten yet that day. Banks hadn't eaten much in the past two days, in fact, ever since he had heard of the fifth missing teenager in the wee hours of Saturday morning.

Over the past two months, he had sometimes thought his head would explode under pressure of the sheer amount of detail he carried around in it. He would awaken in the early hours of the morning, at three or four o'clock, and the thoughts would spin around his mind and prevent him from going back to sleep. Instead, he would get up and brew a pot of tea and sit at the pine kitchen table in his pajamas making notes for the day ahead as the sun came up and spilled its liquid honey light through the high window or rain lashed against the panes.

These were lonely, quiet hours, and while he had got used to, even embraced, solitude, sometimes he missed his previous life with Sandra and the kids in the Eastvale semi. But Sandra was gone, about to marry Sean, and the kids had grown up and were living their own lives. Tracy was in her second year at the University of Leeds, and Brian was touring the country with his rock band, going from strength to strength after the great reviews their first independently produced CD had received. Banks had neglected them both, he realized, over the past couple of months, especially his daughter.

They ordered the last two portions of lamb stew and rice and pints of Tetley's bitter at the bar. It was warm enough to sit outside at one of the tables next to the cricket field. A local team was out practicing, and the comforting sound of leather on willow punctuated their conversation.

Banks lit a cigarette and told Blackstone about AC Hartnell giving North Yorkshire the PC Taylor investigation, and his certainty that it would go to Annie.

"She'll love that," said Blackstone.

"She's already made her feelings quite clear."

"You've told her?"

"I tried to put a positive spin on it to make her feel better, but . . . it sort of backfired."

Blackstone smiled. "Are you two still an item?"

"I think so, sort of, but half the time I'm not sure, to be honest. She's very . . . elusive."

"Ah, the sweet mystery of woman."

"Something like that."

"Maybe you're expecting too much of her?"

"What do you mean?"

"I don't know. Sometimes when a man loses his wife he starts looking for a new one in the first woman who shows any interest in him."

"Marriage is the last thing on my mind, Ken."

"If you say so."

"I do. I haven't bloody time, for a start."

"Talking about marriage, how do you think the wife, Lucy Payne, fits in?" Blackstone asked.

"I don't know."

"She must have known. I mean, she *was* living with the bloke."

"Maybe. But you saw the way things were set up back there. Payne could have sneaked anyone in through the garage and taken them straight into the cellar. If he kept the place locked and barred, nobody need have known. It was pretty well soundproofed."

"I'm sorry, but you can't convince me that a woman lives with a killer who does what Payne did and she hasn't a clue," said Blackstone. "What does he do? Get up after dinner and tell her he's just off down to the basement to play with a teen-age girl he's abducted?"

"He doesn't have to tell her anything."

"But she *must* be involved. Even if she wasn't his accomplice, she must at least have *suspected* something."

Someone gave the cricket ball a hell of a whack and a cheer went up from the field.

Banks stubbed out his cigarette. "You're probably right. Anyway, if there's anything at all to connect Lucy Payne to what happened in the cellar, we'll find out. For the moment, she's not going anywhere. Remember, though, unless we find out differently, we'd better remember that she's a victim first and foremost."

The SOCO teams might be spending weeks at the scene, Banks knew, and very soon number 35 The Hill would resemble a house undergoing major structural renovations. They would be taking in metal detectors, laser lights, infrared, UV, high-powered vacuums and pneumatic drills; they would be collecting fingerprints, flaked skin, fibers, dried secretions, hairs, paint chips, Visa bills, letters, books and personal papers; they would strip the carpets and punch holes in the walls, break up the cellar and garage floors and dig up the gardens. And everything they gathered, perhaps more than a thousand exhibits, would have to be tagged, entered in HOLMES and stored in the evidence room at Millgarth.

Their meals arrived and they tucked right in, waving away the occasional fly. The stew was hearty and mildly spiced. After a few mouthfuls, Blackstone shook his head slowly. "Funny Payne's got no form, don't you think? Most of them have *something* odd in their background. Waving their willies at schoolkids, or a touch of sexual assault."

"More than his job's worth. Maybe he's just been lucky."

Blackstone paused. "Or we've not been doing our jobs properly. Remember that series of rapes out Seacroft way two years or so back?"

"The Seacroft Rapist? Yes, I remember reading about it."

"We never did catch him, you know."

"You think it might have been Payne?"

"Possible, isn't it? The rapes stopped, then girls started disappearing."

"DNA?"

"Semen samples. The Seacroft Rapist was an excretor, and he didn't bother wearing a condom."

"Then check them against Payne's. And check where he was living at the time."

"Oh, we will, we will. By the way," Blackstone went on, "one of the DCs who interviewed Maggie Forrest, the woman who phoned in the domestic, got the impression that she wasn't telling him everything."

"Oh. What did he say?"

"That she seemed deliberately vague, holding back. She

admitted she knew the Paynes but said she knew nothing about them. Anyway, he didn't think she was telling the complete truth as far as her relationship with Lucy Payne went. He thinks they're a lot closer than she would admit."

"I'll talk to her later," said Banks, glancing at his watch. He looked around at the blue sky, the white and pink blossoms drifting from the trees, the men in white on the cricket pitch. "Christ, Ken, I could sit here all afternoon," he said, "but I'd better get back to the house to check on developments."

As she had feared, Maggie was unable to concentrate on her work for the rest of that day and alternated between watching the police activity out of her bedroom window and listening to the local radio for news reports. What came through was scant enough until the area commander in charge of the case gave a press conference, in which he confirmed that they had found the body of Kimberley Myers, and that it appeared she had been strangled. More than that, he wouldn't say, except that the case was under investigation, forensic experts were on the scene and more details would be available shortly. He stressed that the investigation was not yet over and appealed for anyone who had seen Kimberley after eleven o'clock on Friday evening to come forward.

When the knock on her door and the familiar call, "It's all right, it's only me," came after half-past three, Maggie felt relieved. For some reason, she had been worried about Claire. She knew that she went to the same school as Kimberley Myers and that Terence Payne was a teacher there. She hadn't seen Claire since Kimberley's disappearance but imagined she must have been frantic with worry. The two were about the same age and surely must know each other.

Claire Toth often called on her way home from school, as she lived two doors down, both her parents worked, and her mother didn't get home until about half-past four. Maggie also suspected that Ruth and Charles had suggested Claire's visits as a sneaky way of keeping an eye on her. Curious about the newcomer, Claire had first just dropped in to say hello. Then, intrigued by Maggie's accent and her work, she had become a regular visitor. Maggie didn't mind. Claire was a good kid, and a breath of fresh air, though she talked a mile a minute and Maggie often felt exhausted when she left.

"I don't think I've ever felt so awful," Claire said, dropping her backpack on the living room floor and plunking herself down on the sofa, legs akimbo. This was odd, for a start, as she usually headed straight for the kitchen, to the milk and chocolate chip cookies Maggie fed her. She pulled back her long tresses and tucked them behind her ears. She was wearing her school uniform, green blazer and skirt, white blouse and gray socks, which had slipped down around her ankles. She had a couple of spots on her chin, Maggie noticed: bad diet or time of the month.

"You know?"

"It was all around school by lunchtime."

"Do you know Mr. Payne?"

"He's my biology teacher. And he lives across the street from us. How *could* he? The pervert. When I think of what must have been going through his mind while he was teaching us about reproductive systems and dissecting frogs and all that stuff . . . ugh." She gave a shudder.

"Claire, we don't know that he did anything yet. All we know is that Mr. and Mrs. Payne had a fight and that he hit her."

"But they've found Kim's body, haven't they? And there wouldn't be all those policemen over the road if all he'd done was hit his wife, would there?"

If all he'd done was hit his wife. Maggie was often amazed at the casual acceptance of domestic violence, even by a girl-child such as Claire. True enough, she didn't mean it the way it sounded and would be horrified if she knew the details of

Maggie's life back in Toronto, but still, the language came so easily. *Hit his wife.* Minor. Not important.

"You're quite right," she said. "It *is* more than that. But we don't know that Mr. Payne was responsible for what happened to Kimberley. Someone else might have done it."

"No. It's him. He's the one. He killed all those girls. He killed Kim."

Claire started crying and Maggie felt awkward. She found a box of tissues and went to sit next to her on the sofa. Claire buried her head in Maggie's shoulder and sobbed, her thin veneer of teenage cool stripped away in a second. "I'm sorry," she said, sniffling. "I don't usually act like such a baby."

"What is it?" Maggie asked, still stroking her hair. "What is it, Claire? You can tell me. You were her friend, weren't you? Kim's?"

Claire's lip trembled. "I just feel so awful."

"I can understand that."

"But you don't. You can't! Don't you see?"

"See what?"

"That it was my fault. It was my fault that Kim got killed. I should have been with her on Friday. *I should have been with her!*"

And when Claire buried her face in Maggie's shoulder again, there came a loud knock at the door.

DI Annie Cabbot sat at her desk still cursing Banks under her breath and wishing she had never accepted the appointment to Complaints and Discipline, even though it had been the only divisional opening available for her at the level of inspector after passing her boards. Of course, she could have stayed in CID as a detective sergeant, or gone back to uniform for a while as an inspector in Traffic, but she had decided that C & D would be a worthwhile temporary step up until a suitable position became available in CID, which Banks had assured her wouldn't be long. The Western Division was still undergoing some structural reorganization, part of which involved staffing levels, and for the moment CID was taking a backseat to more visible on-the-street and in-your-face policing. But their day would come. This way, at least, she would gain experience at the rank of inspector.

The one good thing about the new appointment was her office. Western Division had taken over the building adjoining the old Tudor-fronted headquarters, part of the same structure, knocked through the walls and redone the interior. While Annie didn't have a large room to herself like Detective Superintendent Chambers, she did have a partitioned space in the general area, which gave her some degree of privacy and looked out over the marketplace, like Banks's office.

Beyond her frosted-glass compartment sat the two detective sergeants and three constables who, along with Annie and Chambers, made up the entire Western Division Complaints and Discipline Department. After all, police corruption was hardly a hot issue around Eastvale, and about the most serious case she had worked on so far was that of a beat policeman accepting free toasted teacakes from the Golden Grill. It turned out that he had been going out with one of the waitresses there and she was finding the way to his heart. Another waitress had become jealous and reported the matter to Complaints and Discipline.

It probably wasn't fair to blame Banks, Annie thought, standing at the window and looking down on the busy square, and perhaps she was only doing so because of the vague dissatisfaction with their relationship that she was already feeling. She didn't know what it was, or why, only that she was beginning to feel a little uncomfortable with it. They hadn't seen each other that often because of the Chameleon case, of course, and Banks had sometimes been so tired that he had fallen asleep even before . . . but it wasn't *that* that bothered her so much as the easy familiarity their relationship seemed to be attaining. When they were together, they were behaving more and more like an old married couple and Annie, for one, didn't want that. Ironic as it seemed, the comfort and familiarity were making her feel distinctly *uncomfortable*. All they needed was the slippers and the fireplace. Come to think of it, in Banks's cottage they even had those, too.

Annie's phone rang. It was Detective Superintendent Chambers summoning her to his office next door. She knocked and went in when he said, "Enter," the way he liked it. Chambers sat behind his messy desk, a big man with the waistcoat buttons of his pinstripe suit stretched tight across his chest and belly. She didn't know if his tie was covered with food stains or if it was supposed to look that way. He had the kind of face that seemed to be wearing a perpetual sneer, and small piggy eyes that Annie felt undress her as she walked in. His complexion was like a slab of beef, and his lips were fleshy, wet and red. Annie always half expected him to start drooling and slobbering as he spoke, but he hadn't done it yet. Not one drop of saliva had found its way on to his green blotter. He had a Home Counties accent, which he seemed to think made him posh.

"Ah, DI Cabbot. Please be seated."

"Sir."

Annie sat as comfortably as she could, careful to make certain that her skirt didn't ride too high over her thighs. If she'd known before she left for work that she was going to be summoned to see Chambers, she would have worn trousers.

"I've just been handed a most interesting assignment," Chambers went on. "Most interesting indeed. One that I think will be right up your alley, as they say."

Annie had the advantage of him but didn't want to let it show. "Assignment, sir?"

"Yes. It's about time you started pulling your weight around here, DI Cabbot. How long have you been with us now?"

"Two months."

"And in that time you've accomplished . . . ?"

"The case of Constable Chaplin and the toasted teacakes, sir. Scandal narrowly averted. A satisfactory resolution all around, if I might say so—"

Chambers reddened. "Yes, well, this one might just take the edge off your attitude, Inspector."

"Sir?" Annie raised her eyebrows. She couldn't stop herself baiting Chambers. He had the kind of arrogant, self-important bearing that cried out for pricking. She knew it could be bad for her career, but even with the rekindling of her ambition, Annie had sworn to herself that her career wasn't worth anything if it cost her her soul. Besides, she had an odd sort of faith that good coppers like Banks, Detective Superintendent Gristhorpe and ACC McLaughlin might have more say in her future than pillocks like Chambers, who, everyone knew, was a lazy slob just waiting for retirement. Still, she hadn't been a lot more careful with Banks at first, either, and it was only her good fortune that he had been charmed and seduced by her insubordination rather than angered by it. Gristhorpe, poor man, was a saint, and she hardly ever saw Red Ron McLaughlin, so she didn't get a chance to piss him off.

"Yes," Chambers went on, warming to his task, "I think you'll find this one a bit different from toasted teacakes. This'll wipe the grin off your face."

"Perhaps you'd care to tell me about it, sir?"

Chambers tossed a thin folder toward her. It slipped off the edge of the desk on to Annie's knees and then to the floor before she could catch it. She didn't want to bend over and pick it up so that Chambers could have a bird's-eye view of her knickers, so she left it where it was. Chambers's eyes narrowed and they stared at one another for a few seconds, but finally he eased himself out of his chair and picked it up himself. The effort made his face red. He slammed the file down harder on the desk in front of her.

"Seems a probationary PC in West Yorkshire has overdone it a bit with her baton and they want us to look into it. Trouble is, the chappie she overdid it with is suspected to be that Chameleon killer they've been after for a while, which, as I'm sure even you will realize, puts a different complexion on things." He tapped the folder. "The details, such as they are at the moment, are all in there. Do you think you can handle it?"

"No problem," said Annie.

"On the contrary," said Chambers, "I think there'll be plenty of problems. It'll be what they call a high-profile case, and because of that my name will be on it. I'm sure you understand that we can't have a mere inspector still wet behind the ears running a case of this importance."

"If that's the case," said Annie, "why don't you investigate it yourself?"

"Because I happen to be too busy at the moment," said Chambers, with a twisted grin. "Besides, why own a dog and bark yourself?"

"Absolutely. Why, indeed? Of course," said Annie, who happened to know that Chambers couldn't investigate his way out of a paper bag. "I understand completely."

"I thought you would." Chambers stroked one of his chins. "And as my name's on it, I want no cock-ups. In fact, if any heads roll over this business, yours will be the first. Remember, I'm only a hairsbreadth away from retirement, so the last thing on my mind is career advancement. You, on the other hand . . . Well, I'm sure you catch my drift."

Annie nodded.

"You'll be reporting to me directly, of course," Chambers went on. "Daily reports required, except in the event of any major developments, in which case you're to report to me immediately. Understood?"

"I wouldn't have it any other way," said Annie.

Chambers narrowed his eyes at her. "One day that mouth of yours will get you into serious trouble, young lady."

"So my father told me."

Chambers grunted and shifted his weight in his chair. "There's one more thing."

"Yes?"

"I don't like the way this assignment was delivered to me. There's something fishy about it."

"What do you mean, sir?"

"I don't know." Chambers frowned. "Acting Detective Superintendent Banks from CID is running our part of the Chameleon investigation, isn't he?"

Annie nodded.

"And if my memory serves me well, you used to work with him as a DS before coming over here, didn't you?"

Again, Annie nodded.

"Well, it might be nothing," said Chambers, looking away from her, at a point high on the wall. "Summat and nowt, as they say up here. But on the other hand . . ."

"Sir?"

"Keep an eye on him. Play your cards close to your chest."

He looked at her chest as he spoke and Annie gave an involuntary shudder. She stood up and walked over to the door.

"And another thing, DI Cabbot."

Annie turned. "Sir?"

Chambers smirked. "This Banks. Watch out for him. He's got the reputation for being a bit of a ladies' man, in case you don't know that already."

Annie felt herself flush as she left the office.

* * *

Banks followed Maggie Forrest into the living room, with its dark wainscoting and brooding landscapes in heavy gilt frames on the walls. The room faced west, and the late-afternoon sun cast dancing shadows of twisted foliage on the far walls. It was not a feminine room, but more like the kind to which the men withdrew for port and cigars in BBC period dramas, and Banks sensed that Maggie was uncomfortable in it, though he wasn't quite certain what gave him that impression. Noticing a whiff of smoke in the air and a couple of cigarette ends in the ashtray, Banks lit up, offering Maggie a Silk Cut. She accepted. He looked at the schoolgirl on the sofa, head lowered, bare knees close together, one of them scabbed from a recent fall, thumb in her mouth.

"Aren't you going to introduce us?" he asked Maggie.

"Detective . . . ?"

"Banks. Acting Detective Superintendent."

"Detective Superintendent Banks, this is Claire Toth, a neighbor."

"Pleased to meet you, Claire," said Banks.

Claire looked up at him and mumbled hello, then she took a crumpled packet of ten Embassy Regal from her blazer pocket and joined the adult smokers. Banks knew this was no time for lectures on the dangers of smoking. Something was clearly wrong. He could see by her red eyes and the streaks on her face that she had been crying.

"I've missed something," he said. "Anyone care to fill me in?"

"Claire went to school with Kimberley Myers," said Maggie. "Naturally, she's upset."

Claire grew edgy, her eyes flitting all over the place. She took short, nervous puffs on the cigarette, holding it affectedly, straight out with her first two fingers vertical, letting go as she puffed, then closing her fingers. She didn't seem to be inhaling, just doing it to look and act grown up, Banks thought. Or perhaps even to *feel* grown up, because only God knew what turbulent feelings must be churning inside Claire right now. And it would only get worse. He remembered Tracy's reaction to the murder of an Eastvale girl, Deborah Harrison, just a few years ago. They hadn't even known each other well, had come from differing social backgrounds, but they were about the same age, and they had met and talked on several occasions. Banks had tried to protect Tracy from the truth for as long as he could, but in the end the best he could do was comfort her. She was lucky; she got over it in time. Some never do.

"Kim was my best friend," Claire said. "And I let her down."

"What makes you think that?" Banks asked.

Claire flicked her eyes toward Maggie, as if seeking permission. Maggie nodded almost imperceptibly. She was an attractive woman, Banks noticed, not so much physically, with the slightly long nose and pointed chin, though he also admired her elfin looks and her trim, boyish figure, but it was the air of kindness and intelligence about her that struck him. He could see it in her eyes, and there was an artist's grace in the economy of her simplest movements, such as flicking ash from her cigarette, in her large hands with the long, tapered fingers.

"I should have been with her," Claire said. "But I wasn't."

"Were you at the dance?" Banks asked.

Claire nodded and bit her lip.

"Did you see Kimberley there?"

"Kim. I always called her Kim."

"All right: Kim. Did you see Kim there?"

"We went together. It's not far. Just up past the roundabout and along Town Street, near the Rugby ground."

"I know where you mean," said Banks. "It's the Congregational church opposite Silverhill Comprehensive, right?"

"Yes."

"So you went to the dance together."

"Yes, we walked up there and . . . and . . ."

"Take your time," said Banks, noticing that she was about to cry again.

Claire took a final puff at her cigarette, then stubbed it out. She didn't do a good job, and the ashes continued to smolder. She sniffled. "We were going to walk home together. I mean . . . people had said . . . you know . . . it was on the radio and television and my father told me . . . we had to be careful, stick together."

Banks had been responsible for the warnings. There was a fine line between panic and caution, he knew, and while he wanted to avert the kind of widespread paranoia that the Yorkshire Ripper case had whipped up for years in the early eighties, he also wanted to make it clear that young women should be cautious after dark. But short of instituting a curfew, you can't force people to be careful.

"What happened, Claire? Did you lose sight of her?"

"No, it wasn't that. I mean, not really. You don't understand."

"Help us to understand, Claire," said Maggie, holding her hand. "We want to. Help us."

"I should have been with her."

"Why weren't you?" Banks asked. "Did you have an argument?"

Claire paused and looked away. "It was a boy," she said finally.

"Kim was with a boy?"

"No, *me*. I was with a boy." Tears streamed down her cheeks, but she pressed on. "Nicky Gallagher. I'd fancied him for weeks and he asked me to dance. Then he said he wanted to walk me home. Kim wanted to leave just before eleven, she had a curfew, and normally I'd have gone with her, but Nicky . . . he wanted to stay for a slow dance . . . I thought there would be lots of people around . . . I . . ." Then she broke down in tears again and buried her head in Maggie's shoulder.

Banks took a deep breath. Claire's pain and guilt and grief were so real they broke over him in waves and made his breath catch in his chest. Maggie stroked her hair and muttered words of comfort, but still Claire let it all pour out. Finally, she came to the end of her tears and blew her nose in a tissue. "I'm sorry," she said. "Really, I am. I'd give *anything* to live that night over again and do it differently. I *hate* Nicky Gallagher!"

"Claire," said Banks, who was no stranger to guilt himself. "It's not his fault. And it's certainly not yours."

"I'm a selfish bitch. I had Nicky to walk me home. I thought he might kiss me. I *wanted* him to kiss me. See? I'm a slut, too."

"Don't be silly," said Maggie. "The superintendent is right. It's not your fault."

"But if I'd only—"

"*If. If. If,*" said Banks.

"But it's true! Kim had no one, so she had to walk home by herself and Mr. Payne got her. I bet he did awful things to her before he killed her, didn't he? I've read about people like him."

"Whatever happened that night," said Banks, "is not your fault."

"Then whose fault is it?"

"Nobody's. Kim was in the wrong place at the wrong time. It could have been—" Banks stopped. Not a good idea. He hoped Claire hadn't picked up on the implication, but she had.

"Me? Yes, I know that. I wish it had been."

"You don't mean that, Claire," said Maggie.

"Yes, I do. Then I wouldn't have to live with it. It was be-

cause of me. Because she didn't want to be a gooseberry."
Claire started crying again.

Banks wondered if it *could* have been Claire. She was the
right type: blond and long-legged, as so many young northern girls were. Was it as random as that? Or had Payne had
his eyes on Kimberley Myers all along? Jenny might have
some theories on that.

He tried to picture what had happened. Payne parked in
his car, near the youth club, perhaps; knowing there was a
dance on that night, knowing the one he'd had his eye on
would be there. He couldn't count on her going home alone,
of course, but nothing ventured, nothing gained. There was
always a chance. A risk, of course, but it would have been
worth it to him. His heart's desire. All the others were practice. This was the real thing, the one he had wanted right
from the start, there at school under his very eyes, tormenting
him, day after day.

Terence Payne would also have known, as Banks did, that
Kimberley lived about two hundred yards farther down The
Hill than her friend Claire Toth, under the railway bridge,
and that there was a dark, desolate stretch of road there, nothing but a wasteland on one side and a Wesleyan chapel on the
other, which would have been in darkness at that hour, Wes-
leyans not being noted for their wild late-night parties. When
Banks had walked down there on Saturday afternoon, the day
after Kimberley had disappeared, following the route she
would have taken home from the dance, he had thought it
would have made an ideal pickup place.

Payne would have parked his car a little ahead of Kimberley and either jumped her or said hello, the familiar, *safe* Mr.
Payne from school, somehow maneuvered her inside, then
chloroformed her and taken her back through the garage to
the cellar.

Perhaps, Banks realized now, Payne couldn't believe his
luck when Kimberley started walking home alone. He would

have expected her to be with her friend Claire, if not with others, and could only hope that the others would live closer to the school than Kimberley did and that she would end up alone for that final short but desolate stretch. But with her being alone right from the start, if he was careful and made sure that nobody could see, he could even have offered her a lift. She *trusted* him. Perhaps he had even, being the good, kind neighbor, given her a lift before.

"Get in the van, Kimberley, you know it's not safe for a girl your age to be walking the streets alone at this hour. I'll take you home."

"Yes, Mr. Payne. Thank you very much, Mr. Payne."

"You're lucky I happened by."

"Yes, sir."

"Now fasten your seat belt."

"Superintendent?"

"I'm sorry," said Banks, who had been lost in his imaginings.

"Is it all right if Claire goes home? Her mother should be back by now."

Banks looked at the child. Her world had shattered into pieces around her. All weekend she must have been terrified that something like this had happened, dreading the moment when the shadow of her guilt was made substance, when her nightmares proved to be reality. There was no reason to keep her here. Let her go to her mother. He knew where she was if he needed to talk to her again. "Just one more thing, Claire," he said. "Did you see Mr. Payne at all on the evening of the dance?"

"No."

"He wasn't at the dance?"

"No."

"He wasn't parked outside the youth club?"

"Not that I saw."

"Did you notice anyone at all hanging around?"

"No. But I wasn't really looking."

"Did you see Mrs. Payne at all?"

"*Mrs.* Payne? No. Why?"

"All right, Claire. You can go home now."

"Is there any more news of Lucy?" Maggie asked after Claire had left.

"She's comfortable. She'll be fine."

"You wanted to see me?"

"Yes," said Banks. "Just a few loose ends from this morning's interview, that's all."

"Oh?" Maggie fingered the neck of her T-shirt.

"Nothing important, I shouldn't think."

"What is it?"

"One of the officers who interviewed you gave me the impression that he thought you weren't telling the full story about your relationship with Lucy Payne."

Maggie raised her eyebrows. "I see."

"Would you describe the two of you as close friends?"

"Friends, yes, but close, no. I haven't known Lucy long."

"When did you last see her?"

"Yesterday. She dropped by in the afternoon."

"What did you talk about?"

Maggie looked down at her hands on her lap. "Nothing, really. You know, the weather, work, that sort of thing."

Kimberley Myers was tied naked in the cellar of the Payne house, and Lucy had dropped by to talk about the weather. Either she really was innocent, or her evil went way beyond anything Banks had experienced before. "Did she ever give you any cause to suspect that anything was wrong at home?" he asked.

Maggie paused. "Not in the way you're suggesting. No."

"What way am I suggesting?"

"I assume it's to do with the murder? With Kimberley's murder?"

Banks leaned back in his armchair and sighed. It had been

a long day, and it was getting longer. Maggie wasn't a convincing liar. "Ms. Forrest," he said, "right now anything at all we can find out about life at number thirty-five The Hill would be useful to us. And I mean *anything*. I'm getting the same impression as my colleague—that you're keeping something back."

"It's nothing relevant."

"How the hell would you know!" Banks snapped at her. He was shocked by the way she flinched at his harsh tone, at the look of fear and submission that crossed her features and the way she wrapped her arms around herself and drew in. "Ms. Forrest . . . Maggie," he said more softly. "Look, I'm sorry, but I've had a bad day, and this is becoming very frustrating. If I had a penny for every time someone told me their information was irrelevant to my investigation I'd be a rich man. I know we all have secrets. I know there are some things we'd rather not talk about. But this is a murder investigation. Kimberley Myers is dead. PC Dennis Morrisey is dead. God knows how many more bodies we'll unearth there, and I have to sit here and hear you tell me that you know Lucy Payne, that she may have shared certain feelings and information with you and that you don't think it's *relevant*. Come on, Maggie. Give me a break here."

The silence seemed to go on for ages, until Maggie's small voice broke it. "She was being abused. Lucy. He . . . her husband . . . he hit her."

"Terence Payne abused his wife?"

"Yes. Is that so strange? If he can murder teenage girls, he's certainly capable of beating his wife."

"She told you this?"

"Yes."

"Why didn't she do something about it?"

"It's not as easy as you think."

"I'm not saying it's easy. And don't assume that you know what I think. What did you advise her?"

"I told her to seek professional help, of course, but she was dragging her heels."

Banks knew enough about domestic violence to know that victims of it often find it very difficult to go to the authorities or get out: they feel shame, feel it's their own fault, feel humiliated and would rather keep it to themselves, believing it will turn out all right in the end. Many of them have nowhere else to go, no other lives to live, and they are scared of the world outside the home, even if the home is violent. He also got the impression that Maggie Forrest knew firsthand what she was talking about. The way she had flinched at his sharp tone, the way she had been so reluctant to talk about the subject, holding back. These were all signs.

"Did she ever mention that she suspected her husband of any other crimes?"

"Never."

"But she was frightened of him?"

"Yes."

"Did you visit their house?"

"Yes. Sometimes."

"Notice anything unusual?"

"No. Nothing."

"How did the two of them behave together?"

"Lucy always seemed nervous, edgy. Anxious to please."

"Did you ever see any bruises?"

"They don't always leave bruises. But Lucy seemed afraid of him, afraid of putting a foot wrong. That's what I mean."

Banks made some notes. "Is that all?" he asked.

"What do you mean?"

"Is that all you were holding back, or is there something else?"

"There's nothing else."

Banks stood up and excused himself. "Do you see now," he said at the door, "that what you've told me *is* relevant, after all? Very relevant."

"I don't see how."

"Terence Payne has serious brain injuries. He's in a coma from which he may never recover, and even if he does, he might remember nothing. Lucy Payne will mend quite easily. You're the first person who's given us any information at all about her, and it's information from which she could benefit."

"How?"

"There are only two questions as regards Lucy Payne. First, was she involved? And second, did she know and keep quiet about it? What you've just told me is the first thing that tips the scales in her favor. By talking to me, you've done your friend a service. Good evening, Ms. Forrest. I'll make sure there's an officer keeping an eye on the place."

"Why? Do you think I'm in danger? You said Terry—"

"Not that sort of danger. The press. They can be very persistent, and I wouldn't want you telling them what you've just told me."

Chapter 5

*L*eanne Wray was sixteen when she disappeared from Eastvale on Friday, the thirty-first of March. She was five feet two inches tall, weighed only six stone twelve pounds, and was an only child living with her father, Christopher Wray, a bus driver, and her stepmother Victoria, who stayed home, in a terrace house just north of Eastvale town center. Leanne was a pupil at Eastvale Comprehensive.

Leanne's parents later told police that they saw nothing wrong in letting their daughter go to the pictures that Friday night, even though they had heard of the disappearances of Kelly Matthews and Samantha Foster. After all, she was going with her friends, and they said she had to be home by half-past ten at the latest.

The one thing Christopher and Victoria might have objected to, had they known about it, was the presence in the group of Ian Scott. Christopher and Victoria didn't like Leanne hanging around with Ian. For one thing, he was two years older than she was, and that meant a lot at her age. For another, Ian had a reputation as a bit of a troublemaker and had even been arrested twice by the police: once for taking and driving away and once for selling Ecstasy in the Bar None. Also, Leanne was a very pretty girl, slim and shapely, with beautiful golden-blond hair, an almost translucent complexion and long-lashed blue eyes, and they thought an older boy like Ian could be interested in her for only one thing. That he had his own flat was another black mark against him.

But Leanne just liked to hang out with Ian's crowd. Ian's girlfriend, also with them that night, was Sarah Francis, age seventeen, and the fourth in the party was Mick Blair, age eighteen, just a friend. They all said they had walked around the center for a while after the film, then gone for a coffee at the El Toro—though the police discovered on further investigation that they had actually been drinking in the Old Ship Inn, in an alley between North Market Street and York Road, and lied about it because both Leanne and Sarah were under age. When pressed, they all said that Leanne had left them just outside the pub and headed home on foot at about a quarter past ten, a journey that should have taken her no more than ten minutes. But she never arrived.

Leanne's parents, though angry and worried, gave her until morning before calling the police, and an investigation, headed by Banks, soon went into full swing. Eastvale was papered with posters of Leanne; everyone who had been at the cinema, in the Old Ship Inn and in the town center that evening was questioned. Nothing. They even ran a reconstruction, but still nothing came of it. Leanne Wray had vanished into thin air. Not one person reported seeing her since she left the Old Ship.

Her three friends said they went to another pub, The Riverboat, a crowded place that stayed open late, and ended up at the Bar None on the market square. The closed-circuit TV cameras showed them turning up there at about half-past twelve. Ian Scott's flat was given the full SOCO treatment to see if any evidence of Leanne's presence could be found there, but there was nothing. If she had been there, she had left no trace.

There were hints of tension in the Wray home, Banks soon discovered, and according to a school friend, Jill Brown,

Leanne didn't get on well with her stepmother. They argued a lot. She missed her real mother, who had died of cancer two years ago, and Leanne had told her friend that she thought Victoria ought to go out and get a job instead of "sponging off her dad," who didn't make a lot of money anyway. Things were always a bit tough financially, Jill said, and Leanne had to wear sturdier clothes than she thought fashionable and make them last longer than she would have wished. When she was sixteen, she got a Saturday job in a town center boutique, so she was able to buy nice clothes at a discount.

There was, then, the faintest hope that Leanne had run away from a difficult situation and somehow hadn't heard the appeals. Until her shoulder bag was found in the shrubbery of a garden she would have passed on her route home. The owners of the house were questioned, but they turned out to be a retired couple in their seventies and were soon exonerated.

After the third day, Banks contacted his assistant chief constable, Ron McLaughlin, and discussions with Area Commander Philip Hartnell of West Yorkshire Police followed. Within days, the Chameleon task force was created and Banks was put in charge of North Yorkshire's part. It meant more resources, more man-hours and more concentrated effort. It also meant, sadly, that they believed a serial killer was at work, and this was something the newspapers lost no time in speculating about.

Leanne was an average pupil, so her teachers said. She could probably do better if she tried harder, but she didn't want to make the effort. She intended to leave school at the end of the year and get a job, maybe in a clothes shop or a music shop like Virgin or HMV. She loved pop music, and her favorite group was Oasis. No matter what people said about them, Leanne was a loyal fan. Her friends thought her a rather shy but easygoing person, quick to laugh at people's jokes and not given much to introspection. She also suffered from mild asthma and carried an inhaler, which had been found along with the rest of her personal things in the abandoned shoulder bag.

If the second victim, Samantha Foster, was a little eccentric, Leanne Wray was about as ordinary a lower-middle-class Yorkshire lass as you could get.

"Yeah, I'm all right to talk, sir. Really. Come on in."

PC Janet Taylor didn't *look* all right to Banks when he called at her flat after six that evening, but then anyone who had, that morning, both fought off a serial killer and cradled her dying partner's head on her lap had every right to look a bit peaky. Janet was pale and drawn, and the fact that she was dressed all in black only served to accentuate her pallor.

Janet's flat was above a hairdresser's on Harrogate Road, not far from the airport. Banks could smell the setting lotion and herbal shampoo inside the ground-floor doorway. He followed her up the narrow staircase. She moved listlessly, dragging her feet. Banks felt almost as weary as Janet seemed. He had just attended Kimberley Myers's postmortem, and while it had yielded no surprises—death by ligature strangulation—Dr. Mackenzie had found traces of semen in the vagina, anus and mouth. With any luck, DNA would link that to Terence Payne.

Janet Taylor's living room showed signs of neglect typical to a single police officer's dwelling. Banks recognized it all too well. He tried to keep his own cottage clean as best he could, but it was difficult sometimes when you couldn't afford a cleaning lady and you didn't have time yourself. When you did have a bit of free time, the last thing you wanted to do was housework. Still, the small room was cozy enough despite the patina of dust on the low table and the T-shirt and bra slung over the back of the armchair, the magazines and occasional half-empty teacups. There were three framed posters of old Bogie movies on the walls—*Casablanca, The Maltese Falcon* and *The African Queen*—and some photos on the mantelpiece, including one of Janet looking proud in her uniform, standing between an older couple Banks took to be her mother and father. The potted plant on the windowsill looked to be on its last legs, wilting and brown around the edges of the leaves. A television set flickered in one corner, the sound turned down. It was a local news program, and Banks recognized the scene around the Payne house.

Janet moved the T-shirt and bra from the back of the armchair. "Sit down, sir."

"Can we have the sound on for a minute?" Banks asked. "Who knows, maybe we'll learn something."

"Sure." Janet turned the volume up, but all they got was a repeat of AC Hartnell's earlier press statement. When it was over, Janet got up and turned off the TV. She still seemed slow in her movements, slurred in her speech, and Banks imagined it was something to do with the tranquilizers the doctor would have given her. Or maybe it was the half-empty bottle of gin on the sideboard.

A plane took off from Leeds and Bradford Airport, and while the noise didn't actually shake the flat, it was enough to rattle a glass and make conversation impossible for a minute or so. It was also hot in the small room, and Banks felt the sweat gather on his forehead and under his arms.

"It's why the place is so cheap," Janet said after the noise had waned to a distant drone. "I don't mind it that much. You get used to it. Sometimes I sit here and imagine I'm up there in one of them, flying off to some exotic country." She got up and poured herself a small gin, adding some tonic from an open bottle of Schweppes. "Fancy a drink, sir?"

"No, thanks. How are you coping?"

Janet sat down again and shook her head. "The funny thing is, I don't really know. I'm all right, I suppose, but I feel sort of numb, as if I've just come around from an anesthetic and I'm still all padded in cotton wool. Or like I'm in a dream and I'm going to wake up tomorrow morning and everything will be different. It won't, though, will it?"

"Probably not," said Banks. "It might even be worse."

Janet laughed. "Well, thanks for not giving me a load of bollocks."

Banks smiled. "My pleasure. Look, I'm not here to question your actions, but I need to know what happened in that house. Do you feel up to talking about it?"

"Sure."

Banks noticed her body language, the way she crossed her arms and seemed to draw in on herself, and guessed that she wasn't up to it, but he had to press on nonetheless.

"I felt like a criminal, you know," she said.

"What do you mean?"

"The way the doctor examined me, bagged my clothes, scraped under my fingernails."

"It's routine. You know it is."

"I know. I know. That's not what it feels like on the receiving end, though."

"I suppose not. Look, I'm not going to lie to you, Janet. This could be a serious problem. It could be over in no time at all, a minor bump in the road, but it could stick around, cause you problems with your career—"

"I think that's pretty much over, don't you, sir?"

"Not necessarily. Not unless you want it to be."

"I must admit I haven't given it a lot of thought since . . . you know." She gave a harsh laugh. "Funny thing is, if this was America, I'd be a hero."

"What happened when you first received the call?"

Janet told him about the car fire and the call and finding Lucy Payne unconscious in the hallway in short, halting sentences, occasionally pausing for a sip of gin and tonic, once or twice losing her thread and staring toward the open window. Sounds of evening traffic came up from the busy road and occasionally a plane landed or took off.

"Did you think she was seriously hurt?"

"Serious enough. Not life-threatening. But I stayed with her while Dennis checked around upstairs. He came back with a blanket and a pillow, I remember that. I thought that was nice of him. It surprised me."

"Dennis wasn't always nice?"

"It's not a word I'd use to describe him, no. We disagreed a lot, but I suppose we got on okay. He's all right. Just a bit of a Neanderthal. And full of himself."

"What did you do next?"

"Dennis went in back, the kitchen. I mean, someone had hit her, and if it was her husband, the odds were he was still in the house somewhere. Right? Probably feeling sorry for himself."

"You stayed with Lucy?"

"Yes."

"Then what happened?"

"Dennis called me, so I left her. She was as comfortable as I could make her, with the blanket and the pillow. The bleeding had pretty much stopped. I didn't think she was in any real danger. The ambulance was on its way . . ."

"You didn't sense any danger in the house?"

"Danger? No, not at all. I mean, no more than you do in any domestic. They can turn on you. It's happened. But no."

"Okay. What made you go down to the cellar? Did you think her husband might be there?"

"Yes, I suppose we must have."

"Why did Dennis call you?"

Janet paused, clearly embarrassed.

"Janet?"

Finally she looked at him. "You've been there? Down the cellar?"

"Yes."

"That picture on the door. The woman."

"I saw it."

"Dennis called me to see it. It was his idea of a joke. That's what I mean. Neanderthal."

"I see. Was the door open? The door to the cellar?"

"No, it was closed. But there was light showing under it, a sort of flickering light."

"You didn't hear anyone in there?"

"No."

"Did either of you call out before you went in, identifying yourselves as police officers?"

"I don't remember."

"Okay, Janet. You're doing fine. Carry on."

Janet's knees were pressed tight together and she was twisting her hands on her lap as she spoke. "Like I said, there was this flickering light."

"The candles."

Janet looked at him and gave a little shudder. "There was a bad smell, too, like drains."

"Did you have any reason to be afraid at this point?"

"Not particularly. It was creepy, but we were proceeding cautiously, as we always do in such situations. Routine. He could have been armed. The husband. We were aware of that possibility. But if you mean did we have any inkling of what we'd find in there, then no. If we had, we'd have been out of there like a shot and brought in the troops. Dennis and me, we're neither of us the hero types." She shook her head.

"Who went in first?"

"I did. Dennis kicked the door in and stood back, like, you know, making a bow. Taking the piss."

"What happened next?"

She gave a sharp jerk of her head. "It was all so fast. It was a blur. I remember candles, mirrors, the girl, crude drawings on the walls, things I saw out of the corners of my eyes. But they're like images from a dream. A nightmare." Her breathing became sharper and she curled up on the armchair, legs under her, arms wrapped around herself. "Then he came. Dennis was right behind me. I could feel his breath warm on my neck."

"Where did he come from?"

"I don't know. Behind. A corner. So fast."

"What did Dennis do?"

"He didn't have time to do anything. He must have heard or sensed something to make him turn, and the next thing I knew he was bleeding. He screamed out. That's when I pulled my baton. He cut Dennis again, and the blood sprayed over me. It was as if he hadn't noticed me, or he didn't care, he'd get to me later. But when he did, I had my baton out and he tried to slash me but I deflected it. Then I hit him . . ." She started to sob and rubbed the backs of her hands against her eyes. "Sorry. Dennis, I'm so sorry."

"It's all right," Banks said. "Take it easy, Janet. You're doing fine."

"He had his head on my lap. I was trying to hold the artery closed, like they teach in First Aid. But I couldn't do it. I'd never done it before, not with anyone real. The blood just kept seeping out. So much blood." She sniffed and ran the back of her hand across her nose. "Sorry."

"That's okay. You're doing fine, Janet. Before that. Before you tried to save Dennis, what else did you do?"

"I remember handcuffing the man to one of the pipes."

"How many times did you hit him?"

"I don't remember."

"More than once?"

"Yes. He wouldn't stop coming, so I hit him again."

"And again?"

"Yes. He kept getting up." She started sobbing again. When she'd calmed, she asked, "Is he dead?"

"Not yet."

"The bastard killed Dennis."

"I know. And when a man's partner is killed he's supposed to do something about it, right? If you don't, it's bad for business, bad for detectives everywhere."

Janet looked at him as if he were crazy. "What?"

Banks looked up at Bogart as Sam Spade. Clearly the posters were there for show, not as a result of any great passion for the films themselves, and his pathetic attempt at lightening things up fell flat. "Never mind," he said. "I was just wondering what went through your mind."

"Nothing. I didn't have time to stop and think. He'd cut Dennis and he was going to cut me. Call it self-preservation if you like, but it wasn't a conscious thought. I mean, I didn't think I'd better hit him again or he might get up and cut me. It wasn't like that."

"What *was* it like?"

"I told you. A blur. I disabled the killer, handcuffed him to one of the pipes and then I tried to keep Dennis alive. I didn't even look in Payne's direction again. To be honest, I didn't give a damn what shape he was in. Only Dennis." Janet paused and looked down at her hands clasped around the glass. "You know what really gets me? I'd just been nasty to him. All because he'd been telling his damn sexist jokes to that fireman."

"What do you mean?"

"We'd been arguing, that's all. Just before we got to the house. I told him his mole was probably cancerous. It was cruel of me. I know he's a hypochondriac. Why did I do that? Why am I such a horrible person? Then it was too late. I couldn't tell him I didn't mean it." She cried again and Banks thought it best to let her get it all out. It would take more than one tearful session to purge her of her guilt, but at least it was a start.

"Have you been in touch with the Federation?"

"Not yet."

"Do it tomorrow. Talk to your rep. They'll be able to help with counseling, if you want it, and . . ."

"Legal representation?"

"If it comes to that, yes."

Janet got to her feet a bit more unsteadily and went to pour herself another drink.

"Are you sure that's wise?" Banks asked.

Janet poured herself a stiff measure and sat down again. "Tell me what else I should be doing, sir. Should I be going to sit with Dennis's wife and kids? Should I try to explain to them how it happened, how it was all my fault? Or should I just smash up my flat and go out on the town and pick a fight in some anonymous pub somewhere, the way I feel like doing? I don't think so. This is by far the least harmful alternative to *anything* else I'd rather be doing right now."

Banks realized that she had a point. He had felt that way himself more than once, and had even given in to the urge to go out on the town and pick a fight. It hadn't helped. He would be a hypocrite if he said he didn't understand plenty about finding oblivion at the bottom of a bottle. There had been two periods in his life when he had sought solace that way. The first was when he felt he was fast approaching burnout those last few months in London, before the transfer to Eastvale, and the second was more than a year ago, after Sandra had left him.

The thing was, people said it didn't work, but it did. As a short-term solution, for temporary oblivion, there was nothing to match the bottle, except perhaps heroin, which Banks hadn't tried. Maybe Janet Taylor was right, and tonight drinking was the best thing she could do. She was hurting, and sometimes you had to do your hurting by yourself. Booze helped dull the pain for a while, and eventually you passed out. The hangover would be painful, but that was for tomorrow.

"Right you are. I'll let myself out." On impulse, Banks leaned over and kissed the top of Janet's head as he left. Her hair tasted of burned plastic and rubber.

That evening, Jenny Fuller sat in her home office, where she kept all the files and notes on the investigation on her computer, no office having been made available to her at Millgarth. The office looked out over The Green, a narrow stretch of parkland between her street and the East Side Estate. She could just see the lights of the houses through the spaces between the dark trees.

Working so closely with Banks had made Jenny remember a lot of their history. She had once tried to seduce him, she recalled with embarrassment, and he had resisted politely, claiming to be a happily married man. But he was attracted to her; she knew that much. He wasn't a happily married man anymore, but now he had "The Girlfriend," as Jenny had come to call Annie Cabbot, though she had never met her. That had come about because Jenny had spent so much time out of the country and hadn't even been around when Banks and Sandra separated. If she had been . . . well, things might have been different. Instead, she had embarked on a series of disastrous relationships.

One of the reasons she had spent so much time away, she had finally admitted to herself after coming back from California this last time with her tail between her legs, was to get away from Banks, from the easy proximity to him that tormented her so much while she pretended to be casual about the whole thing, and much cooler than she felt. And now they were working closely together.

With a sigh, Jenny returned her attention to her work.

Her main problem thus far, she realized, had been an almost complete lack of forensic and crime scene information, and without them, it was damn near impossible to produce a decent threshold analysis—an initial review that could serve as an investigative compass, help the police know where to look—let alone a more complex profile. About all she had been able to work on was the victimology. All this, of course, had given her detractors on the task force—and they were legion—plenty of ammunition.

England was still in the dark ages as far as the use of consultant psychologists and criminal profiling went, Jenny believed, especially as compared to the USA. Partly this was because the FBI is a national force with the resources to develop national programs and Britain has fifty or more separate police forces, all operating piecemeal. Also, profilers in the USA tend to be cops and are therefore more readily accepted. In Britain, profilers are usually psychologists or psychiatrists and, as such, are distrusted by the police and the legal system in general. Consultant psychologists would be lucky to make it to the witness box in an English court, Jenny knew, let alone be accepted as expert witnesses, the way they are in the USA. Even if they did get in the box, whatever evidence they gave would be looked at askance by judge and jury, and the defense would wheel in another psychologist with a different theory.

The dark ages.

When it came right down to it, Jenny was well aware that most of the police she worked with regarded her as perhaps only one step up from a clairvoyant, if that, and that they only brought her in because it was easier than not doing so. But still she struggled on. While she was prepared to admit that profiling was still, perhaps, more of an art than a science, and while a profile could rarely, if ever, point the finger at a specific killer, she believed that it could narrow the field and help focus an investigation.

Looking at pictures on a screen just didn't do it for Jenny, so she spread out the photographs again on her desk, though she knew them all by heart: Kelly Matthews, Samantha Foster, Leanne Wray, Melissa Horrocks and Kimberley Myers, all attractive blond girls between the ages of sixteen and eighteen.

There had been too many assumptions for Jenny's liking right from the start, the prime one being that all five girls had been abducted by the same person or persons. She could, she had told Banks and the team, make out almost as good a case for their not being linked, even on such little information as she possessed.

Young girls go missing all the time, Jenny had argued; they have arguments with their parents and run away from home. But Banks told her that detailed and exhaustive interviews with friends, family, teachers, neighbors and acquaintances showed that all the girls—except perhaps Leanne Wray—came from stable family backgrounds and, apart from the usual rows about boyfriends, clothes, loud music and what have you, nothing unusual or significant had happened in their lives prior to their disappearance. These, Banks stressed, were not your common or garden-variety teenage runaways. There was also the matter of the shoulder bags found abandoned close to where the girls had last been seen. With the botched Yorkshire Ripper investigation still hanging like an albatross around its neck, West Yorkshire was taking no chances.

The number became four, then five, and no traces whatsoever could be found of any of the girls through the usual channels: youth support groups, the National Missing Persons Helpline, *Crimewatch UK* reconstructions, MISSING: CAN-U-HELP posters, media appeals and local police efforts.

In the end, Jenny accepted Banks's argument and proceeded as if the disappearances were linked, at the same time keeping clear notes of any differences between the individual circumstances. Before long, she found that the similarities by far overwhelmed the differences.

Victimology. What did they have in common? All the girls

were young, had long blond hair, long legs and trim, athletic figures. It seemed to indicate the type of girl he liked, Jenny had said. They all have different tastes.

By victim number four, Jenny had noticed the pattern of escalation: nearly two months between victims one and two, five weeks between two and three, but only two and a half weeks between three and four. He had been getting needier, she thought at the time, which meant he might also become more reckless. Jenny was also willing to bet that there was a fair degree of personality disintegration going on.

The criminal had chosen his haunts well. Open-air parties, pubs, dances, clubs, cinemas and pop concerts were all places where you were very likely to find young people, and they all had to get home one way or another. She knew that the team referred to him as the "Chameleon" and agreed that he showed a very high level of skill in taking his pick of victims without being seen. All had been abducted at night in urban settings—desolate stretches of city streets, ill-lit and deserted. He had also managed to stay well beyond the range of the CCTV cameras that covered many city centers and town squares these days.

A witness said she saw Samantha, the Bradford victim, talking to someone through the window of a dark car, and that was the only information Jenny had about his possible method of abduction.

While the New Year's Eve party, the Harrogate pop concert, the cinema and university pub were common knowledge, and obvious hunting grounds, one question that had bothered Jenny since Saturday morning was how the killer had known about the youth-club dance after which Kimberley Myers had been abducted. Did he live in the neighborhood? Was he a church member? Had he simply happened to be passing at the time? As far as she knew, these things weren't advertised outside the immediate community, or even beyond the club's actual members.

Now she knew: Terence Payne lived just down the street, taught at the local comprehensive. Knew the victim.

Also, now, some of the things she had learned that day were making sense of some of the other puzzling facts and questions she had gathered over the weeks. Of the five abductions, four had occurred on a Friday night, or in the early hours of Saturday morning, which had led Jenny to believe that the killer worked a regular five-day week, and that he devoted his weekends to his hobby. The odd one out, Melissa Horrocks, had bothered her, but now that she knew Payne was a schoolteacher, the Tuesday, eighteenth of April, abduction made sense, too. It was the Easter holidays, and Payne had more spare time on his hands.

From this scant information—all this before the Kimberley Myers abduction—Jenny had surmised that they were dealing with an abductor who struck opportunistically. He cruised suitable locations looking for a certain type of victim, and when he found one, he struck as fast as lightning. There was no evidence that any of the girls had been stalked either on the evening of, or prior to, their abductions, though it was a possibility she had to bear in mind, but Jenny was willing to bet that he had scouted the locations, studied every way in and out, every dark nook and cranny, all the sight lines and angles. There was always a certain level of risk involved in things such as this. Just enough, perhaps, to guarantee that quick surge of adrenaline that was probably part of the thrill. Now Jenny knew that he had used chloroform to subdue his victims; that decreased the level of risk.

Jenny had also not been able until now to take into account any crime scene information because there hadn't been a crime scene available. There could be plenty of reasons why no bodies turned up, Jenny had said. They could have been dumped in remote locations and not discovered yet, buried in the woods, dumped in the sea or in a lake. As the number of disappearances increased, though, and as time went on and *still* no bodies were found, Jenny found herself moving toward the theory that their man was a collector, someone who plucks and savors his victims and perhaps then disposes of them the way a butterfly collector might gas and pin his trophies.

Now she had seen the anteroom, where the killer had buried, or partially buried, the bodies, and she didn't think that had been done by chance or done badly. She didn't think that the toes of one victim were sticking through the earth because Terence Payne was a sloppy worker; they were like that because he wanted them that way, it was part of his fantasy, because he *got off on it,* as they said back in America. They were part of his collection, his trophy room. Or his *garden*.

Now Jenny would have to rework her profile, factoring in all the new evidence that would be pouring out of number 35 The Hill over the next few weeks. She would also have to find out all she could about Terence Payne.

And there was another thing. Now Jenny also had to consider Lucy Payne.

Had Lucy known what her husband was doing?

It was possible, at least, that she had her suspicions.

Why didn't she come forward?

Because of some misguided sense of loyalty, perhaps—this was her *husband,* after all—or fear. If he had hit her with a vase last night, he could have hit her at other times, too, warned her of the fate that awaited her if she told anyone the truth. It would have been a living hell for Lucy, of course, but Jenny could believe her doing that. Plenty of women lived their whole lives in such hells.

But was Lucy more involved?

Again, possible. Jenny had suggested, tentatively, that the method of abduction indicated the killer might have had a helper, someone to lure the girl into the car, or distract her while he came up from behind. A woman would have been perfect for that role, would have made the actual abduction easier. Young girls wary of men are far more likely to lean in the window and help when a woman pulls over at the curb.

Were women capable of such evil?

Definitely. And if they were ever caught, the outrage against them was far greater than against any male. You only had to look at the public's reactions to Myra Hindley, Rosemary West and Karla Homolka to see that.

So was Lucy Payne a killer?

Banks felt bone-weary when he pulled up in the narrow lane outside his Gratly cottage close to midnight that night. He knew he should have probably taken a hotel room in Leeds, as he had done before, or accepted Ken Blackstone's offer of the sofa, but he had very much wanted to go home tonight, even if Annie had refused to come over, and he didn't mind the drive too much. It helped relax him.

There were two messages waiting for him on the machine. The first was from Tracy, saying she'd heard the news and hoped he was all right, and the second was from Leanne Wray's father, Christopher, who had seen the press conference and the evening news and wanted to know if the police had found his daughter's body at the Payne house.

Banks didn't answer either of them. For one thing, it was too late, and for another, he didn't want to talk to anybody. He could deal with them all in the morning. Now that he was home, he was even glad that Annie *wasn't* coming. The idea of company tonight, even Annie's, didn't appeal, and after all he'd seen and thought about today, the idea of sex held about as much interest as a trip to the dentist's.

Instead, he poured himself a generous tumbler of Laphroaig and tried to find some suitable music. He needed to listen to something, but he didn't know what. Usually he had no trouble finding what he wanted in his large collection, but tonight he rejected just about every CD he picked out. He

knew he didn't want to listen to jazz or rock or anything too
wild and primitive like that. Wagner and Mahler were out, as
were all the Romantics: Beethoven, Schubert, Rachmaninoff
and the rest. The entire twentieth century was out, too. In the
end, he went for Rostropovich's rendition of Bach's cello
suites.

Outside the cottage, the low stone wall between the dirt
lane and the beck bulged out and formed a little parapet over
Gratly Falls, which was just a series of terraces, none more
than a few feet in height, running diagonally through the village and under the little stone bridge that formed its central
gathering place. Since he had moved into the cottage the previous summer, Banks had got into the habit of standing out
there last thing at night if the weather was good enough, or
even sitting on the wall, dangling his legs over the beck and
enjoying his nightcap and a cigarette before bed.

The night air was still and smelled of hay and warm grass.
The Dale below him was sleeping. One or two farmhouse
lights shone on the far valley side, but apart from the sounds
of sheep in the field across the beck and night animals from
the woods, all was quiet. He could just make out the shapes
of distant fell sides in the dark, humpbacked or jagged
against the night sky. He thought he heard a curlew's eerie
trill from high up on the moors. The new moon gave sparse
light, but there were more stars than he had seen in a long
time. As he watched, a star fell through the darkness, leaving
a thin milky trail.

Banks didn't make a wish.

He felt depressed. The elation he had expected to feel on
finding the killer somehow eluded him. He had no sense of
an ending, of an evil purged. In some odd way, he felt, the
evil was just beginning. He tried to shake off his sense of
apprehension.

He heard a meow beside him and looked down. It was the
skinny marmalade cat from the woods. Starting that spring, it

had come over on several occasions when Banks was outside alone late at night. The second time it appeared, he had brought it some milk, which it lapped up before disappearing back into the trees. He had never seen it anywhere else, or at any other time than night. Once, he had even bought some cat food, to be more prepared for its visit, but the cat hadn't touched it. All it would do was meow, drink the milk, strut around for a few minutes and go back where it came from. Banks fetched a saucer of milk and set it down, refilling his own glass at the same time. The cat's eyes shone amber in the darkness as it looked up at him before bending to drink.

Banks lit his cigarette and leaned against the wall, resting his glass on its rough stone surface. He tried to purge his mind of the day's terrible images. The cat rubbed against his leg and ran off back into the woods. Rostropovich played on, and Bach's precise, mathematical patterns of sound formed an odd counterpoint to the wild roaring music of Gratly Falls, so recently swelled by the spring thaw, and for a few moments, at least, Banks succeeded in losing himself.

Chapter 6

According to her parents, Melissa Horrocks, aged seventeen, who failed to return home after a pop concert in Harrogate on the eighteenth of April, was going through a rebellious phase.

Steven and Mary Horrocks had only the one daughter, a late blessing in Mary's mid-thirties. Steven worked in the office of a local dairy, while Mary had a part-time job in an estate agent's office in the city center. Around the age of sixteen, Melissa developed an interest in the kind of theatrical pop music that used Satanism as its main stage prop.

Though friends advised Steven and Mary that it was harmless enough—just youthful spirits—and that it would soon pass, they were nonetheless alarmed when she started altering her appearance and letting her schoolwork and athletics slip. Melissa first dyed her hair red, got a stud in her nose and wore a lot of black. Her bedroom wall was adorned with posters of skinny, satanic-looking pop stars, such as Marilyn Manson, and occult symbols her parents didn't understand.

About a week before the concert, Melissa decided she didn't like the red hair, so she reverted to her natural blond coloring. There was a good chance, Banks thought later, that if she'd kept it red, that might have saved her life. Which also led Banks to think that she hadn't been stalked before her abduction—or at least not for long. The Chameleon wouldn't stalk a redhead.

Harrogate, a prosperous Victorian-style North Yorkshire city of about seventy thousand, known as a conference center and a magnet for retired people, wasn't exactly the typical venue for a Beelzebub's Bollocks concert, but the band was new and had yet to win a major recording contract; they were working their way up to bigger gigs. There had been the usual calls for a ban from retired colonels and the kind of old busybodies who watch all the filth on television so they can write letters of protest, but in the end this came to no avail.

About five hundred kids wandered into the converted theater, including Melissa and her friends Jenna and Kayla. The concert ended at half-past ten and the three girls stood around outside for a while talking about the show. The three of them split up at about a quarter to eleven and went their separate ways. It was a mild night, so Melissa said she was going to walk. She didn't live far from the city center, and most of her walk home took her along the busy, well-lit Ripon Road. Two people later came forward to say they saw her close to eleven o'clock walking south by the junction of West Park and Beech Grove. To get home, she would turn down Beech Grove and then turn off after about a hundred yards, but she never got there.

At first there was a faint hope that Melissa might have run away from home, given the running battle with her parents. But Steven and Mary, along with Jenna and Kayla, assured Banks this could not be the case. The two friends in particular said they shared everything, and they would have known if she was planning on running away. Besides, she had none of her valued possessions with her, and she told them she was looking forward to seeing them the next day at the Victoria Centre.

Then there was the satanic element, not to be lightly dismissed when a girl had disappeared. The members of the band were interviewed, along with as many audience members as could be rounded up, but that went nowhere, too. Even Banks had to admit when examining the statements later that the whole thing had been pretty tame and harmless, the black magic merely theater, as it had been for Black Sabbath and Alice Cooper in his day. Beelzebub's Bollocks didn't even bite the heads off chickens on stage.

When Melissa's black leather shoulder bag was found in some bushes two days after her disappearance, as if it had been tossed from the window of a moving car, money still intact, the case came to the attention of Banks's Chameleon task force. Like Kelly Matthews, Samantha Foster and Leanne Wray before her, Melissa Horrocks had disappeared into thin air.

Jenna and Kayla were devastated. Just before Melissa had walked off into the night, they had joked, Kayla said, about perverts, but Melissa had pointed to her chest and said the occult symbol on her T-shirt would ward off evil spirits.

The incident room was crowded at nine o'clock on Tuesday morning. Over forty detectives sat on the edges of their desks or leaned against the walls. Smoking was not permitted in the building, and many of them chewed gum or fidgeted with paper clips or rubber bands instead. Most had been on the task force since the beginning, and they had all put in long hours, invested a lot of themselves in the job, emotionally as well as physically. It had taken its toll on all of them. Banks happened to know that one unfortunate DC's marriage had broken up over the hours he spent away from home and the neglect he displayed toward his wife. It would have happened some other time, anyway, Banks told himself, but an investigation like this one can put the pressure on, can push events to a crisis point, especially if that crisis point isn't too far away to start with. These days, Banks also felt that he was approaching his own crisis point, though he had no idea where it was or what would happen when he got there.

Now there was at least some sense of progress, no matter how unclear things still seemed, and the air buzzed with speculation. They all wanted to know what had happened. The mood was mixed: on the one hand, it looked as if they had their man; on the other, one of their own had been killed and his partner was about to be put through the hoops.

When Banks strode in somewhat the worse for wear after another poor night's sleep, despite a third Laphroaig and the second disc of Bach's cello sonatas, the room hushed, everyone waiting to hear the news. He stood next to Ken Blackstone, beside the photographs of the girls pinned to the corkboard.

"Okay," he said, "I'll do my best to explain where we are with this. The SOCOs are still at the scene, and it looks as if they'll be there for a long time yet. So far, they've uncovered three bodies in the cellar anteroom, and it doesn't look as if there's room for any more. They're digging in the back garden for the fourth. None of the victims has been identified yet, but DS Nowak says the bodies are all young and female, so it's reasonable to assume for the moment that they're the young girls who went missing. We should be able to make some headway on identification later today by checking dental records. Dr. Mackenzie performed the postmortem on Kimberley Myers late yesterday and found that she had been subdued by chloroform but death was due to vagal inhibition caused by ligature strangulation. Yellow plastic fibers from the clothesline were embedded in the wound." He paused, then sighed and went on. "She was also raped anally and vaginally and forced to perform fellatio."

"What about Payne, sir?" someone asked. "Is the bastard going to die?"

"The last I heard was that they had to operate on his brain. Terence Payne is still in a coma, and there's no telling how long that might last, or how it will end. By the way, we now know that Terence Payne lived and taught in Seacroft before he moved to west Leeds in September the year before last, at the start of the school year. DCI Blackstone has him in the frame for the Seacroft Rapist, so we're already checking

DNA. I'll want a team to go over the casework on that one with the local CID. DS Stewart, can you get that organized?"

"Right away, sir. That'll be Chapeltown CID."

Chapeltown would be hot to trot on this, Banks knew. It was a "red inker" for them—an easy way of closing several open case files at one fell swoop.

"We've also checked Payne's car registration with DVLA in Swansea. He was using false plates. His own plates end in KWT, just like the witness in the Samantha Foster disappearance saw. The SOCOs found them hidden in the garage. That means Bradford CID must have already interviewed him. I'd imagine it was after that he switched to the false ones."

"What about Dennis Morrisey?" someone asked.

"PC Morrisey died of blood loss caused by the severing of his carotid artery and jugular vein, according to Dr. Mackenzie's examination at the scene. He'll be doing the PM later today. As you can imagine, there's getting to be quite a queue down at the mortuary. He's looking for assistance. Anyone interested?"

Nervous laughter rippled through the room.

"What about PC Taylor?" one of the detectives asked.

"PC Taylor's coping," said Banks. "I talked to her yesterday evening. She was able to tell me what happened in the cellar. As you all probably know, she'll be under investigation, so let's try to keep that one at arm's length."

A chorus of boos came up from the crowd. Banks quieted them down. "It's got to be done," he said. "Unpopular as it is. We're none of us above the law. But let's not let that distract us. Our job is far from over. In fact, it's just beginning. There's going to be a mountain of stuff coming out of forensics examinations at the house. It'll all have to be tagged, logged and filed. HOLMES is still in operation, so the green sheets will have to be filled out and fed in."

Banks heard Carol Houseman, the trained HOLMES operator, groan, "Oh, *bugger* it!"

"Sorry, Carol," he said, with a sympathetic smile. "Needs must. In other words, despite what's happened, we're still very much in business for the time being. We need to gather the evidence. We need to prove beyond a shadow of a doubt that Terence Payne is the killer of all five missing girls."

"What about his wife?" someone asked. "She must have known."

Just what Ken Blackstone had said. "We don't know that," said Banks. "For the moment she's a victim. But her possible involvement is one of the things we'll be looking into. We're already aware that he *might have had* an accomplice. She should be able to talk to me later this morning." Banks glanced at his watch and turned to DS Filey. "In the meantime, Ted, I'd like you to put a team together to go over all the statements and reinterview everyone we talked to when the girls were first reported missing. Family, friends, witnesses, everyone. Okay?"

"Right you are, Guv," said Ted Filey.

Banks hated being called "Guv," but he let it go by. "Get some photographs of Lucy Payne and show one to everyone you talk to. See if anyone remembers seeing her in connection with any of the missing girls."

More mutterings broke out, and Banks quieted them down again. "For the moment," he said, "I want you all to keep in close touch with our office manager, DS Grafton here—"

A cheer went up and Ian Grafton blushed.

"He'll be issuing actions and TIEs, and there'll be plenty of them. I want to know what Terence and Lucy Payne eat for breakfast and how regular their bowel movements are. Dr. Fuller suggested that Payne would have kept some sort of visual record of his deeds—videos, most likely, but maybe just ordinary still photographs. Nothing's been found at the scene yet, but we'll need to know if the Paynes ever owned or rented video equipment."

Banks noticed a number of skeptical looks at the mention

of Jenny Fuller. Typical narrow-minded thinking, in his opinion. Consultant psychologists might not be possessed with magic powers and able to name the killer within hours, but in Banks's experience, they could narrow the field and target the area where the offender may live. Why not use them? At best they could help, and at worst they did no harm. "Remember," he went on, "five girls were abducted, raped and murdered. *Five* girls. You don't need me to tell you any one of them could have been *your* daughter. We think we've got the man responsible, but we can't be sure he acted alone, and until we can *prove* it was him, no matter what shape he's in, there'll be no slacking on this team. Got it?"

The assembled detectives muttered, "Yes, sir," then the group started to split up, some drifting outside for a much-needed cigarette, others settling back at their desks.

"One more thing," said Banks. "DCs Bowmore and Singh. In my office. Now."

After a brief meeting with Area Commander Hartnell—who *definitely* gave her the eye—and Banks, who seemed uncomfortable about the whole thing, DI Annie Cabbot read over PC Janet Taylor's file as she waited in the small office assigned her. Hartnell himself had decided that as Janet Taylor was coming in voluntarily, and as she wasn't under arrest, an office would be a far less threatening environment for the preliminary talk than a standard grungy interview room.

Annie was impressed by PC Taylor's record. There was little doubt that she would find a place in the Accelerated Promotion Course and make the rank of inspector within five years if she was cleared of all charges. A local girl, from Pudsey, Janet Taylor had four A-levels and a degree in sociology from the University of Bristol. She was just twenty-three years old, unmarried and living alone. Janet had high scores on all her entrance exams, and in the opinions of those who had examined her she showed a clear grasp of the complexities of policing a diverse society, along with the sort of cognitive skills and problem-solving abilities that augured well for a detective. She was in good health and listed her hobbies as squash, tennis and computers. Throughout her student career she had spent her summers working for security at the White Rose Centre, in Leeds, both manning the cameras and patrolling the shopping precinct. Janet had also done voluntary community work for her local church group, helping the elderly.

All of this sounded quite dull to Annie, who grew up in an artists' commune near St. Ives surrounded by oddballs, hippies and weirdos of all sorts. Annie had also come late to the police, and though she had a degree, it was in art history, not much use in the force, and she hadn't got on the APC because of an incident at her previous county, when three fellow officers had attempted to rape her at a party following her promotion to sergeant. One succeeded before she had managed to fight them off. Traumatized, Annie had not reported the incident until the following morning, by which time she had spent hours in the bath washing away all evidence. The DCS had accepted the words of the three officers against hers, and while they admitted that things had got a little out of hand, with a drunken Annie leading them on, they said they had retained their control and no sexual assault had taken place.

For a long time, Annie hadn't much cared about her career, and no one had been more surprised than she had at the rekindling of her ambition, which had meant dealing with the rape and its aftermath—more complicated and traumatic than anyone but her really knew—but it had happened, and now she was a fully fledged inspector investigating a politically dodgy case for Detective Superintendent Chambers, who was clearly scared stiff of the assignment himself.

A brief tap at the door was followed by the entry of a young woman with short black hair, which looked rather dry and lifeless. "They told me you were in here," she said.

Annie introduced herself. "Sit down, Janet."

Janet sat and tried to make herself comfortable on the hard chair. She looked as if she hadn't slept all night, which didn't surprise Annie in the least. Her face was pale and there were dark semi-circles under her eyes. Perhaps beyond the ravages of sleeplessness and abject terror, Janet Taylor was an attractive young woman. She certainly had beautiful eyes, the color of loam, and the kind of cheekbones that models hang their careers on. She also seemed a very serious person, weighed down by the gravity of life, or perhaps that was a result of recent events.

"How is he?" Janet asked.

"Who?"

"You know. Payne."

"Still unconscious."

"Will he survive?"

"They don't know yet, Janet."

"Okay. I mean, it's just that . . . well, I suppose it makes a difference. You know, to my case."

"If he dies? Yes, it does. But don't let's worry about that for the time being. I want you to tell me what happened in the Paynes' cellar, then I'll ask you a few questions. Finally, I want you to write it all down in a statement. This isn't an interrogation, Janet. I'm sure you went through hell down in that cellar, and nobody wants to treat you like a criminal. But there are procedures to be followed in cases like this, and the sooner we get going, the better." Annie wasn't being entirely truthful, but she wanted to set Janet Taylor as much at ease as possible. She knew she would have to push and prod a bit, maybe even go in hard now and again. It was her interrogation technique; after all, it was often under pressure of some sort that the truth slipped out. She would play it by ear, but if she needed to badger Janet Taylor a bit, then so be it. Damn Chambers and Hartnell. If she was going to do the bloody job, she was going to do it properly.

"Don't worry," said Janet. "I haven't done anything wrong."

"I'm sure you haven't. Tell me about it."

As Janet Taylor spoke, sounding rather bored and detached, as if she had been through this all too many times already, or as if she were recounting someone else's story, Annie watched her body language. Janet shifted in her chair often, twisted her hands on her lap, and when she got to the real horror, she folded her arms and her voice became flatter, lacking expression. Annie let her go on, making notes on points she thought relevant. Janet didn't so much come to a definite end as trail off after she said she had settled to wait for the ambulance, cradling PC Morrisey's head on her lap and feeling the warm blood seep through on her thighs. As she spoke about this, her eyebrows rose and wrinkled the center of her forehead, and tears formed in her eyes.

Annie let the silence stretch for a while after Janet had fallen silent, then she asked if Janet would like a drink. She asked for water and Annie brought her some from the fountain. The room was hot and Annie got some for herself, too.

"Just a couple of things, Janet; then I'll leave you alone to write your statement."

Janet yawned. She put her hand to her mouth but didn't apologize. Normally Annie would have taken a yawn as a sign of fear or nervousness, but Janet Taylor had good reason to be tired, so she didn't make too much of it on this occasion.

"What were you thinking about while it was happening?" Annie asked.

"Thinking? I'm not sure I was thinking at all. Just reacting."

"Did you remember your training?"

Janet Taylor laughed, but it was forced. "Training doesn't prepare you for something like *that*."

"What about your baton training?"

"I didn't have to *think* about that. It was instinctive."

"You were feeling threatened."

"Damn right I was. He was killing Dennis and he was going to kill me next. He'd already killed the girl on the bed."

"How did you know she was dead?"

"What?"

"Kimberley Myers. How did you know she was dead? You said it all happened so fast, you barely caught a glimpse of her before the attack."

"I . . . I suppose I just assumed. I mean, she was lying there naked on the bed with a yellow rope around her neck. Her eyes were open. It was a reasonable assumption to make."

"Okay," said Annie. "So you never thought of yourself as saving her, as rescuing her?"

"No. It was what was happening to Dennis that concerned me."

"And what you thought was going to happen to you next?"

"Yes." Janet sipped some more water. A little of it dripped down her chin on to the front of her gray T-shirt, but she didn't seem to notice.

"So you got your baton out. What next?"

"I told you. He came at me with this crazy look in his eye."

"And he lashed out at you with his machete?"

"Yes. I deflected the blow with my baton, the side against my arm, like they taught us. And then when he'd swung, before he could bring it back into position again, I swung out and hit him."

"Where did the first blow land?"

"On his head."

"Where exactly on his head?"

"I don't know. I wasn't concerned about that."

"But you wanted to put him out of commission, didn't you?"

"I wanted to stop him from killing me."

"So you'd want to hit him somewhere effective?"

"Well, I'm right-handed, so I suppose I must have hit him on the left side of his head, somewhere around the temple."

"Did he go down?"

"No, but he was dazed. He couldn't get his machete in position to strike again."

"Where did you hit him next?"

"The wrist, I think."

"To disarm him?"

"Yes."

"Did you succeed?"

"Yes."

"What did you do next?"

"I kicked the machete into the corner."

"What did Payne do?"

"He was holding his wrist and cursing me."

"You'd hit him once on the left temple and once on the wrist by this time?"

"That's right."

"What did you do next?"

"I hit him again."

"Where?"

"On the head."

"Why?"

"To incapacitate him."

"Was he standing at this point?"

"Yes. He'd been on his knees trying to get the machete, but he got up and came at me."

"He was unarmed now?"

"Yes, but he was still bigger and stronger than me. And he had this insane look in his eyes, as if he had strength to spare."

"So you hit him again?"

"Yes."

"Same spot?"

"I don't know. I used my baton in the same way. So yes, I suppose so, unless he was half turned away."

"Was he?"

"I don't think so."

"But it's possible? I mean, it was you who suggested it."

"I suppose it's possible, but I don't see why."

"You didn't hit him on the *back* of his head at any point?"

"I don't think so."

Janet had started to sweat now. Annie could see beads of it around her hairline and a dark stain spreading slowly under her arms. She didn't want to put the poor woman through much more, but she had her job to do, and she could be hard when she needed to be. "What happened after you hit Payne on the head a second time?"

"Nothing."

"What do you mean, nothing?"

"Nothing. He kept coming."

"So you hit him again."

"Yes. I took the baton in both hands, like a cricket bat, so I could hit him harder."

"He had nothing to defend himself with at this time, right?"

"Only his arms."

"But he didn't raise them to ward off the blow?"

"He was holding his wrist. I think it was broken. I heard something crack."

"So you had free rein to hit him as hard as you liked?"

"He kept coming at me."

"You mean he kept moving toward you?"

"Yes, and calling me names."

"What sort of names?"

"Filthy names. And Dennis was groaning, bleeding. I wanted to go to him, to see if I could help, but I couldn't do anything until Payne stopped moving."

"You didn't feel you could restrain him with handcuffs at this point?"

"No way. I'd already hit him two or three times, but it seemed to have no effect. He kept coming. If I'd gone in close and he'd got hold of me he'd have strangled the life out of me."

"Even with his broken wrist?"

"Yes. He could have got his arm across my throat."

"Okay." Annie paused to make some notes on the pad in front of her. She could almost smell Janet Taylor's fear, and she wasn't sure if it was residual, from the cellar, or because of present circumstances. She drew out the note-making process until Janet started shifting and fidgeting, then she asked, "How many times do you think you hit him in all?"

Janet turned her head to one side. "I don't know. I wasn't counting. I was fighting for my life, defending myself against a maniac."

"Five times? Six times?"

"I told you. *I don't remember.* As many times as I needed. To make him stop coming. He just wouldn't stop coming at me." Janet broke into sobs and Annie let her cry. It was the first time emotion had broken through the shock and it would do her good. After a minute or so, Janet collected herself and sipped some more water. She seemed embarrassed to have broken down in front of a colleague.

"I've almost finished now, Janet," said Annie. "Then I'll leave you be."

"Okay."

"You managed to get him to stay down, didn't you?"

"Yes. He fell against the wall and slid down."

"Was he still moving then?"

"Not very much. He was sort of twitching and breathing heavily. There was blood on his mouth."

"Final question, Janet: Did you hit him again after he went down?"

Her eyebrows shot together in fear. "No. I don't think so."

"What did you do?"

"I handcuffed him to the pipe."

"And then?"

"Then I went to help Dennis."

"Are you sure you didn't hit him again after he went down? Just to make sure?"

Janet looked away. "I told you. I don't think so. Why would I?"

Annie leaned forward and rested her arms on the desk. "*Try* to remember, Janet."

But Janet shook her head. "It's no good. I don't remember."

"Okay," said Annie, getting to her feet. "Interview over." She pushed a statement sheet and a pen in front of Janet. "Write out what you've told me in as much detail as you can remember."

Janet grasped the pen. "What happens next?"

"When you've finished, love, go home and have a stiff drink. Hell, have two."

Janet managed a weak but genuine smile as Annie left and shut the door behind her.

DCs Bowmore and Singh looked shifty when they walked into Banks's temporary Millgarth office, as well they might, he thought.

"Sit down," he said.

They sat. "What is it, sir?" asked DC Singh, attempting lightness. "Got a job for us?"

Banks leaned back in his chair and linked his hands behind his head. "In a manner of speaking," he said. "If you call sharpening pencils and emptying the wastepaper baskets a job."

Their jaws dropped. "Sir—" Bowmore began, but Banks held his hand up.

"A car number plate ending in KWT. Ring any bells?"

"Sir?"

"KWT. Kathryn Wendy Thurlow."

"Yes, sir," said Singh. "It's the number Bradford CID got in the Samantha Foster investigation."

"Bingo," said Banks. "Now, correct me if I'm wrong, but didn't Bradford send us copies of all their files on the Samantha Foster case when this team was set up?"

"Yes, sir."

"Including the name of everyone in the area who owned a dark car with the number plate ending in KWT."

"Over a thousand, sir."

"Over a thousand. Indeed. Bradford CID interviewed them all. And guess who's among that thousand."

"Terence Payne, sir," answered Singh again.

"Bright lad," said Banks. "Now, when Bradford CID were working on that case, did they have any links to any similar crimes?"

"No, sir," answered Bowmore this time. "There was the girl went missing from the New Year's party in Roundhay Park, but there was no reason to link them together at the time."

"Right," said Banks. "So why do you think I issued an action shortly after this task force was set up to go over all the evidence on the previous cases, including the disappearance of Samantha Foster?"

"Because you thought there was a link, sir," said DC Singh.

"Not just me," said Banks. "But, yes, three girls, as it was then. Then four. Then five. The possibility of a link was becoming stronger and stronger. Now guess who was assigned to go over the evidence in the Samantha Foster case."

Singh and Bowmore looked at each other, then frowned and looked at Banks. "We were, sir," they said as one.

"Including reinterviewing the list of car owners Bradford CID got from the DVLA."

"Over a thousand, sir."

"Indeed," said Banks, "but am I correct in assuming that you had plenty of help, that the action was split up and that the letter *P* was among those alphabetically assigned to you? Because that's what it says in my files. *P* for Payne."

"There were still a lot to go, sir. We haven't got around to them all yet."

"You haven't got around to them yet? This was at the beginning of April. Over a month ago. You've been dragging your feet a bit, haven't you?"

"It's not as if it was the only action assigned us, sir," said Bowmore.

"Look," said Banks, "I don't want any excuses. For one reason or another, you failed to reinterview Terence Payne."

"But it wouldn't have made any difference, sir," Bowmore argued. "I mean, Bradford CID didn't exactly mark him down as their number one suspect, did they? What was he going to tell us that he didn't tell them? He wasn't going to decide to confess just because we went to talk to him, was he?"

Banks ran his hand over his hair and muttered a silent curse. He was not a natural authoritarian—far from it—and he hated this part of the job, dishing out bollockings, having been on the receiving end of plenty himself, but if anyone ever did, these two prize pillocks deserved the worst he could give. "Is this supposed to be an example of you using your initiative?" he said. "Because if it is, you'd have been better advised to stick to procedure and follow orders."

"But, sir," Singh said, "he was a schoolteacher. Newly married. Nice house. We *did* read over all the statements."

"I'm sorry," said Banks, shaking his head. "Am I missing something here?"

"What do you mean, sir?"

"Well, I'm not aware that Dr. Fuller had given us any sort of profile of the person we were looking for at this point."

DC Singh grinned. "Hasn't given us much of anything when you get right down to it, has she, sir?"

"So what made you think you could rule out a recently married schoolteacher with a nice house?"

Singh's jaw opened and shut like a fish mouth. Bowmore looked down at his shoes.

"Well?" Banks repeated. "I'm waiting."

"Look, sir," said Singh, "I'm sorry, but we just hadn't got around to him yet."

"Have you talked to *any* of the people on your list?"

"A couple, sir," muttered Singh. "The ones Bradford CID had marked down as possibles. There was one bloke had a previous for flashing, but he had a solid alibi for Leanne Wray and Melissa Horrocks. We checked that out, sir."

"So when you'd nothing better to do, you'd fill in a bit of overtime by ticking a name or two off the list, names that Bradford CID had put question marks beside. Is that it?"

"That's not fair, sir," Bowmore argued.

"Not fair. I'll tell you what's not bloody fair, DC Bowmore. It's not bloody fair that at least five girls that we know of so far have most likely died at the hands of Terence Payne. That's what's not fair."

"But he wouldn't have admitted it to us, sir," Singh protested.

"You're supposed to be detectives, aren't you? Look, let me put it simply. If you'd gone around to Payne's house when you were supposed to, say last month, then one or two more girls might not have died."

"You can't put that down to us, sir," Bowmore protested, red in the face. "That's just not on."

"Oh, isn't it? What if you'd seen or heard something suspicious while you were in the house interviewing him? What if your finely developed detective's instinct had picked up on something and you'd asked to have a look around?"

"Bradford CID didn't—"

"I don't give a damn what Bradford CID did or didn't do. They were examining a single case: the disappearance of Samantha Foster. You, on the other hand, were investigating a case of serial abductions. If you'd had any reason at all to look in the cellar you'd have had him, believe me. Even if you'd poked around his video collection it might have raised your suspicions. If you'd looked at his car, you'd have noticed the false plates. The ones he's using now end in NGV, not KWT. That might have rung a few alarm bells, don't you think? Instead you decide on your own that this action isn't worth rushing on. God knows what else you thought was so much more important. Well?"

They both looked down.

"Nothing to say for yourselves?"

"No, sir," muttered a tight-lipped DC Singh.

"I'll even give you the benefit of the doubt," said Banks. "I'll assume that you were pursuing other angles and not just skiving off. But you still screwed up."

"But he must've lied to Bradford CID," Bowmore argued. "He'd only have lied to us, too."

"You just don't get it, do you?" said Banks. "I've told you. You're supposed to be *detectives*. You don't take anything at face value. Maybe you'd have noticed something about his body language. Maybe you'd have caught him out in a lie. Maybe—God forbid—you might have even checked one of his alibis and found it didn't hold up. Maybe just something might have made you a little bit suspicious about Terence Payne. Am I making myself clear? You had at least two, maybe three, more things to go on than Bradford had, and you blew it. Now you're off the case, both of you, and this is going on your records. Clear?"

Bowmore looked daggers at Banks, and Singh seemed close to tears, but Banks had no sympathy for either of them at that moment. He felt a splitting headache coming on. "Get the hell out of here," he said. "And don't let me see you in the incident room again."

* * *

Maggie hid herself away in the sanctuary of Ruth's studio. Spring sunshine spilled through the window, which she opened an inch or two to let in some air. It was a spacious room at the back of the house, originally the third bedroom, and while the view through the window left a lot to be desired—a grotty, litter-strewn back passage and the council estate beyond—the room itself was perfect for her needs. Upstairs, in addition to the three rooms, toilet, and bathroom, there was also a loft, accessed by a pull-down ladder, that Ruth said she used for storage. Maggie didn't store anything there; in fact, she never even went up there, as she felt disturbed by spidery, dusty, neglected places, the mere thought of which made her shiver. She had allergies, too, and the slightest hint of dust made her eyes burn and her nose itch.

Another bonus today was that upstairs at the back of the house, she wasn't constantly distracted by all the activity out on The Hill. It was open to traffic again, but number 35 was screened off and people kept coming and going, bringing out boxes and bags of God knew what. She couldn't quite put it out of her mind, of course, but she didn't read the newspaper that morning, and she tuned the radio to a classical station that had few news breaks.

She was preparing to illustrate a new coffee-table selection of *Grimm's Fairy Tales,* working on thumbnails and preliminary sketches, and what nasty, gruesome little stories they were, she discovered on reading through them for the first time since childhood. Back then, they had seemed remote, cartoonish, but now the horror and the violence seemed all too real. The sketch she had just finished was for "Rumpelstiltskin," the poison dwarf who helped Anna spin straw into gold in exchange for her firstborn. Her illustration was a bit too idealized, she thought: a sad-looking girl-child at a spinning wheel, with just the suggestion of two burning eyes and the distorted shadow of the dwarf in the background. She could hardly use the scene where he stamped so hard his foot went through the floor and his leg came off as he tried to pull it out. Matter-of-fact violence, no dwelling on blood and guts the way so many films did these days—special effects for the sake of it—but violence nonetheless.

Now she was working on "Rapunzel" and her preliminary sketches showed the young girl—another firstborn taken from her true parents—letting her long blond hair down from the tower where she was held captive by a witch. Another happy ending, with the witch being devoured by a wolf, except for her talon-like hands and feet, which it spat out to be eaten by worms and beetles.

She was just trying to get the rope of hair and the angle of Rapunzel's head right, so that it would at least *look* as if she might be able to support the prince's weight, when the telephone rang.

Maggie picked up the studio extension. "Yes?"

"Margaret Forrest?" It was a woman's voice. "Am I speaking to Margaret Forrest?"

"Who's asking?"

"Is that you, Margaret? My name's Lorraine Temple. You don't know me."

"What do you want?"

"I understand that it was you who dialed in the emergency call on The Hill yesterday morning? A domestic disturbance."

"Who are you? Are you a reporter?"

"Oh, didn't I say? Yes, I write for the *Post*."

"I'm not supposed to talk to you. Go away."

"Look, I'm just down the street, Margaret. I'm calling on my mobile. The police won't let me near your house, so I wondered if you'd care to meet me for a drink or something. It's almost lunchtime. There's a nice pub—"

"I've nothing to say to you, Ms. Temple, so there's no point in our meeting."

"You *did* report a domestic disturbance at number thirty-five The Hill early yesterday morning, didn't you?"

"Yes, but—"

"Then I *have* got the right person. What made you think it was a domestic?"

"I'm sorry, I don't understand. I don't know what you mean."

"You heard noises, didn't you? Raised voices? Breaking glass? A thud?"

"How do you know all this?"

"I'm just wondering what made you jump to the conclusion that it was a domestic disturbance, that's all. I mean, why couldn't it have been someone grappling with a burglar, for example?"

"I don't know what you're getting at."

"Oh, come on, Margaret. It's Maggie, isn't it? Can I call you Maggie?"

Maggie said nothing. She had no idea why she didn't just hang up on Lorraine Temple.

"Look, Maggie," Lorraine went on, "give me a break here. I've got my living to make. Were you a friend of Lucy Payne's, is that it? Do you know something about her background? Something the rest of us don't know?"

"I can't talk to you anymore," Maggie said, and then she did hang up. But something Lorraine Temple had said struck a chord, and she regretted doing so. Despite what Banks had told her, if she were to be Lucy's friend, then the press might prove an ally, not an enemy. She might have to speak to them, to mobilize them in Lucy's support. Public sympathy would be very important, and in that the media might be able to help her. Of course, all this depended on the approach the police took. If Banks believed what Maggie had told him about the abuse, and if Lucy confirmed it, as she would, then they would realize that she was more of a victim than anything else and just let her go as soon as she was well again.

Lorraine Temple was persistent enough to call back a couple of minutes later. "Come on, Maggie," she said. "Where's the harm?"

"All right," said Maggie, "I'll meet you for a drink. Ten minutes. I know the place you mean. It's called The Woodcutter. At the bottom of The Hill, right?"

"Right. Ten minutes. I'll be there."

Maggie hung up. While she was still close to the phone, she took out the yellow pages and looked up a local florist. She arranged to have some flowers delivered to Lucy in her hospital bed, along with a note wishing her well.

Before she left, she had one last quick look at her sketch and noticed something curious about it. Rapunzel's face. It wasn't the all-purpose fairy-tale princess sort of face you saw in so many illustrations; it was individual, unique, something Maggie prided herself on. More than that, though, Rapunzel's face, half-turned to the viewer, resembled Claire Toth's, even down to the two spots on her chin. Frowning, Maggie picked up her rubber and erased them before she went off to meet Lorraine Temple from the *Post*.

Banks hated hospitals, hated everything about them, and he had done so ever since he'd had his tonsils out at the age of nine. He hated the smell of them, the colors of the walls, the echoing sounds, the doctors' white coats and the uniforms the nurses wore, hated the beds, thermometers, syringes, stethoscopes, IVs, and the strange machines glimpsed behind half-open doors. *Everything.*

If truth be told, he had hated it all since well before the tonsil experience. When his brother, Roy, was born, Banks was five, seven years too young to be allowed inside a hospital at visiting time. His mother had some problems with the pregnancy—those unspecified *adult* problems that grown-ups always seemed to be whispering about—and spent an entire month there. Those were the days when they'd let you hang on to a bed that long. Banks was sent away to live with his aunt and uncle in Northampton and went to a new school for the whole period. He never settled in, and being the new boy, he had to stick up for himself against more than one bully.

He remembered his uncle driving him to the hospital to see his mother one dark, cold winter's night, holding him up to the window—thank God she was on the ground floor—so he could wipe the frost off with his wool mitten and see her swollen shape halfway along the ward and wave to her. He felt so sad. It must be a horrible place, he remembered thinking, that would keep a mother from her son and make her sleep in a room full of strange people when she was so poorly.

The tonsillectomy had only confirmed what he already knew in the first place, and now he was older, hospitals still scared the shit out of him. He saw them as last resorts, places where one *ends up,* where one goes to die, and where the well-intentioned ministrations, the probing, pricking, slicing and all the various *ectomies* of medical science only postpone the inevitable, filling one's last days on earth with torture, pain and fear. Banks was a veritable Philip Larkin when it came to hospitals, could think only of "the anesthetic from which none come round."

Lucy Payne was under guard at Leeds General Infirmary, not far from where her husband lay in intensive care after emergency surgery to remove skull splinters from his brain. The PC sitting outside her room, a dog-eared Tom Clancy paperback on the chair beside him, reported no comings or goings other than hospital staff. It had been a quiet night, he said. Lucky for some, Banks thought as he entered the private room.

The doctor was inside waiting. She introduced herself as Dr. Landsberg. No first name. Banks didn't want her there, but there was nothing he could do about it. Lucy Payne wasn't under arrest, but she *was* under the doctor's care.

"I'm afraid I can't give you very long with my patient," she said. "She has suffered an extremely traumatic experience, and she needs rest more than anything."

Banks looked at the woman in the bed. Half her face, including one eye, was covered with bandages. The eye that he could see was the same shiny black as the ink he liked to use in his fountain pen. Her skin was pale and smooth, her raven's-wing hair spread out over the pillow and sheets. He thought of Kimberley Myers's body spread-eagled on the mattress. That had happened *in Lucy Payne's house,* he reminded himself.

Banks sat down beside Lucy, and Dr. Landsberg hovered like a lawyer waiting to interrupt when Banks overstepped his PACE bounds.

"Lucy," he said, "my name's Banks, Acting Detective Superintendent Banks. I'm in charge of the investigation into the five missing girls. How are you feeling?"

"Not bad," Lucy answered. "Considering."

"Is there much pain?"

"Some. My head hurts. How's Terry? What's happened to Terry? Nobody will tell me." Her voice sounded thick, as if her tongue were swollen and her words were slurred. The medication.

"Perhaps if you just told me what happened last night, Lucy. Can you remember?"

"Is Terry dead? Someone told me he was hurt."

The concern of the abused wife for her abuser—if that was what he was witnessing—didn't surprise Banks very much at all; it was an old sad tune, and he had heard it many times before, in all its variations.

"Your husband was very badly injured, Lucy," Dr. Landsberg cut in. "We're doing all we can for him."

Banks cursed her under his breath. He didn't want Lucy

Payne to know what kind of shape her husband was in; if she thought he wasn't going to survive, she could tell Banks whatever she wanted, knowing he'd have no way of checking whether it was true or not. "Can you tell me what happened last night?" he repeated.

Lucy half closed her good eye; she was trying to remember, or pretending she was trying to remember. "I don't know. I can't remember."

Good answer, Banks realized. Wait and see what happens to Terry before admitting to anything. She was sharp, this one, even in her hospital bed, under medication.

"Do I need a lawyer?" she asked.

"Why would you need a lawyer?"

"I don't know. When the police talk to people . . . you know, on television . . ."

"We're not on television, Lucy."

She wrinkled her nose. "I know that, silly. I didn't mean . . . never mind."

"What's the last thing you remember about what happened to you?"

"I remember waking up, getting out of bed, putting on my dressing gown. It was late. Or early."

"Why did you get out of bed?"

"I don't know. I must have heard something."

"What?"

"A noise. I can't remember."

"What did you do next?"

"I don't know. I just remember getting up and then it hurt and everything went dark."

"Do you remember having an argument with Terry?"

"No."

"Did you go in the cellar?"

"I don't think so. I don't remember. I might have done."

Covering all the possibilities. "Did you *ever* go in the cellar?"

"That was Terry's room. He would have punished me if I went down there. He kept it locked."

Interesting, Banks thought. She could remember enough to distance herself from whatever they might have found in the cellar. Did she know? Forensics ought to be able to confirm whether she was telling the truth or not about going down there. It was the basic rule: wherever you go, you leave something behind and take something with you.

"What did he do down there?" Banks asked.

"I don't know. It was his own private den."

"So you never went down there?"

"No. I didn't dare."

"What do you think he did down there?"

"I don't know. Watched videos, read books."

"Alone?"

"A man needs his privacy sometimes. That's what Terry said."

"And you respected that?"

"Yes."

"What about that poster on the door, Lucy? Did you ever see it?"

"Only from the top of the steps, coming in from the garage."

"It's quite graphic, isn't it? What did you think of it?"

Lucy managed a thin smile. "Men . . . men are like that, aren't they? They like that sort of thing."

"So it didn't bother you?"

She did something with her lips that indicated it didn't.

"Superintendent," Dr. Landsberg cut in, "I really think you ought to be going now and let my patient get some rest."

"Just a couple more questions, that's all. Lucy, do you remember who hurt you?"

"I . . . I . . . it must have been Terry. There was no one else there, was there?"

"Had Terry ever hit you before?"

She turned her head sideways, so the only side Banks could see was bandaged.

"You're upsetting her, Superintendent. I really must insist—"

"Lucy, did you ever see Terry with Kimberley Myers? You do know who Kimberley Myers is, don't you?"

Lucy turned to face him again. "Yes. She's the poor girl that went missing."

"That's right. Did you ever see Terry with her?"

"I don't remember."

"She was a pupil at Silverhill, where Terry taught. Did he ever mention her?"

"I don't think so . . . I . . ."

"You don't remember."

"No. I'm sorry. What's wrong? What's happening? Can I see Terry?"

"I'm afraid you can't, not at the moment," said Dr. Landsberg. Then she turned to Banks. "I'm going to have to ask you to leave now. You can see how agitated Lucy is becoming."

"When can I talk to her again?"

"I'll let you know. Soon. Please." She took Banks by the arm.

Banks knew when he was beaten. Besides, the interview was going nowhere. He didn't know whether Lucy was telling the truth about not remembering or whether she was confused because of her medication.

"Get some rest, Lucy," Dr. Landsberg said as they left.

"Mr. Banks? Superintendent?"

It was Lucy, her small, thick, slurred voice, her obsidian eye fixing him in its gaze.

"Yes?"

"When can I go home?"

Banks had a mental image of what *home* would look like right now, and probably for the next month or more. *Under construction.* "I don't know," he said. "We'll be in touch."

Outside in the corridor, Banks turned to Dr. Landsberg. "Can you help me with something, Doctor?"

"Perhaps."

"Her not remembering. Is that symptomatic?"

Dr. Landsberg rubbed her eyes. She looked as if she got about as much sleep as Banks did. Someone paged a Dr. Thorsen over the PA system. "It's possible," she said. "In cases like this there's often post-traumatic stress disorder, one of the effects of which can be retrograde amnesia."

"Do you think that's the case with Lucy?"

"Too early to say, and I'm not an expert in the field. You'd have to talk to a neurologist. All I can say is that we're pretty certain there's no physical brain damage, but emotional stress can be a factor, too."

"Is this memory loss selective?"

"What do you mean?"

"She seems to remember her husband was hurt and that he was the one who hit her, but nothing else."

"It's possible, yes."

"Is it likely to be permanent?"

"Not necessarily."

"So her complete memory might come back?"

"In time."

"How long?"

"Impossible to say. As early as tomorrow, as late as . . . well, maybe never. We know so little about the brain."

"Thank you, Doctor. You've been very helpful."

Dr. Landsberg gave him a puzzled glance. "Not at all," she said. "Superintendent, I hope I'm not speaking out of turn, but I had a word with Dr. Mogabe—he's Terence Payne's doctor—just before you came."

"Yes."

"He's very concerned."

"Oh?" This was what DC Hodgkins had told Banks the day before.

"Yes. It seems as if his patient was assaulted by a police-woman."

"Not my case," said Banks.

Dr. Landsberg's eyes widened. "Just like that? You're not at all concerned?"

"Whether I'm concerned or not doesn't enter into it. Someone else is investigating the assault on Terence Payne and will no doubt be talking to Dr. Mogabe in due course. My interest is in the five dead girls and the Paynes. Good-bye, Doctor."

And Banks walked off down the corridor, footsteps echoing, leaving Dr. Landsberg to her dark thoughts. An orderly pushed a whey-faced, wrinkled old man past on a gurney, IV hooked up, on his way to surgery, by the look of things.

Banks shuddered and walked faster.

Chapter 7

*O*ne good thing about the family-style chain pubs, thought Maggie, was that nobody raised an eyebrow if you only ordered a pot of tea or a cup of coffee, which was all she wanted when she met Lorraine Temple at The Woodcutter's that Tuesday lunchtime.

Lorraine was a plump, petite brunette with an easy manner and an open face, a face you could trust. She was about Maggie's age, early thirties, wearing black jeans and a jacket over a white silk blouse. She bought the coffees and put Maggie at ease with some small talk and sympathetic noises about the recent events on The Hill, then she got down to business. She used a notebook rather than a tape recorder, Maggie was glad to see. For some reason, she didn't like the idea of her voice, her words, being recorded as sounds; but as squiggles on the page, they hardly seemed to matter.

"Do you use shorthand?" she asked, thinking nobody used that anymore.

Lorraine smiled up at her. "My own version. Would you like something to eat?"

"No, thanks. I'm not hungry."

"Okay. We'll start, then, if that's all right with you?"

Maggie tensed a little, waiting for the questions. The pub was quiet, mostly because it was a weekday and the bottom of The Hill was hardly a tourist area or a business center.

There were a couple of industrial estates nearby, but it wasn't quite lunchtime yet. Pop music played on the jukebox at an acceptable level, and even the few children in the family room seemed more subdued than she would have expected. Maybe the recent events had got to everyone in one way or another. It felt as if a pall lay over the place.

"Can you tell me how it happened?" Lorraine asked first.

Maggie thought for a moment. "Well, I don't sleep very well, and maybe I was awake or it woke me up, I'm not sure, but I heard noises across the street."

"What noises?"

"Voices arguing. A man's and a woman's. Then a sound of glass breaking and then a thud."

"And you know this was coming from across the street?"

"Yes. When I looked out of the window, there was a light on and I thought I saw a shadow pass across it."

Lorraine paused a moment to catch up with her notes. "Why were you so sure it was a domestic incident?" she asked, as she had done over the phone.

"It just . . . I mean . . ."

"Take your time, Maggie. I don't want to rush you. Think back. Try to remember."

Maggie ran her hand over her hair. "Well, I didn't *know* for certain," she said. "I suppose I just assumed, from the raised voices and, you know . . ."

"Did you recognize the voices?"

"No. They were too muffled."

"But it *could* have been someone fighting off a burglar, couldn't it? I understand there's quite a high burglary rate in this area?"

"That's true."

"So what I'm getting at, Maggie, is that maybe there was some other reason you thought you were witnessing a domestic argument."

Maggie paused. Her moment of decision had arrived, and

when it came, it was more difficult than she had thought it would be. For one thing, she didn't want her name splashed all over the papers in case Bill saw it back in Toronto, though she very much doubted that even he would come this far to get at her. There was little likelihood of such exposure with a regional daily like the *Post*, of course, but if the national press got onto it, that would be another matter. This was a big story, and the odds were that it would at least make the *National Post* and the *Globe and Mail* back home.

On the other hand, she had to remember her goal, focus on what was important here: Lucy's predicament. First and foremost she was talking to Lorraine Temple in order to get the image of *Lucy the victim* in people's minds. Call it a preemptive strike: the more the public saw her that way from the start, the less likely they were to believe that she was the embodiment of evil. All people knew so far was that the body of Kimberley Myers had been found in the Paynes' cellar, and a policeman had been killed, most likely by Terence Payne, but everyone knew they were digging there, and everyone knew what they were likely to find. "Maybe there was," she said.

"Could you elaborate on that?"

Maggie sipped some coffee. It was lukewarm. In Toronto, she remembered, they would come around and refill your cup once or twice. Not here. "I might have had reason to believe that Lucy Payne was in danger from her husband."

"Did she tell you that?"

"Yes."

"That her husband abused her?"

"Yes."

"What do *you* think of Terence Payne?"

"Not much, really."

"Do you like him?"

"Not particularly." *Not at all,* Maggie admitted to herself. Terence Payne very much gave her the creeps. She didn't know why, but she would cross the street if she saw him coming rather than meet, say hello and make small talk about the weather, all the time with him looking at her in that curiously empty, dispassionate manner he had, as if she were a butterfly pinned to a felt pad, or a frog on the table ready for dissection.

As far as she knew, though, she was the only one to feel that way. He was handsome and charming on the surface, and according to Lucy he was popular at school, both with the kids and with his colleagues on staff. But there was still something about him that put Maggie off, an emptiness at his center that she found disturbing. With most people, she felt that whatever it was she communicated, whatever radar or sonar beam went out, bounced off something and came back in some way, made some sort of blip on the screen. With Terry, it didn't; it disappeared in the vast, sprawling darkness inside him, where it echoed forever unheard. That was the only way she could explain the way she felt about Terry Payne.

She admitted to herself that she might be imagining it, responding to some deep fear or inadequacy of her own—and God knew, there were enough of those—so she had resolved to try not to criticize him for Lucy's sake, but it had been difficult.

"What did you do after Lucy told you this?"

"Talked to her, tried to persuade her to seek professional help."

"Have you ever worked with abused women?"

"No, not really. I . . ."

"Were you a victim of abuse yourself?"

Maggie felt herself tightening up inside; her head started to spin. She reached for her cigarettes, offered one to Lorraine, who refused, then lit up. She had never talked about the details of her life with Bill—the pattern of violence and remorse, blows and presents—with anyone here except her psychiatrist and Lucy Payne. "I'm not here to talk about me," she said. "I don't want you to write about me. I'm here to talk about Lucy. I don't know what happened in that house, but it's my feeling that Lucy was as much a victim as anything else."

Lorraine put her notebook aside and finished her coffee. "You're Canadian, aren't you?" she asked.

Surprised, Maggie answered that she was.

"Where from?"

"Toronto. Why?"

"Just curious, that's all. I've got a cousin lives there. That house you're living in. Tell me, but doesn't it belong to Ruth Everett, the illustrator?"

"Yes, it does."

"I thought so. I interviewed her there once. She seems like a nice person."

"She's been a good friend."

"How did you meet, if you don't mind my asking?"

"We met professionally, at a convention a few years ago."

"So you're an illustrator, too?"

"Yes. Children's books, mostly."

"Perhaps we can do a feature on you and your work?"

"I'm not very well known. Illustrators rarely are."

"Even so. We're always looking for local celebrities."

Maggie felt herself blush. "Well, I'm hardly that."

"I'll talk with my features editor, anyway, if that's okay with you?"

"I'd rather you didn't, if that's all right."

"But—"

"Please! No. Okay?"

Lorraine held her hand up. "All right. I've never known anyone turn down a bit of free publicity before, but if you insist . . ." She put her notebook and pencil in her handbag. "I must be going now," she said. "Thank you for talking to me."

Maggie watched her leave, feeling oddly apprehensive. She looked at her watch. Time for a little walk around the pond before heading back to work.

"Well, you certainly know how to pamper a girl," Tracy said as Banks led her into the McDonald's at the corner of Briggate and Boar Lane later that afternoon.

Banks laughed. "I thought all kids loved McDonald's."

Tracy nudged him in the ribs. "Enough of the 'kid,' please," she said. "I'm twenty now, you know."

For one horrible moment Banks feared he might have forgotten her birthday. But no. It was back in February, before the task force, and he had sent a card, given her some money and taken her out to dinner at Brasserie 44. A very expensive dinner. "Not even a teenager anymore, then," he said.

"That's right."

And it was true. Tracy was a young woman now. An attractive one at that. It almost broke Banks's heart to see how much she resembled Sandra twenty years ago: the same willowy figure, with the same dark eyebrows, high cheekbones, hair in a long blond ponytail, stray tresses tucked behind her delicate ears. She even echoed some of Sandra's mannerisms, such as biting her lower lip when she was concentrating and winding strands of hair around her fingers as she talked. She was dressed like a student today: blue jeans, white T-shirt with a rock band's logo, denim jacket, carrying a backpack, and she moved with assurance and grace. A young woman, no doubt about it.

Banks had returned her phone call that morning, and they had arranged to meet for a late lunch, after her last lecture of the day. He had also told Christopher Wray that they hadn't found his daughter's body yet.

They stood in line. The place was full of office workers on afternoon break, truant school-kids and mothers with prams and toddlers taking a break from their shopping. "What do you want?" Banks asked. "My treat."

"In that case, I'll have the full Monty. Big Mac, large fries and large Coke."

"Sure that's all?"

"We'll see about a sweet later."

"It'll bring you out in spots."

"No, it won't. I *never* come out in spots."

It was true. Tracy had always had a flawless complexion; school friends had often hated her for it. "You'll get fat, then."

She patted her flat stomach and pulled a face at him. She had inherited his metabolism, which allowed him to live on beer and junk food and still remain lean.

They got their food and sat at a plastic table near the window. It was a warm afternoon. Women wore bright sleeveless summer dresses, and the men had their suit jackets slung over their shoulders and their shirtsleeves rolled up.

"How's Damon?" Banks asked.

"We've decided not to see each other till after exams."

There was something about Tracy's tone that indicated there was more to it than that. Boyfriend trouble? With the monosyllabic Damon, who had spirited her off to Paris last November, when Banks himself should have been with her instead of hunting down Chief Constable Riddle's wayward daughter? He didn't want to make her talk about it; she would get to it in her own time, if she wanted to. He couldn't make her talk, anyway; Tracy had always been a very private person and could be as stubborn as he was when it came to discussing her feelings. He bit into his Big Mac. Special sauce oozed down his chin. He wiped it off with a serviette. Tracy was already halfway through her burger, and the chips were disappearing quickly, too.

"I'm sorry I haven't been in touch very often lately," Banks said. "I've been very busy."

"Story of my life," said Tracy.

"I suppose so."

She put her hand on his arm. "I'm only teasing, Dad. I've got nothing to complain about."

"You've got plenty, but it's nice of you not to say so. Anyway, apart from Damon, how are *you?*"

"I'm fine. Studying hard. Some people say second year's harder than finals."

"Any plans for the summer?"

"I might go to France again. Charlotte's parents have a cottage in the Dordogne but they're going to be in America and they said she can take a couple of friends down if she wants."

"Lucky you."

Tracy finished her Big Mac and sipped some Coke through her straw, looking closely at Banks. "You look tired, Dad," she said.

"I suppose I am."

"Your job?"

"Yes. It's a lot of responsibility. Keeps me awake at night. I'm not at all certain I'm cut out for it."

"I'm sure you're just wonderful."

"Such faith. But I don't know. I've never run such a big investigation before, and I'm not sure I ever want to again."

"But you've caught him," Tracy said. "The Chameleon killer."

"Looks that way."

"Congratulations. I knew you would."

"I didn't do anything. The whole thing was a series of accidents."

"Well . . . the result's the same, isn't it?"

"True."

"Look, Dad, I know why you haven't been in touch. You've been busy, yes, but it's more than that, isn't it?"

Banks pushed his half-eaten burger aside and worked on the chips. "What do you mean?"

"You know what I mean. You probably held yourself personally responsible for those girls' abductions, the way you always do, didn't you?"

"I wouldn't say that."

"I'll bet you thought that if you relaxed your vigilance for just one single moment he'd get someone else, another young woman *just like me,* didn't you?"

Banks applauded his daughter's perception. And she did have blond hair. "Well, there may be a grain of truth in that," he said. "Just a tiny grain."

"Was it really horrible down there?"

"I don't want to talk about it. Not at lunch. Not with you."

"I suppose you think I'm being nosy for sensation like a newspaper reporter, but I worry about you. You're not made of stone, you know. You let these things get to you."

"For a daughter," said Banks, "you do a pretty good impersonation of a nagging wife." Immediately the words were out of his mouth he regretted them. It brought the specter of Sandra between them, again. Tracy, like Brian, had struggled not to take sides in the breakup, but whereas Brian had taken an immediate dislike to Sean, Sandra's new companion, Tracy got along with him quite well and that hurt Banks, though he would never tell her.

"Have you talked to Mum lately?" Tracy asked, ignoring his criticism.

"You know I haven't."

Tracy sipped some more Coke, frowned like her mother and stared out of the window.

"Why?" Banks asked, sensing a change in the atmosphere. "Is there something I should know?"

"I was down there at Easter."

"I know you were. Did she say something about me?" Banks knew he had been dragging his feet over the divorce. The whole thing had just seemed too hurried to him, and he wasn't inclined to hurry, seeing no reason. So Sandra wanted to marry Sean, make it legal. Big deal. Let them wait.

"It's not that," Tracy said.

"What, then?"

"You really don't know?"

"I'd say if I did."

"Oh, shit." Tracy bit her lip. "I wish I'd never got into this. Why do I have to be the one?"

"Because you started it. And don't swear. Now, give."

Tracy looked down at her empty chip carton and sighed. "All right. She told me not to say anything to you yet, but you'll find out eventually. Remember, you asked for it."

"Tracy!"

"Okay. Okay. Mum's pregnant. That's what it's all about. She's three months pregnant. She's having Sean's baby."

Not long after Banks had left Lucy Payne's room, Annie Cabbot strode down the corridors of the hospital to her appointment with Dr. Mogabe. She hadn't been at all satisfied with PC Taylor's statement and needed to check out the medical angle as far as it was possible to do so. Of course, Payne wasn't dead, so there would be no postmortem, at least not yet. If he had done what it very much seemed that he had, then Annie thought it might not be such a bad idea to carry out a postmortem on him while he was still alive.

"Come in," called Dr. Mogabe.

Annie went in. The office was small and functional, with a couple of bookcases full of medical texts, a filing cabinet whose top drawer wouldn't shut, and the inevitable computer on the desk, a laptop. Various medical degrees and honors hung on the cream-painted walls, and a pewter-framed photograph stood on the desk facing the doctor. A family picture, Annie guessed. There was no skull beside it, though; nor was there a skeleton standing in the corner.

Dr. Mogabe was smaller than Annie had imagined, and his voice was higher in pitch. His skin was a shiny purple-black and his short curly hair gray. He also had small hands, but the fingers were long and tapered; a brain surgeon's fingers, Annie thought, though she had nothing for comparison, and the thought of them poking their way through the gray matter made her stomach lurch. Pianist's fingers, she decided. Much easier to live with. Or artist's fingers, like her father's.

He leaned forward and linked his hands on the desk. "I'm glad you're here, Detective Inspector Cabbot," he said, with a voice straight out of Oxford. "Indeed, if the police hadn't seen fit to call, I would have felt obliged to bring them in myself. Mr. Payne was most brutally beaten."

"Always willing to be of service," said Annie. "What can you tell me about the patient? In layman's terms, if you please."

Dr. Mogabe inclined his head slightly. "Of course," he said, as if he already knew the elite, technical mumbo jumbo of his profession would be wasted on an ignorant copper such as Annie. "Mr. Payne was admitted with serious head wounds, resulting in brain damage. He also had a broken ulna. So far, we have operated on him twice. Once to relieve a subdural hematoma. That's—"

"I know what a hematoma is," said Annie.

"Very well. The second to remove skull fragments from the brain. I could be more specific, if you wish?"

"Go ahead."

Dr. Mogabe stood up and started walking back and forth behind his desk, hands clasped behind his back, as if he were delivering a lecture. When he came to name the various parts, he pointed to them on his own skull as he paced. "The human brain is essentially made up of the cerebrum, the cerebellum and the brain stem. The cerebrum is uppermost, divided into two hemispheres by a deep groove at the top, giving what you have probably heard called right brain and left brain. Do you follow?"

"I think so."

"Prominent grooves also divide each hemisphere into lobes. The frontal lobe is the largest. There are also parietal, temporal and occipital lobes. The cerebellum is at the base of the skull, behind the brain stem."

When Dr. Mogabe had finished, he sat down again, looking very pleased with himself.

"How many blows were there?" Annie asked.

"It's difficult to be specific at this stage," said Dr. Mogabe. "I was concerned merely with saving the man's life, you understand, not with conducting an autopsy, but at an estimate I'd say two blows to the left temple, perhaps three. They caused the most damage to begin with, including the hematoma and skull fragments. There is also evidence of one or two blows to the top of the cranium, denting the skull."

"The *top* of his head?"

"The cranium is that part of the head which isn't the face, yes."

"Hard blows? As if someone hit directly down on it?"

"Possibly. But I can't be a judge of that. They would have been incapacitating, but not life-threatening. The top of the cranium is hard, and though the skull there was dented and fractured, as I said, the bone didn't splinter."

Annie made some notes.

"Those weren't the most damaging injuries, though," Dr. Mogabe added.

"Oh?"

"No, the most serious injury was caused by one or more blows to the back of the head, the brain-stem area. You see, that contains the medulla oblongata, which is the heart, blood vessel and breathing center of the brain. Any serious injury to it can be fatal."

"Yet Mr. Payne is still alive."

"Barely."

"Is there a possibility of permanent brain damage?"

"There already *is* permanent brain damage. If Mr. Payne recovers, he may well spend the rest of his life in a wheelchair in need of twenty-four-hour-a-day care. The only good thing is that he probably won't be aware of that fact."

"This injury to the medulla? Could it have occurred as Mr. Payne fell back against the wall?"

Dr. Mogabe rubbed his chin. "Again, it's not my place to do the police's job, or the pathologist's, Detective Inspector. Suffice it to say that in *my* opinion these wounds were caused by the same blunt instrument as the others. Make of that what you will." He leaned forward. "In this simplest layman's terms, this man received a most vicious beating about the head, Detective Inspector. Most vicious. I hope you believe, as I do, that the perpetrator should be brought to justice."

Shit, thought Annie, putting her notebook away. "Of course, Doctor," she said, heading for the door. "You will keep me informed, won't you?"

"You can count on it."

Annie looked at her watch. Time to head back to Eastvale and prepare her daily report for Detective Superintendent Chambers.

After his lunch with Tracy, Banks wandered around Leeds city center in a daze thinking of the news she had given him. The matter of Sandra's pregnancy had hit him harder than he would have expected after so long apart, he realized as he stood and gazed in Curry's window on Briggate, hardly taking in the display of computers, camcorders and stereo systems. He had last seen her in London the previous November, when he was down there searching for Chief Constable Riddle's runaway daughter, Emily. Looking back, he felt foolish for the way he had approached that meeting, full of confidence that because he had applied for a job with the National

Crime Squad that would take him back to live in London, Sandra would see the error of her ways, dump the temporary Sean and run back into Banks's arms.

Wrong.

Instead she had told Banks that she wanted a divorce because she and Sean wanted to get married, and that cathartic event, he thought, had flushed Sandra out of his system forever, along with any thoughts of moving to the NCS.

Until Tracy told him about the pregnancy.

Banks hadn't thought, hadn't suspected for a moment, that they wanted to get married because they wanted to have a baby. What on earth did Sandra think she was playing at? The idea of a half brother or sister for Brian and Tracy, twenty years younger, seemed unreal to Banks. And the thought of Sean, whom he had never met, being the *father* seemed even more absurd. He tried to imagine their conversations leading up to the decision, the lovemaking, the maternal desire rekindled in Sandra after so many years, and even the shadowiest of imaginings made him feel sick. He didn't know her, this woman in her early forties who wanted a baby with a boyfriend she had hardly been with for five minutes, and that also made Banks feel sad.

Banks was in Borders looking at the colorful display of bestsellers, and he didn't even remember walking in the shop, when his mobile rang. He went outside and ducked into the Victoria Quarter before answering, leaning near the entrance across from the Harvey Nichols café. It was Stefan.

"Alan, thought you'd like to know ASAP, we've identified the three bodies in the cellar. Got lucky with the dentists. We'll still run the DNA, though, cross-check with the parents."

"That's great," said Banks, snapping back from his gloomy thoughts of Sandra and Sean. "And?"

"Melissa Horrocks, Samantha Foster and Kelly Matthews."

"What?"

"I said—"

"I know. I heard what you said. I just . . ." People were walking by with their shopping and Banks didn't want to be overheard. To be truthful, he also still felt like a bit of a dickhead talking on his mobile in public, though from what he saw around him, nobody else did. He had even once witnessed a father sitting in a Helmthorpe café phone his daughter in the playground across the road when it was time to go home, and curse because the kid had switched her mobile off so he had to walk across the road and shout to her instead. "I'm just surprised, that's all."

"Why? What's wrong?"

"It's the sequence," Banks said. "It's all wrong." He lowered his voice and hoped that Stefan could still hear him. "Working backward: Kimberley Myers, Melissa Horrocks, Leanne Wray, Samantha Foster, Kelly Matthews. One of the three should be Leanne Wray. Why isn't she there?"

A little girl holding her mother's hand gave Banks a curious look as they passed him by in the arcade. Banks switched off his mobile and headed toward Millgarth.

Jenny Fuller was surprised to find Banks ringing her doorbell that evening. It was a long time since he had visited her at home. They had met many times, for coffee or drinks, even lunch or dinner, but rarely had he come here. Jenny had often wondered whether this was anything to do with that clumsy attempt at seduction the first time they had worked together.

"Come in," she said, and Banks followed her through the narrow hall into the high-ceilinged living room. She had redecorated and rearranged the furniture since his last visit and noticed him glancing around in that policeman's way of his, checking it out. Well, the expensive stereo was the same, and the sofa, she thought, smiling to herself, was the very same one where she had tried to seduce him.

She had bought a small television and video when she got back from America, having picked up the habit of watching there, but apart from the wallpaper and carpeting, nothing much else had changed. She noticed his gaze settle on the Emily Carr print over the fireplace, a huge dark, steep mountain dominating a village in the foreground. Jenny had fallen in love with Emily Carr's work when she was doing post-graduate work in Vancouver and had bought that print to bring back as a reminder of her three years there. Happy years, for the most part.

"Drink?" she asked.

"Whatever you're pouring."

"Knew I could count on you. I'm sorry I don't have any Laphroaig. Is red wine okay?"

"Fine."

Jenny went to pour the wine and noticed Banks walk over to the window. The Green looked peaceful enough in the golden evening sunlight—long shadows, dark green leaves, people walking their dogs, kids holding hands. Perhaps he was re-membering the second time he visited her, Jenny thought with a shudder as she poured the Sainsbury's Côtes du Rhône.

A drugged-out kid called Mick Webster had held her hostage with a handgun and Banks had managed to defuse the situation. The kid's mood swings had been extreme, and the whole thing had been touch and go for a while. Jenny had been terrified. Ever since that day, she had been unable to lis-ten to *Tosca,* which had been playing in the background at the time. When she had poured the wine, she shook off the bad memory, put a CD of Mozart string quartets on and car-ried the glasses over to the sofa.

"Cheers." They clinked glasses. Banks looked as tired as Jenny had ever seen him. His skin was pale and even his nor-mally sharp and lean features seemed to be sagging on the bone the way his suit sagged on his frame, and his eyes seemed more deeply set than usual, duller, lacking their usual sparkle. Still, she told herself, the poor sod probably hasn't had a decent night's sleep since he was put in charge of the task force. She wanted to reach out and touch his face, smooth away the cares, but she didn't dare risk rejection again.

"So? To what do I owe the honor?" Jenny said. "I'm assuming it's not just my irresistible company that's brought you here?"

Banks smiled. It made him look a little better, she thought. A little. "I'd like to say it was," he answered, "but I'd be a liar if I did."

"And God forbid you should ever be a liar, Alan Banks. Such an honorable man. But couldn't you be a bit *less* honorable sometimes? The rest of us human beings, well, we can't help the occasional untruth, but you, no, you can't even lie to give a girl a compliment."

"Jenny, I just couldn't stay away. Some inner force drove me to your house, compelled me to seek you out. I just knew I had to come—"

Jenny laughed and waved him down. "All right, all right. That's enough. Honorable is much better." She ran her hand through her hair. "How's Sandra?"

"Sandra's pregnant."

Jenny shook her head as if she had been slapped. "She's *what?*"

"She's pregnant. I'm sorry to state it so abruptly, but I can't think of a better way."

"That's all right. I'm just a bit gob-smacked."

"You and me both."

"How do you feel about it?"

"You sound like a psychologist."

"I *am* a psychologist."

"I know. But you don't have to sound like one. How do I

feel about it? I don't know yet. When you get right down to it, it's none of my business, is it? I let go the night she asked for a divorce so she could marry Sean."

"Is that why . . . ?"

"Yes. They want to get married, make the kid legal."

"Did you talk to her?"

"No. Tracy told me. Sandra and I . . . well, we don't communicate much anymore."

"That's sad, Alan."

"Maybe."

"There's still a lot of anger and bitterness?"

"Funnily enough, there isn't. Oh, I know I might sound a bit upset, but it was the shock, that's all. I mean, there was a lot of anger, but it was sort of a revelation when she asked for the divorce. A release. I knew then that it was really over and that I should just get on with my life."

"And?"

"And I have done, for the most part."

"But residual feelings surprise you sometimes? Creep up behind you and hit you on the back of your head?"

"I suppose you could say that."

"Welcome to the human race, Alan. You ought to know by now that you don't stop having feelings for someone just because you split up."

"It was all new to me. She was the only woman I'd been with for any length of time. The only one I wanted. Now I know what it feels like. Naturally, I wish them all the best."

"*Meow.* There you go again."

Banks laughed. "No. Really, I do."

Jenny sensed that there was something he wasn't telling her, but she also knew that he guarded his feelings when he wanted to and she would get nowhere if she pushed him. Best move on to the business at hand, she thought. And if he wants to say anything more about Sandra, he'll say it in his own time. "That wasn't why you came to see me, either, was it?"

"Not really. Maybe partly. But I do want to talk to you about the case."

"Any new developments?"

"Just one." Banks told her about the identification of the three bodies and how he found it puzzling.

"Curious," Jenny agreed. "I would have expected some sort of sequence, too. They're still digging outside?"

"Oh, yes. They'll be out there for a while."

"There wasn't much room in that little cellar."

"Just enough for about three, true," said Banks, "but that still doesn't explain why it isn't the most *recent* three. Anyway, I'd just like to go over some stuff with you. Remember when you suggested, quite early on, that the killer might have had an accomplice?"

"It was only a remote possibility. Despite the inordinate amounts of publicity your Wests and Bradys and Hindleys get, the killer couple is still a rare phenomenon. I assume you're thinking of Lucy Payne?"

Banks sipped some wine. "I talked to her at the hospital. She . . . well, she said she didn't remember much about what happened."

"Not surprising," said Jenny. "Retrograde amnesia."

"That's what Dr. Landsberg said. It's not that I don't believe in it—I've come across it before—it's just so damn . . ."

"Convenient?"

"That's one way of putting it. Jenny, I just couldn't get over the feeling that she was waiting, calculating, stalling in some way."

"Waiting for what?"

"Waiting to see which way the wind was going to blow, as if she can't work out what to say until she knows what's happening with Terry. And it would make sense, wouldn't it?"

"What would?"

"The way the girls were taken. A girl walking home on her own would be most unlikely to stop and give directions, say, to a male driver, but she might stop if a woman called her over."

"And the man?"

"Crouched down in the backseat with the chloroform ready? Jumps out the back door and drags her in? I don't know the details. But it makes sense, doesn't it?"

"Yes, it makes sense. Have you got any other evidence of her complicity?"

"None. But it's early days yet. The SOCOs are still going through the house and the lab boys are working on the clothes she was wearing when she was assaulted. Even that might come to nothing if she says she went down in the cellar, saw what her husband had done and ran away screaming. That's what I mean about her waiting to see which way the wind blows. If Terence Payne dies, Lucy's home free. If he lives, his memory could be damaged irretrievably. He is very badly hurt. And even if he recovers, he might decide to protect her, gloss over what part she played."

"If she played a part. She certainly couldn't rely on his memory being damaged, or his dying."

"That's true. But it might have given her the perfect opportunity to cover up her own involvement, if there was any. You had a look around the house, didn't you?"

"Yes."

"What was your impression?"

Jenny sipped some wine and thought about it: the magazine perfect decor, the little knickknacks, the obsessive cleanliness. "I suppose you're thinking of the videos and books?" she said.

"Partly. There looked to be some pretty raunchy stuff, especially in the bedroom."

"So they're into porn and kinky sex. So what?" She raised her eyebrows. "As a matter of fact, I've got a couple of soft porn videos in my bedroom. I don't mind a little kinkiness, now and then. Oh, don't blush, Alan. I'm not trying to seduce you. I'm simply pointing out that a few videos featuring three-way sex and a bit of mild, consensual S and M don't necessarily make a killer."

"I know that."

"And while it is true," Jenny went on, "that, statistically, most sex killers are into pornography of an extreme kind, it's false logic to argue the opposite."

"I know that, too," said Banks. "What about the occult connection? I wondered about the candles and incense in the cellar."

"Could be just for atmosphere."

"But there *was* a sort of ritual element."

"Possibly."

"I was even wondering if there could be some connection there with the fourth victim, Melissa Horrocks. She was into that satanic rock music stuff. You know, Marilyn Manson and the rest."

"Or maybe Payne just has an extreme sense of irony in his choice of victims. But look, Alan, even if Lucy did get off on the kinky stuff and Satanism, it's hardly evidence of anything else, is it?"

"I'm not asking for court evidence. At the moment I'll take anything I can get."

Jenny laughed. "Clutching at straws again?"

"Maybe so. Ken Blackstone reckons Payne might also be the Seacroft Rapist."

"Seacroft Rapist?"

"Two years ago, between May and August. You were in America. A man raped six women in Seacroft. Never caught. It turns out Payne was living there, single, at the time. He met Lucy that July, and they moved to The Hill around the beginning of September, when he started teaching at Silverhill. The rapes stopped."

"It wouldn't be the first time a serial killer was a rapist first."

"Indeed not. Anyway, they're working on DNA."

"Have a smoke if you want," Jenny said. "I can see you're getting all twitchy."

"Am I? I will, then, if you don't mind."

Jenny brought him an ashtray she kept in the sideboard for the occasional visitor who smoked. Though a non-smoker herself, she wasn't as fanatical about not allowing any smoking in her house, as some of her friends were. In fact, her time in California had made her hate the nico-Nazis even more than the smokers.

"What do you want me to do?" she asked.

"Your job," said Banks, leaning forward. "And the way I see it now is that we've probably got enough to convict Terry Payne ten times over, if he survives. It's Lucy I'm interested in, and time's running out."

"What do you mean?"

Banks drew on his cigarette before answering. "As long as she stays in hospital, we're fine, but as soon as she's released we can only hold her for twenty-four hours. Oh, we can get extensions, maybe in an extreme case like this up to ninety-six hours, but we'd better damn well have something solid to go on if we're going to do that, or she walks."

"I still think it's more than possible that she had nothing to do with the killings. Something woke her up that night and her husband wasn't there, so she looked around the house for him, saw the lights in the cellar, went down and saw—"

"But why hadn't she noticed before, Jenny? Why hadn't she been down there before?"

"She was afraid to. It sounds as if she's terrified of her husband. Look at what happened to her when she did go down."

"I know that. But Kimberley Myers was the fifth victim, for God's sake. The *fifth*. Why did it take Lucy so long to find out? Why did she wake up and go exploring only *this* time? She said she *never* went down in the cellar, that she didn't dare. What was so different about this time?"

"Perhaps she didn't *want* to know before. But, don't forget, the way it looks is that Payne was escalating, unraveling. I'd guess he was fast becoming highly unstable. Perhaps this time even she couldn't look away."

Jenny watched Banks take a contemplative drag on his cigarette and let the smoke out slowly. "You think so?" he said.

"It's possible, isn't it? Earlier, if her husband was behaving strangely, she might have suspected that he had some sort of horrible secret vice, and she wanted to pretend it wasn't there, the way most of us do with bad things."

"Sweep it under the carpet?"

"Or play the ostrich. Bury her head in the sand. Yes. Why not?"

"So we're both agreed that there are any number of possibilities to explain what happened and that Lucy Payne might be innocent?"

"Where are you going with this, Alan?"

"I want you to dig deep into Lucy Payne's background. I want you to find out all you can about her. I want—"

"But—"

"No, let me finish, Jenny. I want you to get to know her inside out, her background, her childhood, her family, her fantasies, her hopes, her fears."

"Slow down, Alan. What's the point of all this?"

"You might come across something that implicates her."

"Or absolves her?"

Banks held his hands out, palms open. "If that's what you find, fine. I'm not asking you to make anything up. Just dig."

"Even if I do, I might not come up with anything useful at all."

"Doesn't matter. At least we'll have tried."

"Isn't this a police job?"

Banks stubbed out his cigarette. "Not really. I'm after an evaluation here, an in-depth psychological profile of Lucy Payne. Of course, *we'll* check out any leads you might stumble across. I don't expect you to play detective."

"Well, I'm grateful for that."

"Think about it, Jenny. If she's guilty, she didn't just start helping her husband abduct and kill young girls out of the blue on New Year's Eve. There has to be some pathology, some background of psychological disturbance, some abnormal pattern of behavior, doesn't there?"

"There usually is. But even if I find out she was a bed wetter, liked to start fires and pulled the wings off flies, it *still* won't give you anything you can use against her in court."

"It will if someone was hurt in the fire. It will if you find out about any other mysterious events in her life that we can investigate. That's all I'm asking, Jenny. That you make a start on the psychopathology of Lucy Payne, and if you turn up anything we should investigate further, you let us know and we do it."

"And if I turn up nothing?"

"Then we go nowhere. But we're already nowhere."

Jenny sipped some more wine and thought for a moment. Alan seemed so intense about it that she was feeling browbeaten, and she didn't want to give in just because of that. But she *was* intrigued by his request; she couldn't deny that the enigma of Lucy Payne interested her both professionally *and* as a woman. She had never had the chance to probe the psychology of a possible serial killer up close before, and Banks was right that if Lucy Payne was complicit in her husband's acts, then she hadn't just come from nowhere. If Jenny dug deeply enough, there was a chance that she might find something in Lucy's past. After that . . . well, Banks had said that was the police's job, and he was right about that, too.

She topped up their wineglasses. "What if I agree?" she asked. "Where do I start?"

"Right here," said Banks, digging out his notebook. "There's a friend from the NatWest branch where Lucy Payne worked. One of our teams went and talked to the employees, and there's only one of them who knows her well.

Name's Pat Mitchell. Then there's Clive and Hilary Liversedge. Lucy's parents. They live out Hull way."

"Do they know?"

"Of course they know. What do you think we are?"

Jenny raised a fine, plucked eyebrow.

"They know."

"How did they react?"

"Upset, of course. Stunned, even. But according to the DC who interviewed them, they weren't much help. They hadn't been in close touch with Lucy since she married Terry."

"Have they been to see her in hospital?"

"No. Seems the mother's too ill to travel and the father's a reluctant caregiver."

"What about *his* parents? Terry's."

"As far as we've been able to work out," Banks said, "his mother's in a mental asylum—has been for fifteen years or so."

"What's wrong with her?"

"Schizophrenia."

"And the father?"

"Died two years ago."

"What of?"

"Massive stroke. He was a butcher in Halifax, had a record for minor sex offenses—exposing himself, peeping, that sort of thing. Sounds a pretty classic background for someone like Terry Payne, wouldn't you say?"

"If there is such a thing."

"The miracle is that Terry managed to become a teacher."

Jenny laughed. "Oh, they'll let anyone in the classroom these days. Besides, that's not the miracle."

"What is?"

"That he managed to hold on to the job for so long. And that he was married. Usually serial sex offenders such as Terence Payne find it hard to hold down a job and maintain a relationship. Our man did both."

"Is that significant?"

"It's intriguing. If I'd been pushed for a profile a month or so ago I'd have said you were looking for a man between twenty and thirty, most likely living alone and working at some sort of menial job, or a succession of such jobs. Just shows how wrong one can be, doesn't it?"

"Will you do it?"

Jenny toyed with the stem of her glass. The Mozart ended and left only the memory of music. A car passed by and a dog barked on The Green. She had the time to do as Banks asked. She had a lecture to give on Friday morning, but it was one she had given a hundred times, so she didn't need to prepare. Then she had nothing until a string of tutorials on Monday. That should give her plenty of time. "As I said, it's intriguing. I'll need to talk to Lucy herself."

"That can be arranged. You *are* our official consultant psychologist, after all."

"Easy for you to say that now you need me."

"I've known it all along. Don't let a few narrow-minded—"

"All right," said Jenny. "You've made your point. I can take being laughed at behind my back by a bunch of thick plods. I'm a big girl. When can I talk to her?"

"Best do it as soon as possible, while she's still only a witness. Believe it or not, but defense lawyers have been known to claim that psychologists have tricked suspects into incriminating themselves. How about tomorrow morning? I've got to be down at the hospital for the next postmortem at eleven, anyway."

"Lucky you. Okay."

"I'll give you a lift if you like."

"No. I'll go straight over to talk to the parents after I've talked to Lucy and her friend. I'll need my car. Meet you there?"

"Ten o'clock, then?"

"Fine."

Banks told her how to find Lucy's room. "And I'll let the parents know you're coming." Banks gave her the details. "You'll do it, then? What I'm asking?"

"Doesn't look as if I have much choice, does it?"

Banks stood up, leaned forward and kissed her swiftly on the cheek. Even though she could smell the wine and smoke on his breath, her heart jumped and she wished his lips had lingered a little longer, moved a little closer to her own. "Hey! Any more of that," she said, "and I'll have you up on sexual harassment charges."

Chapter 8

*B*anks and Jenny walked past the police guard into Lucy Payne's room just after ten o'clock the following morning. There was no doctor standing over them this time, Banks was happy to note. Lucy lay propped against the pillows reading a fashion magazine. The slats of the blinds let in some of the morning sun, lighting the vase of tulips on the bedside table, forming a pattern of bars over Lucy's face and the white bedsheets. Her long glossy black hair was spread out on the pillow around her hospital-pale face. The colors of her bruises had deepened since the previous day, which meant they were on the mend, and she still wore half her head swathed in bandages. Her good eye, long-lashed, dark and sparkling, gazed up at them. Banks wasn't sure what he saw in it, but it wasn't fear. He introduced Jenny as Dr. Fuller.

Lucy looked up and gave them a fleeting wisp of a smile. "Is there any news?" she asked.

"No," said Banks.

"He's going to die, isn't he?"

"What makes you think that?"

"I just have this feeling he's going to die, that's all."

"Would that make a difference, Lucy?"

"What do you mean?"

"You know what I mean. If Terry died, would it make a difference to what you might care to tell us?"

"How could it?"

"You tell me."

Lucy paused. Banks could see her frown as she thought about what to say next. "If I were to tell you, you know, what went on. I mean, if I knew . . . you know . . . about Terry and those girls and all . . . what would happen to me?"

"You'll have to be a bit clearer than that, I'm afraid, Lucy."

She licked her lips. "I can't really be any clearer. Not at this point. I have to think of myself. I mean, if I remembered something that didn't show me in a good light, what would you do?"

"Depends what it is, Lucy."

Lucy retreated into silence.

Jenny sat on the edge of the bed and smoothed her skirt. Banks gave her the go-ahead to pick up the questioning. "Do you remember anything more about what happened?" she asked.

"Are you a psychiatrist?"

"I'm a psychologist."

Lucy looked at Banks. "They can't make me have tests, can they?"

"No," said Banks. "Nobody can force you to undergo testing. That's not why Dr. Fuller's here. She just wants to talk to you. She's here to help." *And the check's in the post,* Banks added silently.

Lucy glanced at Jenny. "I don't know . . ."

"You've got nothing to hide, have you, Lucy?" Jenny asked.

"No. I'm just worried that they'll make things up about me."

"Who'll make things up?"

"Doctors. The police."

"Why would they want to do that?"

"I don't know. Because they think I'm evil."

"Nobody thinks you're evil, Lucy."

"You wonder how I could have lived with him, a man who did what Terry did, don't you?"

"How *could* you live with him?" Jenny asked.

"I was frightened of him. He said he'd kill me if I left him."

"And he abused you, is that right?"

"Yes."

"Physically?"

"Sometimes he hit me. Where the bruises wouldn't show."

"Until Monday morning."

Lucy touched her bandages. "Yes."

"Why was it different that time, Lucy?"

"I don't know. I still can't remember."

"That's okay," Jenny went on. "I'm not here to force you to say anything you don't want. Just relax. Did your husband abuse you in other ways?"

"What do you mean?"

"Emotionally, for example."

"Do you mean like putting me down, humiliating me in front of people?"

"That's the kind of thing I mean."

"Then the answer's yes. Like, you know, if something I cooked wasn't very good or I hadn't ironed his shirt properly. He was very fussy about his shirts."

"What did he do if his shirts weren't ironed properly?"

"He'd make me do them again and again. Once he even burned me with the iron."

"Where?"

Lucy looked away. "Where it wouldn't show."

"I'm curious about the cellar, Lucy. Detective Superintendent Banks here told me you said you never went down there."

"I might have been there the once . . . you know . . . the time he hurt me."

"On Monday morning?"

"Yes."

"But you don't remember?"

"No."

"You never went down there before?"

Lucy's voice took on a strange keening edge. "No. Never. Not since we first moved in, anyway."

"How long after that was it that he forbade you to go there?"

"I don't remember. Not long. When he'd done his conversions."

"What conversions?"

"He told me he'd made it into a den, his own private place."

"Were you never curious?"

"Not much. Besides, he always kept it locked and he carried the key with him. He said if he ever thought I'd been down there he'd thrash me to within an inch of my life."

"And you believed him?"

She turned her dark eye on Jenny. "Oh, yes. It wouldn't have been the first time."

"Did your husband ever mention pornography to you?"

"Yes. He sometimes brought videos home, things he said he'd borrowed from Geoff, one of the other teachers. Sometimes we watched them together." She looked at Banks. "You must have seen them. I mean, you've probably been in the house, searching and stuff."

Banks remembered the tapes. "Did Terry have a camcorder?" he asked her. "Did he make his own tapes?"

"No, I don't think so," she said.

Jenny picked up the thread again. "What sort of videos did he like?" she asked.

"People having sex. Girls together. Sometimes people tied up."

"You said you watched the videos together sometimes. Did *you* like them? What effect did they have on you? Did he force you to watch them?"

Lucy shifted under her thin bedsheets. The outline of her

body stirred Banks in ways he didn't want to be stirred by her. "I didn't really like them much," she said in a sort of husky little-girl voice. "Sometimes, you know, though, even so . . . they . . . they excited me." She moved again.

"Did your husband abuse you sexually, make you do things you didn't want to do?" Jenny asked.

"No," she said. "It was all just normal."

Banks was beginning to wonder if the marriage to Lucy was just a part of Terence Payne's "normal" facade, something to make people think twice about his real proclivities. After all, it had worked on DCs Bowmore and Singh, who hadn't even bothered to reinterview him. Perhaps he went elsewhere to satisfy his more perverse tastes—prostitutes, for example. It was worth looking into.

"Do you know if he went with other women?" Jenny asked, as if reading Banks's mind.

"He never said."

"But did you suspect it?"

"I thought he might have done, yes."

"Prostitutes?"

"I don't know. I didn't like to think about it."

"Did you ever find his behavior bizarre?"

"What do you mean?"

"Did he ever shock you, make you wonder what he was up to?"

"Not really. He had a terrible temper . . . you know . . . if he didn't get his own way. And sometimes, during school holidays, I didn't see him for days."

"You didn't know where he was?"

"No."

"And he never told you?"

"No."

"Weren't you curious?"

She seemed to shrink back into the bed. "Curiosity never did you any good with Terry. 'Curiosity killed the cat,' he'd say, 'and if you don't shut up, it'll kill you, too.' " She shook her head. "I don't know what I did wrong. Everything was fine. It was just a normal life. Until I met Terry. Then everything started to fall apart. How could I be such a fool? I should have *known*."

"Known what, Lucy?"

"What kind of person he was. What a monster he was."

"But you did know. You told me he hit you, humiliated you in public and in private. You did know. Are you trying to tell me you thought that was normal? Did you think that was how everybody lived?"

"No, of course not. But it didn't make him the sort of monster you think he is." Lucy looked away again.

"What is it, Lucy?" Jenny asked.

"You must think I'm such a weak person to let him do all that. A terrible person. But I'm not. I'm a nice person. Everybody says I am. I was frightened. Talk to Maggie. She understands."

Banks stepped in. "Maggie Forrest? Your neighbor?"

"Yes." Lucy looked in his direction. "She sent me those flowers. We talked about it . . . you know . . . about men abusing their wives, and she tried to persuade me to leave Terry, but I was too frightened. Maybe in a while I might have found the courage. I don't know. It's too late now, isn't it? Please, I'm tired. I don't want to talk anymore. I just want to go home and get on with my life."

Banks wondered whether he should tell Lucy that she wouldn't be going home for some time, that her *home* looked like the site of an archaeological dig and would be in the police's hands for weeks, perhaps months, to come. He decided not to bother. She would find out soon enough.

"We'll go now, then," said Jenny, standing up. "Take care, Lucy."

"Would you do me a favor?" Lucy asked as they stood in the doorway.

"What is it?" Banks asked.

"Back at the house, there's a nice little jewelry box on the dressing table in the bedroom. It's a lacquered Japanese box, black with all kinds of beautiful flowers hand-painted on it. Anyway, it's got all my favorite pieces in—earrings I bought on our honeymoon on Crete, a gold chain with a heart Terry bought me when we got engaged. They're my things. Would you bring it to me, please? My jewelry box."

Banks tried to hold in his frustration. "Lucy," he said as calmly as he could manage. "We believe that several young girls were sexually abused and murdered in the cellar of your house, and all you can think about is your jewelry?"

"That's not true," said Lucy, a hint of petulance in her tone. "I'm very sorry for what happened to those girls, of course I am, but it's not *my* fault. I don't see why it should stop me having my jewelry box. The only thing anyone's let me have from there is my handbag and purse, and I could tell someone had even been searching through them first."

Banks followed Jenny out into the corridor and they headed for the lifts. "Calm down, Alan," said Jenny. "Lucy's dissociating. She doesn't realize the emotional significance of what's happened."

"Right," said Banks glancing at the clock on the wall. "That's just bloody fine and dandy. Now I have to go and watch Dr. Mackenzie do his next postmortem, but I'll do my damnedest to remember that none of it is Lucy Payne's fault and that she's managing to dissociate herself from it all, thank you."

Jenny put her hand on his arm. "I can understand why you're frustrated, Alan, but it won't do any good. You can't push her. She won't be pushed. Be patient."

The lift came and they got in. "Trying to have a conversation with that woman is like trying to catch water in a sieve," Banks said.

"She's a weird one, all right."

"Is that your professional opinion?"

Jenny grinned. "Let me think about it. I'll talk to you after I've talked to her coworker and her parents. Bye." They arrived at the ground floor and she hurried off toward the car park. Banks took a deep breath and pressed the "down" button.

Rapunzel was going much better today, Maggie decided as she stood back and examined her work, tip of her tongue between her small white teeth. She didn't look as if one good yank on her hair would rip her head from her shoulders, and she didn't look a bit like Claire Toth.

Claire hadn't turned up as usual yesterday after school, and Maggie wondered why not. Perhaps it was only to be expected that she didn't feel very sociable after what had happened. Maybe she just wanted to be alone to sort out her feelings. Maggie decided she would talk to her psychiatrist, Dr. Simms, about Claire, see if there was something that ought to be done. She had an appointment tomorrow which, despite the events of the week, she was determined to keep.

Lorraine Temple's story hadn't turned up in the morning newspaper, as Maggie had expected it to, and she had felt disappointed when she had searched through every page and not found it. She assumed that the journalist needed more time to check her facts and put the story together. After all, it had only been yesterday when they talked. Perhaps it would be a long article focusing on the plight of abused women, a feature in the weekend paper.

She bent over the drawing board and got back to work on the Rapunzel sketch. She had to turn her desk light on as the morning had turned overcast and muggy.

A couple of minutes later, her phone rang. Maggie put her pencil aside and answered it.

"Maggie?"

She recognized the soft, husky voice. "Lucy? How are you?"

"I'm feeling much better now, really."

Maggie didn't know what to say at first. She felt awkward. Despite her sending the flowers and defending Lucy to the police and with Lorraine Temple, she realized they didn't know each other well and came from very different worlds. "It's good to hear from you," she said. "I'm glad you're feeling better."

"I just wanted to thank you for the flowers," Lucy went on. "They're lovely. They make all the difference. It was a nice thought."

"It's the least I can do."

"You know, you're the only person who's bothered with me. Everyone else has written me off."

"I'm sure that's not true, Lucy."

"Oh, but it is. Even my friends from work."

Though Maggie could hardly bring herself to ask, it was only polite. "How's Terry?"

"They won't even tell me that, but I think he's very badly hurt. I think he's going to die. I think the police are going to try to blame me."

"What makes you think that?"

"I don't know."

"Have they been to talk to you?"

"Twice. Just now there were two of them. One was a psychologist. She asked me all sorts of questions."

"About what?"

"About things Terry did to me. About our sex life. I felt like such a fool. Maggie, I just feel so frightened and alone."

"Look, Lucy, if I can help in any way . . ."

"Thank you."

"Have you got a solicitor?"

"No. I don't even know any."

"Look, Lucy. If the police come bothering you again, don't say *anything* to them. I know how they can twist your words, make something out of nothing. Will you at least let me try to get you someone? One of Ruth and Charles's friends is a solicitor in town. Julia Ford. I've met her, and she seems nice enough. She'll know what to do."

"But I don't have that much money, Maggie."

"Don't worry. We'll sort it out with her somehow. Will you let me call her for you?"

"I suppose so. I mean, if you think it's for the best."

"I do. I'll call her right now and ask her to drop by and talk to you, shall I?"

"Okay."

"Are you sure there's nothing else I can do for you?"

Maggie heard a defeated laugh over the line. "Pray for me, perhaps. I don't know, Maggie. I don't know what they're going to do to me. For the moment, I'd just like to know there's someone on *my* side."

"Count on it, Lucy, there is."

"Thank you. I'm tired. I have to go now."

And Lucy hung up the phone.

After attending Dr. Mackenzie's postmortem on the sad pile of bones and decaying flesh that had once been a young and vibrant girl with hopes and dreams and secrets, Banks felt twenty years older but none the wiser. First on the slab was the freshest because Dr. Mackenzie said it might tell him more, which seemed logical to Banks. Even so, the body had been partially buried under a thin layer of soil in Payne's cellar for about three weeks, Dr. Mackenzie estimated, which was why the skin, hair and nails were loose and easy to pull off. Insects had been at work, and much of the flesh was gone. Where skin remained, it had burst open in places, revealing the glistening muscle and fat beneath. Not much fat, because this was Melissa Horrocks, weighing just a little under seven stone, whose T-shirt bore symbols to ward off evil spirits.

Banks left before Dr. Mackenzie had finished, not because it was too gruesome for him, but because these postmortems were going to go on for some time yet, and he had other business to attend to. It would be more than a day or two, Dr. Mackenzie said, before he would be able to get down to a report, as the other two bodies were in an even worse state of decomposition. Someone from the team had to sit through the postmortems, but this was one job Banks was happy to delegate.

After the sights, sounds and smells of Mackenzie's postmortem, the bland headmaster's office at Silverhill Comprehensive came as a relief. There was nothing about the uncluttered and nondescript room that indicated it had anything to do with education, or anything else, for that matter; it was much the same as any anonymous office in any anonymous building, and it didn't even smell of much except a faint whiff of lemon-scented furniture polish. The head was called John Knight: early forties, balding, stoop-shouldered, dandruff on his jacket collar.

After getting a few general details about Payne's employment history, Banks asked Knight if there had been any problems with Payne.

"There *have* been a few complaints, now that you mention it," Knight admitted.

Banks raised his eyebrows. "From pupils?"

Knight reddened. "Good Lord, no. Nothing like that. Have you any idea what happens at the merest *hint* of something like that these days?"

"No," said Banks. "When I was at school the teachers used to thrash us with just about anything they could lay their hands on. Some of them enjoyed it, too."

"Well, those days are over, thank the Lord."

"Or the law."

"Not a believer?"

"My job makes it difficult."

"Yes, I can understand that." Knight glanced toward the window. "Mine, too, sometimes. That's one of the great challenges of faith, don't you think?"

"So what sort of problems were you having with Terence Payne?"

Knight brought himself back from a long way away and sighed. "Oh, just little things. Nothing important in themselves, but they all add up."

"For example?"

"Tardiness. Too many days off without a valid reason. Teachers may get generous holidays, Superintendent, but they *are* expected to be here during term time, barring some serious illness, of course."

"I see. Anything else?"

"Just a general sort of sloppiness. Exams not marked on time. Projects left unsupervised. Terry has a bit of temper, and he can get quite stroppy if you call him on anything."

"How long has this been going on?"

"According to head of science, only since the new year."

"And before that?"

"No problems at all. Terence Payne is a good teacher—knows his stuff—and he seemed popular with the pupils. None of us can believe what's happened. We're stunned. Just absolutely stunned."

"Do you know his wife?"

"I don't know her. I met her once at the staff Christmas party. Charming woman. A little reserved, perhaps, but charming nonetheless."

"Does Terry have a colleague here called Geoff?"

"Yes. Geoffrey Brighouse. He's the chemistry teacher.

The two of them seemed pretty thick. Went out for a jar or two together every now and again."

"What can you tell me about him?"

"Geoff's been with us six years now. Solid sort of fellow. No trouble at all."

"Can I talk to him?"

"Of course." Knight looked at his watch. "He should be over in the chemistry lab right now, preparing for his next class. Follow me."

They walked outside. The day was becoming more and more muggy as the clouds thickened, threatening rain. Nothing new. Apart from the past few days, it had been raining pretty much every day on and off since the beginning of April.

Silverhill Comprehensive was one the few pre-war Gothic redbrick schools that hadn't been sandblasted and converted into offices or luxury flats yet. Knots of adolescents lounged around the asphalt playground. They all seemed subdued, Banks thought, and a pall of gloom, fear and confusion hung about the place, palpable as a pea-souper. The groups weren't mixed, Banks noticed; the girls stood in their own little conclaves, as if huddled together for comfort and security, staring down and scuffing their shoes on the asphalt as Banks and Knight walked by. The boys were a bit more animated; at least some of them were talking and there was a bit of the usual playful pushing and shoving. But the whole effect was eerie.

"It's been like this since we heard," said Knight, as if reading Banks's mind. "People don't realize how far-reaching and long-lasting the effects will be around this place. Some of the students may never get over it. It'll blight their lives. It's not just that we've lost a cherished pupil, but someone we put in a position of trust seems to be responsible for some abominable acts, if I'm not speaking out of turn."

"You're not," said Banks. "And abominable only scratches the surface. But don't tell the papers."

"My lips are sealed. They've been around already, you know."

"Doesn't surprise me."

"I didn't tell them anything. Nothing *to* tell, really. Here we are. The Bascombe Building."

The Bascombe Building was a modern concrete-and-glass addition to the main school building. There was a plaque on the wall near the door, which read: "This building is dedicated to the memory of Frank Edward Bascombe, 1898–1971."

"Who was he?" Banks asked, as they went in the door.

"A teacher here during the war," Knight explained. "English teacher. This used to be part of the main building then, but it was hit by a stray doodlebug in October of 1944. Frank Bascombe was a hero. He got twelve children and another teacher out. Two pupils were killed in the attack. Just through here." He opened the door to the chemistry lab, where a young man sat at the teacher's desk in front of a sheaf of notes. He looked up. "Geoff. A Detective Superintendent Banks to see you." Then he left, shutting the door behind him.

Banks hadn't been in a school chemistry lab for thirty years or more, and though this one had far more modern fixtures than he remembered from his own school days, much of it was still the same: the high lab benches, Bunsen burners, test tubes, pipettes and beakers; the glass-fronted cabinet on the wall full of stoppered bottles containing sulfuric acid, potassium, sodium phosphate and such. What memories. It even smelled the same: slightly acrid, slightly rotten.

Banks remembered the first chemistry set his parents bought him for Christmas when he was thirteen, remembered the fine powdered alum, the blue copper sulfate and bright purple crystals of potassium permanganate. He liked to mix them all up and see what happened, paying no regard to the instructions or the safety precautions. Once he was heating some odd concoction over a candle at the kitchen table when the test tube cracked, making a mess all over the place. His mother went spare.

Brighouse, wearing a lightweight jacket and gray flannel trousers, not a lab coat, came forward and shook hands. He was a fresh-faced lad, about Payne's age, with pale blue eyes, fair hair and a lobster complexion, as if he'd been able to find some sun and stayed out in it too long. His handshake was firm, dry and short. He noticed Banks looking around the lab.

"Bring back memories, does it?" he asked.

"A few."

"Good ones, I hope?"

Banks nodded. He had enjoyed chemistry, but his teacher, "Titch" Barker, was one of the worst, most brutal bastards in the school. He used the rubber connecting lines of the Bunsen burners in his thrashings. Once he held Banks's hand over a burner and made as if to light it, but he backed off at the last moment. Banks had seen the sadistic gleam in his eye, how much effort it had cost him not to strike the match. Banks hadn't given him the satisfaction of a plea for mercy or an outward expression of fear, but he had been shaking inside.

"Anyway, it's sodium today," said Brighouse.

"Pardon?"

"Sodium. The way it's so unstable in air. Always goes down well. The kids these days don't have much of an attention span, so you have to give them pyrotechnics to keep them interested. Luckily, there's plenty of scope for that in chemistry."

"Ah."

"Sit down." He pointed toward a tall stool by the nearest bench. Banks sat in front of a rack of test tubes and a Bunsen burner. Brighouse sat opposite.

"I'm not sure I can help you in any way," Brighouse began. "I know Terry, of course. We're colleagues, and good mates to some extent. But I can't say I know him well. He's a very private person in many ways."

"Stands to reason," said Banks. "Look at what he was doing in private."

Brighouse blinked. "Er . . . quite."

"Mr. Brighouse—"

"Geoff. Please. Call me Geoff."

"Right, Geoff," said Banks, who always preferred the first name, as it gave him an odd sort of power over a suspect, which Geoff Brighouse certainly was in his eyes. "How long have you known Mr. Payne?"

"Since he first came here nearly two years ago."

"He was teaching in Seacroft before then. Is that right?"

"Yes. I think so."

"You didn't know him then?"

"No. Look, if you don't mind my asking, how is he, by the way?"

"He's still in intensive care, but he's hanging on."

"Good. I mean . . . oh, shit, this is so difficult. I still can't believe it. What am I supposed to say? The man's a friend of mine, after all, no matter . . ." Brighouse put his fist to his mouth and chewed on a knuckle. He seemed suddenly close to tears.

"No matter what he's done?"

"I was going to say that, but . . . I'm just confused. Forgive me."

"It'll take time. I understand. But in the meantime I need to find out all I can about Terence Payne. What sorts of things did you do together?"

"Mostly went to pubs. We never drank a lot. At least I didn't."

"Payne's a heavy drinker?"

"Not until recently."

"Did you say anything to him?"

"A couple of times. You know, when he was in his car."

"What did you do?"

"I tried to take his keys away."

"What happened?"

"He got angry. Even hit me once."

"Terence Payne hit you?"

"Yeah. But he was pissed. He's got a temper when he's pissed."

"Did he give you any reason why he was drinking so much?"

"No."

"He didn't talk about any personal problems he might be having?"

"No."

"Did you know of any problems other than the drinking?"

"He was letting his work slip a bit."

The same thing Knight had said. Like the drinking, it was probably more of a symptom than the problem itself. Jenny Fuller would perhaps be able to confirm it, but Banks thought it made sense that a man who was doing, who felt *compelled* to do, what Payne had been doing would need some sort of oblivion. It seemed almost as if he had *wanted* to be caught, wanted it all to be over. The abduction of Kimberley Myers, when he knew he was already in the system because of his car number plate, was a foolhardy move. If it hadn't been for DCs Bowmore and Singh, he might have been brought to Banks's attention earlier. Even if nothing had come from a second interview, his name would have leaped out of HOLMES as soon as Carol Houseman had entered the new data, that Kimberley Myers was a pupil at Silverhill, where Payne taught, and that he was listed as the owner of a car whose number ended in KWT, despite the false NGV plates.

"Did he ever talk about Kimberley Myers?" Banks asked.

"No. Never."

"Did he ever talk about young girls in general?"

"He talked about girls, not particularly young ones."

"How did he talk about women? With affection? With disgust? With lust? With anger?"

Brighouse thought for a moment. "Come to think of it," he said, "I always thought Terry sounded a bit sort of domineering, the way he talked about women."

"How so?"

"Well, he'd spot a girl he fancied, in a pub, say, and go on about, you know, how he'd like to fuck her, tie her to the bed and fuck her brains out. That sort of thing. I . . . I mean, I'm not a prude, but sometimes it was a bit over-the-top."

"But that's just male crudeness, isn't it?"

Brighouse raised an eyebrow. "Is it? I don't know. I honestly don't know what it means. I'm just saying he sounded rough and domineering when he talked about women."

"Talking about male crudeness, did you ever lend Terry any videos?"

Brighouse looked away. "What do you mean? What sort of videos?"

"Pornographic videos."

It wasn't possible for someone as red as Brighouse to blush, but for a moment Banks could almost have sworn that he did.

"Just some soft stuff. Nothing under the counter. Nothing you can't rent at the corner shop. I lent him other videos, too. War films, horror, science fiction. Terry's a film buff."

"No homemade videos?"

"Of course not. What do you think I am?"

"The jury's still out on that one, Geoff. Does Terry own a camcorder?"

"Not that I know of."

"Do you?"

"No. I can just about manage a basic point-and-shoot camera."

"Did you go to his house often?"

"Once in a while."

"Ever go down in the cellar?"

"No. Why?"

"Are you sure about that, Geoff?"

"Damn it, yes. Surely you can't think . . . ?"

"You do realize we're carrying out a complete forensic examination of the Paynes' cellar, don't you?"

"So?"

"So the first rule of a crime scene is that anyone who's been there leaves something and takes something away. If you were there, we'll find out, that's all. I wouldn't want you looking guilty simply for not telling me you were there on some innocent mission, like watching a porn video together."

"I never went down there."

"Okay. Just so long as you know. Did the two of you ever pick up any women together?"

Brighouse's eyes shifted toward the Bunsen burner, and he fiddled with the test tube rack in front of him.

"Mr. Brighouse? Geoff? It could be important."

"I don't see how."

"Let me be the judge of that. And if you're worried about splitting on a mate, you shouldn't be. Your mate's in hospital in a coma. His wife's in the same hospital with a few cuts and bruises he inflicted on her. And we found the body of Kimberley Myers in the cellar of his house. Remember Kimberley? You probably taught her, didn't you? I've just been to the postmortem of one of his previous victims and I'm still feeling a bit off-color. You don't need to know anymore, and believe me, you don't *want* to."

Brighouse took a deep breath. Some of the bright red coloring seemed to have leached from his cheeks and brow. "Well, okay, yeah, we did. Once."

"Tell me what happened."

"Nothing. You know . . ."

"No, I don't know. Tell me."

"Look, this is . . ."

"I don't care how embarrassing it is. I want to know how

he behaved with this woman you picked up. Carry on. Think of it as confiding in your doctor over a dose of clap."

Brighouse swallowed and went on. "It was at a conference in Blackpool. In April, just over a year ago."

"Before he got married?"

"Yeah. He was seeing Lucy, but they weren't married then. Not till May."

"Go on."

"Not much to tell. There was this cracking young teacher from Aberdeen, and one night, you know, we'd all had a few drinks at the bar and got to flirting and all. Anyway, she seemed game enough after a few gins, so we went up to the room."

"The three of you?"

"Yes. Terry and I were sharing a room. I mean, I'd have stayed away if it was his score, like, but she made it clear she didn't mind. It was her idea. She said she'd always fancied a threesome."

"And you?"

"It had been a fantasy of mine, yes."

"What happened?"

"What do you think? We had sex."

"Did she enjoy it?"

"Well, like I said, it had been mostly her idea in the first place. She was a bit drunk. We all were. She didn't object. Really, she was keen. It was only later . . ."

"What was only later?"

"Look, you know what it's like."

"No, I don't know what it's like."

"Well, Terry, he suggested a Greek sandwich. I don't know if you—"

"I know what a Greek sandwich is. Go on."

"But she didn't fancy it."

"What happened?"

"Terry can be very persuasive."

"How? Violence?"

"No. He just doesn't give up. He keeps on coming back to what he wants and it just wears down people's resistance in the end."

"So you had your Greek sandwich?"

Brighouse looked down and rubbed his fingertips on the rough, scratched lab bench. "Yeah."

"And she was willing?"

"Sort of. I mean, yes. Nobody forced her. Not physically. We'd had a couple more drinks and Terry was at her, you know, just verbally, about how great it would be, so in the end . . ."

"What happened afterward?"

"Nothing, really. I mean she didn't kick up a fuss. But it soured the mood. She cried a bit, seemed down, you know, as if she felt betrayed, used. And I could tell she didn't like it much, when it was happening."

"But you didn't stop?"

"No."

"Did she scream or tell you to stop?"

"No. I mean, she was making noises but . . . well, she was a real screamer to start with. I was even worried about the people next door telling us to keep the noise down."

"What happened next?"

"She went back to her own room. We had a few more drinks, then I passed out. I assume Terry did the same."

Banks paused and made a jotting in his notebook. "I don't know if you realize this, Geoff, but what you've just told me constitutes accessory to rape."

"Nobody raped her! I told you. She was willing enough."

"Doesn't sound like it to me. Two men. Her by herself. What choice did she have? She made it clear that she didn't want to do what Terence Payne was asking for, but he went ahead and did it anyway."

"He brought her around to his way of thinking."

"Bollocks, Geoff. He wore down her resistance and resolve. You said so yourself. And I'll also bet she was worried what might happen if she didn't go along with him."

"Nobody threatened her with violence."

"Maybe not in so many words."

"Look, maybe things went just a little too far . . ."

"Got out of hand?"

"Maybe a little."

Banks sighed. The number of times he'd heard that excuse for male violence against women. It was what Annie Cabbot's assailants had claimed, too. He felt disgusted with Geoffrey Brighouse, but there wasn't much he could do. The incident had taken place over a year ago, the woman hadn't filed a complaint as far as he knew, and Terence Payne was fighting for his life in the infirmary anyway. Still, it was one worth noting down for future reference.

"I'm sorry," said Brighouse. "But you must understand. She never told us to stop."

"Didn't seem as if she had much chance to do that, sandwiched between two strapping lads like you and Terry."

"Well, she'd enjoyed everything else."

Move on, Banks told himself, before you hit him. "Any other incidents like that?"

"No. It was the only time. Believe it or not, Superintendent, but after that night, I was a bit ashamed, even though I did nothing wrong, and I would've been uncomfortable getting into a situation like that with Terry again. He was too much for me. So I just avoided the possibility."

"So Payne was faithful to his wife from then on?"

"I didn't say that."

"What do you mean?"

"Just that the two of us didn't pick up any more girls together. Sometimes he told me, you know, about picking up prostitutes and all."

"What did he do with them?"

"What do you think?"

"He didn't go into detail?"

"No."

"Did he ever talk about his wife in a sexual way?"

"No. Never. He was very possessive about her, and very guarded. He hardly mentioned her at all when we were together. It was as if she were part of a different life altogether. Terry's got a remarkable ability to compartmentalize things."

"So it would seem. Did he ever suggest abducting young girls?"

"Do you seriously believe that I'd have anything to do with that sort of thing?"

"I don't know, Geoff. You tell me. He talked to you about tying them up and fucking their brains out, and he certainly raped that teacher in Blackpool, no matter how willing she might have been to have regular sex with the two of you earlier. I don't know what to think of your part in all this, Geoff, to be quite honest."

Brighouse had lost all his color now, and he was trembling. "But you can't think that I . . . ? I mean . . ."

"Why not? There's no reason you couldn't have been in it with him. More convenient if there were two of you. Easier to abduct your victims. Any chloroform in the lab?"

"Chloroform? Yes. Why?"

"Under lock and key, is it?"

"Of course."

"Who has a key?"

"I do. Terry. Keith Miller, the department head, Mr. Knight. I don't know who else. Probably the caretaker and the cleaners, for all I know."

"Whose prints do you think we'd find on the bottle?"

"I don't know. I certainly can't remember the last time *I* used the stuff."

"What did you do last weekend?"

"Not much. Stayed home. Marked some projects. Went shopping in town."

"Got a girlfriend at the moment, Geoff?"

"No."

"See anyone else over the weekend?"

"Just neighbors—you know, people from the other flats, in the hall, on the stairs. Oh, and I went to the pictures Saturday night."

"On your own?"

"Yes."

"What did you go to see?"

"New James Bond, in the city center. And then I dropped in at my local."

"Anyone see you?"

"A few of the regulars, yes. We had a game of darts."

"How late were you there?"

"Closing time."

Banks scratched his cheek. "I don't know, Geoff. When you get right down to it, it's not much of an alibi, is it?"

"I wasn't aware I'd be needing one."

The lab door opened and two boys poked their heads in. Geoff Brighouse seemed relieved. He looked at his watch, then at Banks, and gave a weak smile. "Time for class, I'm afraid."

Banks stood up. "That's all right, Geoff. I wouldn't want to interfere in the education of the young."

Brighouse beckoned the boys in, and more followed, swarming around the stools at the benches. He walked with Banks over to the door.

"I'd like you to come down to Millgarth and make a statement," Banks said before leaving.

"A statement? Me? But why?"

"Just a formality. Tell the detective exactly what you just told me. And we'll also need to know exactly where you were and what you were doing at the times those five girls were abducted. Details, witnesses, the lot. We'll also need a fingerprint scan and a sample of DNA. It won't be painful, just like brushing your teeth. This evening after school will do fine. Say five o'clock? Go to the front desk and ask for DC Younis. He'll be expecting you." Banks gave him a card and wrote down the name of the bright, if rather judgmental, young DC he had that very second chosen for the task of taking Brighouse's formal statement. DC Younis was active in his local Methodist Chapel and a bit conservative, morally. "Cheers," said Banks, leaving a stunned and worried-looking Geoff Brighouse to teach his class the joys of unstable sodium.

Chapter 9

Pat Mitchell took a break when Jenny turned up at the bank, and they walked to the café in the shopping center over the road, where they sipped rather weak milky tea as they talked. Pat was a vivacious brunette with damp brown eyes and a big engagement ring. All she could do at first was shake her head and repeat, "I still can't believe this. I just can't believe this is happening."

Jenny was no stranger to denial, either as a psychologist or as a woman, so she made sympathetic noises and gave Pat the time to compose herself. Once in a while, someone from one of the other tables would give them a puzzled look, as if he or she recognized them but couldn't quite place them, but for the most part the café was empty and they were able to talk undisturbed.

"How well do you know Lucy?" Jenny asked when Pat had stopped crying.

"We're pretty close. I mean, I've known her for about four years, ever since she started here at the bank. She had a little flat then, just off Tong Road. We're about the same age. How is she? Have you seen her?" All the time she talked, Pat's big brown eyes continued to glisten on the brink of tears.

"I saw her this morning," Jenny answered. "She's doing well. Healing nicely." *Physically,* anyway. "What was she like when you first met?"

Pat smiled at the memory. "She was fun, a laugh. She liked a lark."

"What do you mean?"

"You know. She just wanted to enjoy herself, have a good time."

"What was her idea of a good time?"

"Clubbing, going to pubs, parties, dancing, chatting up lads."

"Just chatting them up?"

"Lucy was . . . well, she was just *funny* when it came to lads back then. I mean, most of them seemed to bore her. She'd go out with them a couple of times and then she'd chuck them."

"Why do you think that was?"

Pat swirled the grayish tea in her cup and looked into it as if she were seeking her fortune in the leaves. "I don't know. It was as if she was *waiting* for someone."

"Mr. Right?"

Pat laughed. "Something like that." Jenny got the impression that her laugh would have been a lot more ready and frequent had it not been for the circumstances.

"Did she ever tell you what her idea of Mr. Right was?"

"No. Just that none of the lads around here seemed to satisfy her in any way. She thought they were all stupid and all they had on their minds was football and sex. In that order."

Jenny had met plenty of lads like that. "What was she after? A rich man? An exciting one? A dangerous one?"

"She wasn't interested in money particularly. Dangerous? I don't know. Maybe. She liked to live on the edge. Back then, like. She could be quite over-the-top."

Jenny made some notes. "How? In what way?"

"It's nothing, really. I shouldn't have spoken."

"Go on. Tell me."

Pat lowered her voice. "Look, you're a psychiatrist, right?"

"Psychologist."

"Whatever. Does that mean if I tell you something it goes no further? It stays between you and me and nobody can make you name your source? I mean, I wouldn't want Lucy to think I'd been talking out of turn."

While Jenny might have some valid defenses for not turning over her patients' files without a court order, in this instance she was working for the police and couldn't promise privacy. On the other hand, she needed to hear Pat's story, and Lucy would probably never find out about it. Without resorting to an outright lie, she said, "I'll do my best. I promise."

Pat chewed on her lower lip and thought for a moment, then she leaned forward and gripped her teacup in both hands. "Well, once she wanted to go to some of those clubs in Chapeltown."

"West Indian clubs?"

"Yes. I mean, most nice white girls wouldn't go near places like that, but Lucy thought it would be exciting."

"Did she go?"

"Yes, she went with Jasmine, a Jamaican girl from the Boar Lane branch. Of course, nothing happened. I think she might have tried some drugs, though."

"Why? What did she say?"

"She just hinted and did that, you know, that *knowing* sort of thing with her eyes, like she'd *been* there and the rest of us had only seen it on television. She can be quite unnerving like that, can Lucy."

"Was there anything else?"

"Yes." Once Pat was in full flow, it seemed there was no stopping her. "She once told me she'd acted as a prostitute."

"She'd *what?*"

"It's true." Pat looked around to make sure no one was interested and lowered her voice even more. "It was over a couple of years ago, before Terry came on the scene. We'd talked about it in a pub one night when we saw one—you know, a prostitute—wondering what it would be like and all, doing it for money, just as a bit of a laugh, really. Lucy said she'd like to try it and find out and she'd let us know."

"Did she?"

"Uh-huh. That's what she told me. About a week later, she said the night before she'd put on some slutty clothes—fish-net tights, high heels, a black leather miniskirt and a low-cut blouse and she sat at the bar of one of those business hotels near the motorway. It didn't take long, she said, before a man approached her."

"Did she tell you what happened?"

"Not all the details. She knows when to hold back, does Lucy. For effect, like. But she said they talked, very business-like and polite and all that, and they came to some financial arrangement, then they went up to his room and . . . and they *did* it."

"Did you believe her?"

"Not at first. I mean, it's *outrageous,* isn't it? But . . ."

"Eventually you did?"

"Well, like I said, Lucy's always capable of surprising you, and she likes danger, excitement. I suppose it was when she showed me the money that tipped the balance."

"She showed you?"

"Yes. Two hundred pounds."

"She could have got it out of the bank."

"She could, but . . . Anyway, that's all I know about it."

Jenny made some more notes. Pat tilted her head to see what she was writing. "It must be a fascinating job, yours," she said.

"It has its moments."

"Just like that woman who used to be on television. *Prime Suspect.*"

"I'm not a policewoman, Pat. Just a consultant psycholo-gist."

Pat wrinkled her nose. "Still, it's an exciting life, isn't it? Catching criminals and all that."

Excitement wasn't the first word that came to Jenny's mind, but she decided to leave Pat to her illusions. Like most people's, they wouldn't do her any real harm. "What about after Lucy met Terry?"

"She changed. But then you do, don't you? Otherwise what's the point of getting married? If it doesn't change you, I mean."

"I see your point. How did she change?"

"She became a lot more reserved. Stopped home more. Terry's a bit of a homebody, so there was no more clubbing. He's the jealous type, too, is Terry, if you know what I mean, so she had to watch herself chatting up the lads. Not that she did that after they were married. It was Terry, Terry, Terry all the way then."

"Were they in love?"

"I'd say. Dotty about each other. At least that's what she said, and she seemed happy. Mostly."

"Let's back up a bit. Were you there when they met?"

"She says so, but I can't for the life of me remember them meeting."

"When was it?"

"Nearly two years ago. July. A warm, muggy night. We were at a girls' night out at a pub in Seacroft. One of those really big places with lots of rooms and dancing."

"How do you remember it?"

"I remember Lucy leaving alone. She said she hadn't enough money for a taxi and she didn't want to miss her bus. They don't run late. I'd had a few drinks, but I remember because I said something about her being careful. The Seacroft Rapist was active around then."

"What did she say?"

"She just gave me that look and left."

"Did you see Terry there that night? Did you see him chatting her up?"

"I think I saw him there, by himself at the bar, but I don't remember seeing them talking."

"What did Lucy say later?"

"That she'd talked to him when she went to the bar for drinks once and quite liked the look of him, then they met again on her way out and went to some other pub together. I can't remember. I was definitely a bit squiffy. Anyway, whatever happened, that was it. From then on it was a different Lucy. She didn't have anywhere near enough time for her old friends."

"Did you ever visit them? Go for dinner?"

"A couple of times, with my fiancé, Steve. We got engaged a year ago." She held up her ring. The diamond caught the light and flashed. "We're getting married in August. We've already booked the honeymoon. We're going to Rhodes."

"Did you get along with Terry okay?"

Pat gave a little shudder. "No. I don't like him. Never did. Steve thought he was all right, but . . . That's why we stopped going over, really. There's just something about him . . . And Lucy, she was sort of like a zombie when he was around. Either that or she acted like she was on drugs."

"What do you mean?"

"Well, it's just a figure of speech. I mean, I know she wasn't *really* on drugs, but just, you know, overexcited, talking too much, mind jumping all over the place."

"Did you ever see any signs of abuse?"

"You mean did he hit her and stuff?"

"Yes."

"No. Nothing. I never saw any bruises or anything like that."

"Did Lucy seem to change in any way?"

"What do you mean?"

"Recently. Did she become more withdrawn, seem afraid of anything?"

Pat chewed on the edge of her thumb for a moment before answering. "She changed a bit the past few months, now you come to mention it," she said finally. "I can't say exactly when it started, but she seemed more nervy, more distracted, as if she had a problem, a lot on her mind."

"Did she confide in you?"

"No. We'd drifted apart quite a bit by then. Was he really beating her? I can't understand it, can you, how a woman, especially a woman like Lucy, can let that happen?"

Jenny could, but there was no point trying to convince Pat. If Lucy sensed that would be her old friend's attitude toward her problem, it was no surprise that she turned to a neighbor like Maggie Forrest, who at least showed empathy.

"Did Lucy ever talk about her past, her childhood?"

Pat looked at her watch. "No. All I know is that she's from somewhere near Hull and it was a pretty dull life. She couldn't wait to get away, and she didn't keep in touch as much as she should, especially after Terry came on the scene. Look, I really have to get back now. I hope I've been of help." She stood up.

Jenny stood and shook her hand. "Thanks. Yes, you've been very helpful." As she watched Pat scurry back to the bank, Jenny looked at her watch, too. She had enough time to drive out to Hull and see what Lucy's parents had to say.

It was several days since Banks had last stopped in at his Eastvale office, and the amount of accumulated paperwork was staggering, since he had temporarily inherited Detective Superintendent Gristhorpe's workload. Consequently, when he did find time to drop by the station late that afternoon, driving straight back after his interview with Geoff Brighouse, his pigeonhole was stuffed with reports, budget revisions, memos, requests, telephone message slips, crime statistics and various circulars awaiting his signature. He decided to clear up some of the backlog of paperwork and take Annie Cabbot for a quick drink at the Queen's Arms to discuss her progress in the Janet Taylor investigation, and maybe build a few bridges in the process.

After leaving a message for Annie to drop by his office at six o'clock, Banks closed the door behind him and dropped the pile of papers on his desk. He hadn't even changed his *Dalesman* calendar from April to May, he noticed, flipping over from a photo of the stone bridge at Linton to the soaring lines of York Minster's east window, pink and white may blossom blurred in the foreground.

It was Thursday, the eleventh of May. Hard to believe it was only three days since the gruesome discovery at number 35 The Hill. Already the tabloids were rubbing their hands with glee and calling the place "Dr. Terry's House of Horrors" and, even worse, "The House of Payne." They had somehow got hold of photographs of both Terry and Lucy Payne—the former cropped from a school class picture, by the look of it, and the latter from an "employee of the month" presentation to Lucy at the NatWest branch where she worked. Both photos were poor in quality, and you'd have to know who they were before you'd recognize either of them.

Banks turned on his computer and answered any E-mail he thought merited a response, then he picked away at the pile of papers. Not much, it seemed, had happened in his absence. The major preoccupation had been with a series of nasty post office robberies, in which one masked man terrorized staff and customers with a long knife and an ammonia spray. No one had been hurt yet, but that didn't mean they wouldn't be. There had been four such robberies in the Western Division over a month. DS Hatchley was out rounding up his ragbag assortment of informants. Apart from the robberies, perhaps the most serious crime on their hands was the theft of a tortoise that happened to be sleeping in a cardboard box nicked from someone's garden, along with a Raleigh bicycle and a lawn mower.

Business as usual. And somehow Banks found an odd sort of comfort in these dull, predictable crimes after the horrors of the Paynes' cellar.

He turned on his radio and recognized the slow movement from a late Schubert piano sonata. He felt a tight pain between his eyes and massaged the spot gently. When that didn't work he swallowed a couple of Paracetamol he kept in his desk for emergencies such as this, washed them down with tepid coffee, then he pushed the mound of papers aside and let the music spill over him in gentle waves. The headaches were coming more frequently these days, along with the sleepless nights and a strange reluctance to go to work. It reminded him of the pattern he went through just before he left London for Yorkshire, when he was on the edge of burnout, and he wondered if he was getting in the same state again. He should probably see his doctor, he decided, when he had time.

The ringing telephone disturbed him, as it had so often before. Scowling, he picked up the offending instrument and growled, "Banks."

"Stefan here. You asked me to keep you informed."

Banks relaxed his tone. "Yes, Stefan. Any developments?" Banks could hear voices in the background. Millgarth, most likely. Or the Payne house.

"One piece of good news. They've lifted Payne's prints from the machete used to kill PC Morrisey, and the lab reports both yellow plastic fibers from the rope in the scrapings taken from under Lucy Payne's fingernails, along with traces of Kimberley Myers's blood on the sleeve of her dressing gown."

"Kimberley's blood on Lucy Payne's dressing gown?"

"Yes."

"So she *was* down there," Banks said.

"Looks like it. Mind you, she could explain away the fibers by saying she hung out the washing. They did use the same kind of clothes-line in the back garden. I've seen it."

"But the blood?"

"Maybe more tricky," said Stefan. "There wasn't very much, but at least it proves that she was down there."

"Thanks, Stefan. It's a big help. What about Terence Payne?"

"The same. Blood and yellow fibers. Along with a fair quantity of PC Morrisey's blood."

"What about the bodies?"

"One more, skeletal, out in the garden. That makes all five."

"Skeletal? How long would that take?"

"Depends on temperature and insect activity," said Stefan.

"Could it have happened in just a month or so?"

"Could have, with the right conditions. It hasn't been very warm this past month, though."

"But is it possible?"

"It's possible."

Leanne Wray had disappeared on the thirty-first of March, which was slightly over a month ago, so there was at least some possibility that it was her remains.

"Anyway," Stefan went on, "there's plenty of garden left. They're digging very slowly and carefully to avoid disturbing the bones. I've arranged for a botanist and an entomologist from the university to visit the scene tomorrow. They should be able to help us with time of death."

"Did you find any clothing with the victims?"

"No. Nothing of a personal nature."

"Get to work on identifying that body, Stefan, and let me know the minute you have anything, even if it's negative."

"Will do."

Banks said good-bye to Stefan and hung up, then he walked over to his open window and sneaked a prohibited cigarette. It was a hot, muggy afternoon, with the sort of tension in the air that meant rain would probably come soon, perhaps even a thunderstorm. Office workers sniffed the air and reached for their umbrellas as they headed home. Shopkeepers closed up and wound back the awnings. Banks thought about Sandra again, how when she used to work at the community center down North Market Street they would often meet for a drink in the Queen's Arms before heading home. Happy days. Or so they had seemed. And now she was pregnant with Sean's baby.

The Schubert piano music played on, the serene and elegiac opening of the final, B-flat sonata. Banks's headache began to subside a little. The one thing he remembered about Sandra's pregnancies was that she hadn't enjoyed them, hadn't glowed with the joys of approaching motherhood. She had suffered extreme morning sickness, and though she didn't drink or smoke much, she continued to do both because back then nobody made such a fuss about it. She also continued to go to galleries and plays and meet with friends, and complained when her condition made it difficult or impossible for her to do so.

While pregnant with Tracy, she had slipped on the ice and broken her leg in her seventh month and spent the rest of her confinement with a cast on. That more than anything had driven her crazy, unable to get out and about with her camera the way she loved to do, stuck in their poky little Kennington flat watching gray day follow gray day all that winter while Banks was working all hours, hardly ever home. Well, perhaps Sean would be around for her more often. Lord only knew, perhaps if Banks had been . . .

But he didn't get to follow that thought to the particular circle of hell he was sure must be reserved for neglectful husbands and fathers. Annie Cabbot tapped at his door and popped her head around, giving him a temporary escape from the guilt and self-recrimination that seemed to be so much his lot these days, no matter how hard he tried to do the right thing.

"You did say six o'clock, didn't you?"

"Yes. Sorry, Annie. Miles away." Banks picked up his jacket, checking the pockets for wallet and cigarettes, then cast a backward glance at the pile of untouched paperwork on his desk. To hell with it. If they expected him to do two, three jobs at once, then they could wait for their bloody paperwork.

As Jenny drove through a shower and looked out at the ugly forest of cranes that rose up from Goole docks, she wondered for the umpteenth time what on earth had induced her to return to England. To Yorkshire. It certainly wasn't family ties. Jenny was an only child and her parents were retired academics living in Sussex. Both her mother and father had been far too wrapped up in their work—he as a historian, she as a physicist—and Jenny had spent more of her childhood with a succession of nannies and *au pairs* than with her parents. Given their natural academic detachment, too, Jenny often felt that she had been far more of an experiment than a daughter.

It didn't bother her—after all, she didn't know any different—and it was very much the way she had lived her life, too: as an experiment. Sometimes she looked back and it all seemed so shallow and self-centered that she felt herself panic; other times it seemed just fine.

She would turn forty that coming December, was still single—had never, in fact, been married—and while a bit shop-soiled, battered and bruised, she was far from down and out for the count. She still had her looks and her figure, though she needed more and more magic potions for the former and had to work harder and harder at the university gym to keep those excess pounds from creeping on, given her taste for good food and wine. She also had a good job, a growing reputation as an offender profiler, publications to her credit.

So why did she sometimes feel so empty? Why did she always feel she was in a hurry to get somewhere she never arrived at? Even now, with the rain lashing against her windscreen, the wipers going as fast as they could go, she was doing ninety kilometers per hour. She slowed down to eighty, but her speed soon started creeping up again, along with the feeling that she was late for something, always late for something.

The shower ended. Elgar's *Enigma Variations* was playing on Classic FM. To the north, a power station with its huge corset-shaped cooling towers squatted against the horizon, the steam it spewed almost indistinguishable from the low cloud. She was nearing the end of the motorway now. The east-bound M62 was like so many things in life; it left you just short of your destination.

Well, she told herself, she had come back to Yorkshire because she was running away from a bad relationship with Randy. Story of her life. She had a nice condo in West Hollywood, rented at a most generous rate by a writer who had made enough money to buy a place way up in Laurel Canyon, and she was within walking distance of a supermarket and the restaurants and clubs on Santa Monica Boulevard. She had her teaching and research at UCLA, and she had Randy. But Randy had a habit of sleeping with pretty twenty-one-year-old graduate students.

After a minor breakdown, Jenny had called it a day and come running back to Eastvale. Perhaps that explained why she was always in a hurry, she thought—desperate to get *home,* wherever that was, desperate to get away from one bad relationship and right into the next one. It was a theory, at any rate. And then, of course, Alan was in Eastvale, too. If he was part of the reason why she had stayed away, could he also be part of the reason why she had come back? She didn't want to dwell on that.

The M62 turned into the A63, and soon Jenny caught a glimpse of the Humber Bridge ahead to her right, stretching out majestically over the broad estuary into the mists and fens of Lincolnshire and Little Holland. Suddenly, a few shafts of sunlight pierced the ragged cloud cover as the "Nimrod" variation reached its rousing climax. A "Yorkshire moment." She remembered the "L.A. moments" Randy was so fond of pointing out in their early days when they drove and drove and drove around the huge, sprawling city: a palm tree silhouetted against a blood-orange sky; a big, bright full moon low over the HOLLYWOOD sign.

As soon as she could, Jenny pulled into a lay-by and studied her map. The clouds were dispersing now, allowing even more sunlight through, but the roads were still swamped with puddles and the cars and lorries swished up sheets of water as they sped by her.

Lucy's parents lived off the A164 to Beverley, so she didn't have to drive through Hull city center. She pressed on through the straggling western suburbs and soon found the residential area she was looking for. Clive and Hilary Liversedge's house was a nicely maintained bay-window semi in a quiet crescent of similar houses. Not much of a place for a young girl to grow up, Jenny thought. Her own parents had moved often throughout her childhood, and though she had been born in Durham, she had at various times lived in Bath, Bristol, Exeter and Norwich, all university towns, and all full of randy young men. She had never been stuck in a dull suburban backwater like this.

A small plump man with a soft gray mustache answered the door. He was wearing a green cardigan, unbuttoned, and dark brown trousers which hugged the underside of his rounded gut. A belt wouldn't be much good with a shape like that, Jenny thought, noticing the braces that held the trousers up.

"Clive Liversedge?"

"Come in, love," he said. "You must be Dr. Fuller."

"That's me." Jenny followed him into the cramped hall, from which a glass-paneled door led to a tidy living room with a red velour three-piece suite, an electric fire with fake coals and striped wallpaper. Somehow, it wasn't the kind of place Jenny had imagined Lucy Payne growing up in; she couldn't get any sense of Lucy living in this environment at all.

She could see what Banks meant about the invalid mother. Pale skin and raccoon eyes, Hilary Liversedge reclined on the sofa, a wool blanket covering her lower half. Her arms were thin and the skin looked puckered and loose. She didn't move when Jenny entered, but her eyes looked lively and attentive enough, despite the yellowish cast of the sclera. Jenny didn't know what was wrong with her, but she put it down to one of those vague chronic illnesses that certain types of people luxuriate in toward the ends of their lives.

"How is she?" Clive Liversedge asked, as if Lucy had perhaps suffered a minor fall or car accident. "They said it wasn't serious. Is she doing all right?"

"I saw her this morning," Jenny said, "and she's bearing up well."

"Poor lass," said Hilary. "To think of what she's been through. Tell her she's welcome to come here and stay with us when she gets out of hospital."

"I just came to get some sense of what Lucy's like," Jenny began. "What sort of a girl she was."

The Liversedges looked at each other. "Just ordinary," said Clive.

"Normal," said Hilary.

Right, thought Jenny. Normal girls go marrying serial killers every day. Even if Lucy had nothing at all to do with the killings, there *had* to be something odd about her, something *out of* the ordinary. Jenny had even sensed that during their brief chat in the hospital that morning. She could couch it in as much psychological gobbledygook as she wanted—and Jenny had come across plenty of that in her career—but what it came down to was the feeling that Lucy Payne was definitely a sausage or two short of the full English breakfast.

"What was she like at school?" Jenny pressed on.

"Very bright," answered Clive.

"She got three A-levels. Good marks, too. As and Bs," added Hilary.

"She could have gone to university," Clive added.

"Why didn't she?"

"She didn't want to," said Clive. "She wanted to get out in the world and make a living for herself."

"Is she ambitious?"

"She's not greedy, if that's what you mean," Hilary answered. "Of course she wants to get on in the world like everyone else, but she doesn't think she needs a university degree to do it. They're overrated, anyway, don't you think?"

"I suppose so," said Jenny, who had a BA and a PhD. "Was she studious when she was at school?"

"I wouldn't really say so," said Hilary. "She did what she had to do in order to pass, but she wasn't a swot."

"Was she popular at school?"

"She seemed to get on all right with the other children. We got no complaints from her, at any rate."

"No bullying, nothing like that?"

"Well, there was one girl, once, but that came to nothing," said Clive.

"Someone bullying Lucy?"

"No. Someone complaining she was being bullied *by* Lucy, accused her of demanding money with threats."

"What happened?"

"Nothing. It was just her word against Lucy's."

"And you believed Lucy?"

"Yes."

"So no action was taken?"

"No. They couldn't prove anything against her."

"And nothing else like that occurred?"

"No."

"Did she take part in any after-school activities?"

"She wasn't much a one for sports, but she was in a couple of school plays. Very good, too, wasn't she, love?"

Hilary Liversedge nodded.

"Was she wild at all?"

"She could be high-spirited, and if she got it in her mind to do something, there was no stopping her, but I wouldn't say she was especially *wild*."

"What about at home? How did you all get along?"

They looked at each other again. It was an ordinary enough gesture, but it unnerved Jenny a bit. "Fine. Quiet as a mouse. Never any trouble," said Clive.

"When did she leave home?"

"When she was eighteen. She got that job at the bank in Leeds. We didn't stand in her way."

"Not that we could have," added Hilary.

"Have you seen much of her lately?"

Hilary's expression darkened a little. "She said she's not been able to get over here as much as she'd have liked."

"When was the last time you saw her?"

"Christmas," answered Clive.

"Last Christmas?"

"The year before."

It was as Pat Mitchell had said; Lucy had become distanced from her parents. "So that's seventeen months?"

"I suppose so."

"Did she telephone or write?"

"She writes us nice letters," said Hilary.

"What does she tell you about her life?"

"About her job and the house. Just normal, ordinary sorts of things."

"Did she tell you how Terry was doing at the school?"

This exchanged look *definitely* spoke volumes. "No," said Clive. "And we didn't ask."

"We didn't approve of her taking up with the first boy she met," said Hilary.

"Did she have other boyfriends before Terry?"

"Nobody serious."

"But you thought she could do better?"

"We're not saying there's anything *wrong* with Terry. He seems nice enough, and he's got a decent job, good prospects."

"But?"

"But he seemed to sort of take over, didn't he, Clive?"

"Yes. It was very odd."

"What do you mean?" Jenny asked.

"It was as if he didn't *want* her to see us."

"Did he or she ever say that?"

Hilary shook her head. The loose skin flapped. "Not in so many words. It was just an impression I got. *We* got."

Jenny made a note. To her, this sounded like one of the stages of a sexually sadistic relationship that she had learned about at Quantico. The sadist, in this case Terry Payne, starts to isolate his partner from her family. Pat Mitchell had also suggested the same sort of progressive separation from her friends.

"They just kept to themselves," said Clive.

"What did you think of Terry?"

"There was something strange about him, but I couldn't put my finger on it."

"What sort of person is Lucy?" Jenny went on. "Is she generally trusting? Naïve? Dependent?"

"I wouldn't really describe her in any of those terms, would you, Hilary?"

"No," said Hilary. "She's very independent, for a start. Headstrong, too. Always makes her own decisions and acts on them. Like about not going to university and getting a job instead. Once she'd made her mind up, she was off. It was the same with marrying Terry. Love at first sight, she said."

"You weren't at the wedding, though?"

"Hilary can't travel anymore," said Clive, going over and patting his wife's inert form. "Can you, love?"

"We sent a telegram and a present," Hilary said. "A nice set of Royal Doulton."

"Do you think Lucy lacks confidence, self-esteem?"

"It depends on what you're talking about. She's confident enough at work, but not so much around people. She often becomes very quiet around strangers, very wary and reserved. She doesn't like crowds, but she used to like going out with a small group of friends. You know, the girls from work. That sort of thing."

"Would you say she's a loner by nature?"

"To some extent, yes. She's a very private person, never told us much about what was going on or what was going through her mind."

Jenny was wondering whether she should ask if Lucy pulled the wings off flies, wet her bed and set fire to the local school, but she couldn't find an easy way to get around to doing it. "Was she like that even as a child?" she asked. "Or did her need for solitude develop later in life?"

"We wouldn't know the answer to that," said Clive, looking over at his wife. "We didn't know her then."

"What do you mean?"

"Well, Lucy wasn't our daughter, not our *natural* daughter. Hilary can't have children, you see. She's got a heart condition. Always has had. Doctor said childbirth could kill her." Hilary patted her heart and gave Jenny a rueful look.

"You adopted Lucy?"

"No. No. We fostered her. Lucy was our foster child. The

third and last, as it turned out. She was with us by far the longest and we came to think of her as our own."

"I don't understand. Why didn't you tell the police this?"

"They didn't ask," said Clive, as if that made it all perfectly reasonable.

Jenny was stunned. Here was an essential piece of information in the puzzle that was Lucy Payne, and nobody else on the team knew it. "How old was she when she came to you?" Jenny asked.

"Twelve," said Clive. "It was in March 1990. I remember the day as if it were yesterday. Didn't you know? Lucy was one of the Alderthorpe Seven."

Annie lounged back in her hard wood chair as if it had been molded to fit her shape, and stretched out her legs. Banks had always envied the way she managed to seem so centered and comfortable in almost any environment, and she was doing it now. She took a sip of her Theakston's bitter and almost purred. Then she smiled at Banks.

"I've been cursing you all day, you know," she said. "Taking your name in vain."

"I thought my ears were burning."

"By rights they should have both burned off by now."

"Point taken. What did Superintendent Chambers have to say?"

Annie gave a dismissive wave. "What you'd expect. That it's *my* career on the line if there's any fallout. Oh, and he warned me about you."

"About me?"

"Yes. Said he thought you might try to pump me for information, to play my cards close to my chest. Which he examined rather too closely for my comfort, by the way."

"Anything else?"

"Yes. He said you're a ladies' man. Is that true?"

Banks laughed. "He did? He really said that?"

Annie nodded.

The Queen's Arms was busy with the after-work crowd and tourists seeking shelter, and Banks and Annie had been lucky to get seats at the small, dimpled copper-topped table in the corner by the window. Banks could see the ghostly images of people with umbrellas drifting back and forth on Market Street beyond the red and yellow panes of glass. Rain spotted the windows, and he could hear it tapping in the pauses between words. Savage Garden were on the jukebox claiming that they loved someone before they met her. The air was full of smoke and animated chatter.

"What do you think of Janet Taylor?" Banks asked. "I'm not trying to pry into your case. I'm just interested in your first impression."

"So *you* say. Anyway, I quite like her, and I feel sorry for her. She's a probationary PC with limited experience put in an impossible position. She did what came naturally."

"But?"

"I'll not let my feelings blinker my judgment. I haven't been able to put it all together yet, but it looks to me as if Janet Taylor lied on her statement."

"Deliberately lied or just didn't remember?"

"I suppose we could give her the benefit of the doubt on that. Look, I've never been in a situation like she was. I can't begin to imagine what it must have been like for her. The fact remains that, according to Dr. Mogabe, she must have hit Payne with her baton at least seven or eight times *after* he was beyond any sort of retaliatory action."

"He was stronger than her. Maybe that's what was required to subdue him. The law allows us *some* latitude on reasonable force in making an arrest."

Annie shook her head. She stretched out her legs sideways from the chair and crossed them. Banks noticed the thin gold chain around her ankle, one of the many things he found sexy about Annie. "She lost it, Alan. It goes way beyond self-defense and reasonable force. There's another thing, too."

"What?"

"I spoke to the paramedics and ambulance attendants who were first at the scene. They hadn't a clue what had happened, of course, but it didn't take them long to work out it was something really nasty and bizarre."

"And?"

"One of them said when he went over to PC Taylor, who was cradling PC Morrisey's body, she looked over at Payne and said, 'Is he dead? Did I kill the bastard?'"

"That could mean anything."

"My point exactly. In the hands of a good barrister it could mean she had intended to kill him all along and was asking if she had succeeded in her aim. It could signify intent."

"It could also just be an innocent question."

"You know as well as I do there's nothing *innocent* about this business at all. Especially with the Hadleigh case on the news every day. And don't forget that Payne was unarmed and down on the floor when she aimed the final few blows."

"How do we know that?"

"PC Taylor had already broken his wrist, according to her statement, and kicked the machete into the corner where it was found later. Also, the angles of the blows and the force behind them indicate she had the advantage of height, which we know she didn't have naturally. Payne's six foot one and PC Taylor's only five foot six."

Banks took a long drag on his cigarette as he digested what Annie had to say, thinking it wouldn't be a hell of a lot of fun to tell AC Hartnell about this. "Not an immediate threat to her, then?" he said.

"Not from where I'm looking." Annie shifted a little in her chair. "It's possible," she admitted. "I'm not saying that wouldn't freak out even the best-trained copper. But I've got to say that it looks to me as if she lost it. I'd still like to have a look at the scene."

"Sure. Though I doubt there's much left to see now the SOCOs have been in there for three days."

"Even so . . ."

"I understand," said Banks. And he did. There was something ritualistic in visiting the scene. Whether you picked up vibrations from the walls or what, it didn't really matter. What mattered was that it *connected* you more closely with the crime. You'd *stood* there, in that place where evil had happened. "When do you want to go?"

"Tomorrow morning. I'll call on Janet Taylor after."

"I'll arrange it with the officers on duty," said Banks. "We can go down there together if you like. I'm off to talk to Lucy Payne again before she disappears."

"They're releasing her from hospital?"

"So I've heard. Her injuries aren't that serious. Besides, they need the bed."

Annie paused, then she said, "I'd rather make my own way."

"Okay. If that's what you want."

"Oh, don't look so crestfallen, Alan. It's nothing personal. It just wouldn't look good. And people *would* see us, no matter what you think."

"You're right," Banks agreed. "Look, if there's any chance of a bit of spare time Saturday night, how about dinner and . . . ?"

The corners of Annie's mouth turned up, and a gleam came to her dark eyes. "Dinner and what?"

"You know."

"I don't. Tell me."

Banks glanced around to make sure no one was eavesdropping, then he leaned forward. But before he could say anything, the doors opened and DC Winsome Jackman walked in. Heads turned: some because she was black, and some because she was a gorgeous, statuesque young woman. Winsome was on duty and Banks and Annie had told her where they would be.

"Sorry to disturb you, sir," she said, pulling up a chair and sitting down.

"That's all right," said Banks. "What is it?"

"A DC Karen Hodgkins from the task force just phoned."

"And?"

Winsome looked at Annie. "It's Terence Payne," she said. "He died an hour ago in the infirmary without recovering consciousness."

"Oh, shit," said Annie.

"Well, that should make life interesting," said Banks, reaching for another cigarette.

"Tell me about the Alderthorpe Seven," said Banks into his phone at home later that evening. He had just settled down to Duke Ellington's *Black, Brown and Beige,* the latest copy of *Gramophone* and two fingers of Laphroaig when Jenny phoned. He turned down the music and reached for his cigarettes. "I mean," he went on, "I vaguely remember hearing about it at the time, but I can't remember many details."

"I don't have a lot yet, myself," said Jenny. "Only what the Liversedges told me."

"Go on."

Banks heard a rustle of paper at the other end of the line. "On the eleventh of February, 1990," Jenny began, "police and social workers made a dawn raid on the village of Alderthorpe, near Spurn Head on the East Yorkshire coast. They were acting on allegations of ritual satanic abuse of children and investigating a missing child."

"Who blew the whistle?" Banks asked.

"I don't know," said Jenny. "I didn't ask."

Banks filed it away for later. "Okay. Carry on."

"I'm not a policeman, Alan. I don't know what sort of questions to ask."

"I'm sure you did just fine. Please, go on."

"They took six children from two separate households into care."

"What exactly was supposed to have been going on?"

"At first it was all very vague. 'Lewd and libidinous behavior. Ritualistic music, dance and costume.' "

"Sounds like police headquarters on a Saturday night. Anything else?"

"Well, that's where it gets interesting. And sick. It seems this was one of the few such cases in which prosecutions went forward and convictions were gained. All the Liversedges would tell me was that there were tales of torture, of kids being forced to drink urine and eat . . . Christ, I'm not squeamish, Alan, but this stuff turns my stomach."

"That's all right. Take it easy."

"They were humiliated," Jenny went on. "Sometimes physically injured, kept in cages without food for days, used as objects of sexual gratification in satanic rituals. One child, a girl called Kathleen Murray, was found dead. Her remains showed evidence of torture and sexual abuse."

"How did she die?"

"She was strangled. She'd also been beaten and half-starved, too. That was what sparked the whistle-blower, her not turning up for school."

"And this was proven in court?"

"Most of it, yes. The killing. The satanic stuff didn't come out in the trial. I suppose the CPS must have thought it would just sound like too much mumbo jumbo."

"How did it come out?"

"Some of the children gave descriptions later, after they'd been fostered."

"Lucy?"

"No. According to the Liversedges, Lucy never spoke about what happened. She just put it all behind her."

"Was it followed up?"

"No. There were similar allegations and raids in Cleveland, Rochdale and the Orkneys, and pretty soon it was all over the papers. Caused a hell of a national outcry. Epidemic of child abuse, that sort of thing. Overzealous social workers. Questions in the House, the lot."

"I remember," said Banks.

"Most of the cases were thrown out, and nobody wanted to talk about the one that *was* true. Well, Alderthorpe wasn't the only one. There was a similar case in Nottingham in 1989 that also resulted in convictions, but it wasn't widely publicized. Then we got the Butler-Schloss report and revisions of the Children's Act."

"What happened to Lucy's real parents?"

"They went to jail. The Liversedges have no idea whether they're still there or what. They haven't kept track of things."

Banks sipped some Laphroaig and flicked his cigarette end into the empty grate. "So Lucy stayed with the Liversedges?"

"Yes. She changed her name, too, by the way. She used to be called Linda. Linda Godwin. Then, with all the publicity, she wanted to change it. The Liversedges assured me it's all legal and aboveboard."

From Linda Godwin to Lucy Liversedge to Lucy Payne, Banks thought. Interesting.

"Anyway," Jenny went on, "after they'd told me all this I pushed them a bit more and at least got them to admit life with Lucy wasn't quite as 'ordinary' and 'normal' as they'd originally said it was."

"Oh?"

"Problems adjusting. Surprise, surprise. The first two years, between the ages of twelve and fourteen, Lucy was as good as gold, a quiet, passive, considerate and sensitive kid. They were worried she was traumatized."

"And?"

"Lucy saw a child psychiatrist for a while."

"Then?"

"From fourteen to sixteen she started to act up, come out of her shell. She stopped seeing the psychiatrist. There were boys, suspicions that she was having sex, and then there was the bullying."

"Bullying?"

"Yes. At first they told me it was an isolated incident and came to nothing, but later they said it caused a few problems with the school. Lucy was bullying younger girls out of their dinner money and stuff like that. It's fairly common."

"But in Lucy's case?"

"A phase. The Liversedges worked with the school authorities, and the psychiatrist entered the picture again briefly. Then Lucy settled down to behave herself. The next two years, sixteen to eighteen, she quieted down, withdrew more into herself, became less active socially and sexually. She did her A-levels, got good results and got a job with the NatWest bank in Leeds. That was four years ago. It seemed almost as if she were planning her escape. She had very little contact with the Liversedges after she left, and I get the impression that they were relieved."

"Why?"

"I don't know why. Call it intuition, but I got the feeling that they ended up being *scared* of Lucy, for the way she seemed able to manipulate them. As I say, it's just a vague feeling."

"Interesting. Go on."

"They saw even less of her after she hooked up with Terence Payne. I thought when they first told me that that he might have been responsible for isolating her from her family and friends, you know, the way abusers often do, but now it seems just as likely that she was isolating herself. Her friend from work, Pat Mitchell, said the same thing. Meeting

Terry really changed Lucy, cut her off almost entirely from her old life, her old ways."

"So she was either under his thrall or she'd found a new sort of life that she preferred?"

"Yes." Jenny told him about the incident of Lucy's prostitution.

Banks thought for a moment. "It's interesting," he said. "*Really* interesting. But it doesn't prove anything."

"I told you that would probably be the case. It makes her *weird,* but being weird's no grounds for arrest or half the population would be behind bars."

"More than half. But hang on a minute, Jenny. You've come up with a number of leads worth pursuing."

"Like what?"

"Like what if Lucy was involved in the Alderthorpe abuse herself? I remember reading at the time that there were cases of some of the older victims abusing their own younger siblings."

"But what would it mean even if we *could* prove that after all this time?"

"I don't know, Jenny. I'm just thinking out aloud. What's your next step?"

"I'm going to talk to someone from the social services tomorrow, see if I can get the names of any of the social workers involved."

"Good. I'll work it from the police angle when I get a spare moment. There are bound to be records, files. Then what?"

"I want to go to Alderthorpe, nose around, talk to people who remember."

"Be careful, Jenny. It's bound to be a very raw nerve still out there, even after all this time."

"I'll be careful."

"And don't forget, there might still be someone who escaped prosecution worried about new revelations."

"That makes me feel really safe and secure."

"The other kids . . ."

"Yes?"

"What do you know about them?"

"Nothing, really, except they were aged between eight and twelve."

"Any idea where they are?"

"No. The Liversedges don't know. And I *did* ask them."

"Don't be defensive. We'll make a detective of you yet."

"No, thanks."

"Let's see if we can find them, shall we? They might be able to tell us a lot more about Lucy Payne than anyone else."

"Okay. I'll see how much the social workers are willing to tell me."

"Not much, I'll bet. Your best chance will be if one of them's retired or moved on to some other line of work. Then spilling the beans won't seem like such a betrayal."

"Hey, I'm supposed to be the psychologist. Leave that sort of thinking to me."

Banks laughed over the phone. "It's a blurred line some-times, isn't it? Detective work and psychology."

"Try and tell some of your oafish colleagues that."

"Thanks, Jenny. You've done a great job."

"And I've only just begun."

"Keep in touch."

"Promise."

When Banks put the phone down, Mahalia Jackson was singing "Come Sunday." He turned up the volume and took his drink outside to his little balcony over Gratly Falls. The rain had stopped, but the downpour had been heavy enough to swell the sound of the falls. It was just after sunset and the deep vermilions, purples and oranges were dying in the west-ern sky, streaked with dark ribs of cloud, while the darkening east went from pale to inky blue. Just across the falls was a field of grazing sheep. In it stood a clump of huge old trees where rooks nested and often woke him early in the morning with their noisy squabbling. Such ill-tempered birds, they seemed. Beyond the field, the daleside sloped down to the river Swain and Banks could see the opposite hillside a mile or more away, darkening in the evening, rising to the long, grinning skeleton's mouth of Crow Scar. The runic patterns of the drystone walls seemed to stand out in relief as the light faded. Just a little to his right, he could see the Helmthorpe Church tower poking up from the valley bottom.

Banks looked at his watch. Still early enough to stroll down there and have a pint or two in the Dog and Gun, maybe chat with one or two of the locals he'd become friendly with since his move. But he decided he didn't fancy company; he had too much on his mind, what with Terence Payne's death, the mystery of Leanne Wray, and the revelations Jenny Fuller had just come through with as regards Lucy's past. Since taking on the Chameleon investigation, he realized, he had become more and more of a loner, less inclined to make small talk at the bar. Partly, he supposed, it was the burden of command, but it was also something more; the proximity to such evil, perhaps, that tainted him somehow and made small talk seem like a completely inadequate response to what was happening.

The news of Sandra's pregnancy was also still weighing on his mind, bringing back some memories he had hoped to forget. He knew he wouldn't be good company, but nor would he be able to get to sleep so early. He nipped inside and poured another shot of whiskey, then picked up his cigarettes and went back outside to lean against the damp wall and enjoy the last of the evening light. A curlew piped up on the distant moors and Mahalia Jackson sang on, humming the tune long after she had run out of words.

Chapter 10

*F*riday morning started badly for Maggie. She had spent a
night disturbed by vague and frightening nightmares
that scuttled away into the shadows the minute she awoke
screaming and tried to grasp them. Getting back to sleep was
difficult not only because of the bad dreams, but also because
of the eerie noises and voices she could hear from across the
road. Didn't the police ever sleep?

Once, getting up to go for a glass of water, she looked out
of her bedroom window and saw some uniformed police officers carrying cardboard boxes into a van waiting with its
engine running. Then some men carried what looked like
electronic equipment through the front door, and a short
while later Maggie fancied she could see a strange ghostly
light sweeping the living room of number 35 behind the
drawn curtains. The digging continued in the front garden,
surrounded by a canvas screen and lit on the inside, so that all
Maggie could see was enlarged and deformed shadows of
men silhouetted against the canvas. These figures carried
over into her next nightmare, and in the end she didn't know
whether she was asleep or awake.

She got up a little after seven o'clock and headed for the
kitchen, where a cup of tea helped soothe her frayed nerves.
This was one English habit that she had slipped into easily.
She planned to spend the day working on Grimm again, per-

haps "Hänsel and Gretel," now that she had satisfactory sketches for "Rapunzel," and trying to put the business of number 35 out of her head for a few hours at least.

Then she heard the paperboy arrive and the newspaper slip through her letter box on to the hall mat. She hurried out and carried it back to the kitchen, where she spread it on the table.

Lorraine Temple's story was prominent on the front page, beside the bigger headline story about Terence Payne's dying without recovering consciousness. There was even a photograph of Maggie, taken without her knowledge, standing just outside her front gate. It must have been taken when she was going down to the pub to talk with Lorraine, she realized, as she was wearing the same jeans and light cotton jacket as she had worn on Tuesday.

HOUSE OF PAYNE: NEIGHBOR SPEAKS OUT, ran the headline, and the article went on to detail how Maggie had heard suspicious sounds coming from across The Hill and called the police. Afterward, calling Maggie Lucy's "friend," Lorraine Temple reported what Maggie had said about Lucy's being a victim of domestic abuse, and how she was scared of her husband. All of which was fine and accurate enough, as far as it went. But then came the sting in the tail. According to sources in Toronto, Lorraine Temple went on to report, Maggie Forrest herself was on the run from an abusive husband: Toronto lawyer, William Burke. The article detailed the time Maggie had spent in hospital and all the fruitless court orders issued to stop Bill's going near her. Describing Maggie as a nervous, mousy sort of woman, Lorraine Temple also mentioned that she was seeing a local psychiatrist called Dr. Simms, who "declined to comment."

Lorraine ended by suggesting that, perhaps because of Maggie's own psychological problems, Maggie had been gullible, and that her identification with Lucy's plight may have blinded her to the truth. Lorraine couldn't come out and say that she thought Lucy was guilty of anything—the laws of libel forbade that—but she did have a very good stab at making her readers think Lucy might just be the sort of manipulative and deceitful person who could twist a weak woman like Maggie around her little finger. It was rubbish, of course, but effective rubbish, nonetheless.

How could she *do* that? Now everybody would know.

Every time Maggie walked down the street to go to the shops or catch the bus into town, the neighbors and shopkeepers would look at her differently, with *pity* and perhaps just the merest hint of *blame* in their eyes. Some people would avoid looking her in the eye and perhaps even stop talking to her, associating her too closely for comfort with the events at number 35. Even strangers who recognized her from the photograph would wonder about her. Perhaps Claire would stop coming to see her altogether, though she hadn't been since the time the policeman turned up, and Maggie was already worried about her.

Perhaps even Bill would find out.

It was her own fault, of course. She had put herself in harm's way. She had been trying to do a favor for poor Lucy, trying to garner her some public sympathy, and the whole thing had backfired. How stupid she had been to trust Lorraine Temple. One lousy article like this and her whole new fragile, protected world would change. Just like that. It wasn't fair, Maggie told herself as she cried over the breakfast table. *It just wasn't fair.*

After a short but satisfying night's sleep—perhaps due to the generous doses of Laphroaig and Duke Ellington—Banks was back in his Millgarth cubbyhole by eight-thirty on Friday morning, and the first news to cross his desk was a note from Stefan Nowak informing him that the skeletal remains dug up in the Paynes's garden were *not* Leanne Wray's. Had

Banks been harboring the slightest hope that Leanne might still be alive and well after all this time, he would have jumped for joy, but as it was, he rubbed his forehead in frustration; it looked as if it was going to be another one of those days. He punched in Stefan's mobile number and got an answer after three rings. It sounded as if Stefan was in the middle of another conversation, but he muttered a few asides and gave his attention to Banks.

"Sorry about that," he said.

"Problems?"

"Typical breakfast chaos. I'm just trying to get out of the house."

"I know what you mean. Look, about this identification—"

"It's solid, sir. Dental records. DNA will take a bit longer. There's no way it's Leanne Wray. I'm just about to set off back to the house. The lads are still digging."

"Who the hell can it be?"

"Don't know. All I've been able to find out so far is that it's a young woman, late teens to early twenties, been there a few months and there's a lot of stainless steel in her dental work, including a crown."

"Meaning?" Banks asked, a faint memory beckoning.

"Possible Eastern European origin. They still use a lot of stainless steel over there."

Right. Banks had come across something like that before. A forensic dentist had once told him that Russians used stainless steel. "Eastern European?"

"Just a possibility, sir."

"All right. Any chance of that DNA comparison between Payne and the Seacroft Rapist turning up before the weekend?"

"I'll get onto them this morning, see if I can give them a prod."

"Okay. Thanks. Keep at it, Stefan."

"Will do."

Banks hung up, more puzzled than ever. One of the first things AC Hartnell had instituted when the team was first put together was a special squad to keep tabs on all missing persons cases throughout the entire country—"mispers," as they were called—particularly if they involved blond teenagers, with no apparent reasons for running away, disappearing on their way home from clubs, pubs, cinemas and dances. The team had monitored scores of cases every day, but none had met the criteria of the Chameleon investigation, except one girl in Cheshire, who had turned up alive and contrite two days later after a brief shack-up with her boyfriend, about which she just happened to forget to tell her parents, and the sadder case of a young girl in Lincoln who, it turned out, had been run over and had not been carrying any identification. Now here was Stefan saying they'd probably got a dead Eastern European girl in the garden.

Banks didn't get very far with his chain of thought before his office door opened and DC Filey dropped a copy of that morning's *Post* on his desk.

Annie parked her purple Astra up the street and walked toward number 35 The Hill, shielding her eyes from the morning sunlight. Crime scene tape and trestles blocked off that section of pavement in front of the garden wall, so that pedestrians had to make a detour on to the tarmac road to get by. One or two people paused to glance over the garden gate as they passed, Annie noticed, but most walked to the other side of the road and averted their eyes. She even saw one elderly woman cross herself.

Annie showed her warrant card to the officer on duty, signed in at the gate and walked down the garden path. She wasn't afraid of seeing gruesome sights, if indeed there were any left inside the house, but she had never before visited a scene so completely overrun with SOCO activity, and just walking into it made her edgy. The men in the front garden ignored her and went on with their digging. The door was ajar, and when Annie pushed gently, it opened into the hall.

The hallway was deserted and at first the house seemed so quiet inside that Annie thought she was alone. Then someone shouted, and the sound of a pneumatic drill ripped through the air, coming up from the cellar, shattering her illusion. The house was hot, stuffy and full of dust, and Annie sneezed three times before exploring further.

Her nerves gradually gave way to professional curiosity, and she noted with interest that the carpets had been taken up, leaving only the bare concrete floors and wooden stairs, and that the living room had been stripped of furniture, too, even down to the light fixtures. Several holes had been punched in the walls, no doubt to ensure that no bodies had been entombed there. Annie gave a little shudder. Poe's "The Cask of Amontillado" was one of the more frightening stories she had read at school.

Everywhere she went she was conscious of the narrow roped-off pathway she knew she was supposed to follow. In an odd way it was like visiting the Brontë parsonage or Wordsworth's cottage, where you could only stand and look beyond the rope at the antique furniture.

The kitchen, where three SOCO officers were working on the sink and drains, was in the same sorry state—tiles wrenched up, oven and fridge gone, cupboards bare, fingerprint dust everywhere. Annie hadn't thought anyone could do so much damage to a place in three days. One of the SOCOs looked over at her and asked her rather testily what she thought she was doing there. She flashed him her warrant card and he went back to ripping out the sink. The pneumatic drill stopped and Annie heard the sound of a vacuum cleaner from upstairs, an eerily domestic sound amidst all the crime scene chaos, though she knew its purpose was far more sinister than getting rid of the dust.

She took the silence from the cellar as her cue to go down there, noting as she did so the door open to the garage, which had been stripped as bare as the rest of the house. The car was gone, no doubt in the police garage being taken apart piece by piece, and the oil-stained floor had been dug up.

She sensed herself becoming hypersensitive as she approached the cellar door, her breath coming in short gasps. There was an obscene poster of a naked woman with her legs spread wide apart on the door which Annie hoped the SOCOs hadn't left there because they enjoyed seeing it. That must have unnerved Janet Taylor to start with, she thought, advancing slowly, as she imagined Janet and Dennis had done. Christ, she felt apprehensive enough herself, even though she knew the only people in there were SOCOs. But Janet and Dennis hadn't known what to expect, Annie told herself. Whatever it was, they hadn't expected what they got. She knew far more than they had, and no doubt her imagination was working overtime on that.

Through the door, much cooler down here, trying to feel the way it was, despite the two SOCO officers and the bright lighting . . . Janet went in first, Dennis just behind her. The cellar was smaller than she had expected. It must have happened so quickly. Candlelight. The figure leaping out of the shadows, wielding a machete, hacking into Dennis Morrisey's throat and arm because he was the closest. Dennis goes down. Janet already has her side-handled baton out, extended, ready to ward off the first blow. So close she can smell Payne's breath. Perhaps he can't believe that a woman, weaker and smaller than him, can thwart him so easily. Before he can recover from his shock, Janet lashes out and hits him on the left temple. Blinded by pain and perhaps by blood, he falls back against the wall. Next he feels a sharp pain on his wrist and he can't hold on to the machete. He hears it skitter away across the floor but doesn't know where. He rears up and goes at her. Angry now because she knows her partner is bleeding to death on the floor, Janet hits him again and again, wanting it to be over so she can tend to Dennis. He scrabbles after where he thought the machete went, blood dripping down his face. She hits him again. And again. How much strength does he have left by now? Annie wondered. Surely not enough to overpower Janet? And how many more times does she hit him now he's down, hand-cuffed to the pipe, not moving at all?

Annie sighed and watched the SOCOs shifting their drill to dig into another spot.

"Are you going to start that thing up again?" she asked.

One of the men grinned. "Want some earmuffs?"

Annie smiled back at him. "No, I'd rather just get out of here before you start. Can you give me another minute or so?"

"Can do."

Annie glanced around at the crude stick figures and occult symbols on the walls and wondered how integral a part of Payne's fantasy they were. Banks had also told her that the place was lit by dozens of candles, but they were all gone now, as was the mattress they had found the body on. One of the SOCOs was on his knees looking at something on the concrete floor over by the door.

"What is it?" Annie asked him. "Found something?"

"Dunno," he said. "Some sort of little scuff marks in the concrete. It hardly shows at all, but there seems to be some sort of pattern."

Annie knelt to look. She couldn't see anything until the SOCO pointed to what looked like small circles in the concrete. There were three of them in all, pretty much equidistant.

"I'll try a few different lighting angles," he said, almost to himself. "Maybe some infrared film to highlight the contrasts."

"Could be a tripod," Annie said.

"What? Bugger me—sorry, love—but you could be right.

Luke Selkirk and that funny little assistant of his were down here. Maybe they left the marks."

"I think they'd have been more professional, don't you?"

"I'd better ask them, hadn't I?"

Annie left him to it and walked through the far door. The ground had been sectioned into grids and the soil had been dug up. Annie knew that three bodies had been found there. She followed the narrow marked path across to the door, opened it and walked up the steps into the back garden. Crime scene tape barred her entrance at the top of the steps, but she didn't need to go any farther. Like the anteroom in the cellar, the overgrown garden had been divided into grids and marked out with rope. Most of them had already been cleared of grass and weeds and topsoil, but some, farther back, remained overgrown. At the far wall, a large waterproof sheet used to protect the garden from yesterday's rain lay rolled up like a carpet.

This was a delicate job, Annie knew from watching the excavation of a skeleton at the village of Hobb's End. It was far too easy to disturb old bones. She could see the hole, about three feet deep, where one body had been dug up, and now there were two men gathered around another hole, taking off the soil with trowels and passing it to a third man, who ran it through a sieve as if he were panning for gold.

"What is it?" Annie asked from the top of the cellar steps.

One of the men looked up at her. She hadn't recognized Stefan Nowak at first. She didn't know him well, as he hadn't been at Eastvale's Western Divisional Headquarters for long, but Banks had introduced them once. Stefan was the man, ACC Ron McLaughlin had said, who would drag North Yorkshire kicking and screaming into the twenty-first century. Annie had found him rather reserved, a bit mysterious, even, as if he were carrying around a grave secret or a great weight of past pain. He affected a cheery enough demeanor on the surface, but she could tell it didn't run very deep. He was tall, over six feet, and handsome in a clean-cut, elegant sort of way. She knew his background was Polish and had often wondered if he was a prince or a count or something. Most of the Poles she had ever met said they were descended from counts or princes at one time or another, and there was something regal and stately in Stefan's bearing.

"It's Annie, isn't it?" he said. "DS Annie Cabbot?"

"DI, now, Stefan. How's it going?"

"Didn't know you were on this case."

"One of them," Annie explained. "Terence Payne. I'm with Complaints and Discipline."

"I can't believe the CPS will even let that one see the light of day," said Stefan. "Justifiable homicide, surely?"

"I hope that's how they'll see it, but you never know with them. Anyway, I just wanted a look at the place."

"I'm afraid we've made rather a mess," said Stefan. "It looks as if we've just found another body. Want a look?"

Annie ducked under the tape. "Yes."

"Be careful," said Stefan. "Follow the marked path."

Annie did as he said and soon found herself standing beside the partially excavated grave. This one was a skeleton. Not quite as stained and filthy as the one she had seen at Hobb's End, but a skeleton nonetheless. She could see part of the skull, one shoulder and part of the left arm. "How long?" she asked.

"Hard to say," Stefan answered. "More than a few months." He introduced the two men who had been poring over the grave with him, one a botanist and the other an entomologist. "These lads should be able to help with that. And we're getting Dr. Ioan Williams to come over from the university and give us a hand."

Annie remembered the young doctor with the long hair and the prominent Adam's apple from the Hobb's End case, the way he had caressed Gloria Shackleton's pelvic bone and leered over it at Annie.

"I know this isn't my case," Annie said, "but isn't this one
body too many?"

Stefan looked up at her and shielded his eyes from the sun.
"Yes," he said. "It is. Rather throws a spanner in the works,
doesn't it?"

"Indeed it does."

Annie walked back toward her car. There was nothing
more to be gained from hanging around The Hill. Besides,
she realized, glancing at her watch, she had a postmortem to
attend.

"What the hell do you mean, talking to press like that?" said
Banks. "Didn't I warn you about it?"

"This is the first I've heard we're living in a police state,"
said Maggie Forrest, arms folded over her chest, eyes angry
and tearful. They stood in her kitchen, Banks brandishing the
Post and Maggie in the midst of clearing away her breakfast
dishes. After seeing the article at Millgarth, he had headed
straight for The Hill.

"Don't give me that adolescent crap about police states.
Who do you think you are, a student protesting some distant
war?"

"You've no right to talk to me like this. I haven't done anything wrong."

"Anything wrong? Have you any idea of the wasp's nest
you could be helping to stir up?"

"I don't know what you mean. All I wanted to do was tell
Lucy's side of the story, but that woman twisted it all."

"Are you so naïve that you didn't expect that?"

"There's a difference between being naïve and caring, but
a cynic like you probably wouldn't understand it."

Banks could see that Maggie was shaking, either with
anger or fear, and he was worried that he had given too free a
rein to his anger. He knew she had been abused by her hus-

band, that she was a bruised soul, so she was probably scared stiff of this man raising his voice in her kitchen. It was insensitive of him, but damn it, the woman irritated him. He sat at the kitchen table and tried to cool things down a bit. "Maggie," he said softly. "I'm sorry, but you could cause us a lot of problems."

Maggie seemed to relax a little. "I don't see how."

"Public sympathy is a very fickle thing, and when you mess with it, it's like dancing with the devil. It's just as likely to reach out and eat you up as anyone else."

"But how would people find out what Lucy went through at her husband's hands? *She* won't talk about it, I can guarantee you that."

"None of us know what went on in Lucy's house. All you're doing is jeopardizing her chance of a fair trial, if—"

"Trial? Trial for what?"

"I was going to say, 'if it comes to that.'"

"I'm sorry, but I don't agree." Maggie put the electric kettle on and sat opposite Banks. "People need to know about domestic abuse. It's not something that should be swept under the carpet for any reason. Especially not just because the police say so."

"I agree. Look, I understand you're prejudiced against us, but—"

"Prejudiced? Right. With your help I ended up in hospital."

"But you have to understand that in many of these matters our hands are tied. We're only as good as the information we have and the laws of the land allow."

"All the more reason for me to speak out about Lucy. After all, you're not exactly here to *help* her, are you?"

"I'm here to find out the truth."

"Well, that's all very high-and-mighty of you."

"Now who's the cynic?"

"We all know the police only want convictions, that they're not overly concerned with the truth, or with justice."

"Convictions help, if they keep the bad guys off the street. Too often they don't. And justice we leave to the courts, but you're wrong about the rest. I can't speak for anyone else, but I'm very much concerned with the truth. I've worked day and night on this case since the beginning of April, and every case I work I want to know what happened, who did it and why. I don't always find out, but you'd be surprised how much I do learn. Sometimes it gets me into trouble. And I have to live with the knowledge, take it into my life, take it home with me. I'm that snowball rolling down the hill, only the pure snow's run out and I'm picking up layer after layer of dirt and gravel just so that you can sit safe and warm at home and accuse me of being some sort of Gestapo officer."

"I didn't mean it like that. And I wasn't always safe and warm."

"Do you know that what you've just done actually stands a good chance of warping the truth, whatever it may be?"

"I didn't do that. It was her. That journalist. Lorraine Temple."

Banks slapped the table and immediately regretted it when Maggie jumped. "Wrong," he said. "*She* was only doing her job. Like it or not, that's what it was. Her job's to sell newspapers. You've got this all backward, Maggie. You think the media's here to tell the truth and the police to lie."

"You're confusing me now." The kettle boiled and Maggie got up to make tea. She didn't offer Banks a cup, but when it was ready, she poured him one automatically. He thanked her.

"All I'm saying, Maggie, is that you might be doing Lucy more harm than good by talking to the press. Look at what happened this time. You say it came out all wrong and that they practically said Lucy is as guilty as her husband. That's hardly helping her, is it?"

"But I *told* you. She twisted my words."

"And I'm saying you should have expected that. It made a better story."

"Then where *am* I supposed to go to tell the truth? Or to find it?"

"Christ, Maggie, if I knew the answer to that I'd—"

But before Banks could finish, his mobile rang. This time it was the PC on duty at the infirmary. Lucy Payne had just been cleared for release, and she had a solicitor with her.

"Do you know anything about this solicitor?" Banks asked Maggie when he'd finished on the phone.

She smiled sheepishly. "As a matter of fact, yes, I do."

Banks said nothing, not trusting himself to respond in a civilized manner. Leaving his tea untouched, he bid Maggie Forrest a hurried farewell and dashed out to his car. He didn't even stop to talk to Annie Cabbot when he saw her walking out of number 35, but managed only a quick wave before jumping in his Renault and roaring off.

Lucy Payne was sitting on the bed painting her toenails black when Banks walked in. She gave him a look and demurely pulled her skirt down over her thighs. The bandages were gone from her head, and the bruises seemed to be healing well. She had rearranged her long black hair so it covered the patch the doctor had shaved for his stitches.

Another woman stood in the room, over by the window: the solicitor. Slight in stature, with chocolate brown hair cropped almost as closely as Banks's, and watchful, serious hazel eyes, she was dressed in a charcoal pinstriped jacket, matching skirt and a white blouse with some sort of ruffled front. She wore dark tights and shiny black pumps.

She walked over and held her hand out. "Julia Ford. I'm Lucy's solicitor. I don't believe we've met."

"A pleasure," said Banks.

"This isn't the first time you've talked to my client, is it, Superintendent?"

"No," said Banks.

"And the last time you were accompanied by a psychologist named Dr. Fuller?"

"Dr. Fuller's our consulting psychologist on the Chameleon task force," said Banks.

"Just be careful, Superintendent, that's all. I'd have very good grounds to argue that anything Dr. Fuller might have got from my client is inadmissible as evidence."

"We weren't gathering evidence," said Banks. "Lucy was questioned as a witness, and as a *victim*. Not as a suspect."

"A fine line, Superintendent, should matters change. And now?"

Banks glanced at Lucy, who had resumed painting her toenails, seeming indifferent to the banter between her solicitor and Banks. "I wasn't aware you thought you needed a solicitor, Lucy," he said.

Lucy looked up. "It's in my best interests. They're discharging me this morning. Soon as the paperwork's done, I can go home."

Banks looked at Julia Ford in exasperation. "I hope you haven't encouraged her in this fantasy?"

Julia raised her eyebrows. "I don't know what you're talking about."

Banks turned back to Lucy. "You can't go home, Lucy," he explained. "Your house is being taken apart brick by brick by forensic experts. Have you any concept of what happened there?"

"Of course I have," said Lucy. "Terry hit me. He knocked me out and put me in hospital."

"But Terry's dead now, isn't he?"

"Yes. So?"

"That changes things, doesn't it?"

"Look," said Lucy. "I've been abused, and I've just lost my husband. Now you're telling me I've lost my home, too?"

"For the time being."

"Well, what am I supposed to do? Where am I supposed to go?"

"How about your foster parents, *Linda?*"

Lucy's look let Banks know that she hadn't missed the emphasis. "I don't seem to have much choice, do I?"

"Anyway, it won't be a problem for a while yet," Banks went on. "We found traces of Kimberley Myers's blood on the sleeves of your dressing gown, along with some yellow fibers under your fingernails. You've got a lot of explaining to do before you go anywhere."

Lucy looked alarmed. "What do you mean?"

Julia Ford narrowed her eyes and looked at Banks. "What he means, Lucy, is that he's going to take you in to the police station for questioning."

"Can he do that?"

"I'm afraid so, Lucy."

"And he can keep me there?"

"Under the PACE regulations, he can, yes, if he's not satisfied with the answers you give him. For twenty-four hours. But there are very strict guidelines. You've got nothing to worry about."

"You mean I could be in *prison* for a whole day? In a cell?"

"Don't be alarmed, Lucy," said Julia, stepping over and touching her client's arm. "Nothing bad will happen to you. Those days are gone now. You'll be well looked after."

"But I'll be in prison!"

"Possibly. It all depends."

"But I *haven't done anything!*" She gave Banks an angry look, black eyes burning like coals. "I'm the victim here. Why are you picking on me?"

"Nobody's picking on you, Lucy," said Banks. "There's a lot

of questions need answering, and we think you can help us."

"I'll answer your questions. I'm not refusing to cooperate. You don't have to take me to the police station for that. Besides, I've already answered them."

"Hardly. There's a lot more we need to know, and there are certain formalities, procedures to be followed. Anyway, it's all changed now that Terry's died, hasn't it?"

Lucy looked away. "I don't know what you mean."

"You can speak freely now. You don't have to be afraid of him."

"Oh, I see."

"What did you think I meant, Lucy?"

"Nothing."

"That you could change your story? Just deny everything?"

"I told you. Nothing."

"But there's the blood to explain now. And the yellow fibers. We know you were in the cellar. We can prove it."

"I don't know anything about that. I don't remember."

"Very convenient. Aren't you sorry Terry's dead, Lucy?"

Lucy packed her nail polish away in her handbag. "Of course I am. But he beat me up. It was him who put me here, him who got me into all this trouble with the police. It's not my fault. None of it's *my* fault. I haven't done anything wrong. Why should I have to be the one who suffers?"

Banks shook his head and stood up. "Maybe we'd better just go."

Lucy looked over to Julia Ford.

"I'll come with you," said Julia. "I'll be present when you're questioned and nearby in case you need me."

Lucy managed a weak smile. "But you won't stay in the cell with me?"

Julia smiled back, then looked at Banks. "I'm afraid they don't make doubles, Lucy."

"That's right," said Banks. "Like girls, do you, Lucy?"

"There was no need for that, Superintendent," Julia Ford said. "And I'll thank you to keep any more questions you might have until we're in the interview room."

Lucy just glared at Banks.

"Anyway," Julia Ford went on, turning back to Lucy. "Let's not be pessimistic. It might not come to that." She turned to Banks. "Might I suggest, Superintendent, that we leave by a discreet exit? You can't have failed to notice the media presence."

"It's a big story for them," Banks said. "But yes, that's a good idea. I've got another one, too."

"Oh?"

"That we take Lucy to Eastvale for questioning. You and I know damn well that Millgarth will be a zoo once the press find out she's there. This way we've got a chance of avoiding all that chaos, at least for a while."

Julia Ford thought for moment, then looked at Lucy. "It's a good idea," she said.

"Will you come to Eastvale with me? I'm scared."

"Of course." Julia looked at Banks. "I'm sure the Superintendent here can recommend a decent hotel?"

"But how could she possibly know I'm seeing you?" Maggie asked Dr. Susan Simms at the start of her session that afternoon.

"I've no idea, but you can be certain I didn't tell anyone. And I told her nothing."

"I know," said Maggie. "Thank you."

"Think nothing of it, dear. It's a matter of professional ethics. This implied support of yours for Lucy Payne, is it true?"

Maggie felt her anger bristle again as she remembered her argument with Banks that morning. She still felt upset by it. "I think Lucy's been a victim of abuse, yes."

Dr. Simms remained silent for a while, gazing out of the window, then she shifted in her chair and said, "Just be careful, Margaret. Just be careful. You seem to be under a lot of stress. Now, shall we begin? I believe last time we were talking about your family."

Maggie remembered. It was their fourth session, and the first time they'd touched on Maggie's own family background. Which surprised her. She'd been expecting Freudian questions about her relationship with her father right from the start, even though Dr. Simms had insisted she wasn't a Freudian analyst.

They were sitting in a small office overlooking Park Square, a peaceful, elegant bit of eighteenth-century Leeds. Birds sang in the trees among the pink and white blossoms, and students sat on the grass reading or simply enjoying the sun again after yesterday's rain. Most of the humidity seemed to have cleared away and the air was crisp and warm. Dr. Simms had her window open, and Maggie could smell flowers from the window box; she didn't know what kind, but they were flowers, all right, red and white and purple. She could just see the top of the town hall dome over the trees and elegant facades of the houses on the opposite side of the square.

The place was just like a doctor's office, Maggie thought, or at least an old-style doctor's office, with a solid desk, diplomas on the wall, fluorescent lights, filing cabinets and bookcases full of psychological journals and textbooks. There was no couch; Maggie and Dr. Simms sat in armchairs, not facing each other, but at a slight angle so that eye contact was easy but not mandatory, cooperative rather than confrontational. Dr. Simms had been recommended by Ruth, and so far she was turning out to be a real find. In her mid-fifties, solidly built, matronly, even, and with a severe look about her, she always wore old-fashioned Laura Ashley–style clothes, and her blue-gray hair was lacquered into whorls and waves that looked razor-sharp. Appearances to the contrary, Dr. Simms had the kindest, most compassionate manner Maggie could wish for, without being soft. For she certainly wasn't soft; sometimes she was downright prickly, especially if Maggie—whom she always called Margaret for some reason—got her defenses up or started whimpering.

"There was never any violence in the home when we were growing up. My father was strict, but he never used his fists or his belt to discipline us. Neither my sister Fiona nor me."

"So what *did* he do for discipline?"

"Oh, the usual things. Grounded us, stopped our pocket money, lectured us, that sort of thing."

"Did he raise his voice?"

"No. I never heard him yell at anyone."

"Did your mother have a violent temper?"

"Good Lord, no. I mean, she might get mad and shout if Fiona or I did something annoying, like not tidying up our rooms, but it'd be all over and forgotten in no time."

Dr. Simms put her fist under her chin and rested on it. "I see. Let's get back to Bill, shall we?"

"If you like."

"No, Margaret, it's not for me to like. It's for you to want." Maggie shifted in her chair. "Yes, all right."

"You told me in our previous session that you'd seen signs of his aggressiveness before you were married. Can you tell me more about that?"

"Yes, but it wasn't directed toward me."

"Toward whom was it directed? The world in general, perhaps?"

"No. Just some people. People who screwed up. Like waiters or delivery men."

"Did he beat them up?"

"He got mad, lost his temper, yelled at them. Called them

idiots, morons. What I meant was that he channeled a lot of aggression into his work."

"Ah, yes. He's a lawyer, right?"

"Yes. For a big firm. And he wanted to make partner very badly."

"He's competitive by nature?"

"Very. He was a high-school sports star, and he might have ended up playing professional football if he hadn't ripped his knee apart in a championship game. He still walks with a slight limp, but he hates it if anyone notices it and mentions it. It doesn't stop him playing with the firm's softball team. But I don't see what this has to do with anything."

Dr. Simms leaned forward and lowered her voice. "Margaret, I want you to see, to understand, where your husband's anger and violence come from. They didn't come from you; they came from him. They didn't come out of your family background in any way, either. They came from his. Only when you see that, when you see that it was *his* problem and not yours, will you start to believe that it wasn't your fault, and will you find the strength and courage to go on and live your life as fully as you can, rather than continue in this shadow existence you have at the moment."

"But I already see that," Maggie protested. "I mean, I know it was *his* aggression, not mine."

"But you don't *feel* it."

Maggie felt disappointed; Dr. Simms was right. "Don't I?" she said. "I suppose not."

"Do you know anything about poetry, Margaret?"

"Not much, no. Only what we did at school, and one of my boyfriends at art college used to write me stuff. Terrible drivel, really. He just wanted to get in my pants."

Dr. Simms laughed. Another surprise, for it came out as a loud, horsey guffaw. "Samuel Taylor Coleridge wrote a poem called 'Dejection: An Ode.' It was partly about his inability to *feel* anything, and one of the quotes that has always stuck in my mind was when he wrote about looking at the clouds, the moon and the stars and ended up saying, 'I see, not feel, how beautiful they are.' I think that applies to you, Margaret. And I think you know it. Intellectual awareness of something, through *reason,* does not guarantee emotional acceptance. And you are a very intellectual person, despite your obvious creative inclinations. If I were a Jungian, which I am not, I would probably classify you as the introverted, thinking type. Now tell me more about this courtship."

"There's not much to tell." A door opened and closed out in the corridor. Two male voices rose and fell. Then only the birdsongs and the sounds of distant traffic on The Headrow and Park Lane remained. "I suppose he swept me off my feet," she went on. "It was about seven years ago, and I was just a young art school graduate without a career, still wet behind the ears, hanging out with the artsy crowd in bars and arguing philosophy in Queen Street West pubs and coffee-houses, thinking one day some rich patron would appear and discover my genius. I'd had a few affairs in college, slept with a few boys, nothing satisfactory, then along came this tall, dark, intelligent, handsome man in an Armani suit who wanted to take me to concerts and expensive restaurants. It wasn't the money. That wasn't it at all. Not even the restaurants. I wasn't even eating much then. It was his style, his panache, I suppose. He dazzled me."

"And did he prove to be the patron of the arts you'd been dreaming of?"

Maggie looked down at the scuffed knees of her jeans. "Not really. Bill was never very much interested in the arts. Oh, we had all the requisite subscriptions: symphony, ballet, opera. But somehow I . . ."

"Somehow you what?"

"I don't know. Perhaps I'm being unfair. But I think maybe it was just some sort of a business thing. Being *seen*.

Like going to a client's box at the Skydome. I mean, he'd be excited about going to the opera, for example, take ages getting dressed up in his tux and fuss about what he wanted me to wear, then we'd have drinks in the members' bar beforehand, rub shoulders with colleagues and clients, all the local bigwigs. But I just got the impression that the music itself *bored* him."

"Did any problems manifest themselves early on in your relationship?"

Maggie twisted her sapphire ring around her finger, the "freedom" ring she had bought after she had thrown Bill's wedding and engagement rings into Lake Ontario. "Well," she said, "it's easy to identify things as problems in retrospect, isn't it? Claim that you saw it coming, or should have, after you've found out where things were leading. They might not have seemed strange at the time, might they?"

"Try."

Maggie continued twisting at her ring. "Well, I suppose the main problem was Bill's jealousy."

"About what?"

"Most things, really. He was very possessive, he didn't like me talking to other men for too long at parties, that sort of thing. But mostly he was jealous of my friends."

"The artists?"

"Yes. You see, he never had much time for them, he thought them all a bunch of deadbeats, losers, and he felt he'd somehow *rescued* me from them." She laughed. "And they, on their part, didn't want to mix with corporate lawyers in Armani suits."

"But you continued to see your friends?"

"Oh, yes. Sort of."

"And how did Bill react to this?"

"He used to make fun of them to me, put them down, criticize them. He called them pseudo-intellectuals, no-brainers and layabouts. If we ever met any of them when we were together, he'd just stand there, looking up at the sky, shifting from foot to foot, glancing at his Rolex, whistling. I can see him now."

"Did you defend them?"

"Yes. For a while. Then there seemed no point." Maggie remained silent for a moment, then she went on. "You have to remember that I was head over heels in love with Bill. He took me to movie premieres. We'd go for weekends in New York, stay at the Plaza, take horse-and-buggy rides in Central Park, go to cocktail parties full of stockbrokers and CEOs, you name it. There was a romantic side to it all. Once we even flew down to L.A. for a movie premiere the firm's entertainment lawyers had been involved with. We went to the party, too, and Sean Connery was there. Can you believe it? I actually met *Sean Connery!*"

"How did *you* handle all this high living?"

"I fit in well enough. I was good at mixing with them—businessmen, lawyers, entrepreneurs, the movers and shakers. Believe it or not, many of them are far more cultured than the artsy crowd thinks. A lot of them sponsored corporate art collections. My friends believed that everyone in a suit was dull and conservative, and a philistine to boot. But you can't always go by appearances. I knew that. I think they were being very immature about it all. I think Bill saw me as a positive enhancement to his career, but he saw my friends as dead weights that would drag me down with them if they could. Maybe him, too, if we weren't careful. And I didn't feel anywhere near as uncomfortable in his world as he did in mine. I began to feel I'd only been playing the *starving* artist role, anyway."

"What do you mean by that?"

"Well, my dad's a pretty important architect, and we always moved in elevated circles. Traveled around the continent a fair bit on commissions, too, when I was younger, just after we emigrated from England. Sometimes, if it was school holidays, he'd take me with him. So I didn't come from a blue collar background, or a bohemian one. Dad appreciates the arts, but he's very conservative. And we weren't poor. Anyway, as time went on, I suppose I began to agree with Bill. He wore down my defenses, like he did in a lot of other ways. I mean, all my friends seemed to do was drift from one social security check to the next without making any attempt to *do* anything because it would compromise their precious art. The greatest sin in our crowd was to sell out."

"Which you did?"

Maggie stared out of the window for a moment. The blossoms were falling from the trees in slow motion. She suddenly felt cold and hugged herself. "Yes," she said. "I suppose I did. As far as my friends were concerned I was lost to them. I'd been seduced by the almighty dollar. And all because of Bill. At one of his firm's parties I met a small publisher who was looking for an illustrator for a children's book. I showed him my work and he loved it. I got the job, then that led to another, and so on."

"How did Bill react to your success?"

"He was pleased at first. Thrilled. Proud that the publisher liked my work, proud when the book was published. He bought copies for all his nephews and nieces, his clients' kids. His boss. Dozens of copies. And he was pleased that it was because of him all this had happened. As he never ceased to tell me, it would never have happened if I'd chosen to stay with my deadbeat friends."

"This was at first. What about later?"

Maggie felt herself shrinking in the chair, her voice becoming smaller. "That was different. Later, after we were married and Bill still hadn't made partner, I think he started to resent my success. He started referring to art as my 'little hobby' and suggested I might have to give it up at any time and start having babies."

"But you chose not to have babies?"

"No. I had no choice. I can't have babies." Maggie felt herself slipping down the rabbit hole, just like Alice, darkness closing around her.

"Margaret! Margaret!"

She could hear Dr. Simms's voice only as if from a great distance, echoing. With great effort, she struggled up toward it, toward the light, and felt herself burst out like a drowning person from the water, gasping for air.

"Margaret, are you all right?"

"Yes. I'm . . . I . . . But it wasn't me," she said, aware of the tears flowing down her cheeks. "It isn't *me* who can't have babies. *Bill* can't. It's Bill. It's something to do with his sperm count."

Dr. Simms gave Maggie a little time to dry her eyes, calm down and compose herself.

When she had done so, Maggie laughed at herself. "He used to have to masturbate into a Tupperware container and take it in for testing. Somehow that seemed so . . . well, Tupperware, I mean, it all seemed so *Leave It to Beaver*."

"Pardon?"

"An old American TV program. Mom at home, pop at the office. Apple pie. Happy families. Perfect children."

"I see. Couldn't you have adopted a child?"

Maggie was back out in the light now. Only it felt too bright. "No," she said. "That wouldn't do for Bill. The child wouldn't be *his* then, you see. No more than if I'd had someone else's sperm in artificial insemination."

"Did the two of you discuss what to do?"

"At first, yes. But not after he found out it was *his* physical problem, and not mine. After that, if I ever mentioned children again, he hit me."

"And around this time he came to resent your success?"

"Yes. Even to the point of committing little acts of sabotage so I'd be behind on a deadline. You know, throwing away some of my colors or brushes, misplacing an illustration or a package for the courier, accidentally wiping images from the computer, from *my* computer, forgetting to tell me about an important phone call, that sort of thing."

"So at this time he wanted to have children but discovered that he couldn't father any, and he also wanted to be a partner in his law firm, but he didn't get to be?"

"That's right. But that's no excuse for what he did to me."

Dr. Simms smiled. "True, Margaret. Very true. But it's a pretty volatile combination, don't you think? I'm not making excuses, but can you imagine the stress he must have been under, how it might have *triggered* his violent feelings?"

"I couldn't see it coming at the time. How could I?"

"No, you couldn't. No one could expect you to. It's as you said. Hindsight. Retrospect." She leaned back in her chair, crossed her legs and looked at the clock. "Now, I think that's enough for today, don't you?"

Now was the time. "I've got a question," Maggie blurted out. "Not about me."

Dr. Simms raised her eyebrows and looked at her watch.

"It won't take a minute. Honest it won't."

"All right," said Dr. Simms. "Ask away."

"Well, it's this friend of mine. Not really a friend, I suppose, because she's too young, just a schoolgirl, but she drops by, you know, on her way home from school."

"Yes?"

"Claire's her name, Claire Toth. Claire was a friend of Kimberley Myers."

"I know who Kimberley Myers was. I read the newspapers. Go on."

"They were friends. They went to the same school. Both of them knew Terence Payne. He was their biology teacher."

"Yes. Go on."

"And she felt responsible, you know, for Kimberley. They were supposed to walk home together that night, but a boy asked Claire to dance. A boy she liked, and . . ."

"And her friend walked home alone. To her death?"

"Yes," said Maggie.

"You said you had a question to ask me."

"I haven't seen Claire since she told me this on Monday afternoon. I'm worried about her. Psychologically, I mean. What would something like this do to someone like her?"

"Not knowing the girl in question, I can't possibly say," said Dr. Simms. "It depends on her inner resources, on her self-image, on family support, on many things. Besides, it seems to me that there are two separate issues here."

"Yes?"

"First, the girl's proximity to the criminal and to one victim in particular, and second, her feeling of responsibility, of guilt. As far as the first is concerned, I can offer a few general considerations."

"Please do."

"First of all, tell me how *you* feel about it all."

"Me?"

"Yes."

"I . . . I don't know yet. Afraid, I suppose. Not so trusting. He was my neighbor, after all. I don't know. I haven't been able to work it all out yet."

Dr. Simms nodded. "Your friend probably feels the same way. Mostly confused for the moment. Only she's younger than you, and she probably has fewer defenses. She'll certainly be more mistrustful of people. After all, this man was her *teacher,* a figure of respect and authority. Handsome, well-dressed, with a nice house and a pretty young wife. He didn't look at all like the sort of monster we usually associate in our minds with crimes such as these. And she'll experience a heightened sense of paranoia. She may not feel comfortable going out alone, for example, may feel she's being stalked or watched. Or her parents might not let her go out. Sometimes parents take control in these situations, especially if they feel they've been guilty of any sort of neglect."

"So her parents might be keeping her at home? Keeping her from visiting *me?*"

"It's possible."

"What else?"

"From what I can gather so far, these are sex crimes, and as such they are bound to have some effect on a vulnerable young schoolgirl's burgeoning sexuality. Exactly what effect is hard to say. It takes different people different ways. Some girls might become more childlike, suppress their sexuality, because they think that will afford them some kind of protection. Others may even become more promiscuous because being good girls didn't help the victims. I can't tell you which way she'll go."

"I'm sure Claire wouldn't become promiscuous."

"She may become withdrawn and preoccupied with the case. I think it's most important that she doesn't keep these feelings bottled up, that she struggles to understand what happened. I know that's difficult, even for us adults, but we can help her."

"How?"

"By accepting its effect on her but also reassuring her that it was some sort of aberration, not the natural course of things. There's little doubt the effects will be deep and long-lasting, but she will have to learn how to readjust to the way her worldview has altered."

"What do you mean?"

"We're always saying that teenagers feel immortal, but any immortality your friend felt she had will have been stripped away by what's happened. That's a hard adjustment to make, that what happened to someone close to you could happen to you, too. And the full horror of it hasn't even come out yet."

"What can I do?"

"Probably nothing," said Dr. Simms. "You can't make her come to you, but if she does you should encourage her to talk, be a good listener. But don't push her, and don't try to tell her how to feel."

"Should she be seeing a psychologist?"

"Probably. But that's her decision. Or her parents'."

"Could you recommend someone? I mean, if they're interested."

Dr. Simms wrote a name on a slip of paper. "She's good," she said. "Now, off you go. I've got my next patient waiting."

They arranged another appointment and Maggie walked out into Park Square thinking about Claire and Kimberley and human monsters. That numb sensation had come back, the feeling that the world was at a distance, through mirrors and filters, cotton wool, through the wrong end of the telescope. She felt like an alien in human form. She wanted to go back to where she came from, but she didn't know where it was anymore.

She walked down to City Square, past the statue of the Black Prince and the nymphs bearing their torches, then she leaned against the wall near the bus stop on Boar Lane and lit a cigarette. The elderly woman beside her gave her a curious look. Why was it, Maggie wondered, that she always felt worse after these sessions with Dr. Simms than she did before she went?

The bus arrived. Maggie trod out her cigarette and got on.

Chapter 11

The drive to Eastvale went smoothly enough. Banks ordered an unmarked car and driver from Millgarth and left through a side exit with Julia Ford and Lucy Payne. They didn't run into any reporters. During the journey Banks sat in the front with the driver, a young female DC, and Julia Ford and Lucy Payne sat in the back. Nobody spoke a word. Banks was preoccupied by the discovery of another body in the Payne's back garden, news he had just received from Stefan Nowak on his mobile as they set off from the infirmary. That made one body too many, and by the sound of it, he didn't think this one was Leanne Wray's either.

Occasionally, Banks caught a glimpse of Lucy in the rearview mirror and saw that she was mostly gazing out of the window. He couldn't read her expression. Just to be on the safe side, they entered the Eastvale Police Station through the rear entrance. Banks settled Lucy and Julia in an interview room and went to his office, where he walked over to the window and lit a cigarette and prepared himself for the coming interview.

He had been so preoccupied with the extra body on the journey up that he had hardly noticed it was another gorgeous day out there. There were plenty of cars and coaches parked on the cobbled market square, family groups milling about, holding on to their children's hands, women with cardigans fastened loosely by the sleeves around their necks, just in case a cool breeze sprang up, clutching umbrellas against the possibility of rain. Why is it we English can never quite entrust ourselves to believe that fine weather will last? Banks wondered. We're always expecting the worst. That was why the forecasters covered all bases: sunny with cloudy periods and chance of a shower.

The interview room smelled of disinfectant because its last inhabitant, a drunken seventeen-year-old joyrider, had puked up a take-away pizza all over the floor. Other than that, the room was clean enough, though very little light filtered in through the high barred window. Banks inserted tapes in the machine, tested them, and then went through the immediate formalities of time, date and those present.

"Right, Lucy," he said when he'd finished. "Ready to begin?"

"If you like."

"How long have you been living in Leeds?"

"What?"

Banks repeated the question. Lucy looked puzzled by it but said, "Four years, more or less. Ever since I started working at the bank."

"And you came from Hull, from your foster parents Clive and Hilary Liversedge?"

"Yes. You know that already."

"Just getting the background clear, Lucy. Where did you live before then?"

Lucy started to fidget with her wedding ring. "Alderthorpe," she said quietly. "I lived at number four Spurn Road."

"And your parents?"

"Yes."

"Yes what?"

"Yes, they lived there, too."

Banks sighed. "Don't play games with me, Lucy. This is a serious business."

"Don't you think I know that?" Lucy snapped. "You drag me out of hospital all the way up here for no reason, and then you start asking about my childhood. You're not a psychiatrist."

"I'm just interested, that's all."

"Well, it wasn't very interesting. Yes, they abused me, and yes, I was taken into care. The Liversedges were good to me, but it's not as if they were my *real* parents or anything. When the time came, I wanted to go out on my own in the world, put my childhood behind me and make my own way. Is there anything wrong with that?"

"No," said Banks. He wanted to find out more about Lucy's childhood, especially the events that occurred when she was twelve, but he knew he wasn't likely to find out much from her. "Is that why you changed your name from Linda Godwin to Lucy Liversedge?"

"Yes. Reporters kept bothering me. The Liversedges arranged it with the social services."

"What made you choose to move to Leeds?"

"That's where the job was."

"The first one you applied for?"

"That I really wanted. Yes."

"Where did you live?"

"I had a flat off Tong Road at first. When Terry got the job at Silverhill, we bought the house on The Hill. The one you say I can't go back to, even though it's my home. I suppose you expect me to keep making the mortgage payments while your men rip the place apart, too?"

"You moved in together before you were married?"

"We already knew we were getting married. It was such a good deal at the time that we'd have been fools to turn it down."

"When did you marry Terry?"

"Just last year. The twenty-second of May. We'd been going out together since the summer before."

"How did you meet him?"

"What does that matter?"

"I'm just curious. Surely it's a harmless question."

"In a pub."

"Which pub?"

"I can't remember what it was called. It was a big one, though, with live music."

"Where was it?"

"Seacroft."

"Was he by himself?"

"I think so. Why?"

"Did he chat you up?"

"Not in so many words. I don't remember."

"Did you ever stay at his flat?"

"Yes, of course I did. It wasn't wrong. We were in love. We were going to get married. We were engaged."

"Even then?"

"It was love at first sight. You might not believe me, but it was. We'd only been going out two weeks when he bought me my engagement ring. It cost nearly a thousand pounds."

"Did he have other girlfriends?"

"Not when we met."

"But before?"

"I suppose so. I didn't make a fuss about it. I assumed he's led a pretty normal life."

"Normal?"

"Why not?"

"Did you ever see any evidence of other women in his flat?"

"No."

"What were you doing in Seacroft when you lived off Tong Road? It's a long way."

"We'd just finished a week's training course in town and one of the girls said it was a good place for a night out."

"Had you heard of the man the papers at the time called the Seacroft Rapist?"

"Yes. Everybody had."

"But it didn't stop you going to Seacroft."

"You have to live your life. You can't let fear get the better of you, or a woman wouldn't even dare go out of the house alone."

"That's true enough," said Banks. "So you never suspected that this man you met might be the Seacroft Rapist?"

"Terry? No, of course not. Why should I?"

"Was there nothing at all in Terry's behavior that gave you cause for concern?"

"No. We were in love."

"But he abused you. You admitted this the last time we talked."

She looked away. "That came later."

"How much later?"

"I don't know. Christmas, maybe."

"Last Christmas?"

"Yes. Around then. But it wasn't like that all the time. Afterward, he was wonderful. He always felt guilty. He'd buy me presents. Flowers. Bracelets. Necklaces. I really wish I had them with me now to remember him by."

"In time, Lucy. So he always made up to you after he hit you?"

"Yes, he was wonderful to me for days."

"Was he drinking more these past few months?"

"Yes. He was out more, too. I didn't see him as much."

"Where was he?"

"I don't know. He didn't tell me."

"Didn't you ever ask him?"

Lucy looked away demurely, turning her bruised side on him. Banks got the message.

"I think we can move on, can't we, Superintendent," said Julia Ford. "My client's clearly getting upset with this line of questioning."

Pity for her, Banks wanted to say, but he had plenty more ground to cover. "Very well." He turned to Lucy again. "Did you have anything to do with the abduction, rape and murder of Kimberley Myers?"

Lucy met his gaze, but he couldn't see anything in her dark eyes; if the eyes were the windows of the soul, then Lucy Payne's were made of tinted glass and her soul wore sunglasses. "No, I didn't," she said.

"What about Melissa Horrocks?"

"No. I had nothing to do with any of them."

"How many were there, Lucy?"

"You know how many."

"Tell me."

"Five. That's what I read in the papers, anyway."

"What did you do with Leanne Wray?"

"I don't understand."

"Where is she, Lucy? Where's Leanne Wray? Where did you and Terry bury her? What made her different from the others?"

Lucy looked in consternation at Julia Ford. "I don't know what he's talking about," she said. "Ask him to stop."

"Superintendent," Julia said, "my client has already made it clear she knows nothing about this person. I think you should move on."

"Did your husband ever mention any of these girls?"

"No, Terry never mentioned any of them."

"Did you ever go in that cellar, Lucy?"

"You've asked me all this before."

"I'm giving you a chance to change your answer, to go on record."

"I told you, I don't remember. I might have done, but I don't remember. I've got retrograde amnesia."

"Who told you that?"

"My doctor at the hospital."

"Dr. Landsberg?"

"Yes. It's part of my post-traumatic shock disorder."

It was the first Banks had heard of it. Dr. Landsberg had told him she was no expert on the subject. "Well, I'm very glad you can put a name to what's wrong with you. On how many occasions *might* you have gone down in the cellar, if you could remember?"

"Just the once."

"When?"

"The day it happened. When I got put in hospital. Early last Monday morning."

"So you admit that you *may* have gone down there?"

"If you say so. I can't remember. If I ever did go down, it was then."

"It's not me who says so, Lucy. It's the scientific evidence. The lab found traces of Kimberley Myers's blood on the sleeves of your dressing gown. How did it get there?"

"I . . . I don't know."

"There's only two ways it could have got there: either *before* she was in the cellar or *after* she was in the cellar. Which is it, Lucy?"

"It must be after."

"Why?"

"Because I never saw her before."

"But she didn't live far away. Hadn't you seen her around?"

"In the street, maybe. Or the shops. Yes. But I never talked to her."

Banks paused and shuffled some papers in front of him. "So you admit now that you might have been in the cellar?"

"But I don't remember."

"What do you think *might* have happened, hypothetically speaking?"

"Well, I might have heard a noise."

"What sort of noise?"

"I don't know." Lucy paused and put her hand to her throat. "A scream, maybe."

"The only screams Maggie Forrest heard were yours."

"Well, maybe you could only hear it if you were inside the house. Maybe it came up from the cellar. When Maggie heard me I was in the hall."

"You remember that? Being in the hall?"

"Only very vaguely."

"Go on."

"So I might have heard a noise and gone down to investigate."

"Even though you knew it was Terry's private den and he'd kill you if you did?"

"Yes. Maybe I was disturbed enough."

"By what?"

"By what I heard."

"But the cellar was very well soundproofed, Lucy, and the door was closed when the police got there."

"Then I don't know. I'm just trying to find a reason."

"Go on. What might you have found there if you did go down?"

"That girl. I might have gone over to her to see if there was anything I could do."

"What about the yellow fibers?"

"What about them?"

"They were from the plastic clothesline that was wrapped around Kimberley Myers's neck. The pathologist determined ligature strangulation by that line as cause of death. Fibers were also embedded in Kimberley's throat."

"I must have tried to get it off her."

"Do you remember doing this?"

"No, I'm still imagining how it might have happened."

"Go on."

"Then Terry must have found me and chased me upstairs and then hit me."

"Why didn't he drag you back down the cellar and kill you, too?"

"I don't know. He was my husband. He loved me. He couldn't just kill me like . . ."

"Like some teenage girl?"

"Superintendent," Julia Ford cut in, "I don't think speculation about what Mr. Payne did or didn't do is relevant here. My client says she *might* have gone down in the cellar and surprised her husband at . . . at whatever he was doing, and thus provoked him. That should explain your findings. It should also be enough."

"But you said Terry would kill you if you went in the cellar. Why didn't he?" Banks persisted.

"I don't know. Maybe he was going to. Maybe he had something else to do first."

"Like what?"

"I don't know."

"Kill Kimberley?"

"Maybe."

"But wasn't she already dead?"

"I don't know."

"Get rid of her body?"

"Maybe. I don't know. I was unconscious."

"Oh, come on, Lucy! This is rubbish," said Banks. "The next thing you'll be trying to convince me is you did it while you were sleepwalking. *You* killed Kimberley Myers, didn't you, Lucy? You went down in the cellar and saw her lying there and you strangled her."

"I didn't! Why would I do a thing like that?"

"Because you were jealous. Terry wanted Kimberley more than he wanted you. He wanted to keep her."

Lucy banged the table with her fist. "That's *not* true! You're making it up."

"Well, why else did he have her staked out there naked on the mattress? To give her a biology lesson? It was quite a biology lesson, Lucy. He raped her repeatedly, both vaginally and anally. He forced her to fellate him. Then he—or *someone*—strangled her with a length of yellow plastic fiber clothesline."

Lucy put her head in her hands and sobbed.

"Is this kind of gruesome detail really necessary?" asked Julia Ford.

"What's wrong?" Banks asked her. "Afraid of the truth?"

"It's just a bit over-the-top, that's all."

"*Over-the-top?* I'll tell you what's over the bloody top." Banks pointed at Lucy. "Kimberley's blood on the sleeves of *her* dressing gown. Yellow fibers under *her* fingernails. *She* killed Kimberley Myers."

"It's all circumstantial," said Julia Ford. "Lucy's already explained to you how it might have happened. She doesn't remember. That's not her fault. The poor woman was traumatized."

"Either that or she's a damn good actress," said Banks.

"Superintendent!"

Banks turned back to Lucy. "Who are the other girls, Lucy?"

"I don't know what you're talking about."

"We've found two unidentified bodies in the back garden. Skeletal remains, at any rate. That makes six altogether, including Kimberley. We were only looking into five disappearances, and we haven't even found all of those yet. We don't know these two. Who are they?"

"I've no idea."

"Did you ever go out in the car with your husband and pick up a teenage girl?"

The change of direction seemed to shock Lucy into silence, but she soon found her voice and regained her composure. "No, I did not."

"So you knew nothing about the missing girls?"

"No. Only what I read in the papers. I told you. I didn't go in the cellar and Terry certainly didn't tell me. So how *could* I know?"

"How indeed?" Banks scratched the little scar beside his right eye. "I'm more concerned with how you could possibly *not* have known. The man you're living with—your own husband—abducts and brings home *six* young girls that we know of so far, keeps them in the cellar for . . . God knows how long . . . while he rapes and tortures them, then he buries them either in the garden or in the cellar. And all this time you're living in the house, only one floor away, two at the most, and you expect me to believe you didn't know anything, didn't even *smell* anything? Do I look as if I was born yesterday, Lucy? I don't see how you could fail to know."

"I told you I never went down there."

"Didn't you notice when your husband was missing in the middle of the night?"

"No. I always sleep very heavily. I think Terry must have been giving me sleeping pills with my cocoa. That's why I never noticed anything."

"We didn't find any sleeping pills at the house, Lucy."

"He must have run out. That must be why I woke up on Monday morning and thought something was wrong. Or he forgot."

"Did either of you have a prescription for sleeping tablets?"

"I didn't. I don't know if Terry did. Maybe he got them from a drug pusher."

Banks made a note to look into the matter of sleeping tablets. "Why do you think he might have forgotten to drug you *this* time? Why did you go down to the cellar *this* time?" he went on. "What was so different about *this* time, about Kimberley? Was it because she was too close to home for comfort? Terry must have known he was taking a huge risk in abducting Kimberley, mustn't he? Was he obsessed with her, Lucy? Was that it? Were the others merely practice, substitutes until he could no longer stop himself from taking the one he really wanted? How did you feel about that, Lucy? That Terry wanted Kimberley more than you, more than life itself, more than freedom?"

Lucy put her hands to her ears. "Stop it! It's lies, all lies! I don't know what you mean. I don't understand what's going on. Why are you persecuting me like this?" She turned to Julia Ford. "Get me out of here now. Please! I don't have to stay and listen to any more of this, do I?"

"No," said Julia Ford, standing up. "You can leave whenever you like."

"I don't think so." Banks stood up and took a deep breath. "Lucy Payne, I'm arresting you as an accessory in the murder of Kimberley Myers."

"This is ludicrous," shot Julia Ford. "It's a travesty."

"I don't believe your client's story," said Banks. He turned to Lucy again. "You don't have to say anything, Lucy, but if you fail to say something now that you later rely on in court, it might be held against you. Do you understand?"

Banks opened the door and got two uniformed officers to take her down to the custody officer. When they came toward her she turned pale.

"Please," she said. "I'll come back whenever you want. Please, I'm begging you, don't lock me all alone in a dark cell!"

For the first time in his dealings with her, Banks got the sense that Lucy Payne was genuinely afraid. He remembered what Jenny had told him about the Alderthorpe Seven. *Kept in cages without food for days.* He almost faltered, but there was no going back now. He forced himself to remember Kimberley Myers spread-eagled on the bed in Lucy Payne's dark cellar. Nobody had given *her* a chance. "The cells aren't dark, Lucy," he said. "They're well-lit and very comfortable. They regularly get four stars in the police accommodation guide."

Julia Ford gave him a disgusted look. Lucy shook her head. Banks nodded toward the guards. "Take her down."

He'd managed it by the skin of his teeth, and he didn't even feel as good about it as he had thought he would, but he'd got Lucy Payne where he wanted her for twenty-four hours. *Twenty-four hours to find some real evidence against her.*

Annie felt only indifference toward Terence Payne's corpse laid out naked on the steel autopsy table. It was simply the shell, the deceptive outer human form of an aberration, a changeling, a demon. Come to think about it, though, she wasn't even certain she believed *that*. Terence Payne's evil was all too human. Over the centuries men had raped and mutilated women, whether as acts of plunder in wartime, for dark pleasures in the back alleys and cheap rooms of decaying cities, in the isolation of the countryside, or in the drawing rooms of the rich. It hardly needed a demon in human form to do what men themselves already did so well.

She turned her attention to events at hand: Dr. Mackenzie's close examination of the exterior of Terence Payne's skull. Identity and time of death had not been a problem in this case: Payne had been pronounced dead by Dr. Mogabe at Leeds General Infirmary at 8:13 P.M. the previous evening. Naturally, Dr. Mackenzie would do a thorough job—his assistant had already carried out the weighing and measuring, and photographs and X rays had been taken—indeed, Annie guessed Mackenzie to be the kind of doctor who would do a thorough postmortem on a man shot dead right in front of his very eyes. It didn't do to make assumptions.

The body was clean and ready for cutting, as there's no

man cleaner than one who has just been through surgery. Luckily, the police surgeon had been dispatched to take fingernail scrapings, bloodstained clothing and blood samples when Payne had first arrived at the infirmary, so no evidence had been lost due to the scruples of hospital hygiene.

At the moment, Annie was interested only in the blows to Payne's head, and Dr. Mackenzie was paying particular attention to the cranium before performing the full postmortem. They had already examined the fractured wrist and determined that it was broken by a blow from PC Janet Taylor's baton—which lay on the lab bench by the white-tiled wall—and there were also several defense bruises on Payne's arms, where he had tried to ward off PC Taylor's blows.

Unless Payne had been murdered by a nurse or doctor while he was in hospital, PC Janet Taylor's actions were most likely directly responsible for his death. What had yet to be determined was just *how* culpable she was. An emergency operation to relieve a subdural hematoma had complicated matters, Dr. Mackenzie had told Annie, but it should be easy enough to separate the surgical procedure from the unskilled bludgeoning.

Payne's head had already been shaved before his surgery, which made the injuries easier to identify. After a close examination, Mackenzie turned to Annie and said, "I'm not going to be able to tell you the exact sequence of blows, but there are some interesting clusters."

"Clusters?"

"Yes. Come here. Look."

Dr. Mackenzie pointed toward Payne's left temple, which looked to Annie, with its shaved hair and bloody rawness, rather like a dead rat in a trap. "There are at least three distinct wounds overlapping here," Dr. Mackenzie went on, tracing the outlines as he went, "from the first one—this indentation here—followed by a later wound superimposed and a third, here, which overlaps parts of both."

"Could they have been delivered in quick succession?" Annie asked, remembering what Janet Taylor had told her about the flurry of blows, and the way she had imagined it all herself when she visited the scene.

"It's possible," Dr. Mackenzie admitted, "but I'd say any one of these blows would have incapacitated him for a while, and perhaps changed his position in relation to his attacker."

"Can you explain?"

Dr. Mackenzie brought his hand around gently to the side of Annie's head and pushed. She went with the light pressure and stepped back, head turned. When he reached out again, his hand was closer to the back of her head. "Had that been a real blow," he said, "you would have been turned even farther away from me, and the blow would have stunned you. It might have taken you a little time to get back to the same position."

"I see what you mean," Annie said. "So that would lead you to believe that perhaps other blows came between?"

"Mmm. There's the angles to consider, too. If you look very closely at the indentations, you'll see that the first blow came when the victim was standing." He glanced toward the baton. "See. The wound is relatively smooth and even, allowing for the differences in height between PC Taylor and the victim. I've measured the baton, by the way, and matched it closely to each wound, and that, along with the X rays, gives me a better idea of the victim's position at the time of each blow." He pointed again. "At least one of those blows to the temple was delivered when the victim was on his knees. You can see the way the impression deepens. It's even clearer on the X ray."

Dr. Mackenzie led Annie over to the X ray viewer on the wall, slipped in a sheet of film and turned on the light. He was right. When he pointed to it, Annie could see how the wound was deeper toward the back, indicating that the baton had come down at an angle. They went back to the table.

"Could he have got up again after a blow like that?" Annie asked.

"It's possible. There's no telling with head wounds. People have been known to walk around for days with a bullet in their brains. The main problem would be the rate of blood loss. Head wounds bleed an awful lot. That's why we usually leave the brain until last in a postmortem. Most of the blood has drained off by then. Less messy."

"What are you going to do with Payne's brain?" Annie asked. "Keep it for scientific study?"

Dr. Mackenzie snorted. "I'd as soon read his character by the bumps on his head," he said. "And speaking of which . . ." He asked his assistants to turn the body over. Annie saw another raw, pulpy area at the back of Payne's head. She thought she could see splinters of bone sticking out, but realized she must be imagining things. Payne had been treated in hospital and they wouldn't leave bone splinters sticking out of the back of his head. There was also some evidence of surgical stitching, which probably gave the impression of splinters. She only shivered because it was cold in the room, she told herself.

"These wounds were almost certainly inflicted when the victim was at an inferior level, say on his hands and knees, and they were delivered from behind."

"As if he were moving away from his attacker on all fours, looking for something?"

"I wouldn't know about that," said Mackenzie. "But it's possible."

"It's just that at one point she says she hit him on the wrist and he dropped his machete, which she kicked into a corner. Apparently he went scrabbling after it on his hands and knees and she hit him again."

"That would concur with this kind of injury," Dr. Mackenzie conceded, "though I count three blows to the same general area: the brain stem, by the way, by far the most dangerous and vulnerable to attack."

"She hit him there three times?"

"Yes."

"Would he have been able to get up after that?"

"Again, I can't say. A weaker man might well have been dead by then. Mr. Payne survived for three days. Perhaps he found his machete and got up again."

"So that *is* a possible scenario?"

"I can't rule it out. But look at these." Dr. Mackenzie directed Annie's attention toward the deep depressions at the top of the skull. "These two wounds, I can say with some certainty, were administered when the victim was in an inferior position to the attacker, perhaps sitting or squatting, given the angle, and they were administered with tremendous power."

"What sort of power?"

Mackenzie stood back, raised both his arms high in the air, behind his head, and clasped his hands, then he brought them down as if wielding an imaginary hammer with all his might on to the head of an imaginary victim. "Like that," he said. "And there was no resistance."

Annie swallowed. *Damn.* This was turning into a real bugger of a case.

Elizabeth Bell, the social worker in charge of the Alderthorpe Seven investigation, hadn't retired, but she had changed jobs and relocated to York, which made it easy for Jenny to drop in on her after a quick stop by her office at the university. She found a narrow parking spot several doors away from the terrace house off Fulford Road, not far from the river, and managed to squeeze her car in without doing any damage.

Elizabeth answered the door as quickly as if she had been standing right behind it, though Jenny had been vague on the phone about her time of arrival. It hadn't mattered, Elizabeth said, as Friday was her day off this week, the kids were at school and she had ironing to catch up with.

"You must be Dr. Fuller," Elizabeth said.

"That's me. But call me Jenny."

Elizabeth led Jenny inside. "I still don't know what you want to see *me* about, but do come on in." She led Jenny into a small living room, made even smaller by the ironing board and basket of laundry balanced on a chair. Jenny could smell the lemon detergent and fabric softener, along with that warm and comforting smell of freshly ironed clothes. The television was on, showing an old black-and-white thriller starring Jack Warner. Elizabeth cleared a pile of folded clothes from the armchair and bade Jenny sit.

"Excuse the mess," she said. "It's such a tiny house, but they're so expensive around here and we do so love the location."

"Why did you move from Hull?"

"We'd been looking to move for a while, then Roger—that's my husband—got a promotion. He's a civil servant. Well, hardly all that civil, if you catch my drift."

"What about you. Job, I mean?"

"Still the social. Only now I work down the benefits office. Do you mind if I carry on ironing while we talk? Only I've got to get it all done."

"No. Not at all." Jenny looked at Elizabeth. She was a tall, big-boned woman wearing jeans and a plaid button-down shirt. The knees of her jeans were stained, Jenny noticed, as if she had been gardening. Under her short, no-nonsense haircut, her face was hard and prematurely lined, but not without kindness, which showed in her eyes and in the expressions that suddenly softened the hardness as she spoke. "How many children do you have?" Jenny asked.

"Only two. William and Pauline." She nodded toward a photograph of two children that stood on the mantelpiece: smiling in a playground. "Anyway, I'm intrigued. Why *are* you here? You didn't tell me very much over the telephone."

"I'm sorry. I wasn't meaning to be mysterious, honestly. I'm here about the Alderthorpe Seven. I understand you were involved?"

"How could I forget. Why do you want to know? It was all over ten years ago."

"Nothing's ever 'all over' in my line of work," said Jenny. She had debated how much to tell Elizabeth and had even spoken with Banks on the phone about this. Useful as ever, he had said, "As much as you have to, and as little as you need to." Jenny had already asked Mr. and Mrs. Liversedge not to reveal Lucy's true origins or name to reporters, but it wouldn't be long before some bright spark came across a slip of paper or recognized a photo from the newspaper's morgue. She knew that she and Banks had a very narrow window of opportunity in which to operate before trainloads of media people got off at York and Hull, and even found their way to sleepy little Alderthorpe. She took a risk that Elizabeth Bell wasn't likely to tip them off, either.

"Can you keep a secret?" she asked.

Elizabeth looked up from the shirt she was ironing. "If I have to. I have done before."

"The person I'm interested in is Lucy Payne."

"Lucy Payne?"

"Yes."

"That name is familiar, but I'm afraid you'll have to jog my memory."

"It's been in the news a lot recently. She was married to Terence Payne, the schoolteacher the police believe was responsible for the murder of six young girls."

"Of course. Yes, I *did* see a mention in the paper, but I must admit that I don't follow such things."

"Understandable. Anyway, Lucy's parents, Clive and Hilary Liversedge, turn out to be *foster* parents. Lucy was one of the Alderthorpe Seven. You'd probably remember her as Linda Godwin."

"Good heavens." Elizabeth paused, holding the iron in midair, as if traveling back in her memory. "Little Linda Godwin. The poor wee thing."

"Perhaps now you can see why I asked you about keeping secrets?"

"The press would have a field day."

"Indeed they would. Probably will, eventually."

"They won't find out anything from me."

A worthwhile risk, then. "Good," said Jenny.

"I think I'd better sit down." Elizabeth propped the iron on its end and sat opposite Jenny. "What do you want to know?"

"Whatever you can tell me. How did it all begin, for a start?"

"It was a local schoolteacher who tipped us off," said Elizabeth. "Maureen Nesbitt. She'd been suspicious about the state of some of the children for some time, and some of the things they said when they thought no one could overhear them. Then, when young Kathleen didn't show up for school for a week and nobody had a reasonable explanation—"

"That would be Kathleen Murray?"

"You know about her?"

"I just did a bit of background research among old newspapers at the library. I know that Kathleen Murray was the one who died."

"Was murdered. Should have been the Alderthorpe *Six,* as one of them was already dead by the time the whole thing blew up."

"Where did Kathleen fit in?"

"There were two families involved: Oliver and Geraldine Murray, and Michael and Pamela Godwin. The Murrays had four children, ranging from Keith, age eleven, to Susan, age eight. The two in the middle were Dianne and Kathleen, age ten and nine respectively. The Godwins had three children: Linda, at twelve, was the eldest, then came Tom, who was ten, and Laura, nine."

"Good Lord, it sounds complicated."

Elizabeth grinned. "It gets worse. Oliver Murray and Pamela Godwin were brother and sister, and nobody was quite sure exactly who fathered whom. Extended-family abuse. It's not as uncommon as it should be, especially in small, isolated communities. The families lived next door to one another in two semis in Alderthorpe, just far enough away from the other houses in the village to be guaranteed their privacy. It's a remote enough part of the world to begin with. Have you ever been there?"

"Not yet."

"You should. Just to get the feel of the place. It's creepy."

"I intend to. Were they true, then? The allegations."

"The police would be able to tell you more about that. I was mostly responsible for separating the children and making sure they were cared for, getting them examined, and for fostering them, too, of course."

"All of them?"

"I didn't do it all on my own, but I was in overall charge, yes."

"Did any of them ever go back to their parents?"

"No. Oliver and Geraldine Murray were charged with Kathleen's murder and are still in jail, as far as I know. Michael Godwin committed suicide two days before the trial and his wife was declared unfit to stand trial. I believe she's still in care. A mental institution, I mean."

"There's no doubt about who did what, then?"

"As I said, the police would know more about that than me, but . . . If ever I've come face-to-face with evil in my life, it was there, that morning."

"What happened?"

"Nothing *happened,* it was just . . . I don't know . . . the aura around the place."

"Did you go inside?"

"No. The police wouldn't let us. They said we'd only contaminate the scene. We had a van, a heated van, and they brought the children out to us."

"What about the satanic angle? I understand it didn't come up in court."

"Wasn't necessary, the lawyers said. Would only confuse things."

"Was there any evidence?"

"Oh, yes, but if you ask me, it was nothing but a load of mumbo jumbo to justify drinking, drug-taking and abusing the children. The police found cocaine and marijuana in both houses, you know, along with some LSD, ketamine and Ecstasy."

"Is that case why you gave up social work?"

Elizabeth paused before answering. "Partly, yes. It was the straw that broke the camel's back, if you like. But I was already close to burning out long before that. It takes it out of you, it does, dealing with ill-treated kids all the time. You lose sight of the humanity, the dignity of life. Do you know what I mean?"

"I think so," said Jenny. "Spending too much time with criminals has a similar effect."

"But these were children. They had no *choice.*"

"I see what you mean."

"You meet some proper losers down at the benefits office, believe me, but it's not like child care."

"What state was Lucy in?"

"Same as the rest. Dirty, hungry, bruised."

"Sexually abused?"

Elizabeth nodded.

"What was she like?"

"Linda? Or I suppose I'd better start calling her Lucy from

now on, hadn't I? She was a sweet little thing. Shy and scared. Standing there with a blanket around her and that look on her face like a grubby little angel. She hardly said a word."

"*Could* she speak?"

"Oh, yes. One of the children, Susan, I think, lost the use of her voice, but not Lucy. She'd been abused in just about every way imaginable, yet she was surprisingly resilient. She'd speak if she wanted to, but I never once saw her cry. In fact, she seemed to have assumed the role of caregiver to the younger ones, though she wasn't in a position to offer much in the way of care. She was the eldest, at least, so maybe she could offer them *some* comfort. You'd know more about this than I do, but I guessed she was repressing the full horror of what she'd been through, holding it back. I often wondered what would become of her. I never suspected anything like this."

"The problem is, Elizabeth—"

"Call me Liz, please. Everyone does."

"Okay. Liz. The problem is that we just don't know what Lucy's role in all this is. She claims amnesia, and she was certainly abused by her husband. We're trying to find out whether she knew anything about his other activities, or to what degree she might have been involved."

"You can't be serious! Lucy involved in something like that? Surely her own experiences—"

"I know it sounds crazy, Liz, but the abused often become the abusers. It's all they know. Power, pain, withholding, tormenting. It's a familiar cycle. Studies have shown that abused children as young as eight or ten have gone on to abuse their younger siblings or neighbors."

"But not Lucy, surely?"

"We don't know. That's why I'm asking questions, trying to fit the psychology together, build a profile of her. Is there anything more you can tell me?"

"Well, as I said, she was quiet, resilient, and the other children, the younger ones, seemed to defer to her."

"Were they afraid of her?"

"I can't say I got that impression."

"But they took notice of her?"

"Yes. She was definitely the boss."

"What else can you tell me about Lucy's personality then?"

"Let me think . . . not much, really. She was a very private person. She'd only let you see what she wanted you to see. You have to realize that these children were probably as much, if not more, shaken up by the raid, by being taken from their parents so abruptly. That was all they knew, after all. It might have been hell, but it was a familiar hell. Lucy always seemed gentle, but like most children she could be cruel on occasion."

"Oh?"

"I don't mean torturing animals or that sort of thing," said Elizabeth. "I assume that is the sort of thing you're looking for, isn't it?"

"Such early patterns of behavior can be a useful guide, but I've always thought they were overrated, myself. To be honest, I once pulled the wings off a fly myself. No, I just want to know about her. How could she be cruel, for example?"

"When we were arranging for foster parents, for example, you realize it was impossible to keep the siblings together, so they had to be split up. It was more important at the time that each child have a stable, possibly long-term caring environment. Anyway, I remember Laura, in particular—Lucy's younger sister—was upset, but all Lucy said was she'd just have to get used to it. The poor girl just wouldn't stop crying."

"Where did she end up?"

"Laura? With a family in Hull, I believe. It's a long time ago, so forgive me if I don't remember all the details."

"Of course. Can you tell me what happened to any of the other children at all?"

"I'm afraid I left there shortly after, so I never got to keep track of them. I often wish I had, but . . ."

"Is there anything more you can tell me?"

Elizabeth stood up and went back to her ironing. "Not that I can think of."

Jenny stood up, took her card from her purse and handed it over. "If you think of anything at all . . ."

Elizabeth peered at the card and set it on the edge of the ironing board. "Yes, of course. I'm only too glad to have been of help."

But she didn't look it, Jenny thought as she maneuvered her car out of the tiny parking spot. Elizabeth Bell had looked like a woman forced to confront memories she would sooner forget. And Jenny didn't blame her. She didn't know if she'd learned anything much of value except confirmation that satanic paraphernalia had been found in the cellar. Banks would certainly be interested in that. Tomorrow, she would go all the way to Alderthorpe and see if she could find anyone who knew the families before the investigation, and, as Elizabeth had suggested, to "get the feel of the place."

Chapter 12

*B*anks hadn't had a break all day, had even missed his lunch interviewing Lucy Payne, so with no real plan in mind, around three o'clock that afternoon, he found himself wandering down an alley off North Market Street toward the Old Ship Inn, heavy with the recent news that the second body discovered in the back garden of 35 The Hill was definitely *not* Leanne Wray's.

Lucy Payne was being held in a cell in the basement of police headquarters and Julia Ford had booked herself in at The Burgundy, Eastvale's best, most expensive hotel. The task force and forensics people were working as fast and as hard as they could, and Jenny Fuller was probing Lucy's past—all looking for that one little chink in her armor, that one little piece of hard evidence that she was more involved with the killings than she let on. Banks knew that if they unearthed nothing more by noon tomorrow, he'd have to let her go. He had one more visit to make today: to talk to George Woodward, the detective inspector who had done most of the legwork on the Alderthorpe investigation, now retired and running a B&B in Withernsea. Banks glanced at his watch. It would take him about two hours: plenty of time to head out there after a drink and a bite to eat and still get back before too late.

The Old Ship was a shabby, undistinguished Victorian watering hole with a few benches scattered in the cobbled alley out front. Not much light got in, as the buildings all around were dark and high. Its claim to fame was that it was well-hidden and known to be tolerant of underage drinkers. Many an Eastvale lad, so Banks had heard, had sipped his first pint at the Old Ship well before his eighteenth birthday. The sign showed an old clipper ship, and the windows were of smoked, etched glass.

It wasn't very busy at that time of day, between the lunch-hour and the after-work crowd. Indeed, the Old Ship wasn't busy very often at all, as few tourists liked the look of it, and most locals knew better places to drink. The interior was dim and the air stale and acrid with more than a hundred years' accumulated smoke and beer spills. Which made it all the more surprising that the barmaid was a pretty young girl with short, dyed red hair and an oval face, a smooth complexion, a bright smile and a cheerful disposition.

Banks leaned against the bar. "I don't suppose there's any chance of a cheese-and-onion sandwich, is there?"

"Sorry," she said. "We don't serve food after two. Packet of chips—sorry, crisps—okay?"

"Better than nothing," said Banks.

"What flavor?"

"Plain will do fine. And a pint of bitter shandy, too, please."

As she was pouring the drink and Banks was dipping into a packet of rather soggy potato crisps, she kept glancing at him out of the corner of her eye and finally said, "Aren't you the policeman who was here about that girl who disappeared a month or so ago?"

"Leanne Wray," said Banks. "Yes."

"I thought so. I saw you here. You weren't the policeman I talked to, but you were here. Have you found her yet?"

"It's Shannon, isn't it?"

She smiled. "You remember my name and you never even talked to me. I'm impressed."

Shannon, Banks remembered from the statement taken by DC Winsome Jackman, was an American student taking a year off from her studies. She had already traveled around most of Europe, and through relatives and, Banks suspected, a boyfriend, she had ended up spending a few months in Yorkshire, which she seemed to like. Banks guessed that she was working at the Old Ship, perhaps, because the manager wasn't concerned about visas and permits, and paid cash in hand. Probably not much of it, either.

Banks lit a cigarette and looked around. A couple of old men sat smoking pipes by the window, not speaking, not even looking at one another. They seemed as if they might have been there since the place first opened in the nineteenth century. The floor was worn stone and the tables scored and wobbly. A watercolor of a huge sailing ship hung crookedly on one wall, and on the opposite one, a series of framed charcoal sketches of seagoing scenes, quite good to Banks's untrained eye.

"I wasn't trying to be nosy," Shannon said. "I was only asking because I haven't seen you since and I've been reading about those girls in Leeds." She gave a little shudder. "It's horrible. I remember being in Milwaukee—that's where I'm from, Milwaukee, Wisconsin—when all the Jeffrey Dahmer stuff was going on. I was only a kid but I knew what it was all about and we were all scared and confused. I don't know how people can do things like that, do you?"

Banks looked at her, saw the innocence, the hope and the faith that her life would turn out to be worth living and that the world wasn't an entirely evil place, no matter what bad things happened in it. "No," he said. "I don't."

"So you haven't found her, then? Leanne?"

"No."

"It's not that I knew her or anything. I only saw her once. But, you know, when something like that happens, like you think you might be the last person to have seen someone, well . . ." She rested her hand on her chest. "It sort of sticks with you, if you know what I mean. I can't get the picture out of my mind. Her sitting over there by the fireplace."

Banks thought of Claire Toth, whipping herself over Kimberley Myers's murder, and he knew that anyone remotely connected with what Payne had done felt tainted by it. "I know what you mean," he said.

One of the old men came up to the bar and plunked his half-pint glass down. Shannon filled it for him; he paid and went back to his chair. She wrinkled her nose. "They're in here every day. You can set your watch by them. If one of them didn't turn up I'd have to call an ambulance."

"When you say you can't get Leanne's image out of your mind, does that mean you've given any more thought to that evening?"

"Not really," said Shannon. "I mean, I thought . . . you know, that she'd been taken, like the others. That's what everyone thought."

"I'm starting to believe that might not be the case," said Banks, putting his fear into words for the first time. "In fact, I'm beginning to think we might have been barking up the wrong tree on that one."

"I don't understand."

"Anyway," Banks went on. "I just thought I'd drop by, see if you remembered anything you forgot to mention before, that sort of thing. It's been a while." And that, he knew, meant that any trail Leanne may had left would have gone cold. If they had screwed up in assuming too quickly that Leanne Wray had been abducted by the same person, or persons, as Kelly Matthews and Samantha Foster, then any clues as to what had *really* happened could well have vanished forever by now.

"I don't know how I can help," said Shannon.

"Tell me," said Banks, "you say they were sitting over there, right?" He pointed to the table by the empty tiled fireplace.

"Yes. Four of them. At that table."

"Did they drink much?"

"No. I told the policewoman before. They only had a drink or two each. I didn't think she was old enough but the landlord tells us not to bother too much, unless it's *really* obvious." She put her hand over her mouth. "Shoot, I probably shouldn't have said that, should I?"

"Don't worry about it. We know all about Mr. Parkinson's practices. And don't worry about what you told us before, Shannon. I know I could go and look it all up in the files if I wanted, but I want you to start again, as if it had never happened before."

It was hard to explain to a civilian, but Banks needed the feel of investigating Leanne's disappearance as if it were a fresh crime. He didn't want to start by poring over old files in his office—though it would no doubt come to that if something didn't turn up soon—he wanted to start by revisiting the place where she had last been seen.

"Did Leanne seem intoxicated at all?" he asked.

"She was a bit giggly, a bit loud, as if maybe she wasn't used to the drink."

"What was she drinking?"

"I can't remember. Not beer. Maybe wine, or it could have been Pernod, something like that."

"Did you get the impression that the four of them had paired off? Anything along those lines?"

Shannon thought for a moment. "No. Two of them were clearly a couple. You could tell by the way they were touching one another casually. I mean, it's not as if they were necking or anything. But the other two, Leanne and . . ."

"Mick Blair," said Banks.

"I don't know their names. Anyway, I got the impression he might have been a bit keen, and she was flirting a bit, maybe because of the drinks."

"Was he bothering her at all?"

"Oh, no, nothing like that, or I'd have made a point of saying so before. No, just the way I caught him looking at her once or twice. They seemed comfortable enough together, but as I say, I just thought maybe he fancied her and she was playing him along a bit, that's all."

"You didn't mention this before."

"It didn't seem important. Besides, nobody asked me. Back then, everyone was more concerned that she'd been abducted by a serial killer."

True enough, Banks thought, with a sigh. Leanne's parents had been adamant that she was a good girl and would never, under any normal circumstances, break a curfew. So certain were they that she must have been attacked or abducted that their certainty influenced the investigation, and the police broke one of their cardinal rules: Don't make assumptions until you've checked out every possible angle. People were also making noises about Kelly Matthews and Samantha Foster at the time, so Leanne's disappearance— another nice, well-adjusted teenager—became linked with theirs. And there was, of course, the matter of the abandoned shoulder bag. In it were Leanne's inhaler, which she needed in case of an asthma attack, and her purse, which contained twenty-five pounds and a handful of change. It made no sense that she would throw away her money if she was running away from home. Surely she would need all she could get?

DC Winsome Jackman had questioned Shannon, and perhaps she should have asked more probing questions, but Banks couldn't blame Winsome for the omissions. She had discovered what mattered at the time: that the group had been well-behaved, that they had caused no problems, that there had been no arguments, that they weren't drunk, and that there had been no unwelcome attention from strangers. "What was their general mood?" Banks asked. "Did they seem quiet, rambunctious, or what?"

"I don't remember anything unusual about them. They weren't causing any trouble, or I'm sure I'd have said. Usually you get that with people who know they're drinking underage. They know they're under sufferance, if you know what I mean, so they tend not to draw attention to themselves."

Banks remembered the feeling well. At sixteen he had sat, proud and terrified, with his mate Steve in a poky little pub a mile or so from the estate where they both lived, drinking their first pints of bitter in a corner by the jukebox, smoking Park Drive tipped. They had felt like real grown-ups, but Banks also remembered being worried in case the police came around, or someone who knew them came in—one of his father's friends, for example—so they tried to fade into the woodwork as much as possible.

He sipped his shandy and crumpled up the crisp packet. Shannon took it from him and put it in the waste bin behind the bar.

"I do remember that they seemed excited about something just before they left, though," Shannon added. "I mean they were too far away for me to hear anything and they weren't really noisy about it, but I could tell someone had come up with a good idea for something to do."

Banks hadn't heard about this before. "You've no idea what it was?"

"No, it was just like, they were going, 'Yeah, let's do that.' Then a couple of minutes later they left."

"What time was this?"

"Must have been about a quarter to eleven."

"And they were *all* excited about this idea? Including Leanne?"

"I couldn't honestly separate out the reactions for you," Shannon said with a frown. "It was just a general sort of thing, as if someone had an idea for something to do and they all thought it would be fun."

"This great idea, did you get the impression it was something they were going to do right then, after they left here?"

"I don't know. Perhaps. Why?"

Banks finished his drink. "Because Leanne Wray had an eleven-o'clock curfew," he said. "And according to her parents she never stayed out past her curfew. If she was planning on going off anywhere with them *after* they'd been here, she'd have missed it. There's something else, too."

"What?"

"If they were all planning to do something, it means her friends all lied."

Shannon thought for a moment. "I see what you mean. But there was no reason to think she wasn't going home. She might have. I mean, it could have been just the three of them planning something. Look, I'm really sorry . . . I mean, I never thought, you know, last time. I tried to remember everything that was important."

"It's okay," said Banks, smiling. "Not your fault." He looked at his watch. Time to head out for Withernsea. "Must dash."

"Oh. I'm leaving at the end of next week," said Shannon. "I mean, my last night's a week next Wednesday, you know, if you'd like to stop by for a drink, say good-bye."

Banks didn't know how to take the invitation. Was it a come-on? Surely not. Shannon couldn't have been a day over twenty-one. Still, it was nice to think there was even the remotest chance that a younger girl fancied him. "Thanks," he said. "I'm not sure I'll be able to make it, so in case I don't, I'll say *bon voyage* now."

Shannon gave a little "whatever" sort of shrug and Banks walked out into the dismal alley.

* * *

It was only mid-afternoon, but Annie would have sworn that Janet Taylor was drunk. Not totally, falling-down pissed, but emitting a slight buzz, fuzzy around the edges. She'd had a bit of experience with drunks at the artists' commune where she had grown up with her father, Ray. There had once, briefly, been an alcoholic writer, she remembered, a big, smelly man with rheumy eyes and a thick, matted beard. He hid bottles all over the place. Her father told her to stay away from him and once, when the man, whose name she couldn't remember, started talking to her, her father got angry and made him leave the room. It was one of the few times she had ever seen Ray really angry. He liked a drop or two of wine now and then, and no doubt he still smoked a bit of pot, but he wasn't a drunk or a drug addict. Most of the time he was consumed by his work, whatever painting it happened to be at the time, to the exclusion of pretty much everything, including Annie.

Janet's flat was a mess, with clothes strewn everywhere and half-full cups of tea on the windowsill and mantelpiece. It also smelled like a drunk's room, that peculiar mix of stale skin and the sweet-and-sour smell of booze. Gin, in Janet's case.

Janet slumped on to a wrinkled T-shirt and a pair of jeans on the armchair, leaving Annie to fend for herself. She cleared some newspapers off a hard-backed chair and sat.

"So what is it now?" Janet asked. "You come to arrest me?"

"Not yet."

"What, then? More questions?"

"You've heard Terence Payne died?"

"I've heard."

"How are you doing, Janet?"

"How am I doing? Ha. That's a good one. Well, let me see." She started counting off on her fingers as she spoke. "Apart from not being able to sleep, apart from pacing the flat and feeling claustrophobic whenever it gets dark, apart from reliving the moment over and over again whenever I close my eyes, apart from the fact that my career's pretty much fucked, let me see . . . I feel just fine."

Annie took a deep breath. She certainly wasn't there to make Janet feel any better, though in a way she wished she could. "You know, you really should seek some sort of counseling, Janet. The Federation will—"

"No! No, I'm not seeing any shrinks. I'll not have them messing with my head. Not with all this shit going on. When they've done with me, I'll not know whether I'm coming or going. Imagine how that would look in court."

Annie held her hands up. "Okay. Okay. It's your choice." She took some papers from her briefcase. "I've attended Terence Payne's postmortem, and there's a couple of things I'd like to go over on your statement."

"Are you saying I was lying?"

"No, not at all."

Janet ran her hand through her lifeless, greasy hair. "Because I'm not a liar. I might have been a bit confused about the sequence of events—it all happened so fast—but I told it as I remember it."

"Okay, Janet, that's fine. Look, in your statement you say you hit Payne three times on the left temple and once on his wrist, and that one of the blows to the temple was delivered two-handed."

"Did I?"

"Yes. Is that correct?"

"I couldn't remember *exactly* how many times or where I hit him, but that seemed about right, yes. Why?"

"According to Dr. Mackenzie's postmortem, you hit Payne *nine* times. Three on the temple, one to the wrist, one on the cheek, two to the base of the skull while he was crouching or kneeling, and two to the top of his head while he was squatting or sitting."

Janet said nothing, and a jet from the airport streamed into the silence, filling it with the roar of engines and the promise of distant, exotic places. Anywhere but here, Annie was thinking, and she guessed that Janet probably felt the same. "Janet?"

"What? I wasn't aware you'd asked me a question."

"How do you respond to what I just said?"

"I don't know. I told you, I wasn't counting. I was just trying to save my life."

"Are you sure you weren't acting out of revenge for Dennis?"

"What do you mean?"

"The number of blows, the position of the victim, the violence of the blows."

Janet turned red. "*Victim!* Is that what you call the bastard? *Victim.* When Dennis was lying there on the floor with his lifeblood pumping away, you call Terence Payne a victim. How dare you?"

"I'm sorry, Janet, but that's the way a case would be presented in court, and you'd better get used to the idea."

Janet said nothing.

"Why did you say what you did to the ambulance attendant?"

"What did I say?"

" 'Is he dead? Did I kill the bastard?' What did you mean by that?"

"I don't know. I don't even remember saying it."

"It could be construed as meaning you set out to kill him, do you see?"

"I suppose it could be twisted that way, yes."

"Did you, Janet? Did you intend to kill Terence Payne?"

"No! I told you. I was just trying to save my life. Why can't you believe me?"

"What about the blows to the back of his head? When might those have occurred in the sequence of events?"

"I don't know."

"Try harder. You can do better than that."

"Maybe when he was bent over reaching for his machete."

"Okay. But you don't remember delivering them?"

"No, but I suppose I must have done if you say so."

"What about those two blows to the *top* of his head? Dr. Mackenzie tells me they were delivered with a lot of force. They weren't just random hits."

Janet shook her head. "I don't know. I don't know."

Annie leaned forward and held Janet's chin between thumb and forefinger, looking into her blurry, scared eyes. "Listen to me, Janet. Terence Payne was taller than you. By the angle and force of those blows, the *only* way they could have been delivered was if he was sitting and the attacker had plenty of time to take a huge, uninterrupted downward swing and . . . well, you get the picture. Come on, Janet. Talk to me. Believe it or not, I'm trying to help you."

Janet twisted her chin from Annie's grip and looked away. "What do you want me to say? I'd only get myself deeper in trouble."

"Not true. You'll get nowhere if you're perceived as lying or covering up your actions. That'll only lead to perjury. The truth's your best defense. Do you think there's a person on that jury—if that's what it comes to—who won't sympathize with your predicament, even if you did admit to losing it for a few moments? Give yourself a break here, Janet."

"What do you want me to say?"

"Tell the truth. Was that how it happened? Was he down and you just lost your temper, gave him one for Dennis. And, crack, there's another? Is that how it happened?"

Janet jumped up and began pacing, wringing her hands. "So what if I did give him one or two for Dennis? It was nothing less than he deserved."

"That's what you did? You remember now?"

Janet stopped and narrowed her eyes, then she poured herself two fingers of gin and knocked it back. "Not clearly, no, but if you're telling me that's how it happened, I can hardly deny it, can I? Not in the face of the pathologist's evidence."

"Pathologists can be wrong," Annie said, though not, she thought, about the number, strength and angle of the blows.

"But who will they believe in court?"

"I've told you. If it comes to that you'll get a lot of sympathy. But it might not come to court."

Janet sat down again, perched at the edge of the armchair. "What do you mean?"

"It's up to the CPS. I'll be meeting with them on Monday. In the meantime, if you want to alter your statement at all before then, now's the time to do it."

"It's no good," said Janet, holding her head in her hands and weeping. "I don't remember it clearly. It all seemed to happen so fast, it was over before I knew what was happening, and Dennis . . . Dennis was dead, bleeding on my lap. That went on forever, me telling him to hang on, trying to stanch the blood." She looked at her hands as if seeing the same thing Lady Macbeth saw, what she couldn't wash away. "But he wouldn't stop bleeding. I couldn't stop it from coming out. Maybe it happened as you said. Maybe that's the only way it could have happened. All I remember is the fear, the adrenaline, the . . ."

"The anger, Janet? Is that what you were going to say?"

Janet shot her a defiant glance. "What if I was? Wasn't I right to feel anger?"

"I'm not here to judge you. I think I'd have been angry myself, maybe done exactly the same as you. But we've got to get this sorted. There's no way it'll simply disappear. As I say, the CPS might decide not to press charges. At the worst you'd be looking at excusable homicide, maybe even justifiable. We're not talking jail time here, Janet. Thing is, though, we can't hide it, and it won't go away. There's got to be some action." Annie spoke softly and clearly, as if to a frightened child.

"I hear what you're saying," Janet said. "It's like I'm some sort of sacrificial lamb tossed to the slaughter to appease public opinion."

"Not at all." Annie stood up. "Public opinion is far more likely to be on your side. It's just procedure that has to be followed. Look, if you want to get in touch with me about anything, *anything* at all before Monday, here's my card." She wrote her home and mobile numbers on the back.

"Thanks." Janet took the card, glanced at it and set it on the coffee table.

"You know," Annie said at the door, "I'm not your enemy, Janet. Yes, I'd have to give evidence if it came to court, but I'm not against you."

Janet gave her a twisted smile. "Yeah, I know," she said, reaching for the gin again. "Life's a bitch, isn't it?"

"Sure is." Annie smiled back. "Then you die."

"Claire! It's so nice to see you again. Come in."

Claire Toth walked into Maggie's hall and followed her through to the front room, where she slouched on the sofa.

The first things Maggie noticed about her were how pale she was and that she had cut off all her beautiful long blond hair. What was left lay jaggedly over her skull in such a manner as to suggest that she had cut it herself. She wasn't wearing her school uniform but a pair of baggy jeans and a baggy sweatshirt that hid all signs that she was an attractive young woman. She wore no makeup, and her face was dotted with acne. Maggie remembered what Dr. Simms had said about the possible reactions of Kimberley's close friends, that some might suppress their sexuality because they thought that would protect them from predators such as Terence

Payne. It looked as if Claire was trying to do just that. Maggie wondered if she should comment, but decided not to.

"Milk and cookies?" she asked.

Claire shook her head.

"What is it, sweetheart?" Maggie asked. "What's wrong?"

"I don't know," said Claire. "I can't sleep. I just keep thinking of her. I just lie awake all night with it going through my head—what must have happened to her, what she must have felt like . . . I can't bear it. It's awful."

"What do your parents say?"

Claire looked away. "I can't talk to them. I . . . I thought, you know, you might understand better."

"Let me get those cookies, anyway. I could do with one myself." Maggie fetched two glasses of milk and a plate of chocolate chip cookies from the kitchen and put them down on the coffee table. Claire picked up her milk and sipped at it, then reached out and picked up a cookie.

"You read about me in the papers, then?" Maggie said.

Claire nodded.

"And what did you think?"

"At first I couldn't believe it. Not you. Then I realized it could be anybody, that you didn't have to be poor or stupid to be abused. Then I felt sorry for you."

"Well, please don't do that," said Maggie, trying on a smile. "I stopped feeling sorry for myself a long time ago, and now I'm just getting on with life. All right?"

"Okay."

"What sort of things do you think about? Do you want to tell me?"

"How terrible it must have been for Kimberley, with Mr. Payne, you know, doing things to her. *Sex.* The police didn't say anything to the papers about it, but I *know* he did horrible things to her. I can just picture him there, doing it, hurting her, and Kimberley so helpless."

"It's no use imagining what it was like, Claire. It won't do any good."

"Do you think I don't know that? Do you think I do it on purpose?" She shook her head slowly. "And I keep going over the details of that night in my mind. How I just said I was staying for a slow dance with Nicky and Kimberley said that was okay, she'd probably find somebody to walk home with but it wasn't very far anyway and the road was well-lit. I should have known something would happen to her."

"You couldn't know, Claire. How could you possibly know?"

"I *should* have. We knew about those girls, the ones who'd gone missing. We should have stuck together, been more careful."

"Claire, listen to me: it's *not* your fault. And I know this sounds harsh, but if anyone should have been more careful, perhaps it's Kimberley. You can't be blamed for dancing with a boy. If she was concerned, then she should have made sure she had someone to walk home with her and not gone off alone."

"Maybe she didn't."

"What do you mean?"

"Maybe Mr. Payne gave her a lift."

"You told the police you didn't see him. You didn't, did you?"

"No. But he *could* have been waiting outside, couldn't he?"

"I suppose so," Maggie admitted.

"I hate him. I'm glad he's dead. And I hate Nicky Gallagher. I hate all men."

Maggie didn't know what to say to that. She could tell Claire that she'd get over it in time, but a fat lot of good that would do. The best thing she could do, she decided, was have a talk with Mrs. Toth and see if they could persuade Claire to go for counseling before things got worse. At least she seemed to *want* to talk about her thoughts and feelings, which was a good start.

"Was she conscious all the time he was doing stuff with her?" she asked. "I mean, was she *aware* of him doing it to her?"

"Claire, stop it." But Maggie was spared further debate by the phone. She listened, frowning, said a few words and then turned back to Claire, who managed to pull herself out of her absorption with Kimberley's ordeal for a moment and ask her who it was.

"It was the local television station," Maggie said, wondering if she sounded as stunned as she felt.

A flicker of interest. "What did they want?"

"They want me to go on the local news show tonight."

"What did you say?"

"I said yes," said Maggie, as if she couldn't quite believe it herself.

"Cool," said Claire, squeezing out a tiny smile.

There are many English seaside resorts that look as if they have seen better days. Withernsea looked as if it had never seen any good days at all. The sun was shining over the rest of the island, but you wouldn't know it at Withernsea. A vicious cold rain slanted in from the iron sky, and waves from a North Sea the color of stained underwear churned up dirty sand and pebbles on the beach. Set back from the front was a strip of gift shops, amusement arcades and bingo halls, their bright-colored lights garish and lurid in the gloomy afternoon, the bingo caller's amplified "Number nine, doctor's orders!" pathetic as it sounded along the deserted promenade.

The whole thing reminded Banks of long ago childhood holidays at Great Yarmouth, Blackpool or Scarborough. July or August days when it seemed to rain nonstop for two weeks, and all he could do was wander around the amusement arcades losing pennies in the one-armed bandits and watching the mechanical claw drop the shiny cigarette lighter just before it reached the winner's chute. He had never played bingo, but had often watched the hard-faced peroxide women sit there game after game, chain-smoking and staring down at the little numbers on their cards.

On better days, and when he reached his teens, Banks would spend his time searching through the secondhand bookshops for the old Pan books of horror stories or steamy bestsellers such as *The Carpetbaggers* and *Peyton Place*. When he was thirteen or fourteen, feeling way too grown-up to be on holiday with his parents, he would wander off alone for the day, hanging around in coffee bars and browsing through the latest singles in Woolworth's or a local record shop. Sometimes he would meet a girl in the same predicament, and he had had his first adolescent kisses and tentative gropings on these holidays.

Banks parked by the seafront and, without even stopping for a look at the water, hurried to the house directly across from him, where retired DI George Woodward now ran his B&B. The VACANCIES sign swung in the wind and creaked like a shutter on a haunted house. By the time Banks rang the front doorbell he was cold and soaked to the skin.

George Woodward was a dapper man with gray hair, bristly mustache and the watchful eyes of an ex-copper. There was also an aura of the hangdog about him, most noticeable as he looked over Banks's shoulder at the weather and shook his head slowly. "I did suggest Torquay," he said, "but the wife's mother lives here in Withernsea." He ushered Banks in. "Ah, well, it's not that bad. You've just come on a miserable day, that's all. Early in the season, too. You should see it when the sun's shining and the place is full. A different world altogether."

Banks wondered on which day of the year that momentous event occurred, but he kept silent. No point antagonizing George Woodward.

They were in a large room with a bay window and several tables, clearly the breakfast room where the lucky guests hurried down for their bacon and eggs every morning. The tables were laid out with white linen, but there were no knives and forks, and Banks wondered if the Woodwards had any guests at all at the moment. Without offering tea or anything stronger, George Woodward sat at one of the tables and bade Banks sit opposite.

"It's about Alderthorpe, is it, then?"

"Yes." Banks had spoken with Jenny Fuller on his mobile on his way out to Withernsea and learned what Elizabeth Bell, the social worker, had to say. Now he was after the policeman's perspective.

"I always thought that would come back to haunt us one day."

"How do you mean?"

"Damage like that. It doesn't go away. It festers."

"I suppose you've got a point." Like Jenny had with Elizabeth Bell, Banks decided he had to trust George Woodward. "I'm here about Lucy Payne," he said, watching Woodward's expression. "Linda Godwin, as was. But that's between you and me for the moment."

Woodward paled and whistled between his teeth. "My God, I'd never have believed it. Linda Godwin?"

"That's right."

"I saw her picture in the paper, but I didn't recognize her. The poor lass."

"Not anymore."

"Surely you can't think she had anything to do with those girls?"

"We don't know what to think. That's the problem. She's

claiming loss of memory. There's some circumstantial evidence, but not much. You know the sort of thing I mean."

"What's your instinct?"

"That she's more involved than she's saying. Whether she's an accessory or not, I don't know."

"You realize she was only a twelve-year-old girl when I met her?"

"Yes."

"Twelve going on forty, the responsibility she had."

"Responsibility?" Jenny had said something about Lucy taking care of the younger children; he wondered if this was what Woodward meant.

"Yes. She was the eldest. For Christ's sake, man, she had a ten-year-old brother who was being regularly buggered by his father and uncle and there wasn't a damn thing she could do about it. They were doing it to *her,* too. Can you even *begin* to imagine how all that made her feel?"

Banks admitted he couldn't. "Mind if I smoke?" he asked.

"I'll get you an ashtray. You're lucky Mary's over at her mother's." He winked. "She'd never allow it." Woodward produced a heavy glass ashtray from the cupboard by the door and surprised Banks by pulling a crumpled packet of Embassy Regal from the shirt pocket under his beige V-neck sweater. He then went on to surprise him even further by suggesting a wee dram. "Nowt fancy, mind. Just Bell's."

"Bell's would be fine," said Banks. He'd have just the one, as he had a long drive home. The first sip, after they clinked glasses, tasted wonderful. It was everything to do with the cold rain lashing at the bay windows.

"Did you get to know Lucy at all?" he asked.

Woodward sipped his Bell's neat and grimaced. "Barely spoke to her. Or any of the kids, for that matter. We left them to the social workers. We'd enough on our hands with the parents."

"Can you tell me how it went down?"

Woodward ran his hand over his hair, then took a deep drag on his cigarette. "Good Lord, this is going back a bit," he said.

"Whatever you can remember."

"Oh, I remember everything as if it was yesterday. That's the problem."

Banks tapped some ash from his cigarette and waited for George Woodward to focus his memory on the one day he would probably sooner forget.

"It was pitch-black when we went in," Woodward began. "And cold as a witch's tit. The eleventh of February, it was. 1990. There was me and Baz—Barry Stevens, my DS—in one car. The bloody heater didn't work properly, I remember, and we were almost blue with cold when we got to Alderthorpe. All the puddles were frozen. There were about three more cars and a van, for the social workers to isolate the kids, like. We were working off a tip from one of the local schoolteachers who'd got suspicious about some of the truancies, the way the kids looked and behaved and, especially, the disappearance of Kathleen Murray."

"She's the one who was killed, right?"

"That's right. Anyway, there were a couple of lights on in the houses when we got there, and we marched straight up and bashed our way in—we had a warrant—and that was when we . . . we saw it." He was silent for a moment, staring somewhere beyond Banks, beyond the bay window, beyond even the North Sea. Then he took another nip of whiskey, coughed and went on. "Of course, we didn't know who was who at first. The two households were mixed up and nobody knew who'd fathered who anyway."

"What did you find?"

"Most of them were asleep until we bashed the doors in. They had a vicious dog, took a chunk out of Baz as we went in. Then we found Oliver Murray and Pamela Godwin—

brother and sister—in a bed with one of the Godwin girls: Laura."

"Lucy's sister."

"Yes. Dianne Murray, the second-eldest child, was curled up safe and sound in a room with her brother Keith, but their sister, Susan, was sandwiched between the other two adults." He swallowed. "The place was a pigsty—both of them were—smelled terrible. Someone had knocked a hole through the living-room wall so they could travel back and forth without going outside and being seen." He paused a moment to collect his thoughts. "It's hard to get across the sense of squalor, of depravity you could feel there, but it was tangible, something you could touch and taste. I don't just mean the dirt, the stains, the smells, but more than that. A sort of spiritual squalor, if you catch my drift. Everyone was terrified, of course, especially the kids." He shook his head. "Sometimes, looking back, I wonder if we couldn't have done it some other way, some gentler way. I don't know. Too late for that now, anyroad."

"I understand you found evidence of satanic rituals?"

"In the cellar of the Godwin house, yes."

"What did you find?"

"The usual. Incense, robes, books, pentagram, an altar—no doubt on which the virgin would be penetrated. Other occult paraphernalia. You know what my theory is?"

"No. What?"

"These people weren't witches or Satanists; they were just sick and cruel perverts. I'm sure they used the Satanism as an excuse to take drugs and dance and chant themselves into a frenzy. All that satanic rigmarole—the candles, magic circles, robes, music, chanting and whatnot—it was just something to make it all seem like a game to the children. It was just something that played with their minds, like, didn't let the poor buggers know whether what they were doing was what was supposed to be happening—playing with Mummy and Daddy even if it hurt sometimes and they punished you when you were bad—or something way out, way over-the-top. It was both, of course. No wonder they couldn't understand. And all those trappings, they just helped turn it into a kid's game, ring around the roses, that's all."

Satanic paraphernalia had also been found in the Paynes's cellar. Banks wondered if there was a connection. "Did any of them profess any sort of belief in Satan at any time?"

"Oliver and Pamela tried to confuse the jury with some sort of gobbledygook about the Great Horned God and 666 at their trial, but nobody took a blind bit of notice of them. Trappings, that's all it were. A kid's game. Let's all go down in the cellar and dress up and play."

"Where was Lucy?"

"Locked in a cage—we later found out it was a genuine Morrison shelter left over from the war—in the cellar of the Murray house along with her brother, Tom. It was where you got put if you misbehaved or disobeyed, we found out later. We never did find out what the two of them had done to get put there, though, because they wouldn't talk."

"Wouldn't or couldn't?"

"Wouldn't. They wouldn't talk out against the adults, their parents. They'd been abused and messed up in their minds too long to dare put it into words." He paused a moment. "Sometimes, I don't think they could have expressed it all anyway, no matter how much they tried. I mean, where does a nine-year-old or an eleven-year-old find the language and points of reference she needs to explain something like that? They weren't just protecting their parents or shutting up in fear of them—it went deeper than that. Anyway, Tom and Linda . . . They were both naked and dirty, crawling in their own filth, looked as if they hadn't eaten for a couple of days—I mean, most of the children were malnourished and neglected, but they were worse. There was a bucket in the cage, and the smell . . . And Linda, well, she was twelve, and it showed. She was . . . I mean they'd made no provisions for . . . you know . . . time of the month. I'll never forget the look of shame and fear and defiance on that little kid's face when Baz and I walked in on them and turned the light on."

Banks took a sip of Bell's, waited until it had burned all the way down, then asked, "What did you do?"

"First off, we found some blankets for them, as much for warmth's sake as modesty's, because there wasn't much heat in the place, either."

"After that?"

"We handed them over to the social workers." He gave a little shudder. "One of them couldn't handle it. Well-meaning young lass, thought she was tough, but she didn't have the stomach."

"What did she do?"

"Went back to the car and wouldn't get out. Just sat there hunched up, shivering and crying. There was no one to pay her much mind as we all had our hands full. Me and Baz were mostly occupied with the adults."

"Did they have much to say?"

"Nah. Surly lot. And Pamela Godwin—well, there was clearly summat wrong with her. In the head. She didn't seem to have a clue what was going on. Kept on smiling and asking us if we wanted a cup of tea. Her husband, though, Michael, I'll never forget him. Greasy hair, straggly beard and that look in his dark eyes. You ever seen pictures of that American killer, Charles Manson?"

"Yes."

"Like him. That's who Michael Godwin reminded me of: Charles Manson."

"What did you do with them?"

"We arrested them all under the Protection of Children Act, to be going on with. They resisted arrest, of course. Picked up a few lumps and bruises." He gave Banks a challenge-me-on-that-one-if-you-dare look. Banks didn't.

"Later, of course, we came up with a list of charges as long as your arm."

"Including murder."

"That was later, after we found Kathleen Murray's body."

"When did you find her?"

"Later that day."

"Where?"

"Out back in an old sack in the dustbin. I reckon they'd dumped her there until the ground softened a bit and they could bury her. You could see where someone had tried to dig a hole, but they'd given up, the earth was so hard. She'd been doubled over and been there long enough to freeze solid, so the pathologist had to wait till she thawed out before he could do the postmortem."

"Were they all charged?"

"Yes. We charged all four adults with conspiracy."

"And?"

"They were all committed for trial. Michael Godwin topped himself in his cell, and Pamela was found unfit to stand trial. The jury convicted the other two after a morning's deliberation."

"What evidence did you have?"

"What do you mean?"

"Could anyone else have killed Kathleen?"

"Who?"

"I don't know. One of the other kids, maybe?"

Woodward's jaw tightened. "You didn't see them," he said. "If you had, you wouldn't be making suggestions like that."

"Did anyone suggest it at the time?"

He gave a harsh laugh. "Believe it or not, yes. The adults had the gall to try and pin it on the boy, Tom. But nobody fell for that one, thank the Lord."

"What about the evidence? How was she killed, for example?"

"Ligature strangulation."

Banks held his breath. Another coincidence. "With what?"

Woodward smiled as if laying down his trump card. "Oliver Murray's belt. The pathologist matched it to the wound. He also found traces of Murray's semen in the girl's vagina and anus, not to mention unusual tearing. It looks they went too far that once. Maybe she was bleeding to death, I don't know, but they killed her—*he* killed her, with the knowledge and consent of the others, maybe even with their help, I don't know."

"How did they plead? The Murrays?"

"What would you expect? Not guilty."

"They never confessed?"

"No. People like that never do. They don't even think they've done anything wrong, they're so beyond the law, be-yond what's normal for the rest of us folks. In the end, they got less than they deserved, in that they're still alive, but at least they're still locked up, out of harm's way. And that, Mr. Banks, is the story of the Alderthorpe Seven." Woodward put his palms on the table and stood up. He seemed less dapper and more weary than when Banks had first arrived. "Now, if you'll excuse me, I've got the rooms to do before the missus comes back."

It seemed like an odd time to be doing the rooms, Banks thought, especially as they were all probably vacant, but he sensed that Woodward had had enough, wanted to be alone and wanted, if he could, to get rid of the bad taste of his memories before his wife came home. Good luck to him. Banks couldn't think of anything more to ask, so he said his good-byes, buttoned up and walked out into the rain. He could have sworn he felt a few lumps of hail stinging his bare head before he got into his car.

*   *   *

Maggie began to have doubts the moment she got in the taxi to the local television studio. Truth be told, she had been vacillating ever since she first got the call early that afternoon inviting her to participate in a discussion on domestic violence on the evening magazine show at six o'clock, after the news. A researcher had seen the article in the newspaper and thought Maggie would make a valuable guest. This was not about Terence and Lucy Payne, the researcher had stressed, and their deeds were not to be discussed. It was an odd legal situation, she explained, that no one had yet been charged with the murders of the girls, and the main suspect was dead, but not proved guilty. Could you charge a dead man with murder? Maggie wondered.

As the taxi wound down Canal Road, over the bridge and under the viaduct to Kirkstall Road, where the rush hour traffic was slow and heavy, Maggie felt the butterflies begin the flutter in her stomach. She remembered the newspaper article, how Lorraine Temple had twisted everything, and wondered again if she was doing the right thing or if she was simply walking back into the lions' den.

But she *did* have very good, strong reasons for doing it, she assured herself. In the first place, she wanted to atone for, even correct, the image the newspaper had given of Lucy Payne as being evil and manipulative, if she could slip it in somehow. Lucy was a *victim,* and the public should be made to realize that. Secondly, she wanted to rid herself of the mousy, nervous image Lorraine Temple had lumbered her with, both for her own sake and in order to get people to take her seriously. She didn't like being thought of as mousy and nervous, and she was damn well going to do something about it.

Finally, and this was the reason that pushed her to say yes, was the way that policeman, Banks, had come to the house shouting at her, insulting her intelligence and telling her what she could and couldn't do. *Damn him.* She'd show him.

She'd show them all. She was feeling empowered now, and if
it was her lot to become a spokeswoman for battered wives,
then so be it; she was up to the task. Lorraine Temple had let
the cat out of the bag about her past, anyway, so there was
nothing more to hide; she might as well speak out and hope
she could do some good for others in her position. No more
mousy and nervous.

Julia Ford had phoned her that afternoon to tell her that
Lucy was being detained in Eastvale for further questioning
and would probably be kept there overnight. Maggie was
outraged. What had Lucy done to deserve such treatment?
Something was very much out of kilter in the whole business.

Maggie paid the taxi driver and kept the receipt. The TV
people would reimburse her, they had said. She introduced
herself at reception and the woman behind the desk called
the researcher, Tina Driscoll, who turned out to be a cheerful
slip of a lass in her early twenties with short bleached blond
hair and pale skin stretched tight over her high cheekbones.
Like most of the other people Maggie saw as she followed
Tina through the obligatory television studio maze, she was
dressed in jeans and a white blouse.

"You're on after the poodle groomer," Tina said, glancing
at her watch. "Should be about twenty past. Here's Makeup."

Tina ushered Maggie into a tiny room with chairs and mirrors and a whole array of powders, brushes and potions. "Just
here, love, that's right," said the makeup artist, who introduced herself as Charley. "Won't take a minute." And she
started dabbing and brushing away at Maggie's face. Finally,
satisfied with the result, she said, "Drop by when you've finished and I'll wipe it off in a jiffy."

Maggie didn't see a great deal of difference, though she
knew from her previous television experience that the studio
lighting and cameras would pick up the subtle nuances.
"David will be conducting the interview," said Tina, consulting her clipboard on their way to the green room. "David,"

Maggie knew, was David Hartford, half of the male-female team that hosted the program. The woman was called Emma Larson, and Maggie had been hoping that *she* would have been asking the questions. Emma had always come across as sympathetic on women's issues, but David Hartford, Maggie thought, had a cynical and derogatory tone to his questioning of anyone who was passionate about anything. He was also known to be provocative. Still, the way Maggie was feeling, she was quite willing to be provoked.

Maggie's fellow guests were waiting in the green room: the grave, bearded Dr. James Bletchley, from the local hospital; DC Kathy Proctor of the domestic violence unit; and Michael Groves, a rather shaggy-looking social worker. Maggie realized she was the only "victim" on the program. Well, so be it. She could tell them what it was like to be on the receiving end.

They all introduced themselves and then a sort of nervous silence fell over the room, broken only when the poodle emitted a short yap at the entry of the producer, there to check that everyone was present and accounted for. For the remainder of the wait, Maggie chatted briefly with her fellow guests about things in general and watched the hubbub as people came and went and shouted questions at each other in the corridors outside. Like the other TV studio she had been in, this one also seemed to be in a state of perpetual chaos.

There was a monitor in the room, and they were able to watch the show's opening, the light banter of David and Emma and a recap of the day's main local news stories, including the death of a revered councillor, a proposed new roundabout for the city center and a "neighbors from hell" story from the Poplar estate. During the commercial break after the poodle groomer, a set worker got them all in position on the armchairs and sofas, designed to give the feel of a cozy, intimate living room, complete with fake fireplace, wired up their mikes and disappeared. David Hartford made himself comfortable, in a position where he could see the guests without having to move too much, and where the cameras would show him to best advantage.

The silent countdown came to an end, David Hartford straightened his tie and put on his best smile, and they were off. Close up, Maggie thought, David's skin looked like pink plastic, and she imagined it would feel like a child's doll to the touch. His hair was also too impossibly black to be natural.

As soon as David started his introduction to the subject, he swapped his smile for a serious, concerned expression and turned first to Kathy, the policewoman, for a general idea of how many domestic complaints they got and how they dealt with them. After that, it was the social worker's, Michael's, turn to talk about women's shelters. When David turned to Maggie for the first time, she felt her heart lurch in her chest. He was handsome in a TV-host sort of way, but there was something about him that unnerved her. He didn't seem interested in the problems and the issues, but more in making something dramatically appealing out of it all, of which he was the focus. She supposed that was what television was all about when you came right down to it—making things dramatic and making presenters look good, but still it disturbed her.

He asked her when she first knew there was something wrong, and she briefly detailed the signs, the unreasonable demands, flashes of anger, petty punishments and, finally, the blows, right up to the time Bill broke her jaw, knocked out two of her teeth and put her in hospital for a week.

When Maggie had finished, he turned to the next question on his sheet: "Why didn't you leave? I mean, you've just said you put up with this physical abuse for . . . how long . . . nearly two years? You're clearly an intelligent and resourceful woman. Why didn't you just get out?"

As Maggie sought the words to express why it didn't happen as simply as that, the social worker cut in and explained how easy it was for women to get trapped in the cycle of violence and how the shame often prevented them from speaking out. Finally, Maggie found her voice.

"You're right," she said to David. "I could have left. As you say, I'm an intelligent and resourceful woman. I had a good job, good friends, a supportive family. I suppose part of it was that I thought it would go away, that we would work through it. I still loved my husband. Marriage wasn't something I was going to throw away lightly." She paused, and when nobody else dived into the silence, said, "Besides, it wouldn't have made any difference. Even after I did leave, he found me, stalked me, harassed me, assaulted me again. Even after the court order."

This prompted David to go back to the policewoman and talk about how ineffective the courts were in protecting women at risk from abusive spouses, and Maggie had the chance to take stock of what she had said. She hadn't done too badly, she decided. It was hot under the studio lights and she felt her brow moisten with sweat. She hoped it wouldn't rinse away the makeup.

Next David turned to the doctor.

"Is domestic violence specifically directed from men to women, Dr. Bletchley?" he asked.

"There are some cases of husbands being physically abused by their wives," said the doctor, "but relatively few."

"I think you'll find, statistically," Michael butted in, "that male violence against women by far outstrips women's against men, almost enough to make female violence against men seem insignificant. It's built into our culture. Men hunt down and kill their ex-partners, for example, or commit familial massacres in a way that women do not."

"But that aside," David asked next, "don't you think sometimes, that a woman might overreact and ruin a man's life? I mean, once such accusations have been made, they are often very difficult to shake off, even if a court finds the person not guilty."

"But isn't it worth the risk," Maggie argued, "if it saves the ones who really need saving?"

David smirked. "Well, that's rather like saying what's hanging a few innocent people matter as long as we get the guilty ones, too, isn't it?"

"Nobody intentionally set out to hang innocent people," Kathy pointed out.

"But, say, if a man retaliates in the face of extreme provocation," David pressed on, "isn't the woman still far more likely to be seen as the victim?"

"She *is* the victim," Maggie said.

"That's like saying she asked for it," Michael added. "Just what kind of provocation justifies violence?"

"Are there not also women who actually like it rough?"

"Oh, don't be absurd," said Michael. "That's the same sort of thing as suggesting that women ask to be raped by the way they dress."

"But there *are* masochistic personalities, aren't there, Doctor?"

"You're talking about women who like their sex rough, yes?" said the doctor.

David seemed a little embarrassed by the directness of the question—clearly he was a man used to asking, not answering—but he nodded.

Dr. Bletchley stroked his beard before answering. "Well, to answer your question simply: Yes, there are masochistic women, just as there are masochistic men, but you have to understand that we're dealing with a very tiny fragment of society here and not that section of society concerned with domestic violence."

Obviously glad to be done with this line of questioning, David moved on to his next question, phrasing it carefully for

Maggie. "You've recently had some involvement with what's become rather a cause célèbre involving domestic abuse. Now, while we can't discuss the case directly for legal reasons, is there anything you *can* tell us about that situation?"

He looked hungry for an answer, Maggie thought. "Someone confided in me," she said. "Confided that she was being abused by her husband. I offered advice, as much help and support as I could give."

"But you didn't report it to the authorities."

"It wasn't my place to do that."

"What do you think of that, DC Proctor?"

"She's right. There's nothing we can do until the persons themselves report the matter."

"Or until things come to a head, as they did in this instance?"

"Yes. That's often the unfortunate result of the way things work."

"Thank you very much," David said, about to wrap things up.

Maggie realized she had weakened at the end, got sidetracked, so she launched in, interrupting him, and said, "If I might add just one more thing, it's that victims are not always treated with the care, respect and tenderness we all think they deserve. Right now, there's a young woman in the cells in Eastvale, a woman who until this morning was in hospital with injuries she sustained when her husband beat her last weekend. Why is this woman being persecuted like this?"

"Do you have an answer?" Dave asked. He was obviously pissed off at the interruption but excited by the possibility of controversy.

"I think it's because her husband's dead," Maggie said. "They think he killed some young girls, but he's dead, and they can't exact their pound of flesh. That's why they're picking on her. That's why they're picking on Lucy."

"Thank you very much," David said, turning to the camera and bringing out his smile again. "That just about wraps things up . . ."

There was silence when the program ended and the technician removed their mikes, then the policewoman went over to Maggie and said, "I think it was extremely ill-advised of you to say what you did back there."

"Oh, leave her alone," said Michael. "It's about time someone spoke out about it."

The doctor had already left, and David and Emma were nowhere to be seen.

"Fancy a drink?" said Michael to Maggie as they left the studio after having their makeup removed, but she shook her head. All she wanted to do was get a taxi home and climb into a nice warm bath with a good book. It might be the last bit of peace and quiet she got if there was a reaction to what she had said tonight. She didn't think she had broken any laws. After all, she hadn't said Terry was guilty of the killings, hadn't even mentioned his name, but she was also certain that the police could find something to charge her with if they wanted to. They seemed to be good at that. And she wouldn't put it past Banks at all. Let them do it, she thought. Just let them make a martyr of her.

"Are you sure? Just a quick one."

She looked at Michael and knew that all he wanted to do was probe her for more details. "No," she said. "Thank you very much for the offer, but no. I'm going home."

Chapter 13

*B*anks found chaos outside Western Divisional Headquarters early Saturday morning. Even at the back, where the
entrance to the car park was located, reporters and camera-
wielding television news teams pushed against one another
and shouted out questions about Lucy Payne. Banks cursed to
himself, turned off the Dylan CD halfway through "Not Dark
Yet" and edged his way carefully but firmly through the throng.

Inside, things were quieter. Banks slipped into his office
and looked out of the window over the market square. More
reporters. TV station vans with satellite dishes. The works.
Someone had well and truly let the cat out of the bag. First,
Banks walked into the detectives' squad room looking for answers. DCs Jackman and Templeton were at their desks, and
Annie Cabbot was bending over the low drawer in the filing
cabinet, a heartwarming sight in her tight black jeans, Banks
thought, remembering they had a date that night. Dinner,
video and . . .

"What the hell's going on out there?" he asked the room in
general.

Annie looked up. "Don't you know?"

"Know what?"

"Didn't you *see* her?"

"What are you talking about?"

Kevin Templeton and Winsome Jackman kept their heads down, leaving this one well alone.

Annie put her hands on her hips. "Last night, on the television."

"I was over in Withernsea interviewing a retired copper about Lucy Payne. What did I miss?"

Annie walked over to her desk and rested her hip against the edge. "The neighbor, Maggie Forrest, was involved in a television discussion about domestic violence."

"Oh, shit."

"Indeed. She ended up by accusing us of persecuting Lucy Payne because we can't wreak our revenge on her husband, and she informed the viewers in general that Lucy was being detained here."

"Julia Ford," Banks whispered.

"Who?"

"The lawyer. I'll bet she's the one told Maggie where we were holding Lucy. Christ, what a mess."

"Oh, by the way," Annie said with a smile, "AC Hartnell's already phoned twice. Asked if you'd ring him as soon as you get in."

Banks headed for his office. Before phoning Phil Hartnell, he opened his window as wide as it would go and lit a cigarette. Bugger the rules; it was shaping up to be one of those days, and it had only just begun. Banks should have known Maggie Forrest was a loose cannon, that his warning might well just egg her on to more foolish behavior. But what else could he do about her? Not much, apparently. She hadn't committed a criminal offense, and certainly there was nothing to be gained by going around and telling her off again. Still, if he did happen to see her for any reason, he'd give her a piece of his mind. She had no idea what she was playing with.

When he calmed down, he sat at his desk and reached for

the phone, but it rang before he could pick it up and dial Hartnell's number.

"Alan? Stefan here."

"I hope you've got some good news for me, Stefan, because the way this morning's going I could do with some."

"That bad?"

"Getting that way."

"Maybe this'll cheer you up, then. I just got the DNA comparison in from the lab."

"And?"

"A match. Terence Payne was your Seacroft Rapist, all right."

Banks slapped the desk. "Excellent. Anything else?"

"Only minor points. The lads going through all the documents and bills taken from the house have found no evidence of sleeping tablets prescribed for either Terence or Lucy Payne, and they didn't find any illegal ones, either."

"As I thought."

"They did find an electronics catalog, though, from one of those places that put you on their mailing list when you buy something from them."

"What did they buy?"

"There's no record of their buying anything on their credit cards, but we'll approach the company and get someone to go through the purchases, see if they used cash. And another thing: There were some marks on the floor of the cellar that on further investigation look rather like those a tripod would make. I've talked with Luke and he didn't use a tripod, so—"

"Someone else did."

"Looks that way."

"Then where the hell is it?"

"No idea."

"Okay, Stefan, thanks for the good news. Keep looking."

"Will do."

As soon as he'd hung up, Banks dialed Hartnell's number.
The man himself answered on the second ring.

"Area Commander Hartnell."

"It's Alan," said Banks. "Heard you've been trying to get
in touch with me."

"Did you see it?"

"No. I've only just found out. The place is swarming with
media."

"Surprise, surprise. The stupid woman. What's the situation with Lucy Payne?"

"I talked to her yesterday, got nowhere."

"Any more evidence?"

"Not evidence, as such." Banks told him about the
Seacroft Rapist DNA match, the possibility of a camcorder
still being hidden somewhere on the Paynes' property, and
his talk with George Woodward about the satanic paraphernalia in Alderthorpe and the ligature strangulation of Kathleen Murray.

"It's nothing," said Hartnell. "Certainly not evidence
against Lucy Payne. For Christ's sake, Alan, she was a victim
of the most appalling abuse. I remember that Alderthorpe
case. We don't want all that raked up. Think what it will look
like if we start suggesting she killed her own bloody cousin
when she was only twelve."

"I thought I might use it to push her a bit, see where she
goes."

"You know as well as I do that blood and fibers aren't
enough, and as far as evidence goes, they're all we've got.
This speculation about her past will do nothing but gain her
more sympathy from the public."

"There are probably as many people outraged by the
crimes and thinking maybe she had more to do with them
than she admits."

"Probably, but they're nowhere near as vocal as the people

who've already been phoning Millgarth, believe me. Cut her loose, Alan."

"But—"

"We caught our killer and he's dead. Let her go. We can't hold her any longer."

Banks looked at his watch. "We've still got four hours. Something might turn up."

"Nothing will turn up in the next four hours, believe me. Release her."

"What about surveillance?"

"Too bloody expensive. Tell the local police to keep an eye on her, and tell her to stick around; we might want to talk to her again."

"If she's guilty, she'll disappear."

"If she's guilty we'll find the evidence and then we'll find her."

"Let me have one more shot at her first." Banks held his breath as Hartnell paused at the other end.

"All right. Talk to her one more time. If she doesn't confess, let her go. But be bloody careful. I don't want any allegations of Gestapo interrogation tactics."

Banks heard a knock at his door, put his hand over the mouthpiece and called out, "Come in."

Julia Ford entered and gave him a broad smile.

"No worry on that score, sir," Banks said to Hartnell. "Her lawyer will be present at all times."

"Quite the zoo out there, isn't it?" Julia Ford said after Banks had hung up. The fine lines around her eyes crinkled when she smiled. She was wearing a different suit this morning—gray with a pearl blouse—but it looked every bit as business-like. Her hair looked shiny, as if fresh from the shower, and she had applied just enough makeup to take a few years off her age.

"Yes," Banks answered. "Looks as if someone tipped the entire British media off about Lucy's whereabouts."

"Are you going to let her go?"

"Soon. I want another chat first."

Julia sighed and opened the door for him. "Ah, well. Once more unto the breach."

Hull and beyond were parts of Yorkshire Jenny hardly knew at all. On her map there was a tiny village called Kilnsea right at the southern tip of land where the Humber joined the North Sea, just before a thin strip called Spurn Head, designated as a heritage coast, stuck out into the sea like a witch's crooked, wizened finger. It looked so desolate out there that Jenny shuddered just looking at the map, feeling the ceaseless cold wind and the biting salt spray she imagined were all one would find there.

Was it named Spurn Head because someone was spurned there once, she wondered, and her ghost lingered, walking the sands and wailing in the night, or because "spurn" was a corruption of "sperm" and it looked a bit like a sperm wiggling out to sea? It was probably something much more prosaic, like "peninsula" in Viking. Jenny wondered if anybody ever went there. Birders, perhaps; they were crazy enough to go anywhere in search of the elusive lesser-speckled yellow tree warbler, or some such creature. It didn't look as if there were any holiday resorts in the region, except perhaps Withernsea, which Banks had visited yesterday. All the hot spots were much farther north: Bridlington, Filey, Scarborough, Whitby, all the way up to Saltburn and Redcar, in Teeside.

It was a fine day: windy, but sunny with only an occasional high white cloud passing over. It wasn't exactly warm—definitely light-jacket weather—but then it wasn't freezing, either. Jenny seemed to be the only car on the road beyond Patrington, where she stopped briefly for a cup of coffee and a look at St. Patrick's Church, reputed to be one of the finest village churches in England.

It was desolate country, mostly flat farmland, green fields and the occasional flash of bright yellow rapeseed. What villages she passed through were no more than mean assemblages of bungalows and the odd row of redbrick terraces. Soon, the surrealistic landscape of the North Sea Gas Terminal, with its twisted metal pipes and storage units, came into view, and Jenny headed up the coast toward Alderthorpe.

She had been thinking about Banks quite a lot during her journey and came to the conclusion that he wasn't happy. She didn't know why. Apart from Sandra's pregnancy, which was obviously upsetting to him for any number of reasons, he had everything to be thankful for. For a start, his career was back on track, and he had an attractive young girlfriend. At least she assumed that Annie was attractive.

But perhaps it was Annie who was making Banks unhappy? He had never seemed quite certain of their relationship whenever Jenny had questioned him. She had assumed that was mostly due to his innate evasiveness when it came to personal and emotional matters—like most men—but perhaps he was genuinely confused.

Not that she could do anything. She remembered how disappointed she had felt last year when he had accepted her dinner invitation and failed to turn up, or even phone. Jenny had sat there in her most seductive silky outfit, duck à l'orange in the oven, ready to take a risk again, and waited and waited. At last he had phoned. He'd been called to a hostage situation. Well, it was definitely a good excuse, but it didn't do much to dispel her sense of disappointment and loss. Since then, they had been more circumspect with each other, neither willing to risk making an arrangement in case it got screwed up, but still she fretted about Banks and still, she admitted to herself, she wanted him.

The flat, desolate landscape went on and on. How on earth could anybody live in such a remote and backward spot? Jenny wondered. She saw the sign pointing east—ALDERTHORPE 1/2 MILE—and set off down the narrow unpaved track hoping to hell there was no one coming the other way. Still, the landscape was so open—hardly a tree in sight—that she could easily see someone coming from a long way away.

The half-mile seemed to go on forever, as short distances often do on country roads. Then she saw a huddle of houses ahead, and she could smell the sea through her open window, though she couldn't see it yet. When she found herself turning left on to a paved street with bungalows on one side and rows of redbrick terrace houses on the other, she realized this must be Alderthorpe. She saw a small post office-cum–general store with a rack of newspapers fluttering in the breeze, a greengrocer's and a butcher's, a squat gospel hall and a mean-looking pub called the Lord Nelson, and that was it.

Jenny pulled up behind a blue Citroën outside the post office and when she got out of the car she thought she could see curtains twitching over the road, feel curious eyes on her back as she opened the post-office door. *No one comes here,* she imagined the people thinking. *What could she possibly want?* Jenny felt as if she had walked into one of those lost-village stories, the place that time forgot, and she had the illogical sense that by walking into it she was lost too, and all memory of her in the real world was gone. Silly fool, she told herself, but she shivered, and it wasn't cold.

The bell pinged above her head, and she found herself in the kind of shop that she guessed had ceased to exist even before she was born, where jars of barley sugar rubbed shoulders with shoelaces and patent medicines on high shelves, and birthday cards stood on a rack next to the half-inch nails and tins of evaporated milk. It smelled both musty and fruity—pear drops, Jenny thought—and the light that filtered in from the street was dim and cast strips of shadow on the sales counter. There was a small post-office wicket, and the woman standing there in a threadbare brown coat turned and stared at Jenny when she entered. The postmistress herself peered around her customer and adjusted her glasses. They had clearly been having a good natter and were none too thrilled at being interrupted.

"Can I help you?" the postmistress asked.

"I wondered if you could tell me where the old Murray and Godwin houses are," Jenny asked.

"Why would you be wanting to know that?"

"It's to do with a job I'm doing."

"Newspaper reporter, are you?"

"As a matter of fact, no. I'm a forensic psychologist."

This stopped the woman in her tracks. "It's Spurn Lane you want. Just over the street and down the lane to the sea. Last two semis. You can't miss them. Nobody's lived there for years."

"Do you know if any of the children still live around here?"

"I've not seen hide nor hair of any of 'em since it happened."

"What about the teacher, Maureen Nesbitt?"

"Lives in Easington. There's no school here."

"Thank you very much."

As she left, she heard the customer whisper, "Forensic psychologist? Whatever's that when it's at home?"

"Sightseer," muttered the postmistress. "Ghoul, just like all the rest. Anyway, you were saying about Mary Wallace's husband . . ."

Jenny wondered how they would react when the media descended en masse, which they surely would do before long. It's not often a place such as Alderthorpe sees fame more than once in a lifetime.

She crossed the High Street, still feeling as if she were being watched, and found the unpaved lane that led east to the

North Sea. Though there was a chill in the wind, the cloudless sky was such a bright piercing blue that she put on her sunglasses, remembering with a flutter of anger the day she bought them on Santa Monica Pier, with Randy, the two-timing bastard.

There were about five or six bungalows on each side of Spurn Lane near the High Street, but about fifty yards along, there was only rough ground. Jenny could see two dirty brick semis another fifty yards beyond that. They were certainly isolated from the village, which itself was isolated enough to begin with. She imagined that once the reporters and the television cameras had gone ten years ago, the silence and loneliness and sense of grief must have been devastating for the community, the questions and accusations screaming out loud in the air. Even the residents around The Hill, part of a suburb of a large, modern city, would be struggling to understand what had happened there for years, and many of the residents would need counseling. Jenny could only imagine what Alderthorpe folk probably thought of counseling.

As she approached the houses, she became more and more aware of the salt smell of the sea breeze and realized that it was out there, only yards away beyond the low dunes and marram grass. Villages along this coast had disappeared into the sea, Jenny had read; the sandy coastline was always shifting, and maybe in ten or twenty years' time Alderthorpe would have vanished underwater, too. It was a spooky thought.

The houses were beyond repair. The roofs had caved in and the broken windows and doors were boarded up. Here and there, people had spray-painted graffiti: ROT IN HELL, BRING BACK HANGING and the simple, touching, KATHLEEN: WE WILL NOT FORGET. Jenny found herself oddly moved as she stood there playing the voyeur.

The gardens were overgrown with weeds and shrubs, but

she could make her way through the tangled undergrowth closer to the buildings. There wasn't much to see, and the doors had been so securely boarded up that she couldn't get inside even if she wanted to. In there, she told herself, Lucy Payne and six other children had been terrorized, raped, humiliated, tormented and tortured for God knew how many years before the death of one of them—Kathleen Murray—led the authorities to the door. Now the place was just a silent ruin. Jenny felt like a bit of a fraud standing there, the way she had in the cellar of The Hill. What could she possibly do or say to make sense of the horrors that had occurred here? Her science, like all the rest, was inadequate.

Even so, she stood there for some time, then she walked around the buildings, noting that the back gardens were even more overgrown than the front. An empty clothesline hung suspended between two rusty poles in one of the gardens.

As she was leaving, Jenny almost tripped over something in the undergrowth. At first she thought it was a root, but when she bent down and pulled aside the leaves and twigs, she saw a small teddy bear. It looked so disheveled it could have been out there for years, could even have belonged to one of the Alderthorpe Seven, though Jenny doubted it. The police or the social services would have taken everything like that away, so it had probably been left as a sort of tribute later by a local child. When she picked it up it felt soggy, and a beetle crawled out from a rip in its back on to her hand. Jenny let out a sharp gasp, dropped the teddy bear and headed quickly back to the village. She had intended to knock on a few doors and ask about the Godwins and the Murrays, but Alderthorpe had spooked her so much that she decided instead to head for Easington to talk to Maureen Nesbitt.

"Right, Lucy. Shall we start?"

Banks had turned on the tape recorders and tested them.

This time they were in a slightly bigger and more salubrious interview room. In addition to Lucy and Julia Ford, Banks had invited DC Jackman along too, though it wasn't her case, mostly to get her impressions of Lucy afterward.

"I suppose so," Lucy said in a resigned, sulky voice. She looked tired and shaken by her night in the cell, Banks thought, even though the cells were the most modern part of the station. The duty officer said she'd asked to have the light left on all night, so she couldn't have slept much.

"I hope you were comfortable last night," he asked.

"What do you care?"

"It's not my intention to cause you discomfort, Lucy."

"Don't worry about me. I'm fine."

Julia Ford tapped her watch. "Can we get on with this, Superintendent Banks?"

Banks paused, then looked at Lucy. "Let's talk a bit more about your background, shall we?"

"What's that got to do with anything?" Julia Ford butted in.

"If you'll allow me to ask my questions, you might find out."

"If it distresses my client—"

"*Distresses your client!* The parents of five young girls are more than distressed."

"That's irrelevant," said Julia. "It's nothing to do with Lucy."

Banks ignored the lawyer and turned back to Lucy, who seemed disinterested by the discussion. "Will you describe the cellar at Alderthorpe for me, Lucy?"

"The cellar?"

"Yes. Don't you remember it?"

"It was just a cellar," Lucy said. "Dark and cold."

"Was there anything else down there?"

"I don't know. What?"

"Black candles, incense, a pentagram, robes. Wasn't there a lot of dancing and chanting down there, Lucy?"

Lucy closed her eyes. "I don't remember. That wasn't me. That was Linda."

"Oh, come on, Lucy. You can do better than that. Why is it that whenever we come to something you don't want to talk about, you always conveniently lose your memory?"

"Superintendent," Julia Ford said. "Remember my client has suffered retrograde amnesia due to post-traumatic shock."

"Yes, yes, I remember. Impressive words." Banks turned back to Lucy. "You don't remember going into the cellar at The Hill, and you don't remember the dancing and chanting in the cellar at Alderthorpe. Do you remember the cage?"

Lucy seemed to draw in on herself.

"Do you?" Banks persisted. "The old Morrison shelter."

"I remember it," Lucy whispered. "It was where they put us when we were bad."

"How were you bad, Lucy?"

"I don't understand."

"Why were you in the cage when the police came? You and Tom. What had you done to get yourselves put there?"

"I don't know. It was never much. You never had to do much. If you didn't clean your plate—not that there was ever much on it to clean—or if you talked back or said no when they . . . when they wanted to . . . It was easy to get locked in the cage."

"Do you remember Kathleen Murray?"

"I remember Kathleen. She was my cousin."

"What happened to her?"

"They killed her."

"Who did?"

"The grown-ups."

"Why did they kill her?"

"I don't know. They just . . . she just died . . ."

"They said your brother Tom killed her."

"That's ridiculous. Tom wouldn't kill anybody. Tom's gentle."

"Do you remember how it happened?"

"I wasn't there. Just one day they told us Kathleen had gone away and she wouldn't be coming back. I knew she was dead."

"How did you know?"

"I just knew. She cried all the time, she said she was going to tell. They always said they'd kill any of us if they thought we were going to tell."

"Kathleen was strangled, Lucy."

"Was she?"

"Yes. Just like the girls we found in your cellar. Ligature strangulation. Remember, those yellow fibers we found under your fingernails, along with Kimberley's blood."

"Where are you going with this, Superintendent?" Julia Ford asked.

"There are a lot of similarities between the crimes. That's all."

"But surely the killers of Kathleen Murray are behind bars?" Julia argued. "It's got nothing to do with Lucy."

"She was involved."

"She was a victim."

"Always the victim, eh, Lucy? The victim with the bad memory. How does it feel?"

"That's enough," said Julia.

"It feels awful," Lucy said in a small voice.

"What?"

"You asked how it feels, to be a victim with a bad memory. It feels awful. It feels like I have no self, like I'm lost, I have no control, like I don't count. I can't even remember the *bad* things that happened to me."

"Let me ask you once more, Lucy: Did you ever help your husband to abduct a young girl?"

"No, I didn't."

"Did you ever harm any of the girls he brought home?"

"I never knew about them, not until last week."

"Why did you get up and go down in the cellar on that particular night? Why not on any of the previous occasions when your husband was *entertaining* a young girl in the cellar of your house?"

"I never heard anything before. He must have drugged me."

"We found no sleeping tablets in our search of the house, nor do either of you have a prescription for any."

"He must have got them illegally. He must have run out. That's why I woke up."

"Where would he get them?"

"School. There's all sorts of drugs in schools."

"Lucy, did you know that your husband was a rapist when you met him?"

"Did I . . . what?"

"You heard me." Banks opened the file in front of him. "By our count he had already raped four women we know of before he met you at that pub in Seacroft. Terence Payne was the Seacroft Rapist. His DNA matches that left in the victims."

"I—I—"

"You don't know what to say?"

"No."

"How did you meet him, Lucy? None of your friends remember seeing you talk to him in the pub that night."

"I told you. I was on my way out. It was a big pub, with lots of rooms. We went into another bar."

"Why should you be any different, Lucy?"

"I don't know what you mean."

"I mean, why didn't he follow you out into the street and rape you like he did with the others?"

"I don't know. How should I know?"

"You've got to admit it's strange, though, isn't it?"

"I told you, I don't know. He liked me. Loved me."

"Yet he still continued to rape other young women *after* he'd met you." Banks consulted his file again. "At least two more times, according to our account. And they're only the ones who reported it. Some women don't report it, you know. Too upset or too ashamed. See, they blame themselves." Banks thought of Annie Cabbot, and what she'd been through over two years ago.

"What's that got to do with me?"

"Why didn't he rape *you?*"

Lucy gave him an unfathomable look. "Maybe he did."

"Don't be absurd. No woman likes being raped, and she's certainly not going to marry her rapist."

"You'd be surprised what you can get used to if you've got no choice."

"What do you mean, no choice?"

"What I say."

"It was your choice to marry Terry, wasn't it? Nobody forced you to."

"That's not what I mean."

"Then what do you mean?"

"Never mind."

"Come on."

"Never mind."

Banks shuffled his papers. "What was it, Lucy? Did he tell you about what he'd done? Did it excite you? Did he recognize a kindred spirit? Your Hindley to his Brady?"

Julia Ford shot to her feet. "That's *enough,* Superintendent. One more remark like that and this interview's over and I'll be reporting you."

Banks ran his hand over his closely cropped hair. It felt spiky.

Winsome picked up the questioning. "*Did* he rape you, Lucy?" she asked, in her lilting Jamaican accent. "Did your husband rape you?"

Lucy turned to look at Winsome and seemed to Banks to be calculating how to deal with this new factor in the equation.

"Of course not. I would never have married a rapist."

"So you didn't know about him?"

"Of course I didn't."

"Didn't you find *anything* odd about Terry? I mean, I never knew him, but it sounds to me as if there's enough there to give a person cause for concern."

"He could be very charming."

"Did he do or say *nothing* to make you suspicious in all the time you were together?"

"No."

"But, somehow, you ended up married to a man who was not only a rapist but also an abductor and murderer of young girls. How can you explain that, Lucy? You've got to admit it's highly unusual, hard to believe."

"I can't help that. And I can't explain it. That's just how it happened."

"Did he like to play games, sexual games?"

"Like what?"

"Did he like tying you up? Did he like to *pretend* he was raping you?"

"We didn't do anything like that."

Winsome gave Banks a signal to take over again, and her look mirrored his feelings; they were getting nowhere, and Lucy Payne was probably lying.

"Where's the camcorder?" Banks asked.

"I don't know what you're talking about."

"We found evidence in the cellar. A camcorder had been set up at the end of the bed. I think you liked to video what you were doing to the girls."

"I didn't do anything to them. I've told you, I didn't go down there, except maybe the once. I know nothing about any camcorder."

"You never saw your husband with one?"

"No."

"He never showed you any videos?"

"Only rented or borrowed ones."

"We think we know where he bought the camcorder, Lucy. We can check."

"Go ahead. I never saw one, never knew about any such thing."

Banks paused and changed tack. "You say you didn't play sexual games, Lucy, so what made you decide to dress up and act like a prostitute?" Banks asked.

"What?"

"Don't you remember?"

"Yes, but that wasn't it. I mean, I didn't . . . I wasn't on the *street* or anything. Who told you that?"

"Never mind. Did you pick up a man in a hotel bar for sex?"

"What if I did? It was just a lark, a dare."

"So you did like games."

"This was before I knew Terry."

"So that makes it all right?"

"I'm not saying that. It was a lark, that's all."

"What happened?"

Lucy gave a sly smile. "Same as happened often enough if I let myself get chatted up in a pub. Only this time I got paid two hundred pounds. Like I said, it was a lark, that's all. Are you going to arrest me for prostitution?"

"Some lark," said Banks.

Julia Ford looked a bit perplexed by the exchange, but she said nothing.

Banks knew they were still going nowhere. Hartnell was right: they had no real evidence against Lucy beyond the extreme weirdness of her relationship with Payne and the tiny bloodstains and rope fibers. Her answers might not make a lot of sense, but unless she confessed to aiding and abetting her husband in his murders, she was in the clear. He looked at her again. The bruises had almost faded to nothing and she looked quite innocent and lovely with her pale skin and long black hair, almost like a Madonna. The only thing that made Banks persist in his belief that there was far more to events than she would ever care to admit was her eyes: black, reflective, impermeable. He got the impression that if you stared into eyes like hers for too long you'd go mad. But that wasn't evidence; that was an overactive imagination. All of a sudden, he'd had enough. Surprising all three of them, he stood up so abruptly he almost knocked over his chair, said, "You're free to go now, Lucy. Just don't go too far," and hurried out of the interview room.

Easington was a pleasant change from Alderthorpe, Jenny thought as she parked her car near the pub at the center of the village. Though still almost as remote from civilization, it seemed at least to be connected, to be a part of things in a way that Alderthorpe didn't.

Jenny found Maureen Nesbitt's address easily enough from the barmaid and soon found herself on the doorstep facing a suspicious woman with long white hair tied back in a blue ribbon, wearing a fawn cardigan and black slacks a little too tight for someone with such ample hips and thighs.

"Who are you? What do you want?"

"I'm a psychologist," said Jenny. "I want to talk to you about what happened in Alderthorpe."

Maureen Nesbitt looked up and down the street, then turned back to face Jenny. "Are you sure you're not a reporter?"

"I'm not a reporter."

"Because they were all over me when it happened, but I told them nothing. Scavengers." She pulled her cardie tighter over her chest.

"I'm not a reporter," Jenny repeated, digging deep into her handbag for some sort of identification. The best she could come up with was her university library card. At least it identified her as Dr. Fuller and as a member of the staff. Maureen scrutinized the card, clearly unhappy it didn't also bear a photograph, then she finally let Jenny in. Once inside, her manner changed completely, from grand inquisitor to gracious host, insisting on brewing a fresh pot of tea. The living room was small but comfortable, with only a couple of armchairs, a mirror above the fireplace and a glass-fronted cabinet full of beautiful crystal ware. Beside one of the armchairs was a small table, and on it lay a paperback of *Great Expectations* next to a half-full cup of milky tea. Jenny sat in the other chair.

When Maureen brought through the tray, including a plate of digestive biscuits, she said, "I do apologize for my behavior earlier. It's just that I've learned the hard way over the years. A little notoriety can quite change your life, you know."

"Are you still teaching?"

"No. I retired three years ago." She tapped the paperback. "I promised myself that when I retired I would reread all my favorite classics." She sat down. "We'll just let the tea mash for a few minutes, shall we? I suppose you're here about Lucy Payne?"

"You know?"

"I've tried to keep up with them all over the years. I know that Lucy—Linda, as she was back then—lived with a couple called Liversedge near Hull, and then she got a job at a bank and went to live in Leeds, where she married Terence Payne. Last I heard this lunchtime was that the police just let her go for lack of evidence."

Even Jenny hadn't heard that yet, but then she hadn't listened to the news that day. "How do you know all this?" she asked.

"My sister works for the social services in Hull. You won't tell, will you?"

"Cross my heart."

"So what do you want to know?"

"What were your impressions of Lucy?"

"She was a bright girl. Very bright. But easily bored, easily distracted. She was headstrong, stubborn, and once she'd made her mind up you couldn't budge her. Of course, you have to remember that she'd gone on to the local comprehensive at the time of the arrests. I only taught junior school. She was with us until she was eleven."

"But the others were still there?"

"Yes. All of them. It's not as if there's a lot of choice when it comes to local schools."

"I imagine not. Anything else you can remember about Lucy?"

"Not really."

"Did she form any close friendships outside the immediate family?"

"None of them did. That was one of the odd things. They were a mysterious group, and sometimes when you saw them together it gave you a creepy feeling, as if they had their own language and an agenda you knew nothing about. Have you ever read John Wyndham?"

"No."

"You should. He's quite good. For a science-fiction writer, that is. Believe it or not, I encouraged my pupils to read just about anything they enjoyed, so long as they read something. Anyway, Wyndham wrote a book called *The Midwich Cuckoos* about a group of strange children fathered by aliens on an unsuspecting village."

"That sounds vaguely familiar," Jenny said.

"Perhaps you saw the film? It was called *Village of the Damned*."

"That's it," said Jenny. "That one where the teacher planted a bomb to destroy the children and had to concentrate on a brick wall so they couldn't read his thoughts?"

"Yes. Well, it wasn't quite like that with the Godwins and the Murrays, but it still gave you that sort of feeling, the way they looked at you, waited in the corridor till you'd gone by before talking again. And they always seemed to speak in whispers. Linda, I remember, was very distressed when she had to leave and go to the comprehensive before the others, but I gather from her teacher there that she quickly got used to it. She has a strong personality, that girl, despite what happened to her, and she's adaptable."

"Did she show any unusual preoccupations?"

"What do you mean?"

"Anything particularly morbid. Death? Mutilation?"

"Not so far as I noticed. She was . . . how shall I put this . . . an early developer and rather sexually aware for a girl of her age. On average, girls peak in puberty at about twelve, but Lucy was beyond prepubescence at eleven. Her breasts were developing, for example."

"Sexually active?"

"No. Well, as we now know she was being sexually abused in the home. But, no, not in the way you're suggesting. She was just sexually *there*. It was something people noticed about her, and she wasn't above playing the little coquette."

"I see." Jenny made a note. "And it was Kathleen's absence that led you to call in the authorities?"

"Yes." Maureen looked away, toward the window, but she didn't look as if she were admiring the view. "Not my finest moment," she said, bending to pour the tea. "Milk and sugar?"

"Yes, please. Thank you. Why?"

"I should have done something sooner, shouldn't I? It wasn't the first time I'd had my suspicions something was terribly wrong in those households. Though I never saw any bruises or clear outward signs of abuse, the children often looked undernourished and seemed timid. Sometimes—I know this is terrible—but they smelled, as if they hadn't bathed in days. Other children would stay away from them. They'd jump if you touched them, no matter how gently. I should have known."

"What did you do?"

"Well, I talked with the other teachers, and we all agreed there was something odd about the children's behavior. It turned out the social services already had their concerns, too. They'd been out to the houses once before but never got past the front door. I don't know if you knew, but Michael Godwin had a particularly vicious rottweiler. Anyway, when Kathleen Murray went absent without any reasonable explanation, they decided to act. The rest is history."

"You say you've kept track of the children," Jenny said. "I'd really like to talk to some of them. Will you help me?"

Maureen paused a moment. "If you like. But I don't think you'll get much out of them."

"Do you know where they are, how they are?"

"Not all the details, no, but I can give you a general picture."

Jenny sipped some tea and took out her notebook. "Okay, I'm ready."

Chapter 14

"So what do you think of Lucy Payne?" Banks asked DC Winsome Jackman as they walked along North Market Street on their way to talk to Leanne Wray's parents.

Winsome paused before answering. Banks noticed several people gawk at her as they walked. She knew she was a token minority, she had told Banks when he interviewed her, brought in to fulfill a quota demanded in the aftermath of the Stephen Lawrence case. There were to be more police officers from minorities, the ruling stated, even in communities where those minorities were, to all extent, nonexistent, like West Indians in the Yorkshire Dales. But she also told him she didn't care about the tokenism and she'd do a damn good job anyway. Banks didn't doubt her for a moment. Winsome was ACC McLaughlin's golden girl, set for accelerated promotion and all its blessings; she'd probably be a superintendent before she was thirty-five. And Banks liked her. She was easygoing, had a wicked sense of humor, and she didn't let the race thing get in the way of doing her job, even when other people tried to put it in the way. He knew nothing about her personal life except that she enjoyed both climbing and spelunking—the very thought of which gave Banks a severe case of the heebie-jeebies—and that she lived in a flat on the fringe of the Eastvale student area. Whether she had a boyfriend, or a girlfriend, Banks had no idea.

"I think she might have been protecting her husband," Winsome said. "She knew, or she suspected, and she kept quiet. Maybe she didn't even admit it to herself."

"Do you think she was involved?"

"I don't know. I don't think so. I think she was attracted to the dark side, especially the sex, but I'd pull up short of assuming she was involved. Weird, yes. But a killer . . . ?"

"Remember, Kathleen Murray died of ligature strangulation," Banks said.

"But Lucy was only twelve then."

"Makes you think, though, doesn't it? Isn't the house just down here?"

"Yes."

They turned off North Market on to a grid of narrow streets opposite the community center, where Sandra used to work. Seeing the place and remembering the times he dropped in on her there or waited to pick her up after work to go to a play or a film made Banks feel a pang of loss, but it passed. Sandra was gone now, far, far away from the wife he used to have.

They found the house, not at all far from the Old Ship— maybe ten or fifteen minutes' walk, and most of it along the busy, well-lit stretch of North Market Street, with its shops and pubs—and Banks knocked at the front door.

The first thing that assailed his senses as Christopher Wray opened the door was the smell of fresh paint. When Banks and Winsome stepped inside, he saw why. The Wrays were redecorating. All the wallpaper in the hallway had been stripped, and Mr. Wray was painting the living-room ceiling cream. The furniture was covered with sheets.

"I'm sorry for the mess," he apologized. "Shall we go in the kitchen? Have you found Leanne yet?"

"No, not yet," said Banks.

They followed him through to the small kitchen, where he put the kettle on without even asking if they wanted a cup of tea. They all sat at the small kitchen table, and for the short time it took the kettle to boil, Mr. Wray chatted on about the redecoration as if determined to avoid the real subject of their visit. Finally, tea made and poured, Banks decided it was time to steer things around to the subject of Leanne.

"I must say," he began, "that we're at a bit of a loss."

"Oh?"

"As you know, our men have been working at the Payne house for days now. They've recovered six bodies, four of which have been identified, but none of the six is your daughter's. They're running out of places to look."

"Does that mean Leanne might still be alive?" Wray asked, a gleam of hope in his eyes.

"It's possible," Banks admitted. "Though I've got to say, after all this time without contact, especially given the nationwide appeals on TV and in the press, I wouldn't hold out a lot of hope."

"Then . . . what?"

"That's what we'd like to find out."

"I don't see how I can help you."

"Perhaps you can't," Banks said, "but the only thing to do when a case is stalled like this is to go right back to first principles. We've got to go over the ground we covered before and hope we see it from a new perspective this time."

Wray's wife, Victoria, appeared in the doorway and looked puzzled to see Banks and Winsome enjoying a chat and a cup of tea with her husband. Wray jumped up. "I thought you were resting, dear," he said, giving her a peck on the cheek.

Victoria wiped the sleep from her eyes, though she looked to Banks as if she had spent at least a few minutes putting on her face before coming down. Her skirt and blouse were pure Harvey Nichols, and her accent was what she thought sounded like upper class, though he could hear traces of Birmingham in it. She was an attractive woman in her early thirties, with a slim figure and a full head of shiny, natural-brown hair that hung over her shoulders. She had a slightly retroussé nose, arched eyebrows and a small mouth, but the effect of the whole was rather more successful than one might imagine from the separate parts. Wray himself was about forty and pretty much medium in whatever category you might describe him, except for the chin, which slid down toward his throat before it even got started. They were an odd couple, Banks remembered thinking from the first time he had met them: he was a rather basic, down-to-earth bus driver, and she was an affected social climber. What had drawn them together in the first place Banks had no idea, except perhaps that people who have suffered a great loss, as Christopher Wray had, might not necessarily be the best judges of their next move.

Victoria stretched, sat down and poured herself a cup of tea.

"How are you feeling?" her husband asked.

"Not bad."

"You know you've got to be careful, in your condition. The doctor said so."

"I know. I know." She squeezed his hand. "I'll be careful."

"What condition's that?" Banks asked.

"My wife's expecting a baby, Superintendent." Wray beamed.

Banks looked at Victoria. "Congratulations," he said.

She inclined her head in a queenly manner. Banks could hardly imagine Victoria Wray going through anything as messy and painful as childbirth, but life was full of surprises.

"How long?" he asked.

She patted her stomach. "Almost four months."

"So you were pregnant when Leanne went missing?"

"Yes. As a matter of fact, I'd just found out that morning."

"What did Leanne think of it?"

Victoria looked down into her teacup. "Leanne could be

willful and moody, Superintendent," she said. "She certainly wasn't quite as ecstatic as we hoped she would be."

"Now, come on, love, that's not fair," said Mr. Wray. "She'd have got used to it in time. I'm certain she would."

Banks thought about the situation: Leanne's mother dies a slow and painful death from cancer. Shortly afterward, her father remarries—to a woman Leanne clearly can't stand. Not long after that, the stepmother announces she's pregnant. You didn't need to be a psychologist to see that there was a situation ripe for disaster. It was a bit close to the bone for Banks, too, though he had hardly been in Leanne's position. Still, whether it's your father having a baby with your new stepmother or your estranged wife having one with the bearded Sean, the resulting feelings could be similar, perhaps even more intense in Leanne's case, given her age and her grief over her mother.

"So she wasn't happy with the news?"

"Not really," Mr. Wray admitted. "But it takes time to get used to things like that."

"You have to be at least willing to try first," said Victoria. "Leanne's too selfish for that."

"Leanne was willing," Mr. Wray insisted.

"When did you tell her?" Banks asked.

"The morning of the day she disappeared."

He sighed. "Why didn't you tell us this when we interviewed you after Leanne's disappearance?"

Mr. Wray looked surprised. "Nobody asked. It didn't seem important. I mean, it was a private family matter."

"Besides," said Victoria, "it's bad luck to tell strangers until after three months."

Were they really so thick or were they just playing at it? Banks wondered. Trying to keep his tone as calm and neutral as possible, reminding himself that they were the parents of a missing girl, he asked, "What did she say?"

The Wrays looked at each other. "Say? Nothing, really, did she, dear?" said Mr. Wray.

"Acted up, is what she did," said Victoria.

"Was she angry?"

"I suppose so," said Mr. Wray.

"Angry enough to punish you?"

"What do you mean?"

"Listen, Mr. Wray," Banks said, "when you told us that Leanne was missing and we couldn't find her within a day or two, we were all of us willing to think the worst. Now, what you've just told us puts a different light on things."

"It does?"

"If she was angry at you over her stepmother's pregnancy, then she might easily have run away to strike back."

"But Leanne wouldn't run away," Mr. Wray said, slack-jawed. "She loved me."

"Maybe that's the problem," Banks said. He didn't know if it was called the Electra complex, but he was thinking of the female version of the Oedipus complex: Girl loves her father, then her mother dies, but instead of devoting himself to her, the father finds a new woman, and to make things worse, he makes her pregnant, threatening the entire stability of their relationship. He could easily see Leanne doing a bunk under circumstances like that. But the problem still remained that she would have to be a very uncaring child indeed not to let them know she was still alive after all the hue and cry about the missing girls, and she wouldn't have got far without her money and her inhaler.

"I think she'd probably be capable of it," said Victoria. "She could be cruel. Remember that time when she put castor oil in the coffee, the evening of my first book-club meeting? Caroline Opley was sick all over her Margaret Atwood."

"But that was early days, love," Mr. Wray protested. "It all took a bit of getting used to for her."

"I know. I'm only saying. And she didn't value things as she should have. She lost that silver—"

"Do you think she might have at least been angry enough to disobey her curfew?" Banks asked.

"Certainly," answered Victoria without missing a beat. "It's that boy you should be talking to. That Ian Scott. He's a drug dealer, you know."

"Did Leanne take drugs?"

"Not to our knowledge," said Mr. Wray.

"But she could have done, Chris," his wife went on. "She obviously didn't tell us everything, did she? Who knows what she got up to when she was with those sorts of people."

Christopher Wray put his hand over his wife's. "Don't get excited, love. Remember what the doctor said."

"I know." Victoria stood up. She swayed a little. "I think I need to go and lie down again for a while," she said. "But you mark my words, Superintendent, that's the one you should be looking at—Ian Scott. He's no good."

"Thank you," said Banks. "I'll bear that in mind."

When she'd gone, the silence stretched for a while. "Is there anything else you can tell us?" Banks asked.

"No. No. I'm sure she wouldn't do . . . what you say. I'm sure something must have happened to her."

"Why did you wait until morning to call the police? Had she done that sort of thing before?"

"Never. I would have told you if I thought that."

"So why did you wait?"

"I wanted to call earlier."

"Come on, Mr. Wray," said Winsome, touching his arm gently. "You can tell us."

He looked at her, his eyes beseeching, seeking forgiveness. "I would have called the police, honest I would," he said. "She had never stayed out all night before."

"But you'd had an argument, hadn't you?" Banks suggested. "When she reacted badly to the news of your wife's pregnancy."

"She asked me how could I . . . so soon after . . . after her mother. She was upset, crying, saying terrible things about Victoria, things she didn't mean, but . . . Victoria told her to get out if she wanted, and said she could stay out."

"Why didn't you tell us this at the time?" Banks asked, though he knew the answer: embarrassment, that great social fear—something Victoria Wray would certainly be sensitive to—and not wanting the police involved in your private family arguments. The only way they had found out about the tension between Victoria and Leanne in the first place was through Leanne's friends, and Leanne clearly hadn't had time or chance to tell them about Victoria's pregnancy. Victoria Wray was the kind of woman, Banks thought, who would make the police use the tradesman's entrance, if they had a tradesman's entrance—and the fact that they didn't was probably an unbearable thorn in her side.

There were tears in Mr. Wray's eyes. "I couldn't," he said. "I just couldn't. We thought it was as you said, that perhaps she had stayed out all night to spite us, to demonstrate her anger. But no matter what, Superintendent, Leanne isn't a bad girl. She would have come back in the morning. I'm certain of that."

Banks stood up. "May we have another look at her room, Mr. Wray? There may be something we missed."

Wray looked puzzled. "Yes, of course. But . . . I mean . . . it's been redone. There's nothing there."

"You redecorated Leanne's room?" Winsome said.

He looked at her. "Yes. We couldn't stand it with her gone. The memories. And now, with the new baby on the way . . ."

"What about her clothes?" Winsome asked.

"We gave them to the Oxfam shop."

"Her books, belongings?"

"Them, too."

Winsome shook her head. Banks asked, "May we have a peek, anyway?"

They went upstairs. Wray was right. Not an object remained that indicated the room had ever belonged to a teenager like Leanne Wray. The tiny dresser, bedside drawers and matching wardrobe were all gone, as was her bed with the quilt bedspread, little bookcase, the few dolls left over from her childhood. Even the carpet was gone and the pop star posters had been ripped off the walls. Nothing remained. Banks could hardly believe his eyes. He could understand how people want to escape unpleasant memories, don't like being reminded of someone they've loved and lost, but all *this* just over a month after their daughter's disappearance, and without her body having been found?

"Thank you," he said, indicating for Winsome to follow him down the stairs.

"Isn't that weird?" she said when they'd got outside. "Makes you think, doesn't it?"

"Think what, Winsome?"

"That maybe Leanne *did* go home that night. And that maybe when they heard we were digging up the Paynes' garden, Mr. Wray decided it was time for redecoration."

"Hmm," said Banks. "Maybe you're right, or maybe people just have different ways of showing their grief. Either way, I think we'll be looking a bit more closely at the Wrays over the next few days. You can start by talking to their neighbors, see if they've seen or heard anything unusual."

After her chat with Maureen Nesbitt, Jenny decided to visit Spurn Head itself before heading for home. Maybe a good long walk would help her think things over, blow the cobwebs away. Maybe it would also help her get rid of the eerie feeling she had had since Alderthorpe that she was being watched or followed. She couldn't explain it, but every time she turned suddenly to look over her shoulder, she *felt* rather than saw something slip into the shadows. It was irritating because she couldn't quite grasp whether she was being paranoid or whether it was a case of just because she was paranoid it didn't mean someone *wasn't* following her.

She was still feeling it.

Jenny paid her entrance fee and drove slowly along the narrow track to the car park, noticing an old lighthouse, half under water, and guessing that the sands had shifted since it was built and left it stranded there.

Jenny walked down to the beach. The place wasn't quite as desolate as she had imagined it to be. Just ahead, on a platform a little way out to sea, attached to the mainland by a narrow wooden bridge, were a dock and control center for the Humber pilots, who guided the big tankers in from the North Sea. Behind her stood the new lighthouse and a number of houses. Across the estuary, Jenny could see the docks and cranes of Grimsby and Immingham. Though the sun was shining, there was quite a breeze and Jenny felt the chill as she walked the sands around the point. The sea was an odd combination of colors—purple, brown, lavender, everything but blue, even in the sun.

There weren't many people around. Most of those who visited the area were serious birders, and the place was a protected wildlife sanctuary. Even so, Jenny saw a couple or two walking hand in hand, and one family with two small children. As she walked, she still couldn't shake off the feeling of being followed.

When the first tanker came around the head, it took her breath away. Because of the sharp curve, the huge shape seemed to appear there suddenly, moving very fast, and it filled her field of vision for a few moments, then one of the pilot boats nearby guided it over the estuary toward Immingham docks. Another tanker followed only moments later.

As Jenny stood on the sand looking out over the broad waters, she thought of what Maureen Nesbitt had told her about the Alderthorpe Seven.

Tom Godwin, Lucy's younger brother, had stayed with his foster parents until he was eighteen, like Lucy, then he had gone to live with distant relatives in Australia, all thoroughly checked out by the social services, and he now worked on their sheep farm in New South Wales. By all accounts, Tom was a sturdy, quiet sort of boy, given to long walks alone, and a sort of shyness that made him stutter in front of strangers. Often he woke up screaming from nightmares he couldn't remember.

Laura, Lucy's sister, was living in Edinburgh, where she was studying medicine at the university, hoping to become a psychiatrist. Maureen said Laura was well-adjusted, on the whole, after years of therapy, but there was still a timidity and reticence about her that might make it hard for her to face some of the more human challenges of her chosen profession. There was no doubt she was a brilliant and skilled pupil, but whether she could handle the daily pressures of psychiatry was another matter.

Of the three surviving Murray children, Susan had committed suicide, tragically, at the age of thirteen; Dianne was in a sort of halfway house for the mentally disturbed, suffering from severe sleep disorders and terrifying hallucinations. Keith, like Laura, was also a student, though Maureen reckoned he would be about graduation age by now. He had gone to the University of Durham to study history and English. He was still seeing a psychiatrist regularly and suffered from bouts of depression and anxiety attacks, especially in confined places, but he managed to function and do well in his studies.

And that was it: the sad legacy of Alderthorpe. Such blighted lives.

Jenny wondered if Banks wanted her to continue now that he'd let Lucy go. Maureen Nesbitt had said her best bets were clearly Keith Murray and Laura Godwin, and as Keith lived closer to Eastvale, she decided she would try to reach him first. But was there any more point to it all? She had to admit that she hadn't found any psychological evidence that significantly strengthened the case against Lucy. She felt every bit as inadequate as many officers on the task force thought all offender profilers were anyway.

Lucy *could* have sustained the kind of psychological damage that made her a compliant victim of Terence Payne's, but there again, she might not have. Different people subjected to the same horrors often go in completely different directions. Perhaps Lucy was truly a strong personality, strong enough to put the past behind her and get on with life. Jenny doubted that *anyone* had the strength to avoid at least some kind of psychological fallout from the events in Alderthorpe, but it was possible to heal, at least partially, over time, and to function on some level, as Tom, Laura and Keith had also demonstrated. They might be the walking wounded, but at least they were still walking.

When Jenny had covered half the circle of the head, she cut back through the long grass to the car park and set off down the narrow track. As she went, she noticed a blue Citroën in her rearview mirror and felt certain that she had seen it somewhere before. Telling herself to stop being so paranoid, she left the head and drove toward Patrington. When she'd got closer to the edges of Hull, she called Banks on her mobile.

He answered on the third ring. "Jenny, where are you?"

"Hull. On my way home."

"Find out anything interesting?"

"Plenty, but I'm not sure that it gets us any further. I'll try to put it all together into some sort of profile, if you want."

"Please."

"I just heard you had to let Lucy Payne go."

"That's right. We got her out of a side exit without too much fuss, and her lawyer drove her straight to Hull. They did some shopping in the city center, then Julia Ford, the lawyer, dropped Lucy off at the Liversedges'. They welcomed her with open arms."

"That's where she is now?"

"Far as I know. The local police are keeping an eye on her for us. Where else can she go?"

"Where, indeed?" said Jenny. "Does this mean it's over?"

"What?"

"My job."

"No," said Banks. "Nothing's over yet."

After Jenny had hung up, she checked her rearview mirror again. The blue Citroën was keeping its distance, allowing three or four other cars between them, but there was no doubt it was still back there on her tail.

"Annie, have you ever thought of having children?"

Banks felt Annie tense beside him in bed. They had just made love and were basking in the aftermath, the gentle rushing of the falls outside, the occasional night animal calling from the woods and Van Morrison's *Astral Weeks* drifting up from the stereo downstairs.

"I don't mean . . . well, not now. I mean, not you and me. But ever?"

Annie lay still and silent for a while. He felt her relax a little and stir against him. Finally, she said. "Why do you ask?"

"I don't know. It's been on my mind. This case, the poor devils in the Murray and Godwin families, all the missing girls, not much more than kids, really. And the Wrays, her being pregnant." And Sandra, he thought, but he hadn't told Annie about that yet.

"I can't say as I have," Annie answered.

"Never?"

"Maybe I got shortchanged when it came to handing out the maternal instinct, I don't know. Or maybe it's to do with my own past. Anyway, it never came up."

"Your past?"

"Ray. The commune. My mother dying so young."

"But you said you were happy enough."

"I was." Annie sat up and reached for the glass of wine she had put on the bedside table. Her small breasts glowed in the dim light, smooth skin sloping down to the dark brown areolas, slightly upturned where the nipples rose.

"Then why?"

"Good Lord, Alan, surely it's not every woman's duty in life to reproduce or to analyze why she doesn't want to. I'm not a freak, you know."

"I know. Sorry." Banks sipped some of his wine, lay back against the pillows. "It's just . . . well, I had a bit of a shock the other day, that's all."

"What?"

"Sandra."

"What about her?"

"She's pregnant." There, he'd done it. He didn't know why it should have been so difficult, or why he had the sharp, sudden feeling that he would have been wiser to have kept his mouth closed. He also wondered why he had told Jenny straight away but delayed so long before telling Annie. Partly it was because Jenny *knew* Sandra, of course, but there was more to it than that. Annie didn't seem to like the intimacy implied by details of Banks's life, and she had sometimes made him feel that sharing any part of his past was a burden to her. But he couldn't seem to help himself. Since splitting up with Sandra, he had become far more introspective and examined his life much more closely. He saw little point in being with someone if he couldn't share some of that.

At first, Annie said nothing, then she asked, "Why didn't you tell me before?"

"I don't know."

"How did you hear the news?"

"From Tracy, when we went to lunch in Leeds."

"So Sandra didn't tell you herself?"

"You know as well as I do we don't communicate much."

"Still, I would've thought . . . something like this."

Banks scratched his cheek. "Well, it just goes to show, doesn't it?"

Annie sipped more wine. "Show what?"

"How far apart we've grown."

"You seem upset by this, Alan."

"Not really. Not *upset* so much as . . ."

"Disturbed?"

"Perhaps."

"Why?"

"Just the thought of it. Of Tracy and Brian having a little brother or sister. Of . . ."

"Of what?"

"I was just thinking," Banks said, turning toward her. "I mean, it's something I haven't thought about in years, denied it, I suppose, but this has brought it all back."

"All what back?"

"The miscarriage."

Annie froze for a moment, then said, "Sandra had a miscarriage?"

"Yes."

"When was that?"

"Oh, years ago, when we were living in London. The kids were small, too small to understand."

"What happened?"

"I was working undercover at the time. Drugs squad. You know what it's like, away for weeks at a time, can't contact your family. It was two days before my boss let *me* know."

Annie nodded. Banks knew that she understood about the pressures and stresses of undercover work firsthand; a knowledge of the Job and its effects was one of the things they had in common. "How did it happen?"

"Who knows? The kids were at school. She started bleeding. Thank God we had a helpful neighbor, or who knows what might have happened."

"And you blame yourself for not being there?"

"She could have died, Annie. And we lost the baby. Everything might have gone just fine if I'd been there like any other father-to-be, helping out around the place. But Sandra had to do everything, for crying out loud—all the lifting, shopping, odd jobs, fetching and carrying. She was replacing a light-bulb when she first started to feel funny. She could have fallen and broken her neck." Banks reached for a cigarette. He didn't usually indulge in the "one after" for Annie's sake, but this time he felt like it. He still asked, "Is it okay?"

"Go ahead. I don't mind." Annie sipped more wine. "But thanks for asking. You were saying?"

Banks lit up and the smoke drifted away toward the half-open window. "Guilt. Yes. But more than that."

"What do you mean?"

"I was working drugs, like I said, spending most of my time on the streets or in filthy squats trying to get a lead to the big guys from their victims. Kids, for the most part, run-aways, stoned, high, tripping, zonked out, whatever you care to call it. Some of them as young as ten or eleven. Half of them couldn't even tell you their own names. Or wouldn't. I don't know if you remember, but it was around the time the AIDS scare was growing. Nobody knew for sure yet how bad it was, but there was a lot of scare-mongering. And everyone knew you got it through blood, from unprotected sex— mostly anal sex—and through sharing needles. Thing was, you lived in fear. You just didn't know if some small-time dealer was going to lunge at you with a dirty needle, or if some junkie's drool on your hand could give you AIDS."

"I do know what you mean, Alan, though it was a bit before my time as a copper. But I'm not following. What has it got to do with Sandra's miscarriage?"

Banks sucked in some smoke, felt it burn on the way down
and thought he ought to try stopping again. "Probably nothing, but I'm just trying to give you some sense of the life I
was living. I was in my early thirties, with a wife and two
kids, another on the way, and I was spending my life in
squalor, hanging out with scum. My own kids probably
wouldn't have recognized me if they'd seen me in the street.
The kids I saw were either dead or dying. I was a cop, not a
social worker. I mean, I tried sometimes, you know, if I
thought there was a chance a kid might listen, give up the life
and go home, but that wasn't my job. I was there to get information and to track down the big players."

"And?"

"Well, it's just that it has an effect on you, that's all. It
changes you, warps you, alters your attitudes. You start out
thinking you're an ordinary decent family man just doing a
tough job, and you end up not really knowing what you are.
Anyway, my first thought, when I heard Sandra was okay
but that she'd had a miscarriage . . . Know what my first
feeling was?"

"Relief?" said Annie.

Banks stared at her. "What made you say that?"

She gave him a small smile. "Common sense. It's what I'd
feel—I mean if I'd been in *your* boots."

Banks stubbed out the cigarette. He felt somehow deflated
that his big revelation had seemed so obvious to Annie. He
swirled some red wine around in his mouth to wash away the
taste of smoke. Van Morrison was well into "Madame
George," riffing on the words. A cat howled in the woods,
maybe the one that came for milk sometimes. "Anyway," he
went on, "that's what I felt: relief. And of course I felt guilty.
Not for just not being there, but for being almost glad it happened. And relieved that we wouldn't have to go through it
all again. The dirty nappies, the lack of sleep—not that I was

getting much sleep anyway—the extra responsibility. Here was one life I didn't have to protect. Here was one extra responsibility I could easily live without."

"It's not such an uncommon feeling, you know," said Annie. "It's not so terrible, either. It doesn't make you a monster."

"I felt like one."

"That's because you take too much on yourself. You always do. You're not responsible for all the world's ills and sins, not even a fraction of them. So Alan Banks is human; he isn't perfect. So he feels relief when he thinks he should feel grief. Do you think you're the only one that's happened to?"

"I don't know. I haven't asked anyone else."

"Well, you're not. You just have to learn to live with your imperfections."

"Like you do?"

Annie smiled and flicked a little wine at him. Luckily, she was drinking white. "What imperfections, you cheeky bastard?"

"Anyway, after that we decided no more kids, and we never talked about it again."

"But you've carried the guilt around ever since."

"Yes, I suppose so. I mean, I don't think about it very often, but this brought it all back. And do you know what else?"

"What?"

"I loved the Job more. I never for a moment thought of giving it all up and becoming a used-car salesman."

Annie laughed. "Just as well. I can't imagine you as the used-car-salesman type."

"Or something else. Something with regular hours, less chance of catching AIDS."

Annie reached out and stroked his cheek. "Poor Alan," she said, snuggling closer. "Why don't you just try to put it all out of your mind. Just put everything out of your mind, everything except the moment, me, the music, the here and now."

Van was getting into the meandering, sensuous "Ballerina" and Banks felt Annie's lips, soft and moist, running over his chest, down his stomach, lingering, and he managed to do as she said when she reached her destination, but even as he gave himself up to the sensation of the moment, he still couldn't quite get the thought of dead babies out of his mind.

Maggie checked the locks and the windows for the second time before going to bed that Saturday night, and only when she was satisfied that all was secure did she take a glass of warm milk upstairs with her. She had hardly got halfway up when the telephone rang. At first, she wasn't going to answer it. Not at eleven o'clock on a Saturday night. It was probably a wrong number anyway. But curiosity got the better of her. She knew that the police had been forced to let Lucy go that morning, so it might be she, looking for help.

It wasn't. It was Bill. Maggie's heart started to beat fast, and she felt the room closing in on her.

"You're creating quite a stir over there, aren't you?" he said. "Heroine and champion of battered wives everywhere. Or is that championess?"

Maggie felt herself shrinking, shriveling, her heart squeezing into her throat. All her bravado, her *empowerment,* withered and died. She could hardly talk, hardly breathe. "What do you want?" she whispered. "How did you find out?"

"You underestimate your celebrity. You're not only in the *Globe* and the *Post,* you're in the *Sun* and the *Star,* too. Even a picture in the *Sun,* though it's not a very good one, unless you've changed a hell of a lot. They've been giving quite a bit of coverage to the Chameleon case, as they call it, comparing it to Bernardo and Homolka, naturally, and you seem to be caught right up in the thick of it."

"What do you want?"

"Want? Me? Nothing."

"How did you find me?"

"After the newspaper stories, it wasn't difficult. You had an old address book you forgot to take with you. Your friends were in it. Thirty-two, The Hill, Leeds. Am I right?"

"What do you want with me?"

"Nothing. Not at the moment, anyway. I just wanted to let you know that I know where you are, and I'm thinking of you. It must have been very interesting living across the street from a killer. What's Karla like?"

"It's Lucy. Leave me alone."

"That's not very nice. We were married once, remember."

"How could I forget?"

Bill laughed. "Anyway, mustn't run up the firm's phone bill too much. I've been working very hard lately, and even my boss thinks I need a holiday. Just thought I'd let you know I might be taking a trip over to England soon. I don't know when. Might be next week, might be next month. But I think it'd be nice if we could get together for dinner or something, don't you?"

"You're sick," Maggie said, and heard Bill chuckling as she hung up.

Chapter 15

*B*anks had always thought that Sunday morning was a good time to put a little pressure on an unsuspecting villain. Sunday afternoon was good, too, after the papers, the pub and the roast beef and Yorkshire pud have put him in a good mood and he was stretched out in the armchair, newspaper over his head, enjoying a little snooze. But on Sunday morning, if they weren't particularly religious, people were either relaxed and all set to enjoy a day off, or they were hung over. Either way made for a good chat.

Ian Scott was definitely hung over.

His oily black hair stood in spikes on top and lay flat at the sides, plastered to his skull where he had lain on the pillow. One side of his pasty face was etched with crease marks. His eyes were bloodshot and he wore only a grubby vest and underpants.

"Can I come in, Ian?" said Banks, pushing gently past him before he got an answer. "Won't take long."

The flat reeked of last night's marijuana smoke and stale beer. Roaches still lay scattered in the ashtrays. Banks went and opened the window as wide as it would go. "Shame on you, Ian," he said. "A lovely spring morning like this, you ought to be out walking down by the river or having a crack at Fremlington Edge."

"Bollocks," said Ian, scratching those very items as he spoke.

Sarah Francis stumbled in from the bedroom, holding her tousled hair back from her face and squinting through sleep-gummed eyes. She was wearing a white T-shirt with Donald Duck on the front, and nothing else. The T-shirt only came down to her hips.

"Shit," she said, covering herself with her hands as best she could and dashing back into the bedroom.

"Enjoy the free show?" said Ian.

"Not particularly." Banks tossed a heap of clothes from the chair nearest the window and sat down. Ian turned on the stereo, too loud, and Banks got up and turned it off. Ian sat down and sulked and Sarah came back in wearing a pair of jeans. "You could have bloody warned me," she grumbled to Ian.

"Shut up, you silly cunt," he said.

Now Sarah sat down and sulked, too.

"Okay," said Banks. "Are we all comfortable? Can I begin?"

"I don't know what you want with us again," said Ian. "We told you everything that happened."

"Well, it won't do any harm to go over it again, will it?"

Ian groaned. "I don't feel well. I feel sick."

"You should treat your body with more respect," said Banks. "It's a temple."

"What do you want to know? Get it over with."

"First off, I'm puzzled by something."

"Well, you're the Sherlock; I'm sure you can work it out."

"I'm puzzled by why you haven't asked me about Leanne."

"What do you mean?"

"I'd hardly be back here interrupting your Sunday morning, would I, if Leanne had turned up dead and buried in a serial killer's garden?"

"What are you saying? Speak English."

Sarah had curled herself somehow into a fetal position in the other armchair and was watching the exchange intently.

"What I'm saying, Ian, is that you didn't ask about Leanne. That concerns me. Don't you care about her?"

"She was a mate, that's all. But it's nothing to do with us. We don't know what happened to her. Besides, I'd've got around to it eventually. My brain's not working properly yet."

"Does it ever? Anyway, I'm beginning to think you do."

"Do what?"

"Know something about what happened to Leanne."

"That's rubbish."

"Is it, really? Let's back up a bit. First off, we're pretty certain now that Leanne Wray wasn't one of the Chameleon's victims, as we had first thought."

"Your mistake, isn't it?" said Ian. "Don't come looking to us to bail you out."

"Now, if that's not the case, then it stands to reason that something else happened to her."

"You don't need to be a Sherlock to figure that one out."

"Which, discounting the possibility of *another* stranger killing, leaves three possibilities."

"Oh, yeah? And what are those?"

Banks counted off on his fingers. "One, that she ran away from home. Two, that she did go home on time and her parents did something to her. And three, the main reason I'm here, that she didn't, in fact, go home after you left the Old Ship. That the three of you stayed together and *you* did something to her."

Ian Scott showed no expression but scorn as he listened, and Sarah started sucking on her thumb. "We told you what happened," Ian said. "We told you what we did."

"Yes," said Banks. "But The Riverboat was so busy, the people we talked to were very vague about seeing you. They certainly weren't sure about the time and weren't even sure it was that Friday night."

"But you've got the CCTV. For fuck's sake, what's Big Brother watching for if you can't believe what you see?"

"Oh, we believe what we see all right," said Banks. "But all we see is you, Sarah here and Mick Blair entering the Bar None shortly after half-past twelve."

"Well, there's no point going earlier. Things don't start to warm up till after midnight."

"Yes, Ian, but that leaves over two hours unaccounted for. A lot can happen in two hours."

"How was I to know I'd have to account for my every minute?"

"Two hours."

"I told you. We walked around town a bit, dropped in at The Riverboat, then went to the Bar None. I don't know what fucking time it was."

"Sarah?"

Sarah took her thumb from her mouth. "What he says."

"Is that how it usually goes?" Banks asked. "What Ian says. Haven't you got a mind of your own?"

"What he says. We went to The Riverboat, then to the Bar None. Leanne left us just before half-past ten outside the Old Ship. We don't know what happened to her after that."

"And Mick Blair went with you?"

"Yeah."

"How did Leanne seem that night, Sarah?"

"Uh?"

"What sort of mood was she in?"

"All right, I suppose."

"She wasn't upset about anything?"

"No. We were having a good time."

"Leanne didn't confide anything in you?"

"Like what?"

"Oh, I don't know. Some problem with her stepmother, perhaps?"

"She was always having problems with that stuck-up bitch. I was sick of hearing about them."

"Did she ever talk about running off?"

"Not to me. Not that I remember. Ian?"

"Nah. She just whined about the old cow, that's all. She hadn't the bottle to run away. If I was looking at somebody for it, I'd look at the stepmother first."

"Somebody for what?"

"You know. If you think someone did something to Leanne, like."

"I see. What was the idea that excited you all before you left the Old Ship?"

"I don't know what you mean," said Ian.

"Oh, come on. We know you seemed excited by something you were going to do. What was it? Did it include Leanne?"

"We talked about going to the Bar None, but Leanne knew she couldn't come with us."

"That's all?"

"What else could there be?"

"She didn't give you any hint that she might not be going straight home?"

"No."

"Or that she might run off, teach her stepmother a lesson?"

"Dunno. Who can tell what's in a bitch's mind when it comes right down to it, hey?"

"Tut-tut, such language. You've been listening to too much hip-hop, Ian," said Banks, standing to leave. "Nice choice of partner, Sarah," he said on his way out, noticing that Sarah Francis looked distinctly put out and, more to the point, even a little frightened. That might come in useful before too long, he thought.

* * *

"I just had to get out of the flat, that's all," said Janet Taylor. "I mean, I didn't want to drag you halfway across Yorkshire."

"That's all right," said Annie, with a smile. "I don't live that far away. Besides, I like it here."

Here was a rambling old pub on the edge of the moorland above Wensleydale, not far from Banks's cottage, with a solid reputation for Sunday lunch. Janet's call had come shortly after ten o'clock that morning, just as Annie was having a nap to make up for her lack of sleep at Banks's place. Their conversation had bothered her, kept her awake well into the small hours; she didn't like talking about babies.

Trust Banks to hit a nerve. What she also didn't like and didn't seem able to tell him about these personal revelations of his was that they pushed her into examining her own past and her own feelings far more than she felt ready to do right now. She wished he would just lighten up and take it easy.

Anyway, an open-air lunch was just the ticket. The air was pure, and there wasn't a cloud in the sky. From where they sat she could see the lush green dalesides crisscrossed with drystone walls, sheep wandering all over, baaing like crazy if any ramblers passed by. Down in the valley bottom, the river meandered and a group of cottages huddled around a village green, the square-towered church a little to one side, gray limestone bright in the midday sun. She thought she could see the tiny silhouettes of four people walking along the top of the high limestone scar over the dale. Christ, it would be good to be up there, all alone, not a care in the world.

But if the setting was ideal, she might have chosen a different companion. Despite the change of environment, Janet seemed distracted, forever flicking back the lock of hair that fell over her tired brown eyes. There was an unhealthy pallor about her that Annie guessed would take more than a lunch on the moors to dispel. Already Janet was on her second pint of lager and lime, and Annie had to bite her tongue not to say something about drink driving. She was on her first half of bitter, might have another half, then coffee after lunch. Annie, who was a vegetarian, had ordered quiche and a salad, but she was pleased to see that Janet had ordered roast lamb; she looked as if she needed some meat on her bones.

"How are you doing?" Annie asked.

Janet laughed. "Oh, about as well as can be expected." She rubbed her forehead. "I still can't get the sleep thing sorted out. You know, I keep replaying it, but I'm not sure if I'm seeing it the way it really happened."

"What do you mean?"

"Well, in the replays I see his face."

"Terry Payne's?"

"Yes, all twisted and contorted. Fearsome. But I don't think I remember seeing him clearly at the time. My mind must be filling in details."

"Possibly." Annie thought of her own ordeal, the rape carried out by three colleagues after celebrating her passing her sergeant's boards. At the time, she could have sworn she would remember every grunt and groan, every obscene facial expression and every sensation of him—the one who actually succeeded in penetrating her while the others held her down—forcing himself inside her as she struggled, tearing at her clothes, every drop of sweat that dripped from his face on to her skin, but she was surprised to find that much of it had faded, and it wasn't a memory she felt compelled to re-run for herself night after night. Perhaps she was tougher than she thought, or maybe she was compartmentalizing it, as someone had once told her she did, shutting out the pain and humiliation.

"You've changed your mind about the statement, then?" Annie asked. They were sitting far enough away that they couldn't be overheard if they spoke quietly. Not that any of the other diners looked as if they wanted to eavesdrop; they were all family groups talking loudly and laughing, trying to keep track of their adventurous children.

"I wasn't lying," said Janet. "I want you to know that, first off."

"I know that."

"I was just confused, that's all. My memory of that night's a bit shaky."

"Understandable. But you do remember how many times you hit him?"

"No. All I'm saying is that it might have been more than I thought."

Their meals arrived. Janet tucked in as if she hadn't eaten in a week, which she probably hadn't, and Annie picked at her food. The quiche was dry and the salad boring, but that was to be expected in a place that catered mostly to meat-eaters. At least she could enjoy the view. A high plane left a figure eight of white vapor trail across the sky.

"Janet," Annie went on. "What do you want to change in your statement?"

"Well, you know, where I insisted I only hit him, what, two or three times?"

"Four."

"Whatever. And the postmortem found . . . how many?"

"Nine blows."

"Right."

"Do you remember hitting him nine times?"

"No. That's not what I'm saying." Janet sawed off a piece of lamb and chewed on it for a moment.

Annie ate some lettuce. "What *are* you saying, Janet?"

"Just that, well, I suppose I lost it, that's all."

"You're claiming diminished responsibility?"

"Not really. I mean, I knew what was going on, but I was scared and I was upset about Dennis, so I just . . . I don't know, maybe I should have stopped hitting him sooner, after I'd handcuffed him to the pipes."

"You hit him after that?"

"I think so. Once or twice."

"And you remember doing that?"

"I remember hitting him after I'd handcuffed him, yes. Thinking, this one's for Dennis, you bastard. I just don't remember how many times."

"You realize you'll have to come to the station and revise your statement, don't you? I mean, it's okay just telling me here, now, like this, but it has to be done officially."

Janet raised an eyebrow. "Of course I know that. I'm still a copper, aren't I? I just wanted . . . you know . . ." She looked away out over the dale.

Annie thought she did know, and that Janet was too embarrassed to say it. She wanted some company. She wanted someone who would at least try to understand her in a gorgeous setting on a beautiful day, before the three-ringed circus that was likely to be her life for the next while went into full swing.

Jenny Fuller and Banks had lunch together in the slightly less exotic Queen's Arms. The place was bursting at the seams with Sunday tourists, but they bagged a small table—so small there was hardly room for two roast beef and Yorkshire pud specials and the drinks—just before they stopped serving meals at two o'clock. Lager for Jenny and a pint of shandy for Banks because he had to conduct another interview that afternoon. He still looked tired, Jenny thought, and she guessed that the case had been keeping him awake at nights. That and his obvious discomfort over Sandra's pregnancy.

Jenny and Sandra had been friends. Not close, but both had been through harrowing experiences around the same time and these had created some sort of bond between them. Since her travels in America, though, Jenny hadn't seen much of Sandra, and now she supposed she wouldn't see her again. If she had to choose sides, as people did, then she supposed she had chosen Alan's. She had thought he and Sandra had a solid marriage—after all, Alan had turned her down when she tried to seduce him, and that had been a new experience for her—but clearly she was wrong. Never having been married herself, she would have been the first to confess that she knew little about such things, except that outward appearances often belie an inner turmoil.

So what had been going through Sandra's mind in that last little while was a mystery. Alan had said that he wasn't sure whether Sandra met Sean before or after they split up, or whether he was the real reason behind the separation. Jenny doubted it. Like most problems, it hadn't just happened overnight, or when someone else turned up on the scene. Sean was as much a symptom as anything, and an escape hatch. This business had probably been years in the making.

"The car," Banks said.

"A blue Citroën."

"Yes. I don't suppose you got the number?"

"I must admit it never crossed my mind the first time I saw it. I mean, why would I? It was in Alderthorpe and I parked behind it. Coming back from Spurn Head, it always stayed too far behind for me to be able to see."

"And you lost it where?"

"I didn't lose it. I noticed it stopped following me just after I got on to the M62 west of Hull."

"And you never saw it again?"

"No." Jenny laughed. "I must admit I felt rather as if I was being run out of town. You know, like in those cowboy films."

"You didn't get a glimpse of the driver at all?"

"No. Couldn't even tell if it was a man or a woman."

"What next?"

"I've some university work to catch up on and some tutorials tomorrow. I could postpone them, but . . ."

"No, that's okay," said Banks. "Lucy Payne's out, anyway. No real rush."

"Well, on Tuesday or Wednesday I'll see if I can talk to

Keith Murray in Durham. Then there's Laura in Edinburgh. I'm developing a picture of Linda—Lucy, but it's still missing a few pieces."

"Such as?"

"That's the problem. I'm not sure. I just get the feeling that I'm missing something." She saw Banks's worried expression and slapped his arm. "Oh, don't worry, I'll not go putting my intuitions into my profiles. This is just between you and me."

"Okay."

"I suppose you could call it the missing link. The link between Linda's childhood and the possibility of Lucy's being involved in the abductions and murders."

"There's the sexual abuse."

"Yes, there's no doubt that many people who were abused become abusers themselves—it's a cycle—and according to Maureen Nesbitt, Linda was sexually aware at eleven. But none of that's enough in itself. All I can say is that it *could* have created a psychopathology in Lucy that made her capable of becoming the compliant victim of a man like Terence Payne. People often repeat mistakes and bad choices. You just have to look at *my* history of relationships to see that."

Banks smiled. "You'll get it right one day."

"Meet my knight in shining armor?"

"Is that what you want? Someone to fight your battles for you, then pick you up and carry you upstairs?"

"It's not a bad idea."

"And I thought you were a feminist."

"I am. It doesn't mean I might not fight his battles, pick him up and carry him upstairs the next day. All I'm saying is that chance would be a fine thing. Anyway, can't a woman have her fantasies?"

"Depends where they lead. Has it occurred to you that Lucy Payne wasn't the compliant victim at all, and that her husband was?"

"No, it hasn't. I've never come across such a case."

"But not impossible?"

"In human psychology, nothing's impossible. Just very unlikely, that's all."

"But supposing she were the powerful one, the dominant partner . . ."

"And Terence Payne was her sex slave, doing her bidding?"

"Something like that."

"I don't know," said Jenny. "But I very much doubt it. Besides, even if it is true, it doesn't really get us any further, does it?"

"I suppose not. Just speculation. You mentioned that Payne might have used a camcorder when you visited the cellar, didn't you?"

"Yes." Jenny sipped some lager and dabbed her lips with a paper serviette. "It would be highly unusual in such a ritual-ized case of rape, murder and interment for the perpetrator *not* to keep some sort of record."

"He had the bodies."

"His trophies? Yes. And that probably explains why there was no further mutilation, no need to take a finger or a toe to remember them by. Payne had the whole body. But it's not just that. Someone like Payne would have needed more, something that enabled him to relive the events."

Banks told her about the tripod marks and the electronics catalog.

"So if he had one, where is it?" she asked.

"That's the question."

"And why is it missing?"

"Another good question. Believe me, we're looking hard for it. If it's in that house, even if it's buried ten feet down, we'll find out. We won't leave a brick of that place standing until it's given up all its secrets."

"*If* it's in the house."

"Yes."

"And there'll be tapes, too."

"I haven't forgotten them."

Jenny pushed her plate aside. "I suppose I'd better go and get some work done."

Banks looked at his watch. "And I'd better go see Mick Blair." He reached forward and touched her arm lightly. She was surprised at the tingle she felt. "Take care, Jenny. Keep your eyes open, and if you see that car again, phone me right away. Understand?"

Jenny nodded. Then she noticed someone she didn't know approaching them, walking with an easy, confident grace. An attractive young woman, tight jeans emphasizing her long and shapely legs, what looked like a man's white shirt hanging open over a red T-shirt. Chestnut hair cascaded in shiny waves to her shoulders, and the only flaw on her smooth complexion was a small mole to the right of her mouth. Even that wasn't so much an imperfection as a beauty spot. Her serious eyes were almond in shape and color.

When she got to the table, she pulled up a chair and sat down without being invited. "DS Cabbot," she said, stretching out her hand. "I don't think we've met."

"Dr. Fuller." Jenny shook. Firm grasp.

"Ah, the famous Dr. Fuller. A pleasure to meet you at last."

Jenny felt tense. Was this woman, surely *the* Annie Cabbot, staking out her territory? Had she seen Banks touching her arm and thought something of it? Was she here to let Jenny know as subtly as possible to keep her hands off Banks? Jenny knew she was not bad when it came to the looks department, but she couldn't help feeling somehow *clumsy* and even a bit dowdy next to Annie. *Older,* too. Definitely older.

Annie smiled at Banks. "Sir."

Jenny could sense something between them. Sexual tension, yes, but it was more than that. Had they had a disagreement? All of a sudden the table was uncomfortable and she felt she had to leave. She picked up her bag and started rummaging for her car keys. Why did they always sink to the bottom and get lost among the hairbrushes, paper hankies and makeup?

"Don't let me interrupt your lunch," said Annie, smiling again at Jenny, then turning to Banks. "But I just happened to be in the station catching up on some paperwork after lunch. Winsome told me you were here and that she'd got a message for you. I said I'd deliver it."

Banks raised his eyebrows. "And?"

"It's from your mate Ken Blackstone in Leeds. It seems Lucy Payne's done a runner."

Jenny gasped. "What?"

"Local police dropped by her parents' house this morning just to make sure everything was okay. Turns out her bed hadn't been slept in."

"Bloody hell," said Banks. "Another cock-up."

"Just thought you'd want to know as soon as possible," said Annie, untangling herself from the chair. She looked at Jenny. "Nice to meet you."

Then she walked out with the same elegant grace she had walked in with, leaving Banks and Jenny to sit and stare at each other.

Mick Blair, the fourth person in the group on the night Leanne Wray disappeared, lived with his parents in a semi in North Eastvale, near enough to the edge of town for a fine view over Swainsdale, but close enough to the center for easy access. After Annie's revelation about Lucy Payne, Banks wondered whether he should change his plans, but he decided that Leanne Wray was still a priority and Lucy Payne was still a victim in the eyes of the law. Besides, there would be plenty of coppers keeping an eye open for her; it was the most they could do until, and unless, they had anything to charge her with.

Unlike Ian Scott, Mick had never been in trouble with the police, though Banks suspected he might well have been buying drugs from Ian. He had a slightly wasted look about him, not quite all there, and didn't seem to have much time for personal grooming. When Banks called after his lunch with Jenny that Sunday, Mick's parents were out visiting family, and Mick was slouching around in the living room listening to Nirvana loud on the stereo, wearing torn jeans and a black T-shirt with a picture of Kurt Cobain on it, above his birth and death dates.

"What do you want?" Mick asked, turning down the volume and flopping on to the sofa, hands behind his head.

"To talk about Leanne Wray."

"We've already been over that."

"Let's go over it again?"

"Why? Have you found out something new?"

"What would there be to find out?"

"I don't know. I'm just surprised at your coming here, that's all."

"Was Leanne your girlfriend, Mick?"

"No. It wasn't like that."

"She's an attractive girl. Didn't you fancy her?"

"Maybe. A bit."

"But she wasn't having any of it?"

"It was early days, that's all."

"What do you mean?"

"Some girls need a bit of time, a bit of working on. They don't all just jump into bed with you the first time you meet."

"And Leanne needed time?"

"Yes."

"How far had you got?"

"What do you mean?"

"How far? Holding hands? Necking? Tongue or no tongue?" Banks remembered his own adolescent gropings and the various stages you had to pass. After necking usually came touching above the waist, but with clothes on, then under the blouse but over the bra. After that, the bra came off, then it was below the waist, and so on until you got to go all the way. If you were lucky. With some girls it seemed to take forever to move from one stage to another, and some might let you get below the waist but not go all the way. The whole negotiation was a minefield fraught with the danger of being dumped at every turn. Well, at least Leanne Wray hadn't been an easy conquest, and for some odd reason, Banks was glad to know that.

"We necked once in a while."

"What about that Friday night, the thirty-first of March?"

"Nah. We were in a group, like, with Ian and Sarah."

"You didn't neck with Leanne in the cinema?"

"Maybe."

"Is that a yes or a no?"

"I suppose so."

"Might you have had a falling-out?"

"What are you getting at?"

Banks scratched the scar beside his right eye. "It's like this, Mick. I come here to talk to you again, and it seems to bother you, but you don't ask me if we've found Leanne alive, or found her body yet. It was the same with Ian—"

"You've talked to Ian?"

"This morning. I'm surprised he didn't get straight on the phone to you."

"He can't have been very worried."

"Why should he be?"

"I don't know."

"The thing is, you see, that you both *ought* to be asking me if we've found Leanne alive, or if we've found her body, or if we've identified her remains."

"Why?"

"Why else would I come to talk to you?"

"How should I know?"

"But the fact that you *don't* ask makes me wonder if you know something you're not telling me."

Mick folded his arms. "I've told you everything I know."

Banks leaned forward and held Mick's gaze. "Know what? I think you're lying, Mick. I think you're all lying."

"You can't prove anything."

"What would I need to prove?"

"That I'm lying. I told you what happened. We went for a drink in the Old—"

"No. What you told us was that you went for coffee after the film."

"Right. Well . . ."

"That was lying, wasn't it, Mick?"

"So what?"

"If you can do it once, you can do it again. In fact, it gets easier the more you practice. What really happened that night, Mick? Why don't you tell me about it?"

"Nothing happened. I already told you."

"Did you and Leanne have a fight? Did you hurt her? Maybe you didn't mean to. Where is she, Mick? You *know,* I'm certain of it."

And Mick's expression told Banks that he *did* know, but it also told him that he wasn't going to confess to anything. Not today, at any rate. Banks felt pissed off and culpable at the same time. It was *his* fault that this line of inquiry hadn't been properly followed up. So fixated had he become on a serial killer abducting young girls that he had ignored the basics of police work and not pushed hard enough at those in the position to know best what had happened to Leanne: the people she had been with at the time she disappeared. He should have followed up, knowing of Ian Scott's criminal record, and that it involved drugs. But no. Leanne was put down as the third victim of the unidentified serial killer, another pretty young blond victim, and that was that. Winsome Jackman had done a bit of follow-up work, but she had pretty much accepted the official story too. Banks's fault, all of it, just like Sandra's miscarriage. Just like bloody everything, it seemed sometimes.

"Tell me what happened," Banks pushed again.

"I've told you. I've fucking told you!" Mick sat up abruptly. "When we left the Old Ship, Leanne set off home. That was the last any of us saw of her. Some pervert must have got her. All right? That's what you thought, isn't it? Why are you changing your minds?"

"Ah, so you *are* curious," Banks said, standing up. "I'm sure you've been following the news. We've got the pervert who took and killed those girls—he's dead, so he can't tell us anything—but we found no trace of Leanne's body on the premises, and believe me, we've taken the place apart."

"Then it must've been some other pervert."

"Come off it, Mick. The odds against one are wild enough, the odds against two are astronomical. No. It comes down to you. You, Ian and Sarah. The last people she was seen with. Now, I'm going to give you time to think about it, Mick, but I'll be back, you can count on that. Then we'll have a proper talk. No distractions. In the meantime, stick around. Enjoy the music."

When Banks left, he paused just long enough at the garden gate to see Mick, silhouetted behind the lace curtains, jump up from the sofa and head over to the telephone.

Chapter 16

*T*he Monday-morning sunlight spilled through Banks's kitchen window and glinted on the copper-bottomed pans hanging on the wall. Banks sat at his pine table with a cup of coffee, toast and marmalade, the morning newspaper spread out before him and Vaughan Williams's *Variations on a Theme by Thomas Tallis* playing on the radio. But he was neither reading nor listening.

He had been awake since before four, a million details dancing around in his mind, and though he felt dog-tired now, he knew he couldn't sleep. He would be glad when the Chameleon case was all over, when Gristhorpe was back at work, and when he could go back to his normal duties as detective chief inspector. The responsibility of command over the past month and a half had exhausted him. He recognized the signs: lack of sleep, bad dreams, too much junk food, too much booze and too many cigarettes. He was reaching the same near-burnout state as he had been in when he left the Met for North Yorkshire years ago, hoping for a quieter life. He loved detective work, but it sometimes seemed that modern policing was a young man's game. Science, technology and changes in management structure hadn't simplified things; they had only made life more complicated. Banks realized that he had probably come to the limits of his ambition when he actually thought that morning, for the first time, about packing in the Job altogether.

He heard the postman arrive and went out to pick up the letters from the floor. Among the usual collection of bills and circulars, there was a hand-addressed envelope from London, and Banks immediately recognized the neat, looping hand.

Sandra.

Heart beating just a little too fast for comfort, he carried the pile back into the kitchen. This was his favorite room in the cottage, mostly because he had dreamed about it before he had seen it, but what he read in Sandra's letter was enough to darken the brightest of rooms even more than his previous mood had darkened it.

> *Dear Alan,*
>
> *I understand that Tracy told you Sean and I are expecting a baby. I wish she hadn't, but there it is, it's done now. I hope this knowledge will at least enable you to understand the need for expediency in the matter of our divorce, and that you will act accordingly.*
>
> > *Yours sincerely,*
> > *Sandra*

That was it. Nothing more than a cold, formal note. Banks had to admit that he hadn't been responding to the matter of divorce with any great dispatch, but he hadn't seen any need for haste. Perhaps, he was even willing to admit, deep down, he was stubbornly clinging to Sandra, and in some opaque and frightened part of his soul he was holding to the belief that it was all just a nightmare or a mistake, and he would wake up one morning back in the Eastvale semi with Sandra beside him. Not that that was what he wanted, not anymore, but he was at least willing to admit that he might harbor such irrational feelings.

Now this.

Banks put the letter aside, still feeling its chill. Why couldn't he just let go of this and move on, as Sandra clearly had done? Was it because of what he had told Annie, about his guilt over Sandra's miscarriage, about being glad that it happened? He didn't know; it all just felt too strange: his wife of over twenty years, mother of their children, now about to give birth to another man's child.

He tossed the letter aside, picked up his briefcase and headed out for the car.

He intended to go to Leeds later in the morning, but first he wanted to drop by his office, clear up some paperwork and have a word with Winsome. The drive to Eastvale from Gratly was, Banks had thought when he first made it, one of the most beautiful drives in the area: a narrow road about halfway up the daleside, with spectacular views of the valley bottom with its sleepy villages and meandering river to his left and the steeply rising fields with their drystone walls and wandering sheep to his right. But today he didn't even notice all this, partly because he did it so often, and partly because his thoughts were still clouded by Sandra's letter and vague depression over his job.

After the chaos of the weekend, the police station was back to its normal level of activity; the reporters had disappeared, just as Lucy Payne had. Banks wasn't overly concerned about Lucy's going missing, he thought as he closed his office door and turned on the radio. She would probably turn up again, and even if she didn't, there was no real cause for concern. Not unless they came up with some concrete evidence against her. At least in the meantime, they could keep track of her through ATM withdrawals and credit card transactions. No matter where she was, she would need money.

After he had finished the paperwork, Banks went into the squad room. DC Winsome Jackman was sitting at her desk chewing on the end of a pencil.

"Winsome," he said, remembering one of the details that had awoken him so early in the morning, "I've got another job for you."

And when he'd told her what he wanted her to do, he left by the back exit and set off for Leeds.

It was just after lunch when Annie entered the CPS offices, though she hadn't managed to grab a bite to eat herself yet. The Crown solicitor appointed to the case, Jack Whitaker, turned out to be younger than she had expected, late twenties or early thirties, she guessed, prematurely balding, and he spoke with a slight lisp. His handshake was firm, his palm just a little damp. His office was certainly far tidier than Stafford Oakes's in Eastvale, where every file was out of place and stained with an Olympic symbol of coffee rings.

"Any new developments?" he asked after Annie had sat down.

"Yes," said Annie. "PC Taylor changed her statement this morning."

"May I?"

Annie handed him Janet Taylor's revised statement, and Whitaker read it over. When he'd finished, he slid the papers over the desk back toward Annie. "What do you think?" she asked.

"I think," Jack Whitaker said slowly, "that we might be charging Janet Taylor with murder."

"What?" Annie couldn't believe what she'd just heard. "She acted as a policewoman in pursuit of her duty. I was thinking justifiable homicide, or, at the very most, excusable. But *murder?*"

Whitaker sighed. "Oh, dear. I don't suppose you've heard the news, then?"

"What news?" Annie hadn't turned on the radio when she drove down to Leeds, being far too preoccupied with Janet's case and her confused feelings about Banks to concentrate on news or chat.

"The jury came back on the John Hadleigh case just before lunch. You know, the Devon farmer."

"I know about the Hadleigh case. What was the verdict?"

"Guilty of murder."

"Jesus Christ," said Annie. "But even so, surely that's different entirely? I mean, Hadleigh was civilian. He shot a burglar in the back. Janet Taylor—"

Whitaker held his hand up. "The point is that it's a clear message. Given the Hadleigh verdict, we have to be *seen* to be acting fairly toward everyone. We can't afford to have the press screaming at us for going easy on Janet Taylor just because she's a policewoman."

"So it is political?"

"Isn't it always? Justice must be seen to be done."

"Justice?"

Whitaker raised his eyebrows. "Listen," he said, "I can understand your sympathies; believe me, I can. But according to her statement, Janet Taylor handcuffed Terence Payne to a metal pipe *after* she had already subdued him, then she hit him twice with her baton. Hard. Think about it, Annie. That's deliberate. That's murder."

"She didn't necessarily mean to kill him. There was no intent."

"That's for a jury to decide. A good prosecutor could argue that she knew damn well what the effect of two more hard blows to the head would be after she'd already given him seven previous blows."

"I can't believe I'm hearing this," Annie said.

"No one's sorrier than I am," said Whitaker.

"Except Janet Taylor."

"Then she shouldn't have killed Terence Payne."

"What the hell do you know? You weren't there, in that cellar, with your partner bleeding to death on the floor, a dead girl staked out on a mattress. You didn't have just seconds to react to a man coming at you with a machete. This is a bloody farce! It's politics, is all it is."

"Calm down, Annie," said Whitaker.

Annie stood up and paced, arms folded. "Why should I? I don't feel calm. This woman has been going through hell. *I* provoked her into changing her statement because I thought it would go better for her in the long run than saying she couldn't remember. How does this make me look?"

"Is that all you're concerned about? How it makes you look?"

"Of course it's not." Annie lowered herself slowly back into the chair. She still felt flushed and angry, her breath coming in sharp gasps. "But it makes me look like a liar. It makes it look as if I tricked her. I don't like that."

"You were only doing your job."

"Only doing my job. Only obeying orders. Right. Thanks. That makes me feel a whole lot better."

"Look, we might be able to get a bit of leeway here, Annie, but there'll have to be a trial. It'll all have to be a matter of public record. Aboveboard. There'll be no sweeping it under the table."

"That's not what I had in mind, anyway. What leeway?"

"I don't suppose Janet Taylor would plead guilty to murder."

"Damn right she wouldn't, and I wouldn't advise her to."

"It's not exactly a matter of *advising*. Besides, that's not your job. What do you think she *would* plead guilty to?"

"Excusable homicide."

"It wasn't self-defense. Not when she crossed the line and

delivered those final blows *after* Payne was rendered inca-
pable of defending himself or of attacking her further."

"What, then?"

"Voluntary manslaughter."

"How long would she have to serve?"

"Between eighteen months and three years."

"That's still a long time, especially for a copper in jail."

"Not as long as John Hadleigh."

"Hadleigh shot a kid in the back with a shotgun."

"Janet Taylor beat a defenseless man about the head with
a police baton, causing his death."

"He was a serial killer."

"She didn't know that at the time."

"But he came at her with a machete!"

"And after she'd disarmed him, she used more force than
necessary to subdue him, causing his death. Annie, it doesn't
matter that he was a serial killer. It wouldn't matter if he'd
been Jack the bloody Ripper."

"He'd cut her partner. She was upset."

"Well, I'm certainly glad to hear she wasn't calm, cool
and collected when she did it."

"You know what I mean. There's no need for sarcasm."

"Sorry. I'm sure the judge and jury will take the whole
picture into account, her state of mind."

Annie sighed. She felt sick. As soon as this farce was over
she was getting the hell out of Complaints and Discipline,
back to real police work, catching the villains.

"All right," she said. "What next?"

"You know what next, Annie. Find Janet Taylor. Arrest
her, take her to the police station and charge her with voluntary manslaughter."

"Someone asking to see you, sir."

Why was the fresh-faced PC who popped his head around

the door of Banks's temporary office at Millgarth smirking? Banks wondered. "Who is it?" he asked.

"You'd better see for yourself, sir."

"Can't someone else deal with it?"

"She specifically asked to see someone in charge of the missing girls case, sir. Area Commander Hartnell's in Wakefield with the ACC, and DCI Blackstone's out. That leaves you, sir."

Banks sighed. "All right. Show her in."

The PC smirked again and disappeared, leaving a distinct sense of smirk still in the air, rather like the Cheshire cat's smile. A few moments later, Banks saw why.

She tapped very softly on his door and pushed it open so slowly that it creaked on its hinges, then she appeared before him. All five feet nothing of her. She was anorexically thin, and the harsh red of her lipstick and nail polish contrasted with the almost translucent paleness of her skin; her delicate features looked as if they were made out of porcelain carefully glued or painted on her moon-shaped face. Clutching a gold-lamé handbag, she was wearing a bright green crop top, which stopped abruptly just below her breasts—no more than goose pimples despite the push-up bra—and showed a stretch of pale, bare midriff and a belly-button ring, below which came a black PVS micro-skirt. She wore no tights, and her pale thin legs stretched bare down to the knee-highs and chunky platform heels that made her walk as if she were on stilts. Her expression showed fear and nervousness as her astonishingly lovely cobalt-blue eyes roved restlessly about the stark office.

Banks would have put her down for a heroin-addicted prostitute, but he could see no needle tracks on her arms. That didn't mean she wasn't addicted to *something,* and it certainly didn't mean that she *wasn't* a prostitute. There are more ways of getting drugs into your system than through a needle. Something about her reminded him of Chief Constable Riddle's daughter, Emily, but it quickly passed. She bore more resemblance to the famous heroin-chic models of a few years ago.

"Are you the one?" she asked.

"What one?"

"The one in charge. I asked for the one in charge."

"That's me. For my sins," said Banks.

"What?"

"Never mind. Sit down." She sat, slowly and suspiciously, eyes still flicking restlessly around the office, as if she were afraid someone was going to appear and strap her into her chair. It had obviously taken her a lot of courage to come this far. "Can I get you some tea or coffee?" Banks asked.

She looked surprised at the offer. "Er . . . yes. Please. Coffee would be nice."

"How do you take it?"

"What?"

"The coffee? How do you want it?"

"Milk and plenty of sugar," she said, as if unaware that it came any other way.

Banks phoned for two coffees—black for him—and turned back to her. "What's your name?"

"Candy."

"Really?"

"Why? What's wrong with it?"

"Nothing. Nothing, Candy. Ever been in a police station before?"

Fear flashed across Candy's delicate features. "Why?"

"Just asking. You seem ill at ease."

She managed a weak smile. "Well, yes . . . Maybe I am. A little bit."

"Relax. I won't eat you."

Wrong choice of words, Banks realized, when he saw the lascivious, knowing look in her eye. "I mean I won't harm you," he corrected himself.

The coffee arrived, carried in by the same, still-smirking PC. Banks was abrupt with him, resenting the kind of smug arrogance that the smirk implied.

"Okay, Candy," said Banks after the first sip. "Care to tell me what it's all about?"

"Can I smoke?" She opened her handbag.

"Sorry," said Banks. "No smoking anywhere in the station; otherwise I'd have one with you."

"Maybe we could go outside?"

"I don't think that would be a good idea," Banks said. "Let's just get on with it."

"It's just that I really like a ciggie with my coffee. I always have a smoke with my coffee."

"Not this time. Why have you come to see me, Candy?"

She fidgeted awhile longer, a sulky expression on her face, then shut the handbag and crossed her legs, clipping the underside of the desk with her platform and rattling it so much that Banks's coffee spilled over the rim of his mug and made a gathering stain on the pile of papers before him.

"Sorry," she said.

"It's nothing." Banks took out his handkerchief and wiped it up. "You were going to tell me why you're here."

"Was I?"

"Yes."

"Well, look," Candy said, leaning forward in her chair. "First off, you have to grant me that immunization, or whatever. Or I won't say a word."

"You mean immunity?"

She flushed. "If that's what it's called. I didn't go to school much."

"Immunity from what?"

"From prosecution."

"But why would I want to prosecute you?"

Her eyes were everywhere but on Banks, hands twisting

the bag on her bare lap. "Because of what I do," she said. "You know . . . with men. I'm a prostitute, a tom."

"Bloody hell," said Banks. "You could knock me over with a feather."

Her eyes turned to him, shimmering with angry tears. "There's no need to be snarky. I'm not ashamed of what I am. At least I don't go around locking up innocent people and letting the guilty go free."

Banks felt like a shit. Sometimes he just didn't know when to hold his tongue. He had acted no better than the smirking PC when he insulted her with his sarcasm. "I'm sorry, Candy," he said. "But I'm a very busy man. Can we get to the point? If you've got anything to tell me, then say it."

"You promise?"

"Promise what?"

"You won't lock me up."

"I won't lock you up. Cross my heart. Not unless you've come to confess a serious crime."

She shot to her feet. "I haven't done nothing!"

"All right. All right. Sit down, then. Take it easy."

Candy sat slowly, careful with her platforms this time. "I came because you let her go. I wasn't going to come. I don't like the police. But you let her go."

"Who's this about, Candy?"

"It's about that couple in the papers, the ones who took them young girls."

"What about them?"

"Just that they . . . once . . . you know, they . . ."

"They picked *you* up?"

She looked down. "Yes."

"Both of them?"

"Yes."

"How did it happen?"

"I was just, you know, out on the street, and they came by

in a car. He did the talking, and when we'd fixed it up they
took me to a house."

"When was this, Candy?"

"Last summer."

"Do you remember the month?"

"August, I think. Late August. It was warm, anyway."

Banks tried to work out the timing. The Seacroft rapes had
stopped around the time the Paynes moved out of the area,
about a year or so before Candy's experience. That left a period of about sixteen months before Payne abducted Kelly
Matthews. Perhaps during that period he had been trying to
sublimate his urges, relying on prostitutes? And Lucy's role?

"Where was the house?"

"The Hill. It's the same one that's in all the papers. I've
been there."

"Okay. What happened next?"

"Well, first we had a drink and they chatted to me, putting
me at ease, like. They seemed a really nice couple."

"And then?"

"What do you think?"

"I'd still like you to tell me."

"He said let's go upstairs."

"Just the two of you?"

"Yes. That's what I thought he meant at first."

"Go on."

"Well, we went up to the bedroom and I . . . you know . . .
I got undressed. Well, partly. He wanted me to keep certain
things on. Jewelry. My underwear. At first, anyway."

"What happened next?"

"It was dark in there and you could only make out shadows. He made me lie down on the bed, and the next thing I
knew she was there, too."

"Lucy Payne?"

"Yes."

"On the bed with you?"

"Yes. Starkers."

"Was she involved in what went on sexually?"

"Oh, yes. She knew what she was doing, all right. Proper little minx."

"She never seemed to be coerced, a victim in any way?"

"Never. No way. She was in control. And she liked what was happening. She even came up with suggestions of her own . . . you know, different things to do. Different positions."

"Did they hurt you?"

"Not really. I mean, they liked to play games, but they seemed to know how far to go."

"What sort of games?"

"He asked me if I'd mind him tying me to the bed. He promised they weren't going to hurt me."

"You let him do that?"

"They were paying well."

"And they seemed nice."

"Yes."

Banks shook his head in amazement. "Okay. Go on."

"Don't judge me," she said. "You don't know anything about me or what I have to do, so don't you dare judge me!"

"Okay," said Banks. "Go on, Candy. They tied you to the bed."

"She was doing something with hot candle wax. On my belly. My nipples. It hurt a bit, but it doesn't really hurt. You know what I mean?"

Banks hadn't experimented sexually with candle wax but he had spilled some on his hand on more than one occasion and knew the sensation, the brief flash of heat and pain followed by the quick cooling, the setting and drying, the way it pinched and puckered the skin. Not an entirely unpleasant sensation.

"Were you frightened?"

"A bit. Not really, though. I've known worse. But they were a team. That's what I'm telling you. That's why I came forward. I can't believe you've let her go."

"We don't have any evidence against her, any evidence that she had anything to do with killing those girls."

"But don't you see?" Candy pleaded. "She's the same as him. They're a team. They do things together. *Everything together.*"

"Candy, I know it probably took you a lot of courage to come here and talk to me, but what you've said doesn't change things. We can't go and arrest her on—"

"On some *tom's* statement, you mean?"

"I wasn't going to say that. What I was going to say was that we can't just go and arrest her on the evidence of what you've just told me. You consented. You were paid for your services. They didn't hurt you beyond what you were pre-pared for. It's a risky profession you're in. You know that, Candy."

"But surely what I've said makes a difference?"

"Yes, it makes a difference. To me. But we deal in facts, in evidence. I'm not doubting your word, that it happened, but even if we had it on video, it wouldn't make her a murderer."

Candy paused for a moment, then she said, "They did. Have it on video."

"How do you know?"

"Because I saw the camera. They thought it was hidden behind a screen, but I could hear something, a whirring noise, and once when I got up to go to the toilet I glimpsed a video camera set up behind a screen. The screen had a hole in it."

"We didn't find any videos at the house, Candy. And as I said, even if we had, it wouldn't change anything." But the fact that Candy had *seen* a video camera interested Banks. Again, he had to ask himself where was it, and where were the tapes?

"So it's all for nothing, then? My coming here."

"Not necessarily."

"Yes, it is. You're not going to do anything. She's just as guilty as him, and you're going to let her get away with murder."

"Candy, we've got no evidence against her. The fact that she joined in a threesome with her husband and you does *not* make her a murderer."

"Then find some evidence."

Banks sighed. "Why did you come here?" he asked. "Really. You girls never come forward voluntarily and talk to the police."

"What do you mean, *you girls?* You're judging me again, aren't you?"

"Candy, for crying out loud . . . You're a tom. You told me yourself. You sell sex. I'm not judging your profession, but what I am saying is that girls who practice it rarely make themselves helpful to the police. So why are you here?"

She shot him a sly glance so full of humor and intelligence that Banks wanted to get on his soapbox and persuade her to go to university and get a degree. But he didn't. Then her expression quickly changed to one of sadness. "You're right about my *profession,* as you call it," she said. "It's full of risks. Risk of getting some sexually transmitted disease. Risk of meeting the wrong kind of customer. The nasty kind. Things like that happen to us all the time. We deal with them. At the time, these two were no better or worse than anyone else. Better than some. At least they paid." She leaned forward. "But since I've read about them in the papers, what you found in the cellar . . ." She gave a little shudder and hugged her skinny shoulders. "Girls go missing," she went on. "Girls like me. And nobody cares."

Banks attempted to say something but she brushed it aside.

"Oh, you'll say you do. You'll say it doesn't matter who gets raped, beat up or murdered. But if it's some little butter-wouldn't-melt-in-her-knickers schoolgirl, you'll move heaven and earth to find out who did it. If it's someone like me . . . well . . . let's just say we're pretty much low priority. Okay?"

"If that's true, Candy, there are reasons," said Banks. "And it's not because I don't care. Because we don't care."

She studied him for a few moments and seemed to give him the benefit of the doubt. "Maybe *you* do," she said. "Maybe you're different. And maybe there *are* reasons. Not that they get you off the hook. The point is, though, why I came and all that . . . not just that girls do go missing. Girls *have* gone missing. Well, one in particular."

Banks felt the hairs bristle at the back of his neck. "A girl you know? A friend of yours?"

"Not exactly a friend. You don't have many friends in this *profession*. But someone I knew, yes. Spent time with. Talked to. Had a drink with. Lent money to."

"When did this happen?"

"I don't know exactly. Before Christmas."

"Did you report it?"

Her cutting glance said he'd just gone down a lot in her estimation. Curiously, it mattered to him. "Give me a break," she said. "Girls come and go all the time. Move on. Even give up the life sometimes, save up enough money, go to university, get a degree."

Banks felt himself blush as she said the very thing that had crossed his mind some time ago. "So what's to say this missing girl didn't just up and leave like the others?" he asked.

"Nothing," said Candy. "Maybe it's a wild-goose chase."

"But?"

"But you said that what I had to tell you wasn't evidence."

"That's true."

"It made you think, though, didn't it?"

"It gave me pause for thought. Yes."

"Then what if this girl didn't just move on? What if something *did* happen to her? Don't you think you at least ought to look into that possibility? You never know, you might find some evidence there."

"What you're saying makes sense, Candy, but did you ever see this girl with the Paynes?"

"Not exactly with them, no."

"Did you see the Paynes at any time around her disappearance?"

"I did see them sometimes, cruising the street. I can't remember the exact dates."

"Around that time, though?"

"Yes."

"Both of them?"

"Yes."

"I'll need a name."

"No problem. I know her name."

"And not a name like Candy."

"What's wrong with Candy?"

"I don't believe it's your own name."

"Well, well. I can see now why you're such an important detective. Actually, it's not. My real name is Hayley, which, if you ask me, is even worse."

"Oh, I don't know. It's not that bad."

"You can spare me the flattery. Don't you know us toms don't need to be flattered?"

"I didn't mean—"

She smiled. "I know you didn't." Then she leaned forward and rested her arms on the desk, her pale face only a foot or two away from his. He could smell bubble gum and smoke on her breath. "But that girl who disappeared. I know her name. Her street name was Anna, but I know her *real* name. What do you think of that, Mr. Detective?"

"I think we're in business," said Banks, reaching for pad and pen.

She sat back and folded her arms. "Oh, no. Not until I've had that cigarette."

"What now?" asked Janet. "I've already changed my statement."

"I know," said Annie, that sick feeling at the center of her gut. Partly, it was due to Janet's stuffy flat, but only partly. "I've been to talk to the CPS."

Janet poured herself a shot of gin, neat, from an almost empty bottle. "And?"

"And I'm supposed to arrest you and take you down to the station to charge you."

"I see. What are you going to charge me with?"

Annie paused, took a deep breath, then said, "The CPS wanted me to charge you with murder at first, but I managed to get them down to voluntary manslaughter. You'll have to talk to them about this, but I'm sure that if you plead guilty, it'll go easy on you."

The shock and the anger she had expected didn't come. Instead, Janet twisted a loose thread around her forefinger, frowned and took a sip of gin. "It's because of the John Hadleigh verdict, isn't it? I heard it on the radio."

Annie swallowed. "Yes."

"I thought so. A sacrificial lamb."

"Look," Annie went on, "we can work this out. As I said, the CPS will probably work out a deal—"

Janet held her hand up. "No."

"What do you mean?"

"What part of no don't you understand?"

"Janet—"

"No. If the bastards want to charge me, let them. I'll not give them the satisfaction of pleading guilty to just doing my job."

"This is no time for playing games, Janet."

"What makes you think I'm playing games? I mean it. I'll plead innocent to any charges you care to bring."

Annie felt a chill. "Janet, listen to me. You can't do that."

Janet laughed. She looked bad, Annie noticed: hair unwashed and unbrushed, pale skin breaking out in spots, a general haze of stale sweat and fresh gin. "Don't be silly," she said. "Of course I can. The public want us to do our job, don't they? They want people to feel safe in their nice little middle-class beds at night, or when they're driving to work in the morning or going out for a drink in the evening. Don't they? Well, let them find out there's a price for keeping killers off the streets. No, Annie, I'll not plead guilty, not even to voluntary manslaughter."

Annie leaned forward to put some emphasis into what she was saying. "Think about this, Janet. It could be one of the most important decisions you ever make."

"I don't think so. I already made that one in the cellar last week. But I have thought about it. I haven't thought about anything else for a week."

"Your mind's made up?"

"Yes."

"Do you think I want to do this, Janet?" Annie said, standing up.

Janet smiled at her. "No, of course you don't. You're a decent enough person. You like to do the right thing, and you know as well as I do that this stinks. But when push comes to shove, you'll do your job. The bloody Job. You know, I'm almost glad this has happened, glad to be out of it. The fucking hypocrites. Come on, get on with it."

"Janet Taylor, I'm arresting you for the murder of Terence Payne. You do not have to say anything. But it may harm your defense if you do not mention, when questioned, something which you later rely on in court. Anything you do say may be given in evidence."

*   *   *

When Annie suggested they meet for a drink somewhere other than the Queen's Arms, Banks felt immediately apprehensive. The Queen's Arms was their "local." It was where they always went for a drink after work. By naming another pub, the Pied Piper, a tourist haunt on Castle Hill, Annie was telling Banks she had a serious message to deliver, something beyond casual conversation, or so he believed. Either that, or she was worried about Detective Superintendent Chambers's finding out they were meeting.

He got there ten minutes early, bought a pint at the bar and sat at a table near the window, back to the wall. The view was spectacular. The formal gardens were a blaze of purple, scarlet and indigo, and across the river the tall trees of The Green, some of them still in blossom, blocked out most of the eyesore of the East End Estate. He could still see some of the grim maisonettes, and the two twelve-story tower blocks stuck up as if they were giving the finger to the world, but he could also see beyond them to the lush plain with its fields of bright yellow rapeseed, and he even fancied he could make out the dark green humps of the Cleveland Hills in the far distance.

He could see the back of Jenny Fuller's house, too, facing The Green. Sometimes he worried about Jenny. She didn't seem to have much going in her life apart from her work. She had joked about her bad relationships yesterday, but Banks had witnessed some of them, and they were no joke. He remembered the shock, disappointment and—yes—jealousy he had felt some years ago when he went to interrogate a loser called Dennis Osmond and saw Jenny poke her head around his bedroom door, hair in disarray, a thin dressing gown slipping off her shoulders. He had also listened as she spilled out her woes over the unfaithful Randy. Jenny picked losers, cheats and generally unsuitable partners time after time. The sad thing was, she knew it, but it happened anyway.

Annie was fifteen minutes late, which was unlike her, and she lacked the usual spring in her step. When she got herself a drink and joined Banks at the table, he could tell she was upset.

"Rough day?" he asked.

"You can say that again."

Banks felt that he could have had a better one, too. Sandra's letter he could have done without, for a start. And while Candy's information was interesting, it was maddeningly lacking in the hard evidence he needed if he was to track down Lucy Payne and arrest her for anything other than curb-crawling. That was the trouble; the odd things that trickled in—Lucy's childhood, the satanic stuff in Alderthorpe, Kathleen Murray's murder, and now Candy's statement—were all disturbing and suggestive of more serious problems, but ultimately, as AC Hartnell had already pointed out, they added up to nothing.

"Anything in particular?" he asked.

"I just arrested Janet Taylor."

"Let me guess: the Hadleigh verdict?"

"Yes. It seems everyone knew about it except me. The CPS wants justice to be seen to be done. It's just bloody politics, that's all."

"Often is."

Annie gave him a sour look. "I know that, but it doesn't help."

"They'll make a deal with her."

Annie told him what Janet had just said.

"Should be an interesting trial, then. What did Chambers have to say?"

"He doesn't give a damn. He's just marking time till he gets his pension. I'm through with Complaints and Discipline. Soon as there's an opening in CID, I'm back."

"And we'd be happy to have you, as soon as there is," said Banks, smiling.

"Look, Alan," Annie said, looking at the view through the window, "there's something else I wanted to talk to you about."

Just as he'd thought. He lit a cigarette. "Okay. What is it?"

"It's just that . . . I don't know . . . this isn't working out. You and me. I think we should ease off. Cool it. That's all."

"You want to end our relationship?"

"Not end it. Just change its focus, that's all. We can still be friends."

"I don't know what to say, Annie. What's brought this on?"

"Nothing in particular."

"Oh, come on. You can't just expect me to believe you suddenly decided for no apparent reason to chuck me."

"I'm not chucking you. I told you. Things are just changing."

"Okay. Are we going to continue going out for romantic dinners, to galleries and concerts together?"

"No."

"Are we going to continue sleeping together?"

"No."

"Then what, precisely, are we going to do together?"

"Be friends. You know, at work. Be supportive and stuff."

"I'm already supportive and stuff. Why can't I be supportive and stuff and still sleep with you?"

"It's not that I don't like it, Alan. Sleeping with you. The sex. You know that."

"I thought I did. Maybe you're just a damn good actress."

Annie winced and swigged some beer. "That's not fair. I don't deserve that. This isn't easy for me, you know."

"Then why are you doing it? You know it's more than sex with us, anyway."

"I *have* to."

"No, you don't. Is it because of that conversation we had the other night? I wasn't trying to suggest that we should have children. That's the last thing I'd want right now."

"I know. It wasn't that."

"Was it to do with the miscarriage, what I told you I felt?"

"Christ, no. Maybe. Look, okay, I'll admit it threw me, but not in the way you think."

"In what way, then?"

Annie paused, clearly uncomfortable, shifted in her chair and faced away from him, her voice low. "It just made me think about things I'd rather not think about. That's all."

"What things?"

"Do you have to know everything?"

"Annie, I care about you. That's why I'm asking."

She ran her fingers through her hair, turned her eyes on him and shook her head. "After the rape," she said, "over two years ago, well . . . he hadn't . . . the one who did it hadn't . . . Shit, this is more difficult than I thought."

Banks felt understanding dawn on him. "You got pregnant. That's what you're telling me, right? That's why this whole business with Sandra is bothering you so much."

Annie smiled thinly. "Perceptive of you." She touched his hand and whispered, "Yes. I got pregnant."

"And?"

Annie shrugged. "And I had an abortion. It wasn't my best moment, but it wasn't my worst. I didn't feel guilty afterward. I didn't feel much of anything, in fact. But all this . . . I don't know . . . I just want to put it behind me, and being with you always seems to bring it all back, shove it right in my face."

"Annie—"

"No. Let me finish. You've got too much baggage, Alan. Too much for me to handle. I thought it would get easier, go away, maybe, but it hasn't. You can't let it go. You'll never let it go. Your marriage was such a big part of your life for so long that you can't. You're hurt and I can't console you. I don't do consoling well. Sometimes I just feel too over-whelmed by your life, your past, your problems, and all I want to do is crawl away and be on my own. I can't get any breathing space."

Banks stubbed out his cigarette and noticed his hand was shaking a little. "I didn't know you felt like that."

"Well, that's why I'm telling you. I'm not good at commitment, at emotional closeness. Not yet, anyway. Maybe never. I don't know, but it's stifling me and scaring me."

"Can't we work it out?"

"I don't want to work it out. I don't have the energy. This is not what I need in my life right now. That's the other reason."

"What?"

"My career. This Janet Taylor fiasco aside, believe it or not, I do love police work and I do have an aptitude for it."

"I know—"

"No, wait. Let me finish. What we've been doing is unprofessional. It's hard for me to believe that half the station doesn't already know what we're up to in private. I've heard the sniggers behind my back. Certainly all my colleagues in CID and Complaints and Discipline know. I think Chambers was also dropping a hint when he warned me you were a ladies' man. I wouldn't be surprised if ACC McLaughlin knows, too."

"Relationships on the job aren't unusual, and they certainly aren't illegal."

"No, but they *are* seriously discouraged and frowned upon. I want to make chief inspector, Alan. Hell, I want to make superintendent, chief constable. Who knows? I've rediscovered my ambition."

It was ironic, Banks thought, that Annie should rediscover her ambition just when he thought he had come to the limits of his. "And I'm standing in your way?"

"Not standing in my way. Distracting me. I don't need any distractions."

"All work and no play . . ."

"So I'll be dull for a while. It'll be a nice change."

"So that's it, then? Just like that? Over. The end. Because I'm human and I've got a past that sometimes rears its ugly head, and because you've decided you want to put more effort into your career, we stop seeing each other?"

"If you want to put it like that, yes."

"What other way is there to put it?"

Annie hurried her pint. Banks could tell she wanted to leave. Damn it, though, he was hurt and angry and he wasn't going to let her get off that easily.

"Are you sure there's nothing else?" he asked.

"Like what?"

"I don't know. You're not jealous of anyone, are you?"

"Jealous? Of whom? Why should I be?"

"Jenny, perhaps?"

"Oh, for crying out loud, Alan. No, I'm not jealous of Jenny. If I'm jealous of anyone, it's Sandra. Can't you see that? She's got more of a hold on you than anyone."

"That's not true. Not anymore." But Banks remembered the letter, his feelings when he read the cold, business-like words. "Is there someone else? Is that it?" he went on quickly.

"Alan, there's nobody else. Believe me. I've told you. I don't have room for anyone in my life right now. I can't cope with anyone else's emotional demands."

"What about sexual demands?"

"What do you mean?"

"It doesn't have to be emotional, sex, does it? I mean, if it's too much trouble to sleep with someone who actually cares a bit about you, maybe it'd be easier to pick up some stud in a bar for a quick anonymous fuck. No demands. You don't even have to tell one another your names. Is that what you want?"

"Alan, I don't know where you're going with this, but I'd like you to stop right there."

Banks rubbed his temples. "I'm just upset, Annie, that's all. I'm sorry. I've had a bad day, too."

"I'm sorry about that. I really don't want to hurt you."

He looked her in the eye. "Then don't. No matter who you get involved with, you'll have to face things you want to avoid."

He noticed the tears in her eyes. The only time he'd seen her cry before was when she told him about her rape. He reached out to touch her hand on the table, but she jerked it away. "No. Don't."

"Annie—"

"No."

She stood up so abruptly that she banged the table hard and her drink spilled right on to Banks's lap, then she ran out of the pub before he could say another word. All he could do was sit there feeling the cold liquid seep through his trousers, aware of everyone's eyes on him, thankful only that they hadn't been in the Queen's Arms, where everyone knew him. And he'd thought the day couldn't get any worse.

Chapter 17

*A*fter taking her last tutorial group and clearing up some paperwork, Jenny left her office at York early on Tuesday afternoon and headed for the A1 to Durham. The traffic was heavy, especially lorries and delivery vans, but at least it was a pleasant, sunny day, not pouring down with rain.

After talking to Keith Murray—if he agreed to talk to her—Jenny thought she would still have time to continue on to Edinburgh later in the afternoon and look up Laura Godwin. It would mean an overnight stay—either that or a long drive home in the dark—but she could worry about that later. She had an old student friend in the Psychology Department at the University of Edinburgh, and it might be fun to get together and catch up with each other's history. Not that Jenny's recent history was anything to write home about, she thought glumly, and now that she had met Banks's girlfriend, she decided there probably wasn't much hope for her there, either. Still, she was used to that by now; after all, they had known each other for seven years or more, and they hadn't once strayed beyond the bounds of propriety, more was the pity.

She still wasn't certain whether The Girlfriend had been jealous when she came over to them in the Queen's Arms. She must certainly have seen Banks touch Jenny's arm, and though it was merely a friendly, concerned gesture, it was open to misinterpretation, like so much body language. Was The Girlfriend the jealous kind? Jenny didn't know. Annie had seemed self-assured and poised, yet Jenny had sensed something in her attitude that made her feel strangely concerned for Banks, who was probably the only man she had ever met whom she worried about, wanted to protect. She didn't know why. He was independent, strong, private; perhaps he was more vulnerable than he let on, but he certainly wasn't the sort of person you went around feeling you needed to protect or mother.

A white van sped by on her outside lane just as she was turning off, and still lost in thought, she almost hit it. Luckily, instinct kicked in and she had time to swing back abruptly into her own lane without causing anyone else great distress, but she missed the turnoff she wanted. She honked her horn and cursed him out loud—impotent gestures, but all she could come up with—and drove on to the next junction.

When she had got off the A1, she switched the radio channel from a dreary Brahms symphony to some cheerful pop music, tunes she could hum along with and tap out the rhythm on the steering wheel.

Durham was an odd sort of place, Jenny had always thought. Though she had been born there, her parents had moved away when she was only three, and she didn't remember it at all. Very early in her academic career, she had applied for a job at the university, but she got pipped at the post by a man with more publications to his name. She would have liked living here, she thought as she looked at the distant castle high on the hill, and all the greenery surrounding it, but York suited her well enough, and she had no desire to start applying for a new job at this stage in her career.

She had found from her map that Keith Murray lived out by the university sports grounds, so she was able to bypass the central maze around the cathedral and colleges, the city's main tourist area. Even so, she still managed to get lost on a couple of occasions. There was a chance that Keith might be out at lectures, Jenny realized, though she remembered how few lectures she had attended when she was an undergraduate. If he was, she could wait until later if she had to, explore the city, have a pub lunch, and still be in plenty of time to get to Edinburgh to talk to Laura.

She pulled over into a small car park in front of some shops and consulted the map again. Not far away now. She just had to watch out for the one-way streets or she would end up back where she started.

On the second try, she got it right and pulled off the arterial road into an area of narrow streets. She was concentrating so much on finding the right street and the right house number that she almost didn't see the car she parked behind until the last moment. When she did, her heart jumped into her throat. It was a blue Citroën.

Jenny told herself to be calm, that she couldn't be certain it was the *same* blue Citroën that had followed her around Holderness because she hadn't seen the number plate. But it was the exact same model, and she didn't believe in coincidences.

What should she do? Go ahead anyway? If the Citroën belonged to Keith Murray, what had he been doing at Alderthorpe and Spurn Head, and why had he followed her? Was he dangerous?

As Jenny was trying to make up her mind what to do, the front door of the house opened and two people walked over to the car: a young man with keys in his hand and a woman who looked remarkably like Lucy Payne. Just as Jenny decided to pull away, the young man saw her, said something to Lucy, then walked over and jerked open the driver's door of Jenny's car before she had time to lock it.

Well, she thought, you've well and truly done it now, this time, haven't you, Jenny?

* * *

There were no new developments at Millgarth, according to Ken Blackstone on the phone that morning. The SOCOs were getting to the point where there wasn't much left of the Payne house to take apart. Both gardens had been dug up to a depth of between six and ten feet and searched in a grid system. The concrete floors in the cellar and the garage had been ripped up by pneumatic drills. Almost a thousand exhibits had been bagged and labeled. The entire contents of the house had been stripped and taken away. The walls had been punched open at regular intervals. In addition to the crime scene specialists going over all the collected material, forensic mechanics had taken Payne's car apart looking for traces of the abducted girls. Payne might be dead, but a case still had to be answered, and Lucy's role had still to be determined.

The only snippet of information about Lucy Payne was that she had withdrawn two hundred pounds from an ATM on Tottenham Court Road. It figured she would go to London if she wanted to disappear, Banks thought, remembering his search there for Chief Constable Riddle's daughter, Emily. Perhaps he would have to go and search for Lucy, too, although this time he would have all the resources of the Metropolitan Police at his disposal. Maybe it wouldn't come to that; maybe Lucy wasn't involved and would simply ease herself into a new identity and a new look in a new place and try to rebuild her shattered life. *Maybe.*

Banks looked again at the loose sheets of papers on his desk.

Katya Pavelic.

Katya, Candy's "Anna," had been identified through dental records late the previous evening. Fortunately for Banks, she had suffered a toothache shortly before she disappeared, and Candy had directed Katya to her own dentist. Katya had disappeared, according to Candy, sometime last November. At least, she remembered the weather was cool and misty and the Christmas lights had recently been turned on in the city center. That likely made Katya the victim before Kelly Matthews.

Certainly Candy, or Hayley Lyndon, as she was called, had seen both Terence and Lucy Payne driving around the area on a number of occasions but couldn't connect them directly with Katya. The circumstantial evidence was beginning to build up, though, and if Jenny's psychological probing into the old Alderthorpe wounds turned up anything interesting, then it might be time to reel Lucy in. For the moment, let her enjoy the illusion of freedom.

Katya Pavelic had come to England from Bosnia four years ago, when she was fourteen. Like so many young girls there, she had been gang-raped by Serbian soldiers, and then shot, saving herself only by playing dead under a pile of corpses until some Canadian UN peacekeepers found her three days later. The wound was superficial and the blood had clotted. Her only problem was an infection, and that had responded well to antibiotics. Various groups and individuals had seen that Katya got to England, but she was a disturbed and troublesome girl, and she soon ran away from her foster parents when she was sixteen, and they had tried in vain to find her and contact her ever since.

The irony wasn't lost on Banks. After having survived the horrors of the Bosnian war, Katya Pavelic had ended up raped, murdered and buried in the Paynes' back garden. What was the bloody point of it all? he asked. As usual, he got no answer from the Supreme Ironist in the Sky, only a deep hollow laughter echoing through his brain. Sometimes, the pity and the horror of it all were almost too much for him to bear.

And there remained one more unidentified victim, the one who had been buried there the longest: a white woman in her late teens or early twenties, about five feet three inches tall, according to the forensic anthropologist, who was still conducting tests on the bones. There was little doubt in Banks's mind that this could easily be another prostitute victim, and that might make the corpse hard to identify.

Banks had had one brainstorm and pulled in Terence Payne's teacher friend Geoff Brighouse to help him find the Aberdeen schoolteacher the two of them had taken up to their room at the convention. Luckily, Banks turned out to be wrong, and she was still teaching in Aberdeen. Though she expressed some anger about her experience, she had kept quiet mostly because she didn't want to damage her teaching career and had written that one off to experience. She had also been very embarrassed and angry with herself for being so drunk and foolish as to go to a hotel room with two strange men after all the things she had read in the papers. She had almost fainted when Banks told her that the man who had coerced her into having anal sex against her will was Terence Payne. She hadn't made the connection from the photo in the newspapers and had only been on first-name terms with the two.

Banks opened his window on another fine day in the market-square, tourist buses pulling up already, disgorging their hordes on to the gleaming cobbles. A quick glance around the church's interior, a walk up to the Castle, lunch at the Pied Piper—Banks felt depressed just thinking about what had happened there yesterday—then they'd pile back in the coach and be off to Castle Bolton or Devraulx Abbey. How he wished he could go on a long holiday. Maybe never come back.

The gold hands against the blue face of the church clock stood at five past ten. Banks lit a cigarette and planned out the rest of his day, plans that included Mick Blair, Ian Scott and Sarah Francis, not to mention the grieving parents, Christopher and Victoria Wray. Winsome had discovered nothing new from talking to the Wrays' neighbors, none of whom had either seen or heard anything unusual. Banks still had his suspicions about them, though he found it difficult to convince himself that they could actually have *killed* Leanne.

He had suffered yet another restless night, this time partly because of Annie. Now, the more he thought about her decision, the more sense it made. He didn't want to give her up, but if he was to be honest, it was best all around. Looking back at her on-again-off-again attitude toward their relationship, the way she bristled every time other aspects of his life came up, he realized that however much there had been, the relationship had also been a lot of grief, too. If she didn't like the way his past made her face details of her own, like the abortion, then perhaps she was right to end it. Time to move on and stay "just friends," let her pursue her career and let him try to exorcise his personal demons.

Just as he was finishing his cigarette, DC Winsome Jackman tapped at his door and walked in looking particularly elegant in a tailored pinstripe suit over a white blouse. The woman had clothes sense, Banks thought, unlike himself, and unlike Annie Cabbot. He liked Annie's casual high style—it was definitely *her*—but no one could accuse her of making a fashion statement. Anyway, best forget about Annie. He turned toward Winsome.

"Come in. Sit down."

Winsome sat, crossing her long legs, sniffing accusingly and wrinkling her nose at the smoke.

"I know, I know," Banks said. "I'm going to stop soon, honestly."

"That little job you asked me to do," she said. "I thought you'd like to know that your instinct was right. There was a car reported stolen from Disraeli Street between nine-thirty and eleven o'clock on the night Leanne Wray disappeared."

"Was there, indeed? Isn't Disraeli Street just around the corner from the Old Ship Inn?"

"It is, sir."

Banks sat down and rubbed his hands together. "Tell me more."

"Keeper's name is Samuel Gardner. I've spoken to him on the phone. Seems he parked there while he popped into the Cock and Bull on Palmerston Avenue, just for a pint of shandy, he stressed."

"Of course. Perish the thought we should try to do him for drinkdriving two months after the event. What do you think, Winsome?"

Winsome shifted and crossed her legs the other way, straightening the hem of her skirt over her knees. "I don't know, sir. Seems a bit of a coincidence, doesn't it?"

"That Ian Scott's in the neighborhood?"

"Yes, sir. I know there are plenty of kids taking and driving away, but . . . well, the timing fits, and the location."

"Indeed it does. When did he report it missing?"

"Ten past eleven that night."

"And when was it found?"

"Not until the next morning, sir. One of the beat constables came across it illegally parked down by the formal gardens."

"That's not very far from The Riverboat, is it?"

"Ten-minute walk, at the most."

"You know, this is starting to look good, Winsome. I want you to go and have a word with this Samuel Gardner, see if you can find out any more from him. Put him at ease. Make it clear we don't give a damn whether he drank a whole bottle of whiskey as long as he tells us everything he can remember about that night. And have the car taken into the police garage for a full forensic examination. I doubt we'll find anything after all this time, but Scott and Blair aren't likely to know that, are they?"

Winsome smiled wickedly. "Doubt it very much, sir."

Banks looked at his watch. "When you've talked to Gardner and the car's safe in our care, have Mick Blair brought in.

I think a little chat with him in one of the interview rooms might be very productive."

"Right you are."

"And have Sarah Francis brought in at the same time."

"Okay."

"And, Winsome."

"Sir?"

"Make sure they see one another in passing, would you?"

"My pleasure, sir." Winsome smiled, stood up and left the office.

"Look," said Jenny, "I haven't had any lunch yet. Instead of standing around here in the street, is there anywhere nearby we can go?" Though her immediate fears had dispersed somewhat when the young man simply asked her who she was and what she wanted, without showing any particular inclination toward aggression, she still wanted to be with them in a public place, not up in the flat.

"There's a café down the road," he said. "We can go there if you want."

"Fine."

Jenny followed them back to the arterial road, crossed at the zebra and went into a corner café that smelled of bacon. She was supposed to be slimming—she was *always* supposed to be slimming—but she couldn't resist the smell and ordered a bacon butty and a mug of tea. The other two asked for the same and Jenny paid. Nobody objected. Poor students never do. Now that they were closer, sitting at an isolated table near the window, Jenny could see that she was mistaken. While the girl definitely resembled Lucy, had her eyes and mouth and the same shiny black hair, it *wasn't* her. There was something softer, more fragile, more *human* about this young woman, and her eyes weren't quite so black and impenetrable; they were intelligent and sensitive, though their depths flickered with horrors and fears Jenny could barely imagine.

"Laura, isn't it?" she said when they'd settled.

The young woman raised her eyebrows. "Why, yes. How did you know?"

"It wasn't difficult," Jenny said. "You resemble your sister, and you're with your cousin."

Laura blushed. "I'm only visiting him. It's not . . . I mean, I don't want you to get the wrong idea."

"Don't worry," said Jenny. "I don't jump to conclusions." Well, not *many,* she said to herself.

"Let's get back to my original question," Keith Murray cut in. He was more hard-edged than Laura and not one for small talk. "That's who are you and why you're here. You might as well tell me what you were doing at Alderthorpe, too, while you're at it."

Laura looked surprised. "She was in Alderthorpe?"

"On Saturday. I followed her to Easington and then to Spurn Head. I turned back when she got to the M62." He looked at Jenny again. "Well?"

He was a good-looking young man, brown hair a little over his ears and collar, but professionally layered, slightly better-dressed than most of the students she taught, in a light sports jacket and gray chinos, highly polished shoes. Clean-shaven. Clearly a young lad who took some pride in his rather conservative appearance. Laura, in contrast, wore a shapeless sort of shift that hung around her in a haze of material and hid any claims she might have had to the kind of figure men like. There was a reticence and tentativeness about her that made Jenny want to reach out and tell her everything was fine, not to worry, she didn't bite. Keith also seemed very protective of her, and Jenny wondered how their relationship had developed since Alderthorpe.

She told them who she was and what she was doing, about

her forays into Lucy Payne's past, looking for answers to her present, and both Laura and Keith listened intently. When she had finished, they looked at each other, and she could tell they were communicating in some way that was beyond her. She couldn't tell what they were saying, and she didn't believe it was some sort of telepathic trick, just that whatever they had been through all those years ago had created a bond so strong and deep that it went beyond words.

"What makes you think you'll find any answers there?" Keith asked.

"I'm a psychologist," Jenny said, "not a psychiatrist, certainly not a Freudian, but I do believe that our past shapes us, makes us what we are."

"And what *is* Linda, or Lucy, as she calls herself now?"

Jenny spread her hands. "That's just it. I don't know. I was hoping you might be able to help."

"Why should we help you?"

"I don't know," said Jenny. "Maybe there are some issues back there you still have to deal with yourselves."

Keith laughed. "If we lived to be a hundred, we'd still have issues to deal with from *back then*," he said. "But what's that got to do with Linda?"

"She was with you, wasn't she? One of you."

Keith and Laura looked at each other again and Jenny wished she knew what they were thinking. Finally, as if they had come to a decision, Laura said, "Yes, she was *with* us, but in a way she was apart."

"What do you mean, Laura?"

"Linda was the eldest, so she took care of us."

Keith snorted.

"She *did*, Keith."

"All right."

Laura's lower lip trembled, and for a moment Jenny thought she was going to cry. "Go on, Laura," she said. "Please."

"I know Linda was my sister," Laura said, rubbing one hand against the top of her thigh, "but there's three years between us, and that's an awful lot when you're younger."

"Tell me about it. My brother's three years older than me."

"Well, you'll know what I mean, then. So I didn't really *know* Linda. In some ways, she was as distant as an adult to me, and just as incomprehensible. We played together when we were little, but the older we got, the more we drifted apart, especially with . . . you know . . . the way things were."

"What was she like, though?"

"Linda? She was strange. Very distant. Very self-absorbed, even then. She liked to play games, and she could be cruel."

"In what way?"

"If she didn't get her own way, or if you didn't do what she wanted, she could lie and get you in trouble with the adults. Get you put in the cage."

"She did that?"

"Oh, yes," said Keith. "All of us got on her bad side at one time or another."

"Sometimes we just didn't know if she was with us or them," said Laura. "But she could be kind. I remember her treating a cut I had once, putting some TCP on so it didn't get infected. She was very gentle. And sometimes she even stuck up for us against them."

"In what ways?"

"Little ways. If we were, you know, too weak to . . . or just . . . sometimes they listened to her. And she saved the kittens."

"What kittens?"

"Our cat had kittens and D-d-dad wanted to drown them but Linda took them and found them all homes."

"She liked animals, then?"

"She adored them. She wanted to be a vet when she grew up."

"Why didn't she?"

"I don't know. Maybe she wasn't clever enough. Or maybe she changed her mind."

"But she was also their victim, too? The adults."

"Oh, yes," said Keith. "We all were."

"She was their favorite for a long time," Laura added. "That is, until she . . ."

"She what, Laura? Take your time."

Laura blushed and looked away. "Until she became a woman. When she was twelve. Then they weren't interested in her anymore. Kathleen became their favorite then. She was only nine, like me, but they liked her better."

"What was Kathleen like?"

Laura's eyes shone. "She was . . . like a saint. She bore it all without complaining, everything those . . . those people did to us. Kathleen had some sort of inner light, some, I don't know, some spiritual quality that just shone out, but she was very f-f-fragile, very weak, and she was always ill. She couldn't take the kind of punishments and beatings they dished out."

"Like what?"

"The cage. And no food for days. She was too weak and frail to begin with."

"Tell me," said Jenny, "why did none of you tell the authorities what was going on?"

Keith and Laura looked at each other in that intense way again. "We didn't dare," Keith said. "They said they'd kill us if we ever told a soul."

"And they were . . . they were family," Laura added. "I mean, you wanted your mummy and daddy to love you, didn't you, so you had to do, you know, what they wanted, you had to do what the grown-ups said or your d-d-daddy wouldn't love you anymore."

Jenny sipped some tea to cover her face for a moment. She wasn't sure whether anger or pity had brought the tears to her eyes but she didn't want Laura to see them.

"Besides," Keith went on, "we didn't know any different. How could we know life was different for other kids?"

"What about at school? You must have kept yourselves apart, been aware that you were *different?*"

"We kept apart, yes. We were told not to talk about what happened. It was *family,* and nobody else's business."

"What were you doing in Alderthorpe?"

"I'm writing a book," Keith said. "A book about what happened. It's partly therapeutic and partly because I think people should know what goes on, so maybe it can be prevented from happening again."

"Why did you follow me?"

"I thought you might be a reporter or something, poking about the place like that."

"You'd better get used to that idea, Keith. It won't take them long to find out about Alderthorpe. I'm surprised they're not swarming around already."

"I know."

"So you thought I was a reporter. What were you going to do about me?"

"Nothing. I just wanted to see where you were going, make sure you were gone."

"And what if I'd come back?"

Keith spread his hands, palms up. "You did, didn't you?"

"Did you realize it was Linda as soon as the news about the Paynes broke?"

"I did, yes," said Laura. "It wasn't a good photo, but I knew she'd married Terry. I knew where she lived."

"Did you ever get together, keep in touch?"

"Not often. We did, until Susan committed suicide and Tom went to Australia. And Keith and I visit Dianne as often as we can. But as I said, Linda was always distant, older. I mean, we met up sometimes, for birthdays, that sort of thing, but I thought she was weird."

"In what way?"

"I don't know. It was an evil thought. I mean, she'd suffered the same as we had."

"But it seemed to have affected her in a different way," Keith added.

"What way?"

"I didn't see her nearly as often as Laura did," he went on, "but she always gave me the impression that she was up to something bad, something deliciously evil. It was just the way she spoke, the hint of sin. She was secretive, so she never told us exactly what she was doing, but . . ."

"She was into some pretty weird stuff," Laura said, blushing. "S and M. That sort of thing."

"She told you?"

"Once. Yes. She only did it to embarrass me. I'm not comfortable talking about sex." She hugged herself and avoided Jenny's eyes.

"And Linda liked to embarrass you?"

"Yes. Tease me, I suppose."

"Wasn't it a shock to you, what Terry had done, with Linda so close by, especially after the events of your childhood?"

"Of course it was," said Keith. "It still is. We're still trying to come to terms with it."

"That's partly why I'm here," said Laura. "I needed to be with Keith. To talk. To decide what to do."

"What do you mean, what to do?"

"But we didn't want to be rushed," said Keith.

Jenny leaned forward "What is it?" she asked. "What is it you need to do?"

They looked at each other again, and Jenny waited what seemed like ages before Keith spoke. "We'd better tell her, don't you think?" he said.

"I suppose so."

"Tell me what?"

"About what happened. That's what we've been trying to decide, you see. Whether we should tell."

"But I'm sure you can understand," Keith said, "that we don't want the limelight anymore. We don't want it all raked up again."

"Your book will do that," Jenny said.

"I'll deal with that when and if it happens." He leaned forward. "Anyway, you've sort of forced our hand, haven't you? We would probably have told someone soon, anyway, so it might as well be you, now."

"I'm still not sure what you want to tell me," she said.

Laura looked at her, tears in her eyes. "It's about Kathleen. Our parents didn't kill her, Tom didn't kill her. Linda killed her. Linda killed Kathleen."

Mick Blair was surly when Banks and Winsome entered the interview room at three thirty-five that afternoon. As well he might be, Banks thought. He had been dragged away from his job as a clerk in the Tandy shop in the Swainsdale Centre by two uniformed police officers and left waiting in the dingy room for over an hour. It was a wonder he wasn't screaming for his brief. Banks would have been.

"Just another little chat, Mick," said Banks, smiling as he turned on the tape recorders. "But we'll get it on record this time. That way you can be certain there's no funny business from us."

"Very grateful, I'm sure," said Blair. "And why the hell did you have to keep me waiting so long?"

"Important police business," said Banks. "The bad guys just never stop."

"What's Sarah doing here?"

"Sarah?"

"You know who I mean. Sarah Francis. Ian's girlfriend. I saw her in the corridor. What's she doing here?"

"Just answering our questions, Mick, the way I hope you will."

"I don't know why you're wasting your time on me. I can't tell you anything you don't know already."

"Don't underestimate yourself, Mick."

"What's it about this time, then?" He eyed Winsome suspiciously.

"It's about the night Leanne Wray disappeared."

"Again? But we've been over and over all that."

"Yes, I know, but we haven't got to the truth yet. See, it's like peeling off the layers of an onion, Mick. All we've got so far is layer after layer of lies."

"It's the truth. She left us outside the Old Ship and we went our separate ways. We didn't see her again. What else can I tell you?"

"The truth. Where the four of you went."

"I've told you all I know."

"You see, Mick," Banks went on, "Leanne was upset that day. She'd just heard some bad news. Her stepmother was going to have a baby. You might not understand why, but believe me, that upset her. So I should think that night she was in a rebellious mood, ready to say to hell with the curfew, and let's have some fun. Make her parents suffer a bit at the same time. I don't know whose suggestion it was, maybe yours, but you decided to steal a car—"

"Now, wait a minute—"

"A car belonging to Mr. Samuel Gardner, a blue Fiat Brava, to be exact, which was parked just around the corner from the pub."

"That's ridiculous! We never stole no car. You can't pin that on us."

"Shut up and listen, Mick," said Winsome. Blair looked at her, then swallowed and shut up. Winsome's expression was hard and unflinching, her eyes full of scorn and disgust.

"Where did you go on your little joyride, Mick?" Banks asked. "What happened? What happened to Leanne? Was she giving you the come-on? Did you think it was going to be your lucky night? Did you try it on with her and she changed her mind? Did you get a bit rough? Were you on drugs, Mick?"

"No! It's not true. None of it's true. She left us outside the pub."

"You sound like a drowning man clinging to a bit of wood, Mick. Pretty soon you'll have to let go."

"I'm telling the truth."

"I don't think so."

"Then prove it."

"Listen, Mick," said Winsome, standing up and pacing the small room. "We've got Mr. Gardner's car in the police garage right now and our forensics people are going over it inch by inch. Are you trying to tell us that they won't find anything?"

"I don't know what they'll find," said Mick. "How can I? I've never even seen the fucking car."

Winsome stopped pacing and sat down. "They're the best in the business, our forensics team. They don't even need fingerprints. If there's just one hair, they'll find it. And if it belongs to you, Ian, Sarah or Leanne, we've got you." She held a finger up. "One hair. Think about it, Mick."

"She's right, you know," said Banks. "They *are* very good, these scientists. Me, I know bugger-all about DNA and hair follicles, but these lads could find the exact spot on your head the hair came from."

"We didn't steal no car."

"I know what you're thinking," Banks said.

"Mind reader, too, are you?"

Banks laughed. "It doesn't take much. You're thinking how long ago was it we took that car? It was the thirty-first of March. And what's today's date? It's the sixteenth of May. That's a month and a half. Surely there can't be any traces left by now? Surely the car must have been washed, the interior vacuumed? Isn't that what you're thinking, Mick?"

"I've told you. I don't know nothing about a stolen car." He folded his arms and tried to look defiant. Winsome gave a grunt of disgust and impatience.

"DC Jackman's getting restless," said Banks. "And I wouldn't want to push her too far, if I were you."

"You can't touch me. It's all on tape."

"Touch you? Who said anything about touching you?"

"You're threatening me."

"No. You've got it wrong, Mick. See, *I* want to get this all settled, get you back off to work, home in time for the evening news. Nothing I'd like better. But DC Jackman here is, well, let's just say that she'd be more than happy to see you in detention."

"What do you mean?"

"In the cells, Mick. Downstairs. Overnight."

"But I haven't done anything. You can't do that."

"Was it Ian? Is that whose idea it was?"

"I don't know what you're talking about."

"What happened to Leanne?"

"Nothing. I don't know."

"I'll bet Sarah tells us it was all your fault."

"I haven't done anything."

"She'll want to protect her boyfriend, won't she, Mick? I'll bet she doesn't give a damn about you when the chips are down."

"Stop it!"

Winsome looked at her watch. "Let's just lock him up and go home," she said. "I'm getting fed up of this."

"What do you think, Mick?"

"I've told you all I know."

Banks looked at Winsome before turning back to Mick. "I'm afraid, then, we're going to have to hold you on suspicion."

"Suspicion of *what?*"

"Suspicion of the murder of Leanne Wray."

Mick jumped to his feet. "That's absurd. I didn't kill anyone. Nobody *murdered* Leanne."

"How do you know that?"

"I mean *I* didn't murder Leanne. I don't know what happened to her. It's not my fault if somebody else killed her."

"It is if you were there."

"I wasn't there."

"Then tell us the truth, Mick. Tell us what happened."

"I've told you."

Banks stood up and gathered his file folders together. "All right. We'll see what Sarah has to say. In the meantime, I want you to think about two things while you're in the cells for the night, Mick. Time can drag down there, especially in the wee hours, when all you've got for company is the drunk next door singing 'Your Cheating Heart' over and over again; so it's nice to have something to think about, something to distract you."

"What things?"

"First off, if you come clean with us, if you tell us the truth, if it was all Ian Scott's idea and if whatever happened to Leanne was down to Ian, then it'll go a lot easier with you." He looked at Winsome. "I could even see him walking away from this with little more than a reprimand, failing to report, or something minor like that, can't you, DC Jackman?"

Winsome grimaced, as if the idea of Mick Blair's getting off with less than murder appalled her.

"What's the other thing?" Mick asked.

"The other thing? Oh, yes. It's about Samuel Gardner."

"Who?"

"The owner of the stolen car."

"What about him?"

"Man's a slob, Mick. He *never* cleans his car. Inside or out."

Jenny couldn't think of anything to say after what Keith and Laura had just told her. She sat with her mouth half open and an astonished expression on her face until her brain processed the information and she was able to continue. "How do you know?" she asked.

"We saw her," Keith said. "We were with her. In a way, it was all of us. She was doing it for all of us but she was the only one had the guts to do it."

"Are you certain about this?"

"Yes," they said.

"This isn't something you've just remembered?" Like many of her colleagues, Jenny distrusted repressed memory syndrome, and she wanted to make certain that was not what she was dealing with. Linda Godwin might have been kind to animals and never wet the bed or set a fire, but if she had killed when she was twelve, there was something seriously, pathologically wrong with her, and she could have killed again.

"No," said Laura. "We always knew. We just lost it for a while."

"What do you mean?"

"It's like when you put something away where you can find it again easily, but then you don't remember where you put it," said Keith.

Jenny understood that; it happened to her all the time.

"Or when you're carrying something and you remember you have to do something else, so you put it down on your way, and then you can't find it again," Laura added.

"You say you were there?"

"Yes," said Keith. "We were in the room with her. We saw her do it."

"And you've said nothing all these years?"

Laura and Keith just looked at her and she understood that they couldn't have said anything. How could they? They were too used to silence. And why would they? They were all victims of the Godwins and the Murrays. Why should Linda be singled out for more suffering?

"Is that why she was in the cage when the police came?"

"No. Linda was in the cage because it was her period," Keith said. Laura blushed and turned away. "Tom was in the cage with her because they thought *he* did it. They never suspected Linda."

"But *why?*" asked Jenny.

"Because Kathleen just couldn't take any more," said Laura. "She was so weak, her spirit was almost gone. Linda killed her to s-s-save her. She *knew* what it was like to be in that position, and she knew that Kathleen couldn't handle it. She killed her to save her further suffering."

"Are you sure?" Jenny asked.

"What do you mean?"

"Are you certain that's why Linda killed her?"

"Why else?"

"Didn't you think it might have been because she was jealous? Because Kathleen was usurping *her* place?"

"No!" said Linda, scraping back her chair. "That's horrible. How could you say something like that? She killed her to save her more suffering. She killed her out of k-k-kindness."

One or two people in the café had noticed Laura's outburst and were looking over curiously at the table.

"Okay," Jenny said. "I'm sorry. I didn't mean to upset you."

Laura looked at her and a note of defiant desperation came into her tone. "She *could* be kind, you know. Linda *could* be kind."

* * *

The old house was certainly full of noises, Maggie thought, and she was beginning to jump at almost every one: wood creaking as the temperature dropped after dark, a whistle of wind rattling at the windows, dishes shifting in the rack as they dried. It was Bill's phone call, of course, she told herself, and she tried the routines she used to calm herself—deep breathing, positive visualization—but the ordinary noises of the house continued to distract her from her work.

She put a CD compilation of Baroque classics in the stereo Ruth had set up in the studio, and that both cut out the disturbing sounds and helped her to relax.

She was working late on some sketches for "Hänsel and Gretel" because the following day she had to go to London to meet with her art director and discuss the project so far. She also had an interview at Broadcasting House: a Radio Four program about domestic violence, naturally, but she was beginning to warm to being a spokesperson, and if anything she said could help anyone at all, then all the minor irritations, such as ignorant interviewers and provocative fellow guests, were worthwhile.

Bill already knew where she was, so she had no reason to worry about giving that away now. She wasn't going to run away. Not again. Despite his call, and the way it had shaken her, she was determined to continue in her new role.

While she was in London, she would also try to get a ticket for a West End play she wanted to see and stay overnight at the modest little hotel her art director had recommended several visits ago. One of the joys of a country with a decent train service, Maggie thought, was that London was only a couple of hours away from Leeds, a couple of hours that could be spent in reasonable comfort reading a book as the landscape sped by. One thing that amused and intrigued Maggie was the way that the English always complained about their train service, no matter how good it seemed to someone from Canada, where trains were regarded as something of a necessary evil, tolerated but not encouraged. Maggie thought complaining about trains was probably a British institution that had begun long before the days of British Rail, let alone Virgin and Railtrack.

Maggie turned back to her sketch. She was trying to capture the expression on the faces of Hänsel and Gretel when they realized in the moonlight that the trail of crumbs they had left to lead them from the dangers of the forest to the safety of home had been eaten by birds. She liked the eerie effect she had created with the tree trunks, branches and shadows, which with just a little imagination could take the shapes of wild beasts and demons, but Hänsel and Gretel's expressions still weren't quite right. They were only children, Maggie reminded herself, not adults, and their fear would be simple and natural, a look of abandonment and eyes on the verge of tears, not as complex as adult fear, which would include components of anger and the determination to find a way out. Very different facial expressions indeed.

In an earlier version of the sketch, Hänsel and Gretel had come out looking a bit like younger versions of Terry and Lucy, Maggie thought, just as Rapunzel had resembled Claire, so she scrapped it. Now they were anonymous, faces she had probably once spotted in a crowd which, for whatever mysterious reason, had lodged in her unconscious.

Claire. The poor girl. That afternoon Maggie had talked with both Claire and her mother together, and they had agreed that Claire would try the psychologist Dr. Simms had recommended. That was a start, at least, Maggie thought, though it might take Claire years to work through the psychological disturbance brought on by Terry Payne's acts, her friend's murder and her own sense of guilt and responsibility.

Pachelbel's "Canon" played in the background, and Maggie concentrated on her drawing, adding a little chiaroscuro effect here and a silvering of moonlight there. No need to make it too elaborate, as it would only serve as the model for a painting, but she needed these little notes to herself to show her the way when she came to the final version. That would be different in some ways, of course, but would also retain many of the little visual ideas she was having now.

When she heard the tapping over the music, she thought it was another noise the old house had come up with to scare her.

But when it stopped for a few seconds, then resumed at a slightly higher volume and faster rhythm, she turned off the stereo and listened.

Someone was knocking at the back door.

Nobody ever used the back door. It only led into a mean little latticework of gennels and snickets that connected with the council estate behind The Hill.

Not Bill, surely?

No, Maggie reassured herself. Bill was in Toronto. Besides, the door was deadlocked, bolted and chained. She wondered if she should dial 999 right away, but then realized how silly she would look in the eyes of the police if it was Claire, or Claire's mother. Or even the police themselves. She couldn't bear the idea of Banks hearing she had been such a fool.

Instead, she moved very slowly and quietly. Despite the anonymous creaks, the staircase was relatively silent underfoot, partly because of the thick pile carpet. She picked out one of Charles's golf clubs from the hall cupboard and, brandishing it ready to use, edged toward the kitchen door.

The knocking continued.

It was only when Maggie had got to within a few feet away that she heard the familiar woman's voice: "Maggie, is that you? Are you there? Please let me in."

She abandoned the golf club, turned on the kitchen light and fiddled with the various locks. When she finally got the door open, she was confused by what she saw. Appearance and voice didn't match. The woman had short, spiky blond hair, was wearing a T-shirt under a soft black leather jacket and a pair of close-fitting blue jeans. She was carrying a small holdall. Only the slight bruising by one eye, and the impenetrable darkness of the eyes themselves, told Maggie who it was, though it took several moments to process the information.

"Lucy. My God, it *is* you!"

"Can I come in?"

"Of course." Maggie held the door open and Lucy Payne stepped into the kitchen.

"Only I've got nowhere to go and I wondered if you could put me up. Just for a couple of days or so, while I think of something."

"Yes," said Maggie, still feeling stunned. "Yes, of course. Stay as long as you like. It's quite a new look. I didn't recognize you at first."

Lucy gave a little twirl. "Do you like it?"

"It's certainly different."

Lucy laughed. "Good," she said. "I don't want *anyone* else to know I'm here. Believe it or not, Maggie, but not everyone around here is as sympathetic toward me as you are."

"I suppose not," said Maggie, then she locked, bolted and put the chain on the door, turned out the kitchen light and led Lucy Payne into the living room.

Chapter 18

"*I* just wanted to say I'm sorry," Annie told Banks in his Eastvale office on Wednesday morning. He had just been glancing over the garage's report on Samuel Gardner's Fiat. They had, of course, found many hair traces in the car's interior, both human and animal, but they all had to be collected, labeled and sent to the lab, and it would take time to match them with the suspects, or with Leanne Wray. There were plenty of fingerprints, too—it was certainly true that Gardner had been a slob when it came to his car—but Vic Manson, fingerprints officer, could only hurry to a certain degree, and it wasn't fast enough for Banks's immediate needs.

Banks looked at Annie. "Sorry for *what* exactly?"

"Sorry for making a scene in the pub, for acting like a fool."

"Oh."

"What did you think I meant?"

"Nothing."

"No, come on. That I was sorry about what I said, about us? About ending the relationship?"

"I can always live in hope, can't I?"

"Oh, stop feeling sorry for yourself, Alan. It doesn't suit you."

Banks opened up a paper clip. The sharp end pricked his finger and a tiny spot of blood dropped on his desk. Which fairy tale was that? he found himself wondering. "Sleeping Beauty"? But he didn't fall asleep. Chance would be a fine thing.

"Now, are we going to get on with life, or are you just going to sulk and ignore me? Because if you are, I'd like to know."

Banks couldn't help but smile. She was right. He *had* been feeling sorry for himself. He had also decided that she was right about their relationship. Fine as it had been most of the time, and much as he would miss her intimate company, it was fraught with problems on both sides. So *tell* her, his inner voice prompted. Don't be a bastard. Don't put it all down to her, the whole burden. It was difficult; he wasn't used to talking about his feelings. He sucked his bleeding finger and said, "I'm *not* going to sulk. Just give me a little time to get used to the idea, okay? I sort of enjoyed what we had."

"So did I," said Annie, with a hint of a smile tugging at the corners of her lips. "Do you think it's any easier for me, just because I'm the one who's making the move? We want different things, Alan. *Need* different things. It's just not working."

"You're right. Look, I promise I won't sulk or ignore you or put you down as long as you don't treat me like something nasty stuck on your shoe."

"What on earth makes you think I'd do that?"

Banks was thinking of the letter from Sandra, which had made him feel exactly like that, but he was talking to Annie, he realized. Yes, she was right; things were well and truly screwed up. He shook his head. "Ignore me, Annie. Friends and colleagues, okay?"

Annie narrowed her eyes and scrutinized him. "I *do* care, you know."

"I know you do."

"That's part of the problem."

"It'll get better. Over time. Sorry, I can't seem to think of anything to say but clichés. Maybe that's what they're for, situations like this? Maybe that's why there are so many of them. But don't worry, Annie, I mean what I say. I'll do the best I can to behave toward you with the utmost courtesy and respect."

"Oh, bloody hell!" Annie said, laughing. "You don't have to be so damn stuffy! A simple good morning, a smile and a friendly little chat in the canteen every now and then would be just fine."

Banks felt his face burn, then he laughed with her. "Right you are. How's Janet Taylor?"

"Stubborn as hell. I've tried to talk to her. The CPS has tried to talk to her. Her own lawyer has tried to talk to her. Even *Chambers* has tried to talk to her."

"At least she's got a lawyer now."

"The Federation sent someone over."

"What's she being charged with?"

"They're going to charge her with voluntary manslaughter. If she pleads guilty with extenuating circumstances, there's every chance she'll get it down to excusable homicide."

"And if she goes ahead as planned?"

"Who knows? It's up to the jury. They're either going to give her the same as they gave John Hadleigh, despite the vastly different circumstances, or they're going to take her job and her situation into account and give her the benefit of the doubt. I mean, the public doesn't want us hamstrung when it comes to doing our job, but they don't want us to get ideas above our station, either. They don't like to see us acting as if we're beyond that law. It's a toss-up, really."

"How's she bearing up?"

"She's not. She's just drinking."

"Bugger."

"Indeed. How about the Payne investigation?"

Banks told her what Jenny had discovered about Lucy's past.

Annie whistled. "So what are you going to do?"

"Bring her in for questioning in the death of Kathleen

Murray. If we can find her. It's probably a bloody waste of time—after all, it was over ten years ago, and she was only twelve at the time—so I doubt we'll get anywhere with it, but who knows, it might open other doors if a little pressure is judiciously applied."

"AC Hartnell won't like it."

"I know that. He's already made his feelings clear."

"Lucy Payne doesn't suspect you know so much about her past?"

"She has to be aware there was a chance the others would talk, or that we'd find out somehow. In that case, she may have already gone to ground."

"Anything new on the sixth body?"

"No," said Banks. "But we'll find out who it is." The fact that they couldn't identify the sixth victim nagged away at him. Like the other victims, she had been buried naked and no traces of clothing or personal belongings remained. Banks could only guess that Payne must have burned their clothes and disposed of any rings or watches somehow. He certainly hadn't kept them as trophies. The forensic anthropologist working on her remains had so far been able to tell him that she was a white female between the ages of eighteen and twenty-two and that she had died, like the others, of ligature strangulation. Horizontal striations in the tooth enamel indicated inconsistent nutrition during her early years. The regularity of the lines indicated possible seasonal swings in food supplies. Perhaps, like Katya, she had come from a war-torn country in Eastern Europe.

Banks had had a team keeping track of all mispers over the past few months, and they were working overtime now, following up on reports. But if the victim was a prostitute, like Katya Pavelic, then the chances of finding out who she was were slim. Even so, Banks kept telling himself, she was *somebody's* daughter. Somewhere, somebody *must* be missing her. But perhaps not. There were plenty of people out there without friends or family, people who could die in their homes tomorrow and not be found until the rent was long overdue or the smell grew too bad for the neighbors to bear. There were refugees from Eastern Europe, like Katya, or kids who had left home to travel the world and might be anywhere from Katmandu to Kilimanjaro. He had to inure himself to the fact that they might *not* be able to identify the sixth victim for some time, if ever. But still it galled. She should have a name, an identity.

Annie stood up. "Anyway, I've said what I came to say. Oh, and you'll probably be hearing very soon that I've made a formal request to come back to CID. Think there's any chance?"

"You can have my job, if you want."

Annie smiled. "You don't mean that."

"Don't I? Anyway, I don't know if they've changed their minds about CID staffing levels, but I'll talk to Red Ron, if you think that'll help. We don't have a DI right now, so it's probably a good time to make your application."

"Before Winsome catches up with me?"

"She's sharp, that lass."

"Pretty, too."

"Is she? I hadn't noticed."

Annie stuck her tongue out at Banks and left his office. Sad as he felt at the end of their brief romance, he felt some relief, too. He would no longer have to wonder from one day to the next whether they were on or off again; he had been given his freedom yet again, and freedom was a somewhat ambiguous gift.

"Sir?"

Banks looked up and saw Winsome framed in his doorway. "Yes?"

"Just had a message from Steve Naylor, the custody sergeant downstairs."

"Problem?"

"No, not at all." Winsome smiled. "It's Mick Blair. He wants to talk."

Banks clapped his hands and rubbed them together. "Excellent. Tell them to send him straight up. Our best interview room, I think, Winsome."

When she was packed and ready to head for London, Maggie took Lucy a cup of tea in bed the following morning. It was the least she could do after all the poor woman had been through lately.

They had talked well into the previous night, emptying a bottle of white wine between them, and Lucy had hinted at what a terrible childhood she had suffered and how recent events had brought it all back to mind. She had also confided that she was afraid of the police, afraid they might try to fabricate some sort of evidence against her, and that she couldn't stand the thought of going to jail. Just one night in the cell had almost been too much for her to bear.

The police didn't like loose ends, she said, and in this case she was a very serious loose end indeed. She knew they had been watching her and had sneaked out of her foster parents' house after dark and taken the first train from Hull to York, then changed for London, where she had worked on changing her appearance, mostly through hair, makeup and a different style of dress. Maggie had to agree that the Lucy Payne she knew wouldn't have been seen dead in the kind of casual clothes she was wearing now, nor would she have worn the same, slightly tarty makeup. Maggie agreed to tell no one that Lucy was there, and if any of the neighbors saw her and asked who she was, she would tell them she was a distant relative just passing through.

Both bedrooms, the large and the small, looked over The Hill, and when Maggie tapped on the door of the smaller room she had given Lucy and entered, she saw that Lucy was already standing by the window. Stark naked. She turned when Maggie entered with the tea. "Oh, thank you. You're so kind."

Maggie felt herself blush. She couldn't help but notice what a fine body Lucy had: the full, round breasts, taut, flat stomach, gently curving hips and smooth tapered thighs, the dark triangle between her legs. Lucy seemed completely unembarrassed by her own nakedness, but Maggie felt uncomfortable and tried to avert her eyes.

Luckily the curtains were still closed and the light was fairly dim, but Lucy had held them open a little at the top and had clearly been watching the activity across the street. It had let up a bit in the past couple of days, Maggie had noticed, but there was still a great deal of coming and going, and the front garden was still a complete mess.

"Have you seen what they've done over there?" said Lucy, coming forward and accepting the cup of tea. She got back into bed and covered herself with the thin white sheet. Maggie was grateful at least for that.

"Yes," said Maggie.

"That's *my* house, and they've ruined it completely for me. I can't go back there now. Not *ever*." Her lower lip trembled in anger. "I saw through the door into the hall when someone came out. They've taken all the carpets, pulled up the floorboards. They've even punched big holes in the walls. They've just ruined it."

"I suppose they were looking for things, Lucy. It's their job."

"Looking for what? What more could they want? I'll bet they've taken all my nice things, too, all my jewelry and clothes. All my memories."

"I'm sure you'll get it all back."

Lucy shook her head. "No. I don't want it all back. Not now. I thought I did, but now I've seen what they've done, it's tainted. I'll start over again. With just what I've got."

"Are you all right for money?" Maggie asked.

"Yes, thank you. We had a bit put away. I don't know what will happen to the house, the mortgage, but I doubt we'll be able to sell it in that state."

"There must be some sort of compensation," Maggie said. "Surely they can't just take your house and not compensate you?"

"I wouldn't be surprised at *anything* they could do." Lucy blew on the tea. Steam rose around her face.

"Look, I told you last night," Maggie said, "I have to go to London, just for a couple of days. Will you be all right here by yourself?"

"Yes. Of course. Don't worry about me."

"There's plenty of food in the fridge and freezer, you know, if you don't want to go out or order in."

"That's good, thank you," said Lucy. "I think I really would just like to stay in and shut out the world and watch television or something, try to take my mind off what's been happening."

"There's plenty of videotapes in the cupboard under the TV in my bedroom," said Maggie. "Please feel free to watch them there whenever you want."

"Thank you, Maggie. I will."

Though there was a small television set in the living room, the only TV-and-VCR combination in the entire house was set up in the master bedroom, for some reason, and that was Maggie's room. Not that she wasn't thankful. She had often lain in bed unable to sleep and, when there was nothing suitable on television, had watched one of the love stories or romantic comedies Ruth seemed to favor, with actors such as Hugh Grant, Meg Ryan, Richard Gere, Tom Hanks, Julia Roberts and Sandra Bullock; they had helped her through many a long, hard night.

"Are you sure there isn't anything else you need?"

"I can't think of anything," Lucy said. "I just want to feel *safe* and comfortable so I can remember what it's like."

"You'll be fine here. I'm really sorry I have to leave you so soon, but I'll be back before long. Don't worry."

"It's okay, honest," said Lucy. "I didn't come here to interrupt your life or anything. You've got your work. I know that. I'm only asking for sanctuary for a short time, just till I get myself together."

"What *are* you going to do?"

"No idea. I suppose I can change my name and get a job somewhere far away from here. Anyway, not to worry. You go to London and have a good time. I can take care of myself."

"If you're sure."

"I'm sure." Lucy got out of bed again, put her cup of tea on the bedside table and went back toward the window. There she stood, providing Maggie with a rear view of her finely toned body, looking out across the road at what used to be her home.

"I must dash, then," said Maggie. "The taxi will be here soon."

"Bye," said Lucy, without turning round. "Have a good time."

"Okay, Mick," said Banks. "I understand you want to talk to us."

After his night in the cells, Mick Blair didn't at all resemble the cocky teenager they had interviewed yesterday. In fact, he looked like a frightened kid. Clearly the prospect of spending several years in a similar or worse facility had worked on his imagination. He had also, Banks knew through the custody sergeant, had a long telephone conversation with his parents shortly after his detention, and his manner had seemed to change after that. He had *not* asked for a lawyer. Not yet.

"Yeah," he said. "But first tell me what Sarah said."

"You know I can't do that, Mick."

In fact, Sarah Francis had told them nothing at all; she had remained as monosyllabic and as scared and surly as she had in Ian Scott's flat. But that didn't matter, as she had been mainly used as a lever against Mick, anyway.

Banks, Winsome and Mick were in the largest, most comfortable interview room. It had also been painted recently, and Banks could smell the paint from the institutional-green walls. He still had nothing from the lab on Samuel Gardner's car, but Mick didn't know that. He said he wanted to talk, but if he decided to play coy again, Banks could always drop hints about fingerprints and hairs. He *knew* they had been in the car. It was something he should have checked at the time, with Ian Scott having a record for taking and driving away. Given Scott's other offense, he also had a good idea what the four of them had been up to.

"Would you like to make a statement, then?" Banks said. "For the record."

"Yes."

"You've been made aware of all your rights?"

"Yes."

"Okay, then, Mick. Tell us what happened that night."

"What you said yesterday, about it going easier with me . . . ?"

"Yes?"

"You meant it, didn't you? I mean, whatever Sarah said, she might have been lying, you know, to protect herself and Ian."

"The courts and the judges look favorably upon people who help the police, Mick. That's a fact. I'll be honest. I can't give you the exact details of what will happen—it depends on so many variables—but I *can* tell you that you'll have my support for leniency, and that should go some distance."

Mick swallowed. He was about to rat on his friends. Banks had witnessed such moments before and knew how difficult it was, what conflicting emotions must be struggling for primacy inside Mick Blair's soul. Self-preservation usually won out, in Banks's experience, but sometimes at the cost of self-loathing. It was the same for him, the watcher; he wanted the information, and he had coaxed many a weak and sensitive suspect toward informing, but when he succeeded, the taste of victory was often soured by the bile of disgust.

Not this time, though, Banks thought. He wanted to know what had happened to Leanne Wray far more than he cared about Mick Blair's discomfort.

"You did steal that car, didn't you, Mick?" Banks began. "We've already recovered a lot of hair samples and finger-prints. We'll find yours among them, won't we? And Ian's, Sarah's and Leanne's."

"It was Ian," Blair said. "It was all Ian's idea. It was noth-ing to do with me. I can't even fucking drive."

"What about Sarah?"

"Sarah? Ian says jump, Sarah asks how high."

"And Leanne?"

"Leanne was all for it. She was in a pretty wild mood that night. I don't know why. She said something about her step-mother, but I didn't know what the problem was. To be hon-est, I didn't really care. I mean, I didn't want to know about her family problems. We've all got problems, right?"

Indeed we do, thought Banks.

"You just wanted to get into her knickers, then?" said Winsome.

That seemed to shock Blair, coming from a woman, a beautiful woman at that, with a soft Jamaican accent.

"No! I mean, I liked her, yes. But I wasn't trying it on, honest. I wasn't trying to force her or anything like that."

"What happened, Mick?" Banks asked.

"Ian said why don't we take a car and do some E and smoke a couple of spliffs and maybe drive up to Darlington and go clubbing."

"What about Leanne's curfew?"

"She said fuck the curfew, it sounded like a great idea to

her. Like I said, she was a bit wild that night. She'd had a couple of drinks. Not a lot, like, just a couple, but she didn't usually drink, and it was just enough to loosen her up a bit. She just wanted to have some fun."

"And you thought you might get lucky?"

Again, Winsome's interjection seemed to confuse Blair. "No. Yes. I mean, if she was willing. Okay, I fancied her. I thought, maybe . . . you know . . . she seemed different, more devil-may-care."

"And you thought the drugs would make her even more willing?"

"No. I don't know." He looked at Banks in annoyance. "Look, do you want me to go on with this or not?"

"Go on." Banks gave Winsome the signal to keep out of it for the time being. He could imagine the scenario easily enough: Leanne a little drunk, giggly, flirting with Blair a bit, as Shannon the barmaid had said, then Ian Scott offering Ecstasy in the car, maybe Leanne unsure about it, but Blair encouraging her, egging her on, hoping all the time to get her into bed. But all that was something they could deal with later on, if necessary, when they had established the circumstances of Leanne's disappearance.

"Ian stole the car," Blair went on. "I don't know anything about stealing cars, but he said he learned when he was a kid growing up on the East Side Estate."

Banks knew all too well that stealing cars was one of the essential skills for kids growing up on the East Side Estate. "Where did you go?"

"North. Like I said, we were going to Darlington. Ian knows the club scene up there. Soon as we set off, Ian handed out the E and we all gobbled it up. Then Sarah rolled a spliff and we smoked that."

Banks noticed that it was always someone else committing the illegal act, never Blair, but he filed that away for later. "Had Leanne taken Ecstasy or smoked marijuana before?" he asked.

"Not to my knowledge. She always seemed a bit strait-laced to me."

"But not that night?"

"No."

"Okay. Go on. What happened?"

Mick looked down at the table and Banks could tell he was coming to the hard part. "We hadn't got far out of Eastvale—maybe half an hour or so—when Leanne said she felt sick and she could feel her heart was beating way too fast. She was having trouble breathing. She used that inhaler thing she carried with her, but it didn't do any good. Made her worse, if you ask me. Anyway, Ian thought she was just panicking or hallucinating or something, so first he opened the car windows. It didn't do any good, though. Soon she was shaking and sweating. I mean, she was really scared. Me, too."

"What did you do?"

"We were in the country by then, up on the moors above Lyndgarth, so Ian pulled off the road and stopped. We all got out and walked out on the moor. Ian thought the open spaces would be good for Leanne, a breath of fresh air, that maybe she was just getting claustrophobic in the car."

"Did it help?"

Mick turned pale. "No. Soon as we got out she was sick. I mean *really* sick. Then she collapsed. She couldn't breathe, and she seemed to be choking."

"Did you know she was asthmatic?"

"Like I said, I saw her use the inhaler in the car when she first started feeling weird."

"And it didn't enter your mind that Ecstasy might be dangerous for an asthma sufferer, or that it might cause a bad reaction with the inhalant?"

"How could I know? I'm not a doctor."

"No. But you *do* take Ecstasy—I doubt this was your first time—and you must have been aware of some of the adverse publicity. The Leah Betts story, for example, the girl who died about five years ago? A few others since."

"I heard about them, yes, but I thought you just had to be careful about your body temperature when you were dancing. You know, like, drink plenty of water and be careful you don't dehydrate."

"That's only one of the dangers. Did you give her the inhaler again when she became worse out on the moor?"

"We couldn't find it. It must have been back in the car, in her bag. Besides, it had only made her worse."

Banks remembered viewing the contents of Leanne's shoulder bag and seeing the inhaler there among her personal items, doubting that she would have run away without it.

"Didn't it also cross your mind that she might have been choking on her own vomit?" he went on.

"I don't know, I never really . . ."

"What *did* you do?"

"That's just it. We didn't know what to do. We just tried to give her some breathing space, some air, you know, but all of a sudden she sort of twitched, and after that she didn't move at all."

Banks let the silence stretch for a few moments, conscious only of their breathing and the soft electric hum of the tape machines.

"Why didn't you take her to hospital?" he asked.

"It was too late! I told you. She was dead."

"You were certain of that?"

"Yes. We checked her pulse, felt for a heartbeat, tried to see if she was breathing, but there was nothing. She was dead. It all happened so quickly. I mean, we were feeling the E, too, we were panicking a bit, not thinking clearly."

Banks knew of at least three other recent Ecstasy-related deaths in the region, so Blair's account didn't surprise him too much. MDMA, short for methylenedioxymethamphetamine, was a popular drug with young people because it was cheap and kept you going all night at raves and clubs. It was believed to be safe, though Mick was right that you had to be careful about your water intake and body temperature, but it could also be particularly dangerous to people suffering from high blood pressure or asthma, like Leanne.

"Why didn't you take her to a hospital when you were all still in the car?"

"Ian said she'd be okay if we just got out and walked around for a while. He said he'd seen that kind of reaction before."

"What did you do then, after you discovered she was dead?"

"Ian said we couldn't tell anyone what had happened, that we'd all go to jail."

"So what *did* you do?"

"We carried her further out on the moor and buried her. I mean, there was a sort of sinkhole, not very deep, by a bit of broken-down drystone wall, so we put her in there and we covered her up with stones and bracken. Nobody could find her unless they were *really* looking, and there weren't any public footpaths nearby. Even the animals couldn't get to her. It was so desolate, the middle of nowhere."

"And then?"

"Then we drove back to Eastvale. We were all badly shaken up, but Ian said we ought to be seen about the place, you know, acting natural, as if things were normal."

"And Leanne's shoulder bag?"

"That was Ian's idea. I mean, we'd all decided by then that we'd just say she left us outside the pub and set off home and that was the last we saw of her. I found her bag on the backseat of the car, and Ian said maybe if we dumped it in someone's garden near the Old Ship, the police would think she'd been picked up by a pervert or something."

And indeed we did, thought Banks. One simple, spur-of-the-moment action, added to two other missing girls whose bags had also been found close to the scenes of their disappearances, and the entire Chameleon task force had been created. But not in time to save Melissa Horrocks or Kimberley Myers. He felt sick and angry.

There was mile after mile of moorland up beyond Lyndgarth, Banks knew, none of it farmed. Blair was right about the isolation, too. Only the occasional rambler crossed it, and then usually by the well-marked paths. "Can you remember where you buried her?" he asked.

"I think so," said Blair. "I don't know about the exact spot, but within a couple of hundred yards. You'll know it when you see the old wall."

Banks looked at Winsome. "Get a search party together, would you, DC Jackman, and have young Mick here go out with them. Let me know the minute you find anything. And have Ian Scott and Sarah Francis picked up."

Winsome stood up.

"That'll do for now," Banks said.

"What'll happen to me?" Blair asked.

"I don't know, Mick," said Banks. "I honestly don't know."

Chapter 19

*T*he interview had gone well, Maggie thought as she walked out on to Portland Place. Behind her, Broadcasting House looked like the stern of a huge ocean liner. Inside, it had been a maze. She hadn't known how anyone could find their way around, even if they had worked there for years. Thank the Lord the program's researcher had met her in the lobby, then guided her through security to the entrails of the building.

It started to rain lightly, so Maggie ducked into Starbucks. Sitting on a stool by the counter that stretched along the front window, sipping her latte and watching the people outside wrestle with their umbrellas, she reviewed her day. It was after three o'clock in the afternoon and the rush hour already seemed to have begun. If it ever ended in London. The interview she had just given had focused almost entirely on the generalities of domestic abuse—things to watch out for, patterns to avoid falling into—rather than her own personal story, or that of her co-interviewee, an abused wife who had gone on to become a psychological counselor. They had exchanged addresses and phone numbers and agreed to get in touch, then the woman had had to dash off to give another interview.

Lunch with Sally, the art director, had gone well, too. They had eaten at a rather expensive Italian restaurant near

Victoria Station, and Sally had looked over the sketches, making helpful suggestions here and there. Mostly, though, they had talked about recent events in Leeds, and Sally had shown only the natural curiosity that anyone who happened to live across the street from a serial killer might expect. Maggie had been evasive when questioned about Lucy.

Lucy. The poor woman. Maggie felt guilty for leaving her alone in that big house on The Hill, right opposite where the nightmare of her own life had recently come to a head. Lucy had said she would be okay, but was she just trying to put a brave face on things?

Maggie hadn't been able to get tickets for the play she wanted to see. It was so popular it was sold out, even on a Wednesday. She thought she might book into the little hotel anyway and go to the cinema instead, but the more she thought about it, and the more she looked out at the hordes of passing strangers, the more she thought she ought to be there for Lucy.

What she would do, she decided, was wait till the rain stopped—it only looked like a mild shower, and she could already see some blue clouds in the sky over the Langham Hilton across the road—do some shopping on Oxford Street, and then head home in the early evening and surprise Lucy.

Maggie felt much better when she had decided to go home. After all, what was the point going to the cinema by herself when Lucy needed someone to talk to, someone to help take her mind off her problems and help her decide what to do with her future?

When the rain had stopped completely, Maggie drained her latte and set out. She would buy Lucy a little present, too, nothing expensive or ostentatious, but perhaps a bracelet or a necklace, something to mark her freedom. After all, as Lucy had said, the police had taken all her things and she didn't want them back now; she was about to start a new life.

* * *

It was late in the afternoon when Banks got the call to drive out to the Wheaton Moor, north of Lyndgarth, and he took Winsome with him. She had done enough work on the Leanne Wray case to be there at the end. Most of the daffodils were gone, but white and pink blossoms covered the trees, and the hedgerows glowed with the burnished gold stars of celandines. Gorse flowered bright yellow all over the moors.

He parked as close as he could to the cluster of figures, but they still had almost a quarter of a mile to walk over the springy gorse and heather. Blair and the others had certainly carried Leanne a long way from civilization. Though the sun was shining and there were only a few high clouds, the wind was cold. Banks was glad of his sports jacket. Winsome was wearing calf-high leather boots and a herringbone jacket over her black polo-neck sweater. She strode with grace and confidence, whereas Banks caught his ankle and stumbled every now and then in the thick gorse. Time to get out and exercise more, he told himself. And time to stop smoking.

They reached the team that Winsome had dispatched about three hours ago, Mick Blair handcuffed to one of the uniformed officers, greasy hair blowing in the wind.

Another officer pointed down the shallow sinkhole, and Banks saw part of a hand, most of the flesh eaten away, the still-white bone showing. "We tried to disturb the scene as little as possible, sir," the officer went on. "I sent for the SOCOs and the rest of the team. They said they'd get here ASAP."

Banks thanked him. He glanced back toward the road and saw a car and a van pull up, figures get out and make their way across the rough moorland, some of them in white coveralls. The SOCOs had soon roped off an area of several yards around the mound of stones, and Peter Darby, the local crime scene photographer, got to work. Now all they needed was Dr. Burns, the police surgeon. Dr. Glendenning, the

Home Office pathologist, would most likely conduct the PM, but he was too old and important to go scrambling across the moors anymore. Dr. Burns was skilled, Banks knew, and he already had plenty of experience of on-scene examinations.

It was another ten minutes before Dr. Burns arrived. By then Peter Darby had finished photographing the scene intact, and it was time to uncover the remains. This the SOCOs did slowly and carefully, so as not to disturb any evidence. Mick Blair had said that Leanne died after taking Ecstasy, but he could be lying; he could have tried to rape her and choked her when she didn't comply. Either way, they couldn't go around jumping to conclusions about Leanne. Not this time.

Banks began to feel that the whole thing was just too damn familiar, standing out there on the moors with his jacket flapping around him as men in white coveralls uncovered a body. Then he remembered Harold Steadman, the local historian they had found buried under a similar drystone wall below Crow Scar. That had been only his second case in Eastvale, back when the kids were still at school and he and Sandra were happily married, yet it seemed centuries ago now. He wondered what on earth a drystone wall was doing up here anyway, then realized it had probably marked the end of someone's property long ago, property that had now gone to moorland, overgrown with heather and gorse. The elements had done their work on the wall, and nobody had any interest in repairing it.

Stone by stone, the body was uncovered. As soon as he saw the blond hair, Banks knew it was Leanne Wray. She was still wearing the clothes she had gone missing in—jeans, white Nike trainers, T-shirt and a light suede jacket—and that was something in Blair's favor, Banks thought. Though there was some decomposition and evidence of insect and small-animal activity—a missing finger on her right hand, for example—the cool weather had kept her from becoming a complete skeleton. In fact, despite the splitting of the skin to expose the muscle and fat on her left cheek, Banks was able to recognize Leanne's face from the photographs he had seen.

When the body was completely uncovered, everyone stood back as if they were at a funeral paying their last respects before the interment rather than at an exhumation. The moor was silent but for the wind whistling and groaning among the stones like lost souls. Mick Blair was crying, Banks noticed. Either that or the chill wind was making his eyes water.

"Seen enough, Mick?" he asked.

Mick sobbed, then abruptly turned away and vomited noisily and copiously into the gorse.

Banks's mobile rang as he turned away to go back to his car. It was Stefan Nowak, and he sounded excited. "Alan?"

"What is it, Stefan? Identified the sixth victim?"

"No. But I thought you'd like to know immediately. We've found Payne's camcorder."

"Tell me where," said Banks, "and I'll be with you as fast as I possibly can."

Maggie was tired when her train pulled into City Station around nine o'clock that evening, half an hour late due to a cow in a tunnel outside Wakefield. Now she had an inkling of why the British complained so much about their trains.

There was a long queue at the taxi rank, and Maggie only had a light holdall to carry, so she decided to walk around the corner to Boar Lane and catch a bus. There were plenty of them that stopped within a short walk of The Hill. It was a pleasant evening, no sign of rain here, and there were still plenty of people on the streets. The bus soon came and she sat at the back downstairs. Two elderly women sat in front of her, just come from the bingo, one with hair that looked like a sort of blue haze sprinkled with glitter. Her perfume irritated Maggie's nose and made her sneeze, so she moved even farther back.

It was a familiar journey by now, and Maggie spent most of it reading another story in the new Alice Munro paperback she had bought on Charing Cross Road. She had also bought the perfect present for Lucy. It nestled in its little blue box in her holdall. It was an odd piece of jewelry and had immediately caught her eye. Hanging on a thin silver chain, it was a circular silver disc about the size of a ten-penny piece. Inside the circle, made by a snake swallowing its own tail, was an image of the phoenix rising. Maggie hoped that Lucy would like and appreciate the sentiment.

The bus turned the last corner. Maggie rang the bell and got off near the top of The Hill. The streets were quiet and the western sky was still smeared with the reds and purples of sunset. There was a slight chill in the air now, Maggie noticed, giving a little shiver. She saw Mrs. Toth, Claire's mother, crossing The Hill with some fish and chips wrapped in newspaper and said hello, then turned to the steps.

She fumbled for her keys as she made her way up the dark steps overhung with shrubbery. It was hard to see her way. A perfect place for an ambush, she thought, then wished she hadn't. Bill's telephone call still weighed on her mind.

The house seemed to be in darkness. Perhaps Lucy was out? Maggie doubted it. Then she got past the bushes and noticed a flickering light coming from the master bedroom. She was watching television. For a moment, Maggie felt the uncharitable wish that she still had the house to herself. The knowledge that there was someone in her bedroom bothered her. But she had told Lucy she could watch television up there if she wanted, and she could hardly just march in and kick her out, tired as she was. Perhaps they should change rooms if Lucy just wanted to watch television all the time? Maggie would be quite happy in the small bedroom for a few days.

She turned the key in the lock and went inside, then put down her bag and hung up her jacket before heading upstairs to tell Lucy she had decided to come back early. As she glided up on the thick pile carpet she could hear sounds from the television but couldn't make out what they were. It sounded like somebody shouting. The bedroom door was slightly ajar, so without even thinking to knock, Maggie simply pushed it open and walked in. Lucy lay sprawled on the bed naked. Well, that wasn't too much of a surprise after this morning's display, Maggie thought. But when she turned to see what was on television she didn't want to believe her eyes.

At first she thought it was just a porn movie, though why Lucy should be watching something like that and where she had got it from were beyond her, then she noticed the home-made quality, the makeshift lighting. It was some sort of cellar, and there was a girl who appeared to be tied to a bed. A man stood beside her playing with himself and shouting obscenities. Maggie recognized him. A woman lay with her head between the girl's legs, and in the split second it took Maggie to register all this, the woman turned, licked her lips and grinned mischievously at the camera.

Lucy.

"Oh, no!" Maggie said, turning to Lucy, who was looking at her now with those dark, impenetrable eyes. Maggie put her hand to her mouth. She felt sick. Sick and afraid. She turned to leave but heard a sudden movement behind, then felt a splitting pain at the back of her head, and the world exploded.

The pond was gathering the evening light by the time Banks got there after taking Mick Blair back to Eastvale, making sure Ian Scott and Sarah Francis were under lock and key, and picking up Jenny Fuller on his way out of town. Winsome and Sergeant Hatchley could take care of things at Eastvale until tomorrow morning.

The colors shimmered on the water's surface like an oil slick, and the ducks, having noticed so much human activity, were keeping a polite and safe distance, and no doubt wondering where the expected chunks of bread had got to. The Panasonic Super 8 camcorder lay, still attached to its tripod, on a piece of cloth on the bank. DS Stefan Nowak and DCI Ken Blackstone had stayed with it until Banks could get there.

"Are you sure it's the one?" Banks asked Ken Blackstone.

Blackstone nodded. "One of our enterprising young DCs succeeded in tracking down the branch where Payne bought it. He paid cash for it, on the third of March last year. The serial number checks out."

"Any tapes?"

"One in the camera," said Stefan. "Ruined."

"No chance of restoration?"

"All the king's horses . . ."

"Only the one? That's all?"

Stefan nodded. "Believe me, the men went over every inch of the place." He gestured to take in the area of the pond. "If any tapes had been dumped here, we'd have found them by now."

"So where are they?" Banks asked nobody in particular.

"If you want my guess," said Stefan, "I'd say whoever chucked the camcorder in the lake dubbed them on to VHS. There's some loss of quality, but it's the only way you can watch them on a regular VCR, without the camcorder."

Banks nodded. "Makes sense to me. Better take it to Millgarth and lock it up safe in the property room, though what good it's going to do us now, I don't know."

Stefan bent to pick up the camera, wrapping it carefully in

the cloth, as if it were a newborn baby. "You never know."

Banks noticed the pub sign about a hundred yards away: The Woodcutter's. It was a chain pub, that much he could tell even from a distance, but it was all there was in sight. "It's been a long day, and I haven't had my tea yet," he said to Blackstone and Jenny after Stefan had driven off to Millgarth. "Why don't we have a drink and toss a few ideas around?"

"You'll get no objection from me," said Blackstone.

"Jenny?"

Jenny smiled. "Not much choice, have I? I came in your car, remember? But count me in."

They were soon settled at a corner table in the almost empty pub, which Banks found to his delight was still serving food. He ordered a beef burger and chips along with a pint of bitter. The jukebox wasn't so loud that they couldn't hear themselves talk, but it was loud enough to mask their conversation from any nearby tables.

"So what have we got?" Banks asked when he had his burger in front of him.

"A useless camcorder, by the looks of it," said Blackstone.

"But what does it mean?"

"It means that someone—Payne, presumably—chucked it away."

"Why?"

"Search me."

"Come on, Ken, we can do better than this."

Blackstone smiled. "Sorry, it's been a long day for me, too."

"It's an interesting question, though," said Jenny. "Why? And when?"

"Well, it has to have been before PCs Taylor and Morrisey entered the cellar," said Banks.

"But Payne had a captive, remember," said Blackstone. "Kimberley Myers. Why on earth would he ditch his camera when he was doing exactly the sort of things we assume he liked to videotape? And what did he do with the dubbed VHS tapes, if Stefan's right about that?"

"I can't answer those questions," Jenny said, "but I can offer another way of looking at them."

"I think I know what you're getting at," said Banks.

"You do?"

"Uh-huh. Lucy Payne." He took a bite of his beef burger. Not bad, he thought, but he was so hungry he would have eaten just about anything by then.

Jenny nodded slowly. "Why have we still been assuming that this video business was all down to Terence Payne when we've been investigating Lucy as a possible partner in crime all along? Especially after what Laura and Keith told me about Lucy's past, and what that young prostitute told Alan about her sexual proclivities. I mean, doesn't it make sense, psychologically, that she was just as involved as he was? Remember, the girls were killed in exactly the same way as Kathleen Murray: ligature strangulation."

"Are you saying that *she* killed them?" Blackstone asked.

"Not necessarily. But if what Keith and Laura say is true, then Lucy might have seen herself acting as a deliverer, the way it appears she did with Kathleen."

"A mercy killing? But you said earlier she killed Kathleen out of jealousy."

"I said that jealousy certainly *could* have been a motive. One that her sister Laura didn't want to believe. But Lucy's motives could have been mixed. Nothing's simple in a personality like hers."

"But why?" Blackstone went on. "Even if it was her, why would she throw away the camera?"

Banks speared a chip and thought for a moment before answering: "Lucy's terrified of jail. If she thought there was any chance of imminent capture—and it must have entered her mind after the first police visit and the connection between Kimberley Myers and Silverhill school—then might she not start making plans for self-preservation?"

"It all seems a bit far-fetched to me."

"Not to me, Ken," said Banks. "Look at it from Lucy's point of view. She's not stupid. Brighter than her husband, I'd say. Terence Payne kidnaps Kimberley Myers that Friday night—he's out of control, becoming disorganized—but Lucy's still organized, she sees the end coming fast. First thing she does is get rid of as much evidence as possible, including the camcorder. Maybe that's what sets Terry against her, causes the row. Obviously she has no way of knowing that it will end the way it does, at the time it does, so she has to improvise, see which way the wind's blowing. If we find any traces of her being in the cellar—"

"Which we do."

"Which we do," Banks agreed, "then she's got a believable explanation for that, too. She heard a noise and went to investigate, and surprise, surprise, look what she found. The fact that her husband clobbers her with a vase only helps her case."

"And the tapes?"

"She wouldn't throw them away," Jenny answered. "Not if they were a record of what she—of what *they*—had done. The camera's nothing, merely a means to an end. You can buy another camera. But those tapes would be more valuable than diamonds to the Paynes because they're unique and they can't be replaced. They're her trophies. She could watch them over and over again and relive those moments with the victims in the cellar. It's the next best thing to the reality for her. She wouldn't throw them away."

"Then where are they?" said Banks.

"And where is she?" said Jenny.

"Isn't it just remotely possible," Banks suggested, pushing his plate aside, "that the two questions have the same answer?"

* * *

Maggie woke up with a splitting headache and a feeling of nausea deep in the pit of her stomach. She felt weak and disoriented; didn't know at first where she was or how much time had gone by since she lost consciousness. The curtains were open and she could see it was dark outside. As things slowly came into focus, she realized she was still in her own bedroom. There was one bedside lamp turned on; the other lay in pieces on the floor. That must have been what Lucy hit her with, Maggie thought. She could feel something warm and sticky in her hair. Blood.

Lucy hit her! The sudden revelation shocked her closer to consciousness. She had seen the video: Lucy and Terry doing things to that poor girl, Lucy looking as if she were enjoying herself.

Maggie tried to move and found that her hands and feet were bound to the brass bed. She was tied up and spread-eagled, just like the girl on the video. She felt the panic rise in her. She thrashed around, trying to get loose, but only succeeding in making the bedsprings creak loudly. The door opened and Lucy came in. She was dressed in her jeans and T-shirt again.

Lucy shook her head slowly. "Look what you made me do, Maggie," she said. "Just look at what you made me do. You told me you weren't coming back for another day."

"It was *you*," Maggie said. "On that video. It was you. It was vile, disgusting."

"You weren't supposed to see that," said Lucy, sitting at the edge of the bed and stroking Maggie's brow.

Maggie flinched.

Lucy laughed. "Oh, don't worry, Maggie. Don't be such a prude. You're not my type, anyway."

"You killed them. You and Terry together."

"You're wrong there," said Lucy, getting up again and

pacing the room, arms folded. "Terry never killed anyone. He didn't have the bottle. Oh, he liked them tied up naked, all right. He liked to *do* things to them. Even *after* they were dead. But I had to do all the killing myself. Poor things. See, they could only take so much, and then I had to put them to sleep. I was always gentle. Gentle as I could be."

"You're insane," said Maggie, thrashing around on the bed again.

"Keep still!" Lucy sat on the bed again, but this time she didn't touch Maggie. "Insane? I don't think so. Just because you can't understand me doesn't mean I'm insane. I'm different, true. I see things differently. I need different things. But I'm not insane."

"But *why?*"

"I can't explain myself to you. I can't even explain myself to me." She laughed again. "Least of all to me. Oh, the psychiatrists and psychologists would try. They would dissect my childhood and toss around their theories, but even they know when it gets right down to it that they've got no explanations for someone like me. I just am. I happen. Like five-legged sheep and two-headed dogs. Call it what you will. Call me evil, if it helps you understand. More important right now, though, is how am I going to survive?"

"Why don't you just go? Run away. I won't say anything."

Lucy gave her a sad smile. "I wish that were true, Maggie. I wish things were as easy as that."

"They are," Maggie said. "Go. Just go. Disappear."

"I can't do that. You've seen the tape. You *know*. I can't let you just walk around with that knowledge. Look, Maggie, I don't *want* to kill you, but I think I can. And I think I must. I promise I'll be every bit as gentle as I was with the others."

"Why me?" Maggie whimpered. "Why did you pick on me?"

"You? Easy. Because you were so willing to believe that I was a victim of domestic violence, just like you. True enough, Terry had been getting unpredictable and had lashed out on one or two occasions. It's an unfortunate thing that men like him lack the brains, but they don't lack for brawn. No matter, now. Do you know how I met him?"

"No."

"He raped me. You don't believe me, I can tell. How could you? How could anyone? But he did. I was walking to the bus stop after I'd been to a pub with some friends, and he dragged me in an alley and raped me. He had a knife."

"He *raped* you, and you *married* him? You didn't tell the police?"

Lucy laughed. "He didn't know what he was getting into. I gave him the rape of his life. It might have taken him a while to realize it, but I was raping him as much as he was raping me. It wasn't my first time, Maggie. Believe me, I know *all* about rape. From experts. There was nothing he could do that hadn't been done to me before, time after time, by more than one person. He thought he was in control, but sometimes it's the victim who's *really* in control. We had a lot in common, we soon found out. Sexually. And in other ways. He kept on raping girls even after we were together. I encouraged him. I used to make him tell me all the details of what he'd done to them while we were fucking."

"I don't understand." Maggie was crying and trembling, no longer able to keep her horror and fear in check now she knew there was no chance of reasoning with Lucy.

"Of course you don't," Lucy said soothingly, sitting on the edge of the bed and stroking Maggie's brow. "Why should you? But you've been useful, and I'd like to thank you for that. First you gave me somewhere to hide the tapes. I knew they were the only things that might incriminate me other than Terry, and I didn't think he'd talk. Besides, he's dead now."

"What do you mean about the tapes?"

"They were here all along, Maggie. Remember I came to see you that Sunday, before all hell broke loose?"

"Yes."

"I brought them with me and hid them behind some boxes up in the loft when I went up to the toilet. You'd already told me you never went up there. Don't you remember?"

Maggie did remember. The loft was an airless, dusty place, she had discovered on her first and only look, which gave her the willies and aggravated her allergies. She must have mentioned it to Lucy when showing her around the house. "Is that why you made friends with me, because you thought I might be useful?"

"I thought I might have need of a friend somewhere down the line, yes, a defender, even. And you *were* good. Thank you for all you've said on my behalf. Thank you for believing in me. I'm not enjoying this, you know. I get no pleasure from killing. It's a pity it has to end this way."

"But it doesn't," Maggie begged. "Oh, God, please don't. Just go. I won't say anything. I promise."

"Oh, you say that now, now that you're full of fear of death, but if I go, you won't feel that way anymore, and you'll tell the police everything."

"I won't. I *promise.*"

"I wish I could believe you, Maggie, I really do."

"It's true."

Lucy took the belt off her jeans.

"What are you doing?"

"I told you, I'll be gentle. It's nothing to be frightened of, just a little pain, then you'll go to sleep."

"No!"

Someone banged on the front door. Lucy froze and Maggie held her breath. "Be quiet," Lucy hissed, putting her hand over Maggie's mouth. "They'll go away."

But the banging continued. Then came a voice. "Maggie!

Open up, it's the police. We know you're in there. We spoke to your neighbor. She saw you come home. Open up, Maggie. We want to talk to you. It's very important."

Maggie could see fear in Lucy's expression. She struggled to shout, but the hand covered her mouth, almost cut off her breath.

"Is she with you, Maggie?" the voice continued. It was Banks, Maggie realized, the detective who made her angry. If only he stayed, broke down the door and rescued her, she'd apologize; she'd do whatever he wanted. "Is that who it is?" Banks went on. "The blond girl your neighbor saw. Is it Lucy? Did she change her appearance? If it's you, Lucy, we know all about Kathleen Murray. We've got a lot of questions for you. Maggie, come down and open up. If Lucy's with you, don't trust her. We think she hid the tapes in your house."

"Be quiet," Lucy said, and went out of the room.

"I'm here!" Maggie immediately yelled at the top of her lungs, not sure if they could hear her or not. "She's here, too. Lucy. She's going to kill me. Please help me!"

Lucy came back into the bedroom, but she didn't seem concerned by Maggie's screams. "They're out back, too," she said, crossing her arms. "What can I do? I can't go to jail. I couldn't stand to be locked up in the cage for the rest of my days."

"Lucy," Maggie said as evenly as she could manage. "Untie me and open the door. Let them in. I'm sure they'll be lenient. They'll see you need help."

But Lucy wasn't listening. She had started pacing again and muttering to herself. All Maggie could catch was the word "cage" again and again.

Then she heard an almighty crash from downstairs as the police broke the front door, then the sound of men running up the stairs.

"I'm up here!" she yelled.

Lucy looked at her, almost pitifully, Maggie thought, said, "Try not to hate me too much," then she took a run and dived through the bedroom window in a shower of glass.

Maggie screamed.

Chapter 20

*F*or someone who disliked hospitals as much as Banks did, he seemed to have spent more than enough time in the infirmary over the past couple of weeks, he thought as he walked down the corridor to Maggie Forrest's private room on Thursday.

"Oh, it's you," Maggie said when he knocked and walked in. She wouldn't look him in the eye, he noticed, but stared at the wall. The bandage over her forehead held the dressing at the back of her head in place. The wound had been a nasty one, requiring several stitches. She had also lost a lot of blood. When Banks had got to her, the pillow was soaked with it. According to the doctor, though, she was out of the woods and should be okay to go home in a day or so. Now she was being treated for delayed shock as much as anything. Looking at her, Banks thought of the day not so long ago when he first saw Lucy Payne in a hospital bed, one eye bandaged, the other assessing her situation, black hair spread out on the white pillow.

"Is that all the thanks I get?" he said.

"Thanks?"

"For bringing in the cavalry. It was my idea, you know. True, I was only doing my job, but people sometimes feel the need to add a word or two of personal thanks. Don't worry, I don't expect a tip or anything."

"It's easy for you to be flippant, isn't it?"

Banks pulled up the chair and sat at her bedside. "Maybe not as easy as you think. How are you?"

"Fine."

"Really?"

"I'm all right. A bit sore."

"It's hardly surprising."

"Was it really you?"

"Was what really me?"

Maggie looked him in the eye for the first time. Hers were dulled with medication, but he could see pain and confusion there, along with something softer, something less definable. "Who led the rescue party."

Banks leaned back and sighed. "I only blame myself that it took me so long," he said.

"What do you mean?"

"I should have worked it out earlier. I had all the pieces. I just didn't put them together quickly enough, not until the SOCO team found the camcorder in the pond at the bottom of The Hill."

"That's where it was?"

"Yes. Lucy must have dumped it there sometime over that last weekend."

"I go there sometimes to think and feed the ducks." Maggie stared at the wall, then turned to face him again after a few seconds. "Anyway, it's hardly your fault, is it? You're not a mind reader."

"No? People sometimes expect me to be. But I suppose I'm not. Not in this case. We suspected from the start that there must have been a camcorder and tapes, and we knew she wouldn't part with the tapes easily. We also knew that the only person she was close to was you, and that she had visited your house the day before the domestic disturbance."

"She couldn't have known what was going to happen."

"No. But she knew things were coming to a head. She was

working on damage control, and hiding the tapes was part of it. Where were they?"

"The loft," Maggie said. "She knew I didn't go up there."

"And she knew she'd be able to get at them without too much trouble, that you were probably the only person in the whole country who'd give her house room. That was the other clue. There was really nowhere else for her to go. First we talked to your neighbors, and when Claire's mother told us you'd just got home and another neighbor said she'd seen a young woman knocking at your back door a couple of nights ago, it seemed to add up."

"You must think I was *so* stupid to take her in."

"Foolish, maybe, naïve, but not necessarily stupid."

"She just seemed so . . . so . . ."

"So much the victim?"

"Yes. I *wanted* to believe in her, needed to. Maybe as much for me as for her. I don't know."

Banks nodded. "She played the role well. She could do that because it was partially true. She'd had a lot of practice."

"What do you mean?

Banks told her about the Alderthorpe Seven and the murder of Kathleen Murray. When he had finished, Maggie turned pale, swallowed and lay back in silence, staring at the ceiling. It was a minute or so before she spoke again. "She killed her cousin when she was only twelve?"

"Yes. That's partly what set us looking for her again. At last we had a bit of evidence that suggested she was more than she pretended to be."

"But a lot of people have terrible childhoods," said Maggie, some color returning to her face. "Perhaps not as terrible as that, but they don't all turn into killers. What was so different about Lucy?"

"I wish I knew the answer," said Banks. "Terry Payne was a rapist when they met, and Lucy had killed Kathleen. Somehow or other, the two of them getting together the way they did created a special sort of chemistry, acted as a trigger. We don't know why. We'll probably never know."

"And if they'd never met?"

Banks shrugged. "It may never have happened. None of it. Terry finally gets caught for rape and put in jail, while Lucy goes on to marry a nice young man, have two point four children and become a bank manager. Who knows?"

"She told me that *she* killed the girls, that Terry didn't have the nerve."

"Makes sense. She'd done it before. He hadn't."

"She said she did it out of kindness."

"Maybe she did. Or out of self-protection. Or out of jealousy. You can't expect her to understand her own motives any better than we can, or to tell the truth about them. With someone like Lucy it was probably some strange sort of combination of all three."

"She also said they met because he raped her. Tried to rape her. I couldn't really understand. She said she raped him as much as he raped her."

Banks shifted in his chair. He wished he could have a cigarette, even though he had determined to quit before the year was out. "I can't explain it any more than you can, Maggie. I might be a policeman, and I might have seen a lot more of the dark side of human nature than you, but something like this . . . for someone with a past like Lucy's, who knows how topsy-turvy things can get? I should imagine that after the things that had been done to her in Alderthorpe, and given her peculiar sexual tastes, Terence Payne was a bit of a pussycat to deal with."

"She said to think of her as a five-legged sheep."

The image took Banks back to his childhood, when the traveling fair came around at Easter and in autumn and set up on the local recreation ground. There were rides—Waltzers, Caterpillar, Dodgems and Speedway—and stalls where you could throw weighted darts at playing cards or shoot at tin figures with an air rifle to win a goldfish in a plastic bag full of water; there were flashing lights and crowds and loud music; but there was also the freak show, a tent set up on the edge of the fairground, where you paid your sixpence and went inside to see the exhibits. They were ultimately disappointing, not a genuine bearded lady, elephant man, spider woman or pinhead in sight. Those kinds of freaks Banks only saw later in Todd Browning's famous movie. None of these freaks were alive, for a start; they were deformed animals, stillborn or killed at birth, and they floated in the huge glass jars full of preserving fluid—a lamb with a fifth leg sticking out of its side; a kitten with horns; a puppy with two heads; a calf with no eye sockets—the stuff that nightmares were made of.

"Despite what happened," Maggie went on, "I want you to know that I'm not going to let it turn me into a cynic. I know you think I'm naïve, but if that's the choice, I'd rather be naïve than bitter and untrusting."

"You made a mistake in judgment and it almost got you killed."

"Do you think she would have killed me if you hadn't come?"

"Do you?"

"I don't know. I've got a lot of thinking to do. But Lucy was . . . she was as much a victim as anything. You weren't there. You didn't hear her. She didn't *want* to kill me."

"Maggie, for crying out loud, will you just listen to yourself! She murdered God knows how many young girls. She *would* have killed you, believe me. If I were you, I'd put the victim thing right out of my mind."

"I'm not you."

Banks took a deep breath and sighed. "Lucky for both of us, isn't it? What will you do now?"

"Do?"

"Will you stay at The Hill?"

"Yes, I think so." Maggie scratched at her bandages, then squinted at Banks. "I don't really have anywhere else to go. And there's still my work, of course. Another thing I've discovered through all this is that I can also do some good. I can be a voice for people who don't have one, or who don't dare speak out. People listen to me."

Banks nodded. He didn't say so, but he suspected that Maggie's very public championing of Lucy Payne might well tarnish her ability to act as a believable spokesperson for abused women. But perhaps not. About all you could say about the public, when it came right down to it, was that they were a fickle lot. Maybe Maggie would emerge as a heroine.

"Look, you'd better get some rest," Banks said. "I just wanted to see how you were. We'll want to talk to you in some detail later. But there's no hurry. Not now."

"Isn't it all over?"

Banks looked into her eyes. He could tell she wanted it to be over, wanted to stand at a distance and think it through, get her life going again—work, good deeds, the lot. "There still might be a trial," he said.

"A trial? But I don't . . ."

"Haven't you heard?"

"Heard what?"

"I just assumed . . . oh, shit."

"I've been pretty much out of it, what with the drugs and all. What is it?"

Banks leaned forward and rested his hand on her forearm. "Maggie," he said, "I don't know how to say this any other way, but Lucy Payne isn't dead."

Maggie recoiled from his touch and her eyes widened. "Not dead? But I don't understand. I thought . . . I mean, she . . ."

"She jumped out of the window, yes, but the fall didn't kill her. Your front path is overgrown, and the bushes broke her fall. The thing is, though, she landed on the sharp edge of one of the steps and broke her back. It's serious. Very serious. There's severe damage to the spinal cord."

"What does that mean?"

"The surgeons aren't sure of the full extent of her injuries yet—they've got a lot more tests to do—but they think she'll be paralyzed from the neck down."

"But Lucy's not dead?"

"No."

"She'll be in a wheelchair?"

"If she survives."

Maggie looked toward the window again. Banks could see tears glistening in her eyes. "So she *is* in a cage, after all."

Banks stood up to leave. He was finding Maggie's compassion for a killer of teenage girls difficult to take and didn't trust himself not to say something he'd regret. Just as he got to the door, he heard her small voice: "Superintendent Banks?"

He turned, hand on doorknob. "Yes."

"Thank you."

"Are you all right, love?"

"Yes, why shouldn't I be?" said Janet Taylor.

"Nothing," the shopkeeper said, "Only . . ."

Janet picked up her bottle of gin from the counter, paid him and walked out of the off-license. What was up with him? she wondered. Had she suddenly sprouted an extra head or something? It was Saturday evening, and she had hardly been out since her arrest and release on bail the previous Monday, but she didn't think she looked *that* different from the last time she'd been in the shop.

She climbed back up to her flat above the hairdresser's, and when she turned her key in the lock and walked inside she noticed the smell for the first time. And the mess. You didn't notice it so much when you were living in the midst of it, she thought, but you certainly did when you went out and came back to it. Dirty clothes lay strewn everywhere, half-full coffee cups grew mold, and the plant on the windowsill had died and wilted. The smell was of stale skin, rotting cabbage, sweat and gin. And some of it, she realized, turning her nose toward her armpit, came from her own body.

Janet looked in the mirror. It didn't surprise her to see the lank, lifeless hair and the dark bags under her eyes. After all, she had hardly slept since it happened. She didn't like to close her eyes because when she did, it all seemed to play over and over again inside her mind. The only times she could get any rest at all were when she'd had enough gin and passed out for an hour or two. No dreams came then, only oblivion, but as soon as she started to stir, the memory and the depression kicked in again.

She didn't really care what happened to her as long as the nightmares—sleeping and waking—went away. Let them kick her off the Job, put her in jail, even. She didn't care as long as they also wiped out the memory of that morning in the cellar. Didn't they have machines or drugs that could do that, or was that only something she'd seen in a movie? Still, she was better off than Lucy Payne, she told herself. Paralyzed from the neck down in a wheelchair for life, by the sound of it. But it was no less than she deserved. Janet remembered Lucy lying in the hall, blood pooling around her head wound, remembered her own concern for the abused woman, her anger at Dennis's male chauvinism. *Appearances.* Now she'd give anything to have Dennis back and thought even paralysis too slight a punishment for Lucy Payne.

Moving away from the mirror, Janet stripped off her clothes and tossed them on the floor. She would have a bath, she decided. Maybe it would make her feel better. First, she poured herself a large gin and took it into the bathroom with her. She put the plug in and turned on the taps, got the tem-

perature right, poured in a capful of bubble bath. She looked
at herself in the full-length mirror on the back of the bathroom door. Her breasts were starting to sag and the lard-
colored skin was creasing around her belly. She used to take
good care of herself, work out at the police gym at least three
times a week, go out for a run. Not for a couple of weeks,
though.

Before dipping her toes into the water, she decided to
bring the bottle and set it on the edge of the tub. She'd only
have to get out and fetch it soon, anyway. Finally, she lay
back and let the bubbles tickle her neck. At least she could
clean herself. That would be a start. No more off-license
clerks asking her if she was all right because she smelled. As
for the bags under her eyes, well, they wouldn't go away
overnight, but she would work on them. And on tidying up
the flat.

On the other hand, she thought, after a good long sip of
gin, there were razor blades in the bathroom cabinet. All she
had to do was stand up and reach for them. The water was
good and hot. She was certain she would feel no pain. Just a
quick slit on each wrist, then put her arms underwater and let
the blood seep out. It would be like going to sleep, only there
would be no dreams.

As she lay there wrapped in the warmth and softness of
the bubble bath, her eyelids started to droop and she couldn't
keep her eyes open. There she was again, in that stinking cellar with Dennis spurting blood all over the place and that maniac Payne coming at her with a machete. *What could she
have done differently?* That seemed to be the question that
nobody could, or would, answer for her. What *should* she
have done?

She jerked to consciousness, gasping for breath, and at
first the bathtub looked as if it were full of blood. She
reached out for the gin, but she was clumsy and she knocked

the bottle on the bathroom floor. It shattered on the tiles and spilled its precious contents.

Shit!

That meant she'd have to go out and buy more. She picked up the bath mat and shook it hard to get rid of any glass that might have lodged there, then she hauled herself out of the tub. When she stepped on to the mat, she underestimated her capacity for balance and stumbled a little. Her right foot hit the tiles, and she felt the sting of the glass on her sole. Janet winced with pain. Leaving a thin trail of blood on the bathroom floor, she negotiated her way into the living room without further injury, sat down and pulled out a couple of large slivers of glass, then she put on some old slippers and went back for peroxide and bandages. First she sat on the toilet seat and poured the peroxide as best she could over the sole of her foot. She almost screamed out in pain, but soon the waves abated and her foot just started to throb, then turn numb. She swathed it in bandages, then went to her bedroom and got dressed, putting on clean clothes and extra-thick socks.

She had to get out of the flat, she decided, and not just for as long as it took to go to the off-license. A good drive would help keep her awake, the windows wide open, breeze blowing in her hair, rock music and chatter on the radio. Maybe she'd drop in on Annie Cabbot, the only decent copper among them. Or perhaps she'd drive out into the country and find a B&B where nobody knew who she was or what she had done, and stay a night or two. Anything to get away from this filthy, smelly place. She could pick up another bottle on the way. At least now she was clean, and no stuffy off-license clerk was going to turn his nose up at her.

Janet hesitated a moment before she picked up her car keys, then pocketed them anyway. What more could they do to her? Add insult to injury and charge her with drink driving? Fuck the lot of them, Janet thought, laughing to herself as she limped down the stairs.

That same evening, three days since Lucy Payne had jumped out of Maggie Forrest's bedroom window, Banks was at home listening to *Thaïs* in his cozy living room with the melted-Brie ceiling and the blue walls. It was his first escape from the paperwork since he had visited Maggie Forrest in hospital on Thursday, and he was enjoying it immensely. Still uncertain about his future, he had decided that before making any major career decisions, he would first take a holiday and think things over. He had plenty of leave due and had already talked to Red Ron and picked up a few travel brochures. Now it was a matter of deciding *where* to go.

He had also spent quite a lot of time over the past couple of days standing at his office window looking down on the market square and thinking about Maggie Forrest, thinking about her conviction and her compassion, and now he was still thinking about her at home. Lucy Payne had tied Maggie to the bed and was about to strangle her with a belt when the police broke in. Yet Maggie still saw Lucy as the victim, and could shed tears for her. Was she a saint or a fool? Banks didn't know.

When he thought about the girls Lucy and Terry Payne had violated, terrorized and murdered—of Kelly Matthews, Samantha Foster, Melissa Horrocks, Kimberley Myers and Katya Pavelic—paralysis wasn't sufficient; it didn't *hurt* enough. But when he thought of Lucy's violent and abusive childhood at Alderthorpe, then a quick, clean death or a lifetime of solitary confinement seemed a more apt punishment.

As usual, what he thought didn't really matter, because the whole business was out of his hands, the judgment not his to make. Perhaps the best he could hope for was to put Lucy

Payne out of his mind, which he would succeed in doing over time. Partially, at any rate. She would always be there—they all were, killers and victims—but in time she would fade and become a more shadowy figure than she was at the moment.

Banks had not forgotten the sixth victim. She had a name, and unless her childhood was like Lucy Payne's, someone must have once loved her, held her and whispered words of comfort after a nightmare, perhaps, soothed away the pain when she fell and scraped her knee. He would have to be patient. The forensic experts were good at their jobs, and eventually her bones would yield up something that would lead to her identity.

Just as the famous "Meditation" at the end of the first CD started, his phone rang. He was off duty and at first thought of not answering, but curiosity got the better of him, as it always did.

It was Annie Cabbot, and she sounded as if she were standing in the middle of a road, there was so much noise around her: voices, sirens, car brakes, people shouting orders.

"Annie, where the hell are you?"

"Roundabout on the Ripon Road, just north of Harrogate," Annie said, shouting to make herself heard over the noise.

"What are you doing there?"

Somebody spoke to Annie, though Banks couldn't hear what was said. She answered abruptly and then came back on the line. "Sorry, it's a bit chaotic down here."

"What's going on?"

"I thought you ought to know. It's Janet Taylor."

"What about her?"

"She ran into another car."

"She what? How is she?"

"She's dead, Alan. *Dead.* They haven't been able to get her body out of the car yet, but they know she's dead. They got her handbag out and found my card in it."

"Bloody hell." Banks felt numb. "How did it happen?"

"Can't say for sure," Annie said. "The person in the car behind her says she just seemed to speed up at the roundabout rather than slow down, and she hit the car that was going round. A mother driving her daughter home from a piano lesson."

"Oh, Jesus Christ. What happened to them?"

"The mother's okay. Cuts and bruises. Shock."

"The daughter?"

"It's touch and go. The paramedics suspect internal injuries, but they won't know till they get her to hospital. She's still stuck in the car."

"Was Janet pissed?"

"Don't know yet. I wouldn't be surprised if drinking had something to do with it, though. And she was depressed. I don't know. She might have been trying to kill herself. If she did . . . it's . . ." Banks could sense Annie choking up.

"Annie, I know what you're going to say, but even if she did do it on purpose, it's not your fault. You didn't go down there in that cellar, see what she saw, do what she did. All you did was carry out an unbiased investigation."

"Unbiased! Christ, Alan, I bent over backward to be sympathetic toward her."

"Whatever. It's not your fault."

"Easy for you to say."

"Annie, she was no doubt drunk, and she went off the road."

"Maybe you're right. I can't believe that Janet would take someone else with her if she wanted to kill herself. But whichever way you look at it, drunk or not, suicide or not, it's still down to what happened, isn't it?"

"It happened, Annie. Nothing to do with you."

"The politics. The fucking politics."

"Do you want me to come down?"

"No, I'm okay."

"Annie—"

"Sorry, got to go now. They're pulling the girl out of the

car." She hung up, leaving Banks holding the receiver and breathing quickly. Janet Taylor. Another casualty of the Paynes.

The first CD had finished, and Banks had no real desire to listen to the second one after the news he had just heard. He poured himself two fingers of Laphroaig and took his cigarettes outside to his spot by the falls and, as the vivid orange and purple colors streaked the western sky, he drank a silent toast to Janet Taylor and to the nameless dead girl buried in the Paynes' garden.

But he hadn't been out there five minutes when he decided he should go to Annie, *had* to go, no matter what she had said. Their romantic relationship might be over, but he had promised to be her friend and give her support. If she didn't need that right now, when would she? He looked at his watch. It would take him an hour or so to get there, if he moved fast, and Annie would probably still be at the scene. Even if she'd gone, she would be at hospital, and he would be able to find her there easily enough.

He left the tumbler, still half-full, on the low table and went to grab his jacket. Before he could put it on, the phone rang again. Thinking it was Annie calling back with more news, he answered. It was Jenny Fuller.

"I hope I haven't called at an awkward moment," she said.

"I was just going out."

"Oh. An emergency?"

"Sort of."

"Only I was thinking we might have a drink and celebrate, you know, now it's all over."

"That's a great idea, Jenny. I can't do it right now, though. I'll call you later, okay?"

"Story of my life."

"Sorry. Got to go. I'll call. Promise."

Banks could hear the disappointment in Jenny's voice, and he felt like a real bastard for being so abrupt with her—

after all, she had worked on the case as hard as anyone—but he didn't want to explain about Janet Taylor, and he didn't feel like celebrating anything.

Now it's all over, Jenny had said. Banks wondered if it would ever be all over, the aftermath of the Paynes' rampage, if it would ever cease taking its toll. Six teenage girls dead, one still unidentified. Kathleen Murray dead these ten years or more. PC Dennis Morrisey dead. Terence Payne dead. Lucy Payne paralyzed. Now Janet Taylor dead and a young girl seriously injured.

Banks checked for his keys and cigarettes, and headed out into the night.

Acknowledgments

I would like to thank my editor, Patricia Lande Grader, for her help in reshaping the unruly early drafts, and my wife, Sheila Halladay, for her perceptive and helpful comments. Also, many thanks to my agent, Dominick Abel, for all his hard work on my behalf, and to Erika Schmid for her fine copyediting.

As far as research goes, the usual crowd came through: Detective Sergeant Keith Wright, Detective Inspectors Claire Gormley and Alan Young, and Area Commander Philip Gormley. Any mistakes are entirely my own and are, of course, made in the interests of dramatic fiction. Also, thanks to Woitek Kubicki for his advice on Polish names.

A number of books proved invaluable in understanding the "killer couple" phenomenon, and among those to which I owe my greatest debt of gratitude are Emlyn Williams, *Beyond Belief;* Brian Masters, *She Must Have Known;* Paul Britton, *The Jigsaw Man;* Gordon Burn, *Happy Like Murderers;* and Stephen Williams, *Invisible Darkness.*

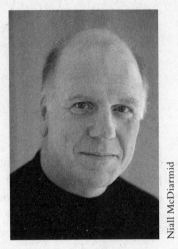

Niall McDiarmid

About the Author

One of the world's most popular and acclaimed writers, **PETER ROBINSON** grew up in the United Kingdom, and now divides his time between Toronto and England. The bestselling, award-winning author of the Inspector Banks series, he has also written two short-story collections and three standalone novels, which combined have sold more than ten million copies around the world. Among his many honors and prizes are the Edgar Award, the CWA (UK) Dagger in the Library Award, and Sweden's Martin Beck Award.